ALL THE

STARS

IN

THE SKY

UNTIL THE END OF THE WORLD
BOOK THREE

SARAH LYONS FLEMING

For Jamie, my first and most favorite fangirl.
And my own personal juker.

And for my parents (again).
Because y'all deserve more than a novella.

CHAPTER 1

It isn't easy to be optimistic when you have thousands of unknown miles ahead of you and an army of zombies at your heels. Especially when the road you've been traveling for hours is barren of all life—except the undead, of course. If I hadn't promised to believe everything will be all right, I might consider jerking the steering wheel out of Peter's hands and sending us all into a tree. It may be unlikely we'll get to Alaska, but I won't be the one to say it.

"Want me to drive?" I ask.

Peter takes his puffy eyes off the road. I've begged him to sleep, but he refuses. I couldn't sleep after Adrian died. "Maybe in a little while."

Peter's the main reason for my optimism. He says we'll make it, and I think that belief is what's holding him together. That and Bits, who sits in the back with Hank, both staring out the window as we follow the RV and pickup through Quebec. Or maybe we're in Ontario now.

I unscrew the cap of my water bottle and offer it to Peter. His dark hair is limp, hanging to his cheekbones, and he pushes it back with a sigh. I want to say something, but there's not much to say to someone when they've just watched the person they love become a zombie. I know this from experience.

The sun bleaches the brown grass to beige and flickers through the trees like a strobe light. I'm too tired to find my sunglasses, so I close my eyes to escape its brightness. A moment later I start awake, heart racing and damp with sweat. I saw Ana, face slack and neck bloody, right before I sent a bullet into her brain. John under a pile of Lexers. Henry's struggle before he fell into the bus. Dan watching us leave from the ambulance's roof.

Dan's dead by now. If he lost the nerve to do it himself, even bolstered by the flask he always carried, enough time has passed that he's one of them. Dead, even if he's walking. I know he didn't lose his nerve, though. I may not have known him as well as I could have, but he wasn't the kind of guy who'd sit around and wait to become a zombie.

I haven't slept in over a day, but I won't sleep until Peter does. He needs the company and, truthfully, so do I. I'm afraid to go to sleep. To dream. Because no matter how optimistic you are when awake, sleep gives your brain free rein to fuck with you. My eyelids threaten to lower and I sit up straight, legs crossed under me. Criss-cross applesauce, Bits calls it.

"Lie down," Peter says.

"I'm fine."

"Cassandra, please."

"You need to rest, too," I say. "I'll keep you company until then."

He doesn't argue, even though I know he wants to by the way he grips the steering wheel. Penny sticks her head between us from the back. "Let me and James take over for a while."

Penny doesn't look much better than Peter, but she uses her teacher voice that leaves no room for argument. She hasn't asked me for more specifics about how I killed her sister. That's a conversation I hope never to have. Peter pulls to the side of the road. The other vehicles stop and Nelly leans out of the pickup's window. When he sees we're switching, he sits with the engine idling until we resume driving. Our last pit stop wasn't too long ago.

There isn't much room for passengers when the VW's bed is open, but Bits and Hank are small kids and they fit on the two seats that are left. I smile at them and even Hank, who lost his dad yesterday, smiles back.

"You guys tired?" I ask. They both shake their heads. "Hungry?" Two more shakes.

I finish working off my boots and dig my fingers into my heel. It may be smarter to sleep with my boots on, but my feet need out. Peter kicks off his boots, places his holster by his side and flops back with an arm over his eyes.

"Are you okay if I sleep?" I ask the kids. "Do you need anything?"

Hank fingers Adrian's knife on his belt, which I officially gave to him last night. I had my Ka-Bar in my bag, and Adrian would have liked for Hank to have it.

"We've got it," he says.

It would almost be funny because he's a skinny ten year-old with big glasses and burgeoning dreadlocks that look more like a clear-cut forest than hair, but his dad is evident in Hank's serious expression. I hope there is such a thing as Heaven, and that Henry's with Corrine and Dottie now. I hope everyone we've lost is up there, having a kick-ass dinner or something. John believed they would be, and if it's true, he's up there.

I kiss the kids' foreheads, then lie down and steel myself for more images: The splatter that flew out the back of Ana's head, hitting the Lexers behind her. The way her hands twitched on the dirt road before going still. But when I close my eyes, it's only blackness. Even my brain is too tired for games right now.

CHAPTER 2

I wake in the late afternoon when Peter kicks me in his sleep. His eyes open. I can see he's remembering Ana by the way he swallows and stares into space. That first wakeup is the worst. They all suck, but the first one—the one where you remember someone is dead—takes the cake. Every once in a while, even months later, you get one that's almost as bad, but you're somewhat used to the letdown by then. You've grown a thicker skin, even if it only feels like a millionth of a millimeter.

"Did I kick you?" he asks. "Sorry."

I rest my cheek on the mattress. "Just don't steal my blankets unless you want to be kicked back."

He tries to smile, and I touch his shoulder before I sit up. Bits and Hank are still in their spots, Sparky the cat perched between them. James is behind the wheel and Penny is asleep in the passenger's seat, hands resting on her round stomach. Penny's always hated naps, but at six months pregnant she craves them. She's not missing anything exciting. The road had been open fields, then an endless wall of trees on either side, and now we're at flat with small groups of trees.

"Well," I say, "Ontario's shaping up to be just as exciting as Quebec."

"Seriously," James agrees. "We're coming up on a town where we're going to look for fuel."

We're sticking to gas stations instead of siphoning or draining fuel from the tanks of abandoned cars. Most have already been emptied, or the gas has oxidized into an engine-destroying muck that even our fuel stabilizer can't save. Add in the time it took to check each car, giving Lexers time to converge on us, and it quickly proved to be an exercise in futility when an hour's work produced four gallons of usable gas.

The pickup has a hundred gallon tank in the bed, but with three vehicles, one an RV, we're blowing through gas like it's water. Which, incidentally, we've also seen plenty of—there's a lake or pond or marsh every time you blink. It's great for drinking and washing up, something I'd really like to do, but water isn't going to get us another 3,600 miles.

We discussed ditching the gas-guzzling RV last night, but we need a vehicle that holds a lot of passengers in case something happens to the pickup or VW. I hope we don't have to ditch Miss Vera the VW. She's not as shiny as she was a day ago, covered as she is in dead bugs and dust, but her wood interior still gleams. The general consensus was that there's no correct answer, so we left it as it is for now.

We cross a small bridge onto a street of plain houses painted various shades of brown. They're unfenced, with only the eternal flatness of this part of Canada as their backyards. We're hoping to make it through the thousands of miles of prairie to the mountains before the Lexers do. Considering that we have no idea where the Lexers are or in what direction they're heading, it may be a stupid and insane plan. But it's all we've got.

The houses are replaced by cheap motels and a few boxy buildings that housed businesses, followed by a stretch of stores with boarded windows and peeling signs. The bodies, garbage and abandoned cars make it clear this place was part of the apocalypse, but it looks as though the apocalypse began long before zombies.

Bits's and Hank's lips are still chocolaty from the MRE dessert they ate while I slept. I reach into one of the bags crammed by the wall. If we get separated we don't want to be without ammo, clothing and food.

"Now eat your carrot," I say, and hand them each one from the gardens we plundered at the Quebec Safe Zone. Their eating junk food is the least of my worries, but I figure I should say something mother-like. I pull on my boots while they crunch their carrots and then grab myself one. We don't have much food spread between twenty people; these and the dessert were rationed for lunch.

"So, what happened while I was asleep?" I ask.

"Trees," Hank says.

"And lakes," Bits adds.

"Not surprising," Peter says, and sits up next to me. I hand him a carrot and he chews slowly. "Any grass? I was hoping for grass."

I smile sideways at Peter when they giggle. He looks better than he did a few hours ago and certainly better than a few minutes ago.

"How're you feeling?" Peter asks me.

I should be the one asking that of him, except I hated when people asked me how I was after Adrian. "I'm fine."

I'm not fine. I just have other things to worry about. Like Hank and Peter and Penny and Maureen, who've all lost someone they loved. I did too, but I don't have time to mourn. I don't *want* time to mourn. I've woven it into the grief I already carried instead of letting it knock me down the way it could have. Staying optimistic may be difficult, but after yesterday I'm pretty sure I can endure anything this world throws at me.

"Are you okay?" I ask.

He keeps his face to the window. "Yeah."

It could be he's holding it together because he doesn't have any other choice. Focusing on patrol or guard helped me to get through this summer, and now we're on the longest patrol ever. I spent two weeks living in a tent and crying after I lost Adrian. I guess that was what can be considered a luxury these days, which is a truly depressing thought.

I eat the last of my carrot and reach for Hank's hand. "How are you, sweetie?"

Hank, the least snuggly ten year-old I've ever met, climbs into my lap like a puppy. Bits knows now that we'd never leave her, and I hope it's only a matter of time before he knows it, too. I'm stuck with these kids, which is both a wonderful and terrifying responsibility. "I'm so glad you're with us," I say. "Don't worry, we'll be there soon."

Hank wipes his nose on his sleeve and nods. He's smart enough to know that it might not happen, but I want him to believe—maybe it'll make the difference between death and survival.

"Gas station," James calls.

The gas pumps sit in a large concrete lot with a convenience store set far behind. We ignore the pumps, pull to the underground tanks and turn off our engines to wait for any unwanted visitors. After a full minute, there's still nothing but empty street on one side and open field and train tracks on the other.

Zeke's head emerges from the RV. "All right. Take your spots."

Penny moves into the driver's seat and waits with the kids. She's there to rescue us or take off with Bits and Hank if she can't. She hates this part but does it with a grim determination I'd only seen on her sister prior to now.

Nelly jumps from the pickup and saunters over, blond hair sticking out at crazy angles and blue eyes sparkling. "You're both looking less shitty. Did you sleep?"

"Is there an ounce of tact in there, Nel?" Adam, his boyfriend, shakes his head.

"You know there isn't," I say. "It's a lost cause. Give up before you go crazy."

"Too late for that," Adam says.

Zeke, Kyle and Shawn work on opening the ground tanks and readying the pump, which resembles a tiny red generator with a gas nozzle on one end and a collection hose on the other, while the rest of us fan out in a circle to keep watch. Once the pump's going you can't hear a thing. I wish we had the small tanker truck from Whitefield that held enough fuel to deposit us in Alaska with barely any stops.

The roar of the pump commences and continues on. That means there's fuel in the tanks and it looks fresh enough to use, although they'll add fuel stabilizer to be sure. If there's enough to fill the tank in the pickup's bed, the vehicle gas tanks and the fuel cans, it'll get us another 800 miles. I grip the axe, a tactical tomahawk, that I found among our spare weapons, and wish for my cleaver. It's gone forever, seeing as I dropped it on the road outside Kingdom Come. I loved that weapon for its versatility, but mainly I loved it because it was handmade by John. I'd gladly give up every weapon I have and a whole lot more to get him back. That he's gone leaves me feeling rudderless, as though we're not traveling to a destination but lost at sea. I'm trying my best to believe Peter when he says we'll make it, but John would've been able to convince me. I tell myself to stop wishing for things that can't be. If there were no zombies, we wouldn't be in this mess in the first place. How's that for a wish?

I grind my teeth. When we get to Alaska I'll allow myself a huge, sobbing, ugly cry. Until then, I'm focusing on the people I do have instead of the people I don't. By the time seven Lexers stumble out from between the businesses across the road, I've managed to swallow back my tears. Those of us on the street side move forward to meet them at the sidewalk.

Five against seven is a fair fight when it comes to people and zombies: We have speed and brains and they have the ability to go forever. I swing my axe. The handle grip sits firmly in my glove and the head is nicely weighted for impact, with one side a hatchet and the other an evil-looking spike.

Peter ventures into the street after one that's strayed from the pack. He finishes it off and then slides his blade through the back of another's head. The metal blade glints in the Lexer's open mouth before he yanks it out. He's taking more chances than he should, and I resolve to keep an eye on him to be sure he doesn't do anything stupid like I did this summer.

The remaining five close in, resembling extras in a horror movie with their open sores and gray skin and tattered clothes. I'm glad the pump masks the noises that must be coming out of their gaping mouths because, along with the smell, those hissing moans can drive you batty. I've held on to the hatred for these things that want to eat us, but they don't scare me as much as they used to. I still get tense and sweaty, but I'd be a fool not to when death is only feet away.

I'm taller than the woman who comes for me, so I swing the spike downward through the top of her head. It's not the optimal spot—you can get a good knife or machete through skull, especially the softer skulls of older zombies, but it's more work for the same payoff and you're better off going for an eye, nose or mouth. I'm pleasantly surprised when the axe's spike punctures with no jarring impact the way a knife would.

Jamie whoops and skewers a tall, skinny Lexer with her spike. The curly ends of her black hair poke out from the knot atop her head and her rosebud lips are curled. Jamie's fairly crazy, even measured against everyone else who's survived thus far, and we're all crazy to some extent.

But no one was crazier than Ana. It's strange to kill Lexers without her to watch my back and make ridiculous comments. She was reckless, but she always survived. I truly thought Ana would outlive us all. Never in a million years did I think she'd end up a zombie.

Adam stands from his corpse, brown eyes sad the way they sometimes are. He takes no satisfaction from this, probably because he had to put a kitchen knife in his boyfriend's head last year. But he does what needs to be done in his quiet way. Nelly puts an arm around his slim shoulders while we return to our positions.

It's only another few minutes before they've filled every container. In the silence, the wind rustles the branches of the only two trees for block after block of concrete. This town was not designed with aesthetics in mind.

"We're just about full up," Zeke says. He smiles under his bushy beard. "We got lucky here, no doubt. Let's look in the store in case there's something."

Margaret, Tony and Shawn head for the store, where the broken windows practically assure us that nothing worth taking remains. Kyle opens the camper door and scoops up his four year-old daughter, Nicki. She rubs a hand on his shaved head and asks, "It's safe now, Daddy?"

"Yeah, baby," Kyle says. "Do you have to go potty before we leave?"

Kyle is average height but wide enough to appear tall, with brown skin, well-sculpted features and nice eyes that he hides behind sunglasses much of the day. He's friendly, but the only time I've ever seen him happy is when he's with Nicki. Otherwise, he acts like a military man on a mission—which I guess is what he is.

"Uh-huh," Nicki says with a bounce of her two puffy pigtails. "Can I go in the RV?"

We only use the bathroom in the RV when we need to, so as not to waste water. We've left a trail of pee between here and Quebec, but since this area doesn't afford much privacy and we don't let the kids out with Lexers nearby, we'll use the toilet and flush only when full.

"I think we could use a little luxury," I say.

"You need me to come?" he asks.

"I've got her." He nods his thanks and sets Nicki on the steps.

Inside, Ashley's dark blond ponytail swings as she struggles to keep Barnaby in one spot on the RV's floor. Barn's so excited by the sight of his leash that he dances in a circle, tail whipping around. "Barn, sit still!" Ash pins him down and clips it to his collar. "This dog is such a dork."

Barnaby is a dork, and he's also not allowed out until we know the coast is clear. He either barks at Lexers or tries to run in a whimpering mess, neither of which is helpful when you're attempting to be quiet and unobtrusive. Ashley, however, has shown herself to be both in the past day, especially for a sixteen year-old.

"We saw a few out there," I say. "So give him to someone else to walk, okay?"

"I'll take him," Maureen says from where she folds blankets. She puts on her coat and takes the leash from Ash.

"Are you sure?" I ask. "I can do it."

Maureen gives me a motherly look. "I may be an old lady, Cassie, but I can walk a dog around a parking lot. Don't worry about me."

"You're not old. Just well-loved."

She spanks my behind as she's dragged out the door by Barn. Maureen's in her fifties and full of energy, although the past days have aged her more than I care to see. I must look like I'm forty instead of thirty, and I feel like I'm ninety.

"Okay, let's go potty," I say to Nicki. "This is so much better than a tree, isn't it?"

"It's really hard to go on a tree," she says, her long-lashed eyes round.

She doesn't know how adorable she is, which makes her even more so. It's no wonder Kyle can barely smile. I'm worried enough about Bits and Hank, but I know they can run. They could fend for themselves for a little while, maybe a long while, whereas a four year-old is as good as dead by herself.

"That it is," I say. "But I still like being a girl."

"Me, too. I think I have to poop. Can you wipe me?"

I sigh inwardly. Of course she has to poop. Everything has to poop. I've spent a lot of time in the past day escorting various life forms—a cat, a dog, small children—to places where they can poop. It's a good thing Penny's baby isn't due until December; cloth diapers would be a nightmare.

"Can't wait!" I say. Nicki dissolves into giggles as we head for the bathroom.

CHAPTER 3

The sun is almost down when we finally make it out of town. I'm behind the wheel of the VW and remembering why I like automatic transmissions. "I hate myself for saying this," I say, "but Miss Vera is possibly not the best car for this journey."

"You think?" Peter asks. I laugh—he's improved his sarcasm in the past year. "Even with Shawn's new engine our top speed will be forty miles per hour once we get to the mountains."

"Say it isn't so!" Penny calls from the back. She loves Vera as much as I do. "We'll have to get a minivan or something."

"Another pickup with an extra gas tank would be good," I say. "I don't mind being squished if we don't have to stop as often."

"Sparky can sit on my lap," Bits says. "I don't want her to ride in a different car. Or I could ride in the RV with her. They have a TV. Hank and I—"

"No," Peter and I say at the same time. Neither of us is letting her ride in a separate vehicle ever again.

"It's not a big deal," Hank says. "We're right next to each other, it's not like—"

"Nope," Peter says. He's answered by two sighs. On the farm, we let them run free within the fences, but if there was ever a time when being an overbearing parent is called for it would be now.

I slow at brake lights ahead. Zeke's voice comes from our handheld radio. "Big traffic jam up ahead. Move to the right shoulder and go slow. Gonna get a little bumpy, but it looks like someone cleared the way."

This part of Canada wasn't very populated, which has worked in our favor so far. But now, with the sides of the roads an inky black, it feels menacingly desolate. I straddle as much of the shoulder as possible and bump over the grass behind the RV.

A heavy fog has rolled in, making the cars in the gloom resemble a deep-ocean shipwreck. Our headlights pass over open doors and a particularly bad collision. Bodies dot the asphalt along with bags and suitcases that have burst open or been rifled through.

"Did you see that?" Hank yells, nearly giving me a heart attack. "There was one in that car! It was pounding on the windows and its face was all white."

I hadn't, but Hank's aspiring-author description gives me plenty to go on. The stopped cars stretch on for another hundred feet before we're back on asphalt. I wonder what became of all the people in those cars—another mystery chalked up to the zombie apocalypse. We spend far too much time trying to work these little mysteries out, almost like a game.

"What do you think happened there?" Penny asks.

"Maybe a pod caused it," James says.

"Yeah," Bits says. "Or the crash was first and there wasn't enough time to move the cars before a pod came."

"Maybe it was a roadblock," Hank says. "We saw a lot of those when we were walking to Whitefield."

A few more suggestions are thrown around. There's never a winner, but it gives everyone something to do besides despair that we'll meet the same fate as those cars and people.

"That's it, gang, I'm not giving Vera up," I say. "We can travel the country, solving mysteries. I'll paint flowers on the side of our Mystery Machine."

James breaks into the *Scooby Doo* theme song, and Bits and Hank join in with the rest of us; Scooby spans many generations. At the end, Peter does a Scooby Doo impression that's so spot on I can't see the road through my tears.

"What the heck?" I ask. "How did I not know you could do Scooby?"

"I'm full of secret talents," he says. "And I would've gotten away with it if it weren't for you meddling kids."

Everyone laughs. This trip sucks on so many levels—we're missing so many, we have no home, we don't have enough fuel or food, we have no idea what awaits us—but I'm in the Mystery Machine with what's left of the best people on Earth, which kind of makes everything all right.

CHAPTER 4

The bus is quiet when Peter takes over driving. Bits and Hank have crammed in with Penny and James on the VW's bed. Midway through the night, Penny and James will drive while we sleep through dawn. I lean my head against the window and watch the taillights of the RV. It's slightly hypnotic, and with the heat blowing I have to fight to stay awake. I'm not afraid to sleep after my nap today; I'm yearning for it.

"Let's turn off the heat," I say quietly. "Just for a bit."

"I know it's your voice," Peter says, "so it must be you, but are *you* really asking to turn off the heat?"

"I was never gladder in all my life than to find out that running a car's heat doesn't use extra fuel, but it's putting me to sleep."

"Sleep, I'll be fine. Our shift's almost over, anyway."

It's tempting, but it's against the rules. The rules that are intended to keep us alive.

"Nope, one to drive and one to watch and keep them awake." I switch off the heat and stretch. "Are you tired?"

"I don't know if I can sleep."

"Yeah."

I don't know what else to say. We drive in silence, but it's not uncomfortable. The spring before last, I never would've guessed Peter and I could do anything comfortably. Now, he's one of the people I love most in the world. We have a special bond in Bits; everyone loves her, but I don't know that anyone else has the drive we feel to keep her safe at any cost. The relief that she's only feet away makes me exhale.

"What's wrong?" Peter asks.

"Nothing. I just...Bits is back there, you know? I really didn't think—"

I see Peter's smile in the lights of the dash before it falls, and then I want to kick myself. Saving Bits is all jumbled up in losing Ana and Dan and John. Peter would never say it, but I'm afraid he's angry at me for being the one to take Ana out of the world for good. Maybe I should have left her like that, but I'd sworn I wouldn't.

"I promised her," I whisper before I can think better of it.

"What?"

It's cooling down quickly, although that's not why I shiver. I clamp my knees together and slip my hands under my thighs.

"Who? What do you mean?" Peter asks again.

"Ana," I whisper. "I promised her I'd do it if...I'm sorry."

There's a long silence, this one not so comfortable. I continue looking out the window and out of the corner of my eye see Peter glance over, but he doesn't say a word.

Penny clears her throat. "Hey, it's almost our turn."

She perches on the folding seat with her legs by the shifter and rests her chin on my shoulder. I'm glad she heard. It saves me from having to say it twice. I pull my hands from under my legs and hold the arm she's wrapped around my middle.

"Love you," Penny says.

I nod because I can't speak. They deserve to cry more than I do, and they're not, so I don't. I wish Peter would say something, anything. Tell me that he hates me or that it's okay. I watch the road until the lead vehicles slow to switch drivers and gas up. The two-lane road is empty and Tony, who's been driving the pickup, has chosen an open spot in which to stop. We leave the kids sleeping and spill out into the cool night air.

Tony has spiky, dark hair and cherubic cheeks when he smiles, which is often. He's pulled the pickup alongside the VW, and now he unhooks the nozzle from the in-bed tank. When the VW is full, he moves to top off the RV while the rest of us watch the fields or get ready for bed.

"We're making good time," Zeke says from where he stands in the headlights. "If we keep this up, we'll get there in a few days."

"Well, now you've jinxed us," Shawn says with a grin. He stands, feet apart, and stretches his beefy arms above his head. "But I'll be asleep, finally, so just let me die and don't wake me."

Jamie hits his side. He drops his arms with an *oof.* "Don't even joke about that, Shawn."

"Why?"

"Because I have you trained and really don't want to go through that again."

Shawn and the others laugh, but Jamie's mouth is tight. I pull on one of her curls when she passes. "I'm just tired," she says. "And I hate when Shawn says stupid shit like that."

She shrugs and climbs into the RV. Peter and I ready ourselves for bed while James drives. I'm glad it's dark, that Peter can't see how distressed I am that he still hasn't spoken. I pull back the covers to find Bits practically on top of Hank. This may be bad for Hank, but it gives us more space. I lie on my side, Peter's warmth on my back, and have just closed my eyes when I feel his shoulders shake. I hesitate before I flip to place my hand on his chest. He may not want me to hear, but I can't ignore his crying now that I have.

Peter's hand covers mine. "I'm glad you promised."

I can't see his expression, but the softness in his voice and touch ease my anxiety. His arm moves under me and I rest my head on his shoulder. It's a comfort to hold on to something, and I know he feels it by the way his heart slows. I wait for its beating to return to normal before I allow myself to sleep.

CHAPTER 5

I jump awake at Penny's frightened yelp in time to see a Lexer bounce off the left corner of the VW. Shadows move on the side of the road just outside the reach of our headlights. A flashlight points from the pickup's side window, illuminating hundreds of Lexers on the south side of the road heading straight for us.

"Keep going, keep going," a voice yells from the radio. "They're behind us, too."

Peter laces up his boots and sits at the ready, his machete glinting in the lights of the dash. I find my gloves and boots in the dark and grip my axe. I don't dare turn on the interior lights in case it attracts more. James accelerates to avoid the onslaught, but the VW is hit by a mass of bodies hard enough to throw us to the right. I slam against Peter and the kids land in a pile on the floor. James curses and yanks the wheel straight. We could have hit a huge pod—one of the pods we think are moving north—and if it's them, we're fucked. I press a flashlight to the window. It's smeared with juices from decaying bodies, but the beam carries far enough to see an end to the sea of white faces.

It's good news, but it doesn't mean we're safe. James fights his way down the clogged road, finding the open spaces so he can push them out of the way without creating a hill of bodies. Out of all our vehicles, the VW is the weakest and lowest to the ground. It would be best to follow in the RV's wake, but we can't speed up to get close.

I order the kids to get on their shoes and coats, and then slip our backpacks on our shoulders. A Lexer slams into James's side window hard enough to crack it with a sound like a gunshot. James curses, but he's calmer than I could ever hope to be. James is always calm.

I hold Bits and clench my teeth so as not to scream the way she does each time the VW swerves. I imagine the worst—that we'll be pushed over or off the road and have to fight our way through to the others—and tell myself that we can do it again, as many times as we have to. We've done it before and we'll do it again.

Another window cracks. I shove Bits into Peter's lap, where he grips her, prepared to run. I raise Hank's hand to my cheek to be sure he's put on his gloves and then hold his gloved hand tight in mine.

Rotten faces appear in the headlights, hit the windshield and fall away. One struggles to stay upright, its hands wrapped around the windshield wiper, before it goes down and takes the wiper with it. A head hits the glass and explodes like a rotten jack-o'-lantern, leaving a starburst in the glass and a flood of whatever filled its brain cavity. James tries the wipers, but the wiper on his side is somewhere on the asphalt and Penny's side becomes only marginally cleaner.

Penny peers through the murky windshield and directs him through the throng in a surprisingly steady voice, until the hailstorm of hands lessens to a gentle patter before it ceases completely. A few miles later, we pull over and exit on shaky legs. I can make out more than just shadows now that the sky is lightening, but I can't see the full extent of the damage until Zeke turns on his flashlight and lets out a low whistle. Miss Vera is destroyed. Windows are cracked and the beautiful paint job that the previous owner must have waxed weekly is marred by Lexer sludge and dents.

"I'm so glad I wasn't driving," Penny says, hand to her mouth.

James puts an arm around her and grimaces. "I wouldn't have gotten out of that without you."

"I think we've learned a valuable lesson," Mark, a compact older man with a trim beard, says. He still acts like the history teacher he was before Bornavirus hit. "Driving at night does not seem to be a viable option. Our lights can be seen for miles. A pod that might have missed us in the day will surely race for us at night. We'll never see them coming."

I know we'd all been thinking the same thing, but it's such a demoralizing thought that I was reluctant to bring it up.

"It'll take us double the time," Mike says. His long face looks as if it's lengthened by a couple of inches. His twenty year-old son, Rohan, nods. "I know we don't have a choice, but we don't have enough food."

The RV that arrived from Whitefield hadn't been a part of their bug out plan, just a place where kids would gather to watch the occasional movie. We have enough food to feed ten people for a week on portions that aren't generous. It was going to be tight feeding twenty for four or five days. Nine or ten days will be even tighter.

"We do have a choice," Mark says. "But prudence pays, especially with the monsters."

The best thing to do is play it safe unless we have a good reason not to. There's the fear that we'll run into a giant pod of Lexers if we travel slowly, but it's close to a certainty that we'll run into a smaller pod at night; they're a dime a dozen.

The sun has risen by the time we've emptied the VW and moved it off the road. Miss Vera has become one of the cars you see by the roadside—abandoned, dented and bloody. A mystery that only we have the answer to. But I don't feel as sad as I expected at her loss: We're still alive, and for all her beauty she is, after all, just an artfully arranged collection of wood and metal.

"Thanks, Miss V," I say to her. I snap a picture with Adrian's phone and put my arms around the kids. "Guess you're gonna get some TV."

CHAPTER 6

"We need better maps," James says from the table in the RV. "There are tons of back roads, but they're not on the map. What we really need is a road atlas."

We've been checking cars and a few houses we've passed, but all we've found are folding maps that show only main roads.

"If we can find a phone book, we can find a bookstore. That's—" I stop. That's what Ana and I did when we saved Nelly from his infection. "It's probably the best way."

James nods. "We're coming up on Thunder Bay. There should be a bookstore there."

"And a new car, maybe," Tony says from the front.

It's tight in the camper. Five adults in the pickup leaves fifteen in here. Even minus the four kids in the bedroom watching a movie and Penny in the bed over the cab, we're cramped. But no one's sold on the idea of using more gas than we need.

I sit with Maureen. Her brown bob is limp, but her cheeks have gone back to plump from where they'd fallen at the news of John's death. She's the caretaking type, and we give her something to do. She's fed us pasta and cleaned up, and now her arm is around me on the couch. I snuggle in and am reminded of Hank on my lap. I wonder at what age you stop wanting your parents when things are rough. Maybe you never do.

"A van," Nelly says. "That way we can all fit if we had to."

"And you can ride with us," I say.

"What makes you think I want to ride with you?"

"My delightful odor?"

Everyone laughs, although it's true. The RV is full of potable water that shouldn't be wasted; otherwise I'd even take a cold shower. I've changed into a spare outfit because the one I wore when we left Kingdom Come was disgusting enough that I left it in Quebec, and I have one more change of clothes after this. Ana's bag is here, but I don't think I can bring myself to wear her clothes. Besides, it's probably leather pants, which are warm when it's cold but sweaty when it's not. It's sunny and in the fifties; I thought September would be colder up here.

"Turn's coming up," James says to Mike, our driver.

"Here goes nothing," Mike mutters. He turns off the highway and slows at two houses with only trees for neighbors. "What do you think?"

It looks safe enough. I follow Peter and Nelly to the blue house, whose door is easily kicked open by one strike of Zeke's heavy boot. Inexpensive but nice furniture and a huge television make up most of the living room's decor. It smells fine, but we call out to be sure nothing's lurking before we step in.

"If you were a phone book, where would you be?" Nelly asks.

"Kitchen," I say. "Maybe office. There were no smartphones when you were growing up. Don't you remember looking things up the old-fashioned way?"

Nelly grunts and moves left to the kitchen, where he drops his machete on the table and searches the cabinets. I poke around in a guest bedroom-slash-office down the hall. There's no phone book in the drawers or closet, but I grab the ream of paper that sits next to the printer and every writing implement I can find. I'm shoving it all into a pillowcase when Peter appears at the doorway.

He sets down a litter box, which he must have emptied, a box of litter, and a bin that he opens to reveal dry cat food. "We won't have to feed Sparky and Barnaby our food."

"Or walk Sparky, thank God." It's not the walking of the cat that's so bad, since she has the harness I made, but she plants her butt on the ground or pounces on waving grass instead of doing her business. "What happened to the cat that was here?"

"You don't want to know."

All the people who've died is a bigger tragedy, but that doesn't stop me from feeling terrible about the animals who must have starved or died of thirst waiting for their owners to return. If they weren't eaten by them.

"Look at all this paper and stuff," I say, rather than think about the cat that's probably curled up in a corner somewhere, desiccated and pathetic. "Bits and Hank can start on their next comic."

"Good thinking. They'll be excited."

Peter takes the pillowcase and throws it on the bin, then leaves for the RV. I look around in the living room for something to read, but these people preferred electronic entertainment.

Zeke stands at the front door, his beard just brushing the arms he's folded over his chest while he keeps watch. "What, no books, sugar?"

"Not a one."

"We'll find you something to read." He points to the coffee table's lower shelf. "Looks like a magazine under there."

I pull out the celebrity magazine. The first few pages inform me that celebrities are just like me—They take out the garbage! They walk down the street!—and I drop it to the floor in disgust. "I'd rather read can labels. Although the thought of all those people becoming zombies is somewhat heartening."

Zeke's laugh follows me into the kitchen, where I find Nelly fighting to open a large drawer. Batteries, scissors, screwdrivers, instruction manuals, and other assorted things leap to the floor.

"It's like your kitchen," he says to me.

"Quiet, you," I say. "Every kitchen needs a junk drawer."

"Except you had junk *drawers*, plural, and junk cabinets and junk—"

I push him out of the way to retrieve the batteries and open the upper cabinets to find plenty of dishes but no food. Nelly checks the cabinet under the drawer and holds up two phone books in triumph. I trace my name in the film of dust on the microwave. Nelly adds his name and then writes *were here* underneath, and I giggle just as Peter comes up behind us.

"How old are you guys?" he asks.

I write his name, too. "We have to leave our marks. That way, one day people will remember us."

"Our names will be known far and wide," Nelly says. "By *all* seven people still alive. Ready to check the fridge?"

I make a face. There's never anything except the smell of death inside. But it's unwise not to check, especially since we're low on food. I hold my nose and pull open the door. The stench fills the kitchen even though I slam it after the few seconds it takes to register exploded containers and a colony of mold.

Peter leans into the living room for fresh air. "That's never once been a good idea."

We trail him to the RV, where James locates a bookstore and a car dealership in town. The houses go from woodsy to houses and apartment complexes. There's plenty of overgrown lawn on which to drive until we hit a length of road that's been dug into rock. Even at a few feet tall, the walls are high enough to prevent skirting around the pileup that blocks the way. The RV won't be able to navigate through the cleared spaces like the pickup can.

Shawn stops alongside in the pickup and leans out the window. "Now what?"

"Some of us take the pickup and meet back here," Kyle says. "I'll go."

I tilt my head to where Nicki stands, thumb in her mouth and eyes wide. Kyle's jaw twitches, but he stays quiet.

"I have to go, we might need my superior mechanical skills," Shawn says.

Jamie sighs from the back of the pickup. "I'll go, if only to volunteer you as bait so we can escape."

I start to speak, but Peter coughs and looks to Bits, who might as well be sucking her thumb by the look on her face. "I'll go," he says.

"Not if I don't," I say.

I'm not chomping at the bit to head into a city that used to have a hundred thousand people and now may have half of that number of zombies post-winter, but I'd feel guilty if I didn't volunteer. And I want to keep an eye on Peter.

Peter frowns. "Why do you have to go for me to go?"

"I'm just saying that—"

"You stay." Mark picks up his bow from where it rests on the counter. "I'll come along."

"I'm four," Zeke says. "That's good enough. If we're not back in four hours, you start down the road again."

CHAPTER 7

Nelly, Peter and I keep watch from the RV's roof. It's a residential neighborhood, and there have to be Lexers in the side streets or backyards, waiting in that trance-like state for a meal. The plan is to make it past Thunder Bay before we find a place for the night. From what we can see on our useless map, there aren't any roads that head north and skirt the town, so it could take hours.

"Let's find a big house," Nelly says. "With lots of bedrooms."

"Bedrooms?" I ask with a wink. "Why? Huh?"

Nelly shakes his head. "You really never made it past ten, did you?"

"I did, just not when it comes to you and Penny."

"Great."

Peter laughs. "I'll help scout out houses. Maybe a few of us should ride ahead and radio back if we see something that looks good."

"You're not going ahead," I say. "No one is splitting up."

"We're split up right now."

"That's because it's unavoidable. Even a few miles are too much if it's not necessary. You can't go without me, and you wouldn't let me go, would you?"

"Why aren't you letting me do anything, Mom?" Peter asks. "And why do you keep looking at me like that?"

"Like what?"

"Like he's about to cannonball into a pool full of Lexers," Nelly says.

I look down because I know I've been caught. "I am not."

"Just stop doing or thinking whatever it is that you're doing or thinking," Peter says.

The supply of people I love in this world is rapidly dwindling, and these two are at the top of the chart of those left. I rub at a scuff on my boot with my gloved finger. I don't want either of them to see how scared I am at the possibility that they won't make it. "I just want to make sure you're okay."

Peter leans into my line of vision. "I'm okay."

I believe him, but that only reassures me that he won't do something dangerous on purpose. I have no control over the rest of the world, which appears to get its kicks out of throwing dangerous things our way. "Fine. But you're not leaving me alone to raise two kids, so we have to do everything together."

"So they'll have no one?" Peter asks. "I fail to see the sense in that plan."

"We'll keep each other safe. Nelly's in charge if we die."

"Hold on," Nelly says. "I'm the gay uncle. I didn't sign up for gay dad."

"Shush," I tell him. I know he'd take the kids in a heartbeat. "The only option is to stay alive, so that's what we're going to do. We'll be freezing our asses off in Alaska in no time."

"Well, someone's turned into Pollyanna Sunshine," Nelly says.

"That's right, so don't fuck with me."

A pounding starts up from the closest house. The glass window of the garage door shatters and the arms and head of a Lexer poke through. It tries to pull back, but it's managed to wedge itself in the small space. It's a perfect kill shot, and we have to take it because its noises will draw any nearby Lexers straight here.

"I got it," I say, and climb down the ladder.

Peter hits the ground a second later and raises his brows when I turn to him. "Everything together, right? I'm sticking like glue."

I snort and walk toward the garage. A year of zombiehood has not been kind to this one. Its skin has toughened into leather and only a wisp of hair remains. Nose gone, ear missing. You'd think the teeth would fall out of rotten gums, but those manage to hang on tight. A world of toothless zombies would be great. Or better. The damn thing keeps moving its head side to side, and I have to get closer than I'd like. I place one hand on his forehead and bring the tomahawk spike into his eye.

"At least he wasn't a gusher," Peter says about the body that now hangs out the window. The older ones usually don't have a lot of muck, but every once in a while you get one that throws out a ton of fluid and it only takes a few drops to make you stink. "I would've done it."

"Now you tell me," I say, and wipe my axe in the long grass.

The sun goes behind a cloud once we're back on the roof. I wrap my arms around myself. It's warmer than I thought it would be, but it's nowhere near the eighty degrees I prefer.

"What time is it?" I ask Nelly.

"Time to get a watch," he says.

"You're hysterical."

He looks at his wrist. "Ten, they've been gone two hours."

Another two hours and we'll have to leave. I stand for a better view, imagining any number of ways they could have died, and see Lexers rounding the corner of a side street.

"About twenty coming," I say.

"Shit," Nelly says. "Now what?"

It's too many to take on foot or from the roof for no good reason, and a waste of good, noisy ammo. Nelly lifts the other handheld and says, "Lexers on their way. We gotta go."

They're over a block away, but we still haul our butts to the door. Barnaby stands at attention and lets out a low bark. It's his warning bark, soon to be followed by his incessant, incredibly loud barks. Tony fires up the engine and rolls back the way we came.

"Zeke'll find us down the road," Kyle yells over Barnaby, who, sure enough, has moved on to stage two.

"Quiet!" I clamp a hand around Barn's snout until the only noise is quiet *moofs*. When he's done, I pat his head with a sigh. I don't want to leave Barn behind, but I'm afraid he'll get us all killed.

Tony stops at the highway. It'll take a couple of hours for that group of Lexers to get here, and by then the others will be back. Or they won't.

"He wasn't too loud, right?" Bits asks, imploring me to agree. "We can't get rid of him."

I don't want to lie, so I make a sound that isn't a yes or no. Immediately, her eyes fill and spill over. Peter rubs his forehead. He gives Bits anything she wants, within reason, and even he's silent.

"Please," Bits begs.

"Don't worry about that," Peter says. "Right now he's fine."

"I promise," I say. "Okay?"

Bits nods, but she's still on course for a sobbing cry when Mike says, "How about a story?"

Hank stops eyeing me and Peter as if we might kill Barn any second and asks, "What kind of story?"

Mike spreads his arms. "A story of wonder and heroes and fantastical creatures. Of dark and light and good and evil."

Mike is a writer. His bug out bag contains mostly notebooks, with survival equipment thrown in as an aside. I get it; I would've loved to have brought art supplies. But as it is, I have enough things in my two bags that aren't sensible.

"I want to hear," Nicki says.

"Well, let's go in the bedroom," Mike says, and herds them away. "Once upon a time there was a princess—"

"This is a good one. My dad told it to me when I was little," Rohan interrupts. He looks like his dad, with his pale skin and shoulder-length dark hair, and has the same good humor.

"That's right," Mike says.

"Was she a fancy princess?" Bits asks. "I don't like princesses that much."

"No," Mike replies. "She didn't wear a crown. In fact, she wore her hair in two buns and carried a gun."

"Like Cassie!" Bits says.

Mike winks at me. "Exactly. Anyway, like I was saying, this princess was strong and fearless. She was being held hostage by the forces of darkness—"

"Is this Star Wars?" Hank asks.

"Are you guys going to let me tell this story or not?" Mike asks. He shuts the door behind them.

I kiss Barn's golden-yellow head and turn away before he can give me a slobbery kiss on the lips. "We'll have to do something if he won't stop barking," I say to Peter.

I don't know what we'd do; I couldn't possibly kill him, and leaving him alone somewhere makes a lump rise in my throat. I know he's only trying to protect us, but these aren't criminals who are deterred by dogs. They *eat* dogs, and his bark rings out like a dinner bell.

"How about a muzzle?" Peter asks.

"They tried that on the farm. He still makes a lot of noise."

"Then I'll train him to be quiet."

"Do you know how many times people have tried to teach him a trick? It never works."

Peter scratches Barn's chin and then wipes his hand on his pants. "I'll figure it out. I've always wanted a dog."

"He's all yours."

Peter looks pleased by the idea. Nut job. He looks up when I rise to my feet. "Where are you going?"

"Have to pee. Want to stick like glue now? Could get messy."

He laughs, and I realize I've made him laugh a few times today. My mother always said that humor is the last refuge of the damned, but I've found it's the first refuge of the zombie apocalypse.

CHAPTER 8

A cheer rises in the RV when the pickup arrives fifteen minutes before our scheduled departure. They don't have another vehicle, but I'm so glad to see them that I don't care. Shawn jumps out of the van and salutes us. He reaches into the door and pulls out a thick book. "One back roads atlas, as promised. Two, actually."

James inspects the book. "Dude, this is perfect. What happened? We were getting worried."

"That place is crawling with Lexers. We tried to lead them away from the dealership, but they wouldn't follow."

Zeke hands me a large shopping bag, and I hug him when I see the books it contains: Everything from kids' books to sci-fi to chick-lit to an astronomy book. "Glad you like them, sugar."

"I'm not hugging you because of the books, although you are my hero. I'm hugging you because you're back. You know I can't live without you."

He dips me low with a booming laugh. Zeke is almost always in a good mood, and if he's not, you only have to wait a few minutes until he is again. He tells me he wasn't always that way, but it's the only Zeke I know.

"You are sweet as sugar." Zeke sets me upright. "Isn't she?"

Peter and Nelly look at him like he's crazy, and I glare at them before I kiss Zeke's cheek. "Only with you, Zeke, because you deserve it."

"It doesn't solve the problem of another vehicle," Zeke says, drawing out the word like *vee-hick-ul*. "But the RV's a place to sleep if we can't find one. Maybe it's better this way."

"This baby ain't breaking down," Shawn says, as he kicks an RV tire.

"Speaking of sleep, the kids are still sleeping," Maureen says. "Why don't we leave before they wake?"

"Your stories always put me to sleep," Rohan says to his dad, who cuffs him good-naturedly.

The kids didn't get much rest last night. Of course, this nap is probably going to lead to kids being awake all night, but cranky daytime kids are worse than happy nighttime kids.

While we drive, James sits at the RV's dinette with his new best friend, flipping pages and muttering. Houses appear through the foliage that borders the highway, and with the increase in population comes abandoned cars. At first we can weave our way through, but then we hit what must have been a mass exodus out of Thunder Bay. Car doors hang open where people ran for their lives, thereby leaving lanes, the shoulder and the median unusable. A few figures rise in the distance and begin stumbling our way.

We sit, engines idling and James muttering, until he has us turn around. We head north on a two-lane road that's seen better days, then a network of dirt roads that deposit us back on the main highway past Thunder Bay.

***

Bits, Hank and Nicki have awakened, and between their longing for another movie and treats, I wish they'd go back to sleep. I hate to say no about the treats, but as far as I'm concerned they can watch movies until their brains implode. Once we get to Alaska movies will be a rare occurrence again.

"Does it drain the battery?" Bits asks for the thousandth time.

"Isn't there solar?" Hank asks. "Doesn't that mean we can watch?"

"Can we, Daddy?" Nicki asks.

Kyle looks to me. Now that they've gotten a taste of movies they're like desert travelers who've been allowed to sip from a full water bottle. "James?" I ask.

"It should be fine," he says with a shrug.

James's jaw-length hair is stringy and greasy. I brushed mine earlier before winding it back into buns and consoled myself with the thought that those natural oils were giving it the deepest conditioning treatment ever, which made me miss Ana. Even a year after the apocalypse I'm accustomed to being relatively clean, which is probably more than other survivors can say.

"Go ahead," I say. Once they've scampered back to the bed, Ash included, I look to the others. "I wonder if we'll see anyone."

There are small groups who've contacted Safe Zones to let them know they're out here. We know of one official Safe Zone on our way. It was a green pin on Whitefield's map—meaning it hadn't been heard from in a while—but we're going to stop anyway.

Adam spins in the passenger's seat where he sits next to Nelly. "They're probably off the main road. And if they see us, they'll probably hide. Wouldn't you?"

"They might shoot first and ask questions later," Kyle says. "Back home, anyone who wanted a piece of us wouldn't take the chance. You think these people are as lucky?"

Kyle's right that it's different out here. I want to believe that most people are basically good, but desperate people do desperate things—I'd probably steal and lie to keep the kids alive if I absolutely had to. Others might want what we have, which isn't much compared to what we had in Vermont, but it's a lot to people living on the edge. We're living on the edge now, and the difference between life and death this winter lies in our gas tanks and weapons and the tiny pantry of the RV.

"There's a lake with a beach up ahead," Nelly says.

We need to wash off the reddish-brown and black juices left by our ride through the pod. We've been opening the vehicle doors with rags, and I freak out whenever Bits or Hank go near the exterior, so this is time well spent in my book. The lake is surrounded by open fields and small clusters of trees that aren't hiding any undead. I make the kids stretch their legs with the promise that the movie will resume after intermission, and then I stand on the shore with Peter while we wait for our turn with the sponges and buckets.

"Sparky doesn't like the water," Bits calls.

She'd insisted Sparky needed exercise, but it's clear she likes the novelty of walking a cat. Sparky sniffs at the water's edge and jumps back. Bits's laugh echoes across the water when Hank picks up Sparky and pretends to walk her across the lake's surface.

"They're good for each other," Peter says.

"Like a brother and sister who don't fight all the time. Eric and I did at that age. It drove my parents crazy." I wish Eric were here to fight with. To do anything with.

"My sister and I did, too. My mother would send us to one of our rooms and tell us to play until we could be friends."

"How'd that work out?" I ask.

"It worked until we got out of the room."

I laugh and watch the kids dry Sparky's paws. Hank folds the towel and drapes it over his shoulder; Bits would've dropped it on the ground and forgotten it immediately. "Henry and I had a deal. I told him I'd take care of Hank if anything happened."

"We will," Peter says.

I nod. The lake is huge and marshy, reflecting the gray of the now overcast sky. I tell myself we will hit the mountains. It's just going to take a little longer than we'd hoped. We'll have time. The more northerly our route, the longer it will take any northbound Lexers to reach us.

"You know, for someone who's a big crybaby, you've hardly cried at all," Peter says.

"When we get to Alaska I'm going to fall apart. So watch out." Maybe he thinks I'm kidding, since he laughs. Boy, is he going to be surprised.

"Just don't do anything stupid," he says. "Promise?"

"I promise I won't. You promise me?"

His nod is comforting. I need him for more than just raising two kids—I never would've gotten through this summer without him. I think at this point Peter might know me better than Nelly and Penny do, and he still likes me in spite of it, even when I've been at my most unlikeable.

"What are you two doing lollygagging over here?" Nelly asks. "I'm not cleaning off that crap without y'all."

"You don't want me on your cleaning detail anyway," I say. "I'm such a slob, with junk drawers everywhere, right? How much help could I be?"

"Nice try," Nelly says. "But no. The soap's been sitting long enough."

He hands us ponchos and rubber gloves. The others fill buckets for us to rinse and scrub until it's as clean as cold water can make it. When we're finished, I walk to where trees grow near the lake, strip to my tank top and roll up my jeans. I pant as I step into the cold water with a bottle of soap. This is an insane idea, but I can't shake the feeling that I have cooties.

"Remember when we washed up in the stream at that campground in Jersey?" Penny asks.

I spin around. Her face is puffy with pregnancy and grief, but her brown eyes are bright. "You even washed your hair," I say. "Want to come in?"

"No freaking way. I'm cleaner than you, anyway. Ha."

We wouldn't let her help with cleanup, and she didn't sweat her way through hundreds of Lexers two days ago. That baby is making it to Alaska. She laughs at my attempt to wash my armpits while not getting wet. I give up once my arms are clean and splash her as I walk out.

"*Coño!*" she yells, and wipes the droplets off her face. "But I'm still cleaner."

"Well, at least I don't have to squeeze the equivalent of an eight-pound ham out of my nether regions in the next few months."

She throws back her head, her laugh mixing with the calls of the birds above, and her eyes are moist when she flings my towel at me. "You win."

CHAPTER 9

The pickup pulls over near Winnipeg, where we've planned to stop for the night before venturing into the city for fuel tomorrow morning. Zeke steps out and points to a thin stream of smoke rising from a group of trees to the west. No house is visible, but two silos sit at the edge of the overgrown farmland. "Looks like people. We'll have to pass, so let's be on our guard."

"Should we stop?" Nelly asks.

Mark taps his chin. "Most people I met on the way to Vermont were sociable, if somewhat desperate. It could be helpful to get some details about Winnipeg."

"I'm not so sure," Zeke says. "They might not want to share details, seeing as how we plan to take what they might think of as *their* gas."

"Winnipeg was a city of 600,000," Mark says. "Getting gas while staying alive is going to be difficult. A little insider knowledge might prove useful."

Zeke points to Kyle, Shawn, Peter and Nelly. "Okay, we'll drive the pickup behind the RV. If they look friendly, we'll circle back while the RV waits up ahead."

"Maybe I should go in the pickup," Jamie says. "I don't know—me, Mark, Margaret and Cassie? They're much less likely to feel threatened by women than men."

I take in Zeke, who's a teddy bear but looks threatening if you don't know him. The others are no better. A bunch of grubby guys are bound to set off anyone's alarms. I don't love the idea of being shot at, to put it mildly, but it's a better plan—I know *I'd* be more frightened of a truck full of men than women.

"Okay," I say. Peter shakes his head. I shrug and wait for him to offer a better idea, but he only tightens his mouth.

"Sure," Margaret says. She's in her early forties, lean and ropy, and always wears a low ponytail, the ends still dyed auburn. Her face has settled into lines that make me think she hasn't had an easy life; she doesn't talk about life before Bornavirus enough for me to know for sure. In fact, she barely speaks. She's the kind of lady you know at a moment's glance not to fuck with, but she gives off a live-and-let-live vibe that keeps her from being scary. Perfect for meeting new friends—or enemies.

"Right, they won't shoot at women, they'll just ra—" Nelly stops at Peter's head tilt toward the kids.

"This is the biggest city we've been to in the past year," Jamie says. "It's huge. We need some help." She quiets Shawn's protest with a scowl. "We'll be in a truck. We'll be out of there before anything happens."

"No." Peter shakes his head like he's the final decision maker. I may not want to do this, but to be told I *can't* is irritating. "We'll figure it out ourselves."

Zeke nods like it's been settled. It was his plan to begin with, but because they don't want the womenfolk to go, it's off the table. I understand their concern, even if I do find it a bit surprising. Chivalry hasn't completely died out in the past year but, at least in our group, chauvinism has taken a back seat to survival. And we need to do something besides stand here and wait to be murdered.

"I think Zeke's plan was best, but Jamie's right, too," I say, even as I want to smack myself for arguing in favor of being one of the first people killed. "Kyle, remember what you said about strangers shooting first and asking questions later? Wouldn't you be less likely to shoot first if you saw women?"

Kyle thinks for a moment, then nods. He talks more than Margaret does, although ninety percent of those words are to Nicki.

"That's all I'm saying," Jamie says with a sweet smile. I swear she bats her eyelashes. "I'm not suggesting we go in there guns blazing or anything. And you'll be just down the road. I won't be worried if you guys are there."

Zeke tugs on his beard. "I guess it's not a bad plan."

Jamie gives me a subtle eye roll when the others agree. Shawn looks half-pleased with the idea of rescuing us, but Peter watches like he's not buying it and then says with a sigh, "I'm driving the pickup."

Once Peter, Mark, Jamie, Margaret and I have situated ourselves in the truck, guns in laps, we follow at a steady pace a short distance behind the RV.

"This is a stupid idea," Peter mutters. "You promised you wouldn't do anything stupid."

"We're in Canada, home of the nicest people on Earth," I joke, although my nervousness grows with each passing second. "What could go wrong, eh?"

Peter pretends he hasn't heard me. The fence that surrounds the house and trees has small wooden doors set at eye level, perfect for killing Lexers, keeping watch and, I suppose, shooting us. The razor wire at the top doesn't exactly scream *welcome*. The RV speeds past. We go a bit slower, and we're halfway there when one of the small doors swings open. Peter hits the accelerator hard enough to give me whiplash. I expect to see the barrel of a shotgun in the side view mirror, but it's a square of white cloth waving at the end of a stick.

"Wait!" I say. "It's a truce flag."

Zeke's voice comes through the radio. "Looks like they want to talk."

The flag hangs limply out of the hole by the time we reach the RV. "Could be a trap," Zeke says out the window, "but I think we should check it out. It's almost dark and they know we're here. They could sneak up on us tonight."

Peter doesn't say a word before pulling the truck around and heading back to where the flag has resumed its waving. He stops on the opposite side of the road and rolls down his window, pistol in his hand out of eyeshot. A head appears in the small square.

"Hello," a man's voice calls. He sounds happy enough to see us.

"Hi," Peter says. His voice gives away nothing. No fear or happiness at the sight of another human being in a world full of zombies. I want to request that he act a bit friendlier, but he'd probably shoot me.

"Where are you heading?" the voice comes again.

"West. Alaska."

"How many are you?"

"Twenty."

"Shouldn't go through Winnipeg at night. Too dangerous. We don't have much to spare, but if you need a safe place until the morning, you're welcome to stay."

"I think we should take him up on his offer," Mark says from the back

I nod at Peter's glance. There's only one way to know if they're as welcoming as they say, and that's to let down our guard. I have a good feeling about this place. Staying behind a fence would be safer. Peter reverses the truck. For a moment it looks as though he's decided against taking them up on their hospitality, but then he pulls ten feet from the door. A man with a thin face peers out at us, his sloped eyes friendly when he smiles.

"Name's Thomas."

"Peter."

"That's a long drive."

"We had to leave the Vermont Safe Zone. The Lex—zombies are coming up north. Thousands of them."

Thomas's eyes leave Peter's face for the south before they return. "I'd like to hear more about that. We've only had a few visitors in the past year."

Peter watches him for another beat, then puts the radio in my lap and says, "Tell them to come."

CHAPTER 10

When Thomas swings open the wooden gate, it becomes apparent that this is no ordinary enclosure. The outside resembles a privacy fence, the type you'd find around any suburban home, but the inside is lined with metal of all types. Everything from highway signs to sheet metal has been screwed into the wood. Rocks have been mortared into walls along the fence, and every three feet or so there's a thick brace made of wood or metal. I'm still apprehensive about their motives, but it's comforting to be inside a barrier again.

Kingdom Come's trench must be packed with enough Lexers to walk across. I'd like to believe that they didn't pull the fences down, since there were no humans left, but the livestock would have been irresistible—we're the preferred snack, although animals will do in a pinch. The grass must be trodden, the barn fences destroyed. I'm sure they're trampling Adrian's grave. It shouldn't matter, but it makes me angry to think they've probably claimed his resting place as well as his life.

The gate swings closed behind us, followed by the loud latching of several bolts. I force myself to stay on high alert once we've hit the dirt. They have a couple of acres fenced off, with a small barn and several tiny sheds within. A large garden sits to the right of the house, dark shapes of low, bushy fruit trees behind it, and the familiar clucking of chickens settling for the night fills the air from our left. I move Bits behind me in case I need to draw my gun and shush her when she barrages me with questions. I would've preferred she stayed in the RV.

Thomas turns at the opening of the house's door. A woman who looks to be his age—forty or so—with shoulder-length brown hair and a round, pleasant face stops on the top step and watches us with her hand on her collarbone. When she sees Bits, Hank and Nicki, she perks up and makes her way down the stairs to join Thomas, who says, "This is my wife, Jessica."

"We appreciate the offer of a place to sleep, ma'am," Zeke says. "We'll stay in the RV and be out of your way in the morning. Name's Zeke."

"We have room in the house," she says. "It's the floor, but it's warm."

"Don't want to be any trouble, ma'am." Zeke's Southern manners are so gracious that he could be giving a courtly bow wearing a seersucker suit instead of boots and a motorcycle jacket.

"Don't call me ma'am again, Zeke," Jessica says, and her wide, friendly smile erases my final bit of uncertainty about their motives.

An elderly man with wispy white hair that has lifted from its comb-over comes to the doorway. "Why don't you come inside? It's cold out here," he says in a gravelly voice.

Just inside the foyer, stairs rise to the second floor. To the left is a dining room with a large table, the kitchen off it to the rear. The scent of food loaded with spices makes my mouth water. I've been able to ignore my hunger much of the day—we're going without lunch now that our travel time has increased—but now I'm famished.

"Make yourselves comfortable," Thomas says. "I have to check on the chickens and then we'll talk."

He gestures toward the living room that takes up the right side of the first floor. The flickering lamps give off warm light, and a woodstove by the far wall throws off gloriously abundant heat. A piano sits in the corner. I wonder if they ever play it or if it sits silent now. My dad used to say that there was always music playing somewhere—maybe this is one of those places.

When we enter, a dozen people rise from the various couches. One, a blond teenage boy, checks out Ashley before examining his own feet. A man holds a pregnant woman's arm protectively. Most are somewhere in their twenties through forties, a mix of men and women. They introduce themselves and we say our names before standing in silence. Maybe they feel as uncomfortable as I do, having invaded their space.

"Well, let them sit. Were you all raised in a barn?" the old man, Gerry, says after he's lowered himself into an easy chair. He waves us in. "Sit down."

I guide Bits and Hank to the wall near the stove. Penny sinks onto a couch cushion. The pregnant woman, Robin, perches beside her and tucks her dark hair behind her ears.

"When are you due?" Robin asks. "I'm due in a few weeks."

"Mid-December." Penny compares their stomachs and groans. "Oh God, I'm already as big as you! Are you positive you don't have another three months?"

The tension in the room dissolves at Robin's laugh. Quiet conversations begin, and I listen to the pregnant ladies commiserate about morning sickness and impending labor. I can only comprehend so many of the joys of pregnancy. The baby part is cool, but the getting there seems like a pain in the ass. Literally, according to Penny. I'll have to take her word for it.

I shove the thought of Adrian and our never-to-be-born children out of my mind. I have Bits and now Hank. It's enough. It'll have to be enough. After Dan, I feel like anyone I touch is doomed to die; I'd rather be alone than wait for the next victim. And I certainly won't have any more children if I can help it. Not in this world.

Peter kisses the top of Bits's head after she scoots into his lap. I have my little family. The fact that it's an adoptive, platonic co-parenting family doesn't make it any less than the conventional kind. For the first time in days I feel safe. Content, even, if I don't think about what's ahead of us or what we left behind. Just for tonight, I'll try to stop worrying. But I can't stop my hunger. Whatever they're cooking in the kitchen is pure torture.

"I'm hungry," Bits says, more fact than complaint. "When are we eating? What are we eating?"

"What do you say we talk after supper?" Zeke asks Thomas, who's just returned. "We'll go and fix our meal while you have yours."

"Don't waste your fuel," Thomas says. "You're welcome to use the stove. One thing we do have is plenty of LP and wood."

"Thank you," Maureen says, and turns to me. "Cassie, want to help?"

Maureen and I search the RV's pantry for something quick and easy. We save the cold stuff like MREs and canned goods for times when we won't be able to cook. There are boxes of pasta, packages of ramen noodles and bags of rice, flour, sugar and oats. The amounts are depressingly small. I place five packages of noodles, a few vegetables from our meager stock and all of our containers in a cloth bag to bring inside.

Maureen stares into the cabinet. "We'll make it work."

With doubling the travel time to account for stopping at night and any difficulties that may arise, we're limiting ourselves to far fewer calories than we need. We're on a strict diet, and none of us needs to be on a diet.

"I know," I say, although I don't.

Maureen's hand tightens into a fist on a box of pasta before her head drops. Her sob is raw, the kind that's impossible to hold back. I wrap my arms around her shoulders. I know how much she cared for John, and he for her. She'd found love again, only to have it taken—again.

"I'm okay," she says.

"You don't have to be. I'm not."

"You are." She swipes at her cheeks. "John knew you would be."

"I don't want you to think I don't care that he's—" I say, and realize I don't know what he is. He's very likely roaming the woods of Vermont, looking for something to eat. John deserves better than that. We all do, but he was so kind and loving that it breaks my heart to think he may have become something to fear.

Maureen takes my hands. "Don't ever think I don't know how much you loved him. We just go on the best we can. We have to."

I blink to stave off tears. That's what she said to me the day we first arrived at Kingdom Come. And here we are, searching for a home again. "He loved you so much," I say. "Enough to admit it to me, even."

John's love was huge, just like his heart, but he wasn't known for his willingness to discuss it. The fine lines around Maureen's eyes turn up. "And I loved him. John used to say, 'The Lord is near to the broken-hearted.' It's from Psalms. I remind myself of that every day. And when I do, I can feel God. And John and my husband and daughter."

I look for signs from those I've lost—there aren't ever any. It doesn't mean I think they've ceased to exist, just that I can't be certain they're somewhere better.

She takes a shaky breath. "And I am okay. Don't you worry about me. It's my job to worry about you."

"How about we worry about each other?"

"Deal. Let's get dinner on."

"You relax," I say. "Enjoy the couch and fire. You're always bustling around, it drives me crazy. I look lazy in comparison."

For the first time in days, I hear Maureen's throaty laugh. "You're such a stinker. But I think I will. Thank you, sweetheart."

Jessica offers a broad smile when I enter the kitchen. "What do you need? Thomas said you'd be cooking in here."

"Just a large pot," I say. "Thank you. Oh, I'll be right back, I forgot water."

"Help yourself, we have no shortage of water. There's a well behind the house."

She points me to a large container with a spigot and then dishes their meal into bowls. It's some sort of grain with beans and what look to be chunks of squash and tomato. It smells of cumin, onions and garlic, which is to say it smells delicious.

I fill the pot with more water than needed. It won't have caloric value, but warm, weakened broth feels more filling than plain water. Jessica leaves to bring food to the rest of her household. I chop carrots and zucchini and ignore the mushrooms that practically scream my name from a basket on the counter.

Nelly enters and watches me chop. "Need help?"

"Yeah, run out to the store and get us some steaks." I dump the veggies in the pot to wait for them to come to a boil.

Nelly groans. He could easily quadruple the calories he's getting on our new diet. He must be starving. "I'm killing and eating the next animal I see. I don't care what it is."

"Well, while we're waiting for that to happen, you can set out bowls. It'd better not be Sparky. Bits would never forgive you."

"How about Barnaby?"

"Maybe we'll get so hungry that he'll start to look like a turkey, with delicious turkey vapors rising off his golden drumsticks. You know, like in cartoons."

Nelly laughs. "Or a roast with those little white hats on the bones."

"Paper frills," Peter says from the kitchen doorway.

"Of course you know what they're called, Pete," Nelly says.

Barnaby trails Peter into the kitchen. "You have a new shadow," I say. "Maybe he knows you're the only thing standing between him and his demise."

Nelly trains his eyes on Barn and licks his lips. "Mm...steak." Barn wags his tail, oblivious to our plot to eat him.

"Maybe we should rename him Steak," I say, "so if the kids ask what we're eating, we can just say, 'Steak.' "

Peter levels a finger at us. "You are not eating my dog. I came to see if you needed help."

"Unless you can do something miraculous like change rocks to bread, I'm good."

We stop discussing food when Jessica reenters. I must not be the only one who doesn't want her to see how little we have and feel obligated to help us.

"You have a nice place," Peter says.

"Thanks. I like it, especially now that we don't have to pay a mortgage," she says with a laugh.

"That's one good thing," I say. "No bills to pay."

Jessica holds out a hand made raw by all the work one has to do these days. "Tell you what I'd love—lotion. It's so dry in the winter."

"I want an endless amount of lip balm," I say. Jessica nods vigorously. "How cold does it get here?"

"In *Winter*peg?" she asks. Peter, Nelly and I laugh. "Really freaking cold. You don't want to know."

I whimper. "Alaska's going to suck." She pats my shoulder and grins before she leaves.

I break the noodles and dump them into the water. Three minutes later, Peter ladles equal portions into our receptacles and Nelly brings out the first round. I take a few noodles and all of the vegetables from my mug and drop them into Penny's, then scoop some of her broth into mine so it looks even. She needs it more than I do. I point James to Penny's mug and watch him do the same with his soup. I'm sure he'd give her his whole meal if he could, but Penny would flip if he tried.

Jessica stops on her way past the table, brow furrowed. "That doesn't look like enough. Are you low on food?"

Peter and I stare at each other instead of meeting her eyes. He speaks first. "We have more people than we thought we would, but we're going into the city for fuel and food tomorrow."

I nod like it's going to be the best time ever to head into a place with hundreds of thousands of zombies. Jessica's mouth moves, but she nods instead of speaking. I wait for her to disappear and gulp down my broth and noodles without a spoon.

"I'm ready for breakfast," I say to Peter, who studies his plastic bowl and nods.

Bits eats delicately while Hank inhales his. He's too well-mannered to complain, but by the way he licks his bowl clean I know he'd like to beg for more. I wish I hadn't eaten what I didn't give to Penny so I could give it to him. I'd be ravenous, but that doesn't seem as bad as watching Hank scrape his bowl. I wash the pot and leave it to dry. When I turn, Peter's dumping the remainder of his soup into the kids' bowls. It's a gesture that makes me want to simultaneously hug and yell at him. He walks his empty bowl over to the sink.

"You need to eat," I say. "A big, strapping lad like yourself."

"So do you. I saw what you did with Penny's soup."

He must think I'm gearing up for an argument by the way his shoulders tense, so I say, "Well, obviously we're both idiots."

"I've always known that. I'm just glad you can finally admit it."

I kick his boot before I turn to wash the dishes. I'm surrounded by freaking comedians.

CHAPTER 11

W e've told Thomas and the others about the pods coming this way, unless they all veered for the Northeast. We answer their questions as best we can, but we lack a vast amount of information. Once they've exhausted our store of knowledge, James asks him about the farm.

"We bought the land to start an organic farm," Thomas says. "Then we found out we would have to wait longer than usual for certification. We were going to lose too much money, so I decided to return to work as an engineer. We'd just listed the farm for sale last spring."

He speaks in a measured voice, the engineer in him evaluating every word before it leaves his mouth. "We shored up the fence and waited it out. As long as we were quiet, we didn't have many visitors. Most people who left the city didn't stop. The few who did stop," he smiles at his housemates, "stayed on. So far, we've been able to find enough food and fuel. We've only seen a few people so far this summer—Robin and Ryan—and some who drove past without stopping."

Thomas thinks for a moment. "If the giant group—pod—was in Iowa over a month ago, they should've been here by now."

James spreads a map of the United States on the coffee table. "If they're walking straight and slow at one mile per hour, then, yeah. But they could be twenty or thirty miles east or west, coming this way. I don't think that pod in Iowa moved east, or they would've hit the Safe Zones in Pennsylvania and New York before us. I think there's more than one pod. Between the Southern U.S. and South America, there are a lot of zombies that didn't freeze this winter."

We had the winter in which to plan, recuperate and regain a sense of security. Down south, where the Lexers ate through the winter, there must be nothing left. If there were, maybe they wouldn't be eating their way north.

"There are some places to get a decent view. A few buildings, I mean, but getting inside won't be easy." Thomas shrugs, but the lines around his eyes have begun to descend.

"You definitely should," James says. "We had a lookout. That's how we got out in time. We couldn't see much from the roads with all the trees and mountains."

"Well, we don't have a problem with mountains or trees." Thomas gives a cheerless laugh. "Have you seen the mold on the bodies?"

"You mean the black moss?" Mark asks. "Is that what it is?"

"That's what Gerry thinks."

"It's mold all right," Gerry says, pushing at his dentures with his tongue. "Not one I've ever seen, but it's mold. Used to do mold removal years ago. It's the only thing that makes sense."

He stops as if we're going to argue; when we don't, he continues. "When you see the black fuzz, now, that's a large colony. But I'd say they all have some spores on them. With all these bodies, the air must be full of 'em."

"Is it dangerous to us?" Penny asks.

"Don't know, but I don't think so. You've all been around it and are fine?" We nod, and he crosses his arms like that's that. I'd like a more conclusive answer, but since we're still alive I suppose it won't kill us.

"Gerry thinks the mold is breaking down the virus in the flesh, allowing for decomposition," Thomas explains, then shrugs. "It's just a theory. Now, as for Winnipeg..." He leans over our atlas.

Jessica leaves for the dining room, where Bits and Hank are belly-down on the floor, working on a comic, while Nicki scribbles beside them. Ash and the teenage boy, Colin, each wear one earbud while they listen to music on my phone. Colin almost fainted when he saw a phone in working order. He may have thought Ash was cute before, but now she's a goddess. I watch Jessica beckon them into the kitchen and then return my attention to Thomas and James.

"We've gone as far into the city on the east side as is safe," Thomas says. "You won't find much unless you venture farther in. There are places where the bodies block the streets and you'll never get them moved before more hear you." He runs a finger along the map. "Here, on the west, is a large subdivision called Whyte Ridge. There are gas stations and shopping centers nearby—Walmart, Costco. I don't know what's left, though. The outbreak started over there."

"If you want to come along, we'll split what we find," Zeke offers. "We have a good fuel pump and long hoses. We can get down in the underground tanks where most people with siphons can't reach."

I'm disappointed when Thomas shakes his head. "I'd like to see if anything's coming before we risk our lives for supplies we won't need."

After he points out a few more stores and marks their locations on the map, we set up our blankets on the living room floor. Jessica runs her fingers along the closed lid of the piano.

"Do you ever get to play?" I ask.

"All winter. I miss it." Her fingers tap the wood, and she looks to where Thomas stands in the doorway. "Maybe I can play something short. If you want."

"Please do," Mark says.

She opens the lid carefully and sits on the bench. Bits settles in my lap, and I smell the rich spices of their dinner on her breath.

"Your tummy full, sweetie?" I ask.

"Yeah. It was really good."

I'm filled with gratitude. I spend much of my day wishing for things, and at least for tonight, the wish that they don't go to bed hungry has come true.

Jessica lowers her fingers to the keys. The music is simple and beautiful and quiet, exactly what I'd like the world to be again. Maybe that's why she chose it. The piece can't be more than a few minutes long, but in those few minutes before the final chord fades away, I believe that we'll make it, that we'll find respite from all the ugliness and noise of the Lexers.

Jessica shrugs off our praise with a shy smile. "See you in the morning."

"That was beautiful," I say to Bits, who nods. "I wonder what it was."

"Bach," Peter says.

"Prelude in C Major," Margaret adds, surprising us with her knowledge. She covers herself with her blankets and doesn't utter another word.

The worry I've kept at bay the past few hours resurfaces. I long for the spell of the music, but there's nothing but the crackling of the fire and the surety that tomorrow is going to suck. I can feel it in my bones, as John would've said.

CHAPTER 12

There's a reason why floors are not celebrated as places to get a restful night's sleep. I wake up stiff and sore, but warm. I have a feeling they kept the stove going all night for us and I appreciate every degree. After I've cleaned up, which involves the outhouse, a toothbrush and a new, ineffective layer of deodorant, I find Jessica in the kitchen.

"Thank you for feeding the kids," I say. "I really appreciate it."

She murmurs something and keeps her eyes on the pot she stirs. It's more of that grain from last night, but she's added maple syrup as you would to oatmeal. My oatmeal is waiting outside, but I wanted to catch her before things got hectic.

"Okay, well, thanks again," I say when no more words are forthcoming.

"Welcome," she whispers.

I leave to eat, wondering why she's aloof when last night she was friendly but put it out of my mind when Jamie hands me my breakfast. I would happily eat a mixing bowl full of oatmeal right now even though I don't love it. Will Jackson—Whitefield's old boss—was right when he said people may bitch about oatmeal but they know they're lucky to get it.

"So, how was the RV?" I ask Jamie, who slept there with Shawn last night.

"Cold," she says, her breath fogging in the morning air, "but private."

"You know what they say." Shawn finishes his final bite of oatmeal and claps his hands for warmth. "If the RV's a rockin', don't come a knock—"

Jamie smacks him. Bits and Hank look up from where they sit on the ground. I focus on my food; there's no way I'm explaining that one. Bits knows about sex, and she knows far too much about its darker side, having spent weeks listening to her mother being used by men before they finally killed her. It still wakes her up at night. But she's been around happy partnerships, although the fact that a few of those were ended by Lexers probably doesn't help. Her amused disgust at the thought of kissing, which she says she'll do when she's older—*maybe*—gives me hope that she hasn't been too damaged by what she's seen.

We say our goodbyes and have just started rolling when Jessica runs from the house with a cloth sack clutched to her chest, calling my name. She thrusts it into my arms on the RV's steps.

"Wheat berries," she says breathlessly. "Twenty pounds. If you soak them the night before, they'll need less time to cook. Use a three to one ratio with water. Toss them with oil or spices if you want." I nod slowly, taken aback by her kindness and trying to put her instructions to memory. She blinks. "I couldn't let you leave without something."

That's why she wouldn't look at me—she felt guilty. I hug her, sack in one arm and eyes burning. "Thank you so much."

"Be careful out there," she says with a final squeeze.

"Wait!" I rush into the RV and grab both my bags from under the bed. I find my lip balm stash, grab two of my four unopened tubes and put them in her hand. "It's not lotion, but I thought you could use it."

Jessica holds the tubes to her heart. I wave as we pass through the gate and then admire the bag of wheat berries. It's worth its weight in gold—more, since gold is worthless. I look around and see I'm not the only one who stares at the unassuming sack with something like awe.

"See?" I say to Peter. "Canadians."

✵✵✵

For a city of over half a million, the outskirts are desolate farmland. The blocked roads into Winnipeg force us to circle around and burn more gas than we'd like. The lack of hills, of any rise at all, allows us to drive on the grass when necessary and to avoid a few smaller pods of Lexers on the road. In mountainous or wooded territory we might have driven around a bend and directly into them.

Now that we've all had a handful of nuts and dried fruit, my hunger— or maybe my fear of hunger—has lessened. We're back on diet rations rather than starvation rations. If we ever head back to the Northeast, I'll stop to give Jessica another hug.

The fields end at a long white fence with an entrance into subdivision. Some houses are still occupied, with cars sitting in their driveways and Lexers beating on the window glass. James directs us to a street of large homes that he's chosen for its multiple exit routes and proximity to the stores. The pickup will go for fuel and those left here will check the houses for anything useful. It doesn't look promising, based on the number of kicked-in doors and broken windows. I didn't argue when Tony, Margaret, Zeke, Mike and Rohan volunteered for the fuel run; I couldn't bring myself to leave the kids in a place so populated, even in hands that I know to be competent.

I wave at the others who have already seated themselves in the pickup and touch Mike's arm. "Careful, please."

"Don't worry," Rohan says. "We'll have the Tantive Four all gassed up in no time, Leia Organa."

Mike laughs at my blank look. "Princess Leia's ship. The Tantive Four."

"That's it, I'm switching to a ponytail," I say.

I pretend to punch Rohan, who ducks into the pickup and grins as they pull away. I send along a wish that they make it back in record time with plenty of gas.

CHAPTER 13

Maureen and Penny watch the kids while we search a house that has shattered windows and a broken door but a minivan out front, which might mean clothes for Hank. We found him a spare outfit in Quebec, but it's all he has except for what he wore outside of Kingdom Come. Even washed out, it still retains the faint scent of death, and I don't want Hank to have to wear a reminder of what happened. I want fresh underwear, as does everyone else. At this point, I've lost the wearing-someone-else's-underwear-is-weird thing. If it's in a drawer and clean, then I'm wearing it.

Nelly, Peter, Adam and I step into a foyer that leads into a living room with vaulted ceilings. I don't know that I'll ever grow accustomed to stepping into someone's life and rummaging through their belongings, although I hope people have done the same in my apartment in Brooklyn. Maria, Penny and Ana's mother, was supposed to go there if she ever escaped the hospital where she was trapped. We left plenty of food in the basement along with camping equipment. If she never made it, someone else might have. Maybe someone is wearing my underwear right now. I smile at the thought instead of contemplating what's almost certainly become of Maria, who was like a mother to me.

"What's funny?" Nelly asks as we cross the carpet for the kitchen.

"I was thinking about a stranger wearing my underwear."

"I should've known."

We speak in hushed tones, partly so we don't attract anything that's outside, but also because you can feel the ghosts of the former inhabitants—the echoes of a once normal life. Dinner every night at six, kids playing in front of the TV, parents talking in the kitchen. There's no room in the RV for the scattered toys and an infant bouncy seat I know Penny would appreciate, but a baby might mean maternity clothes.

A quick look in the kitchen cabinets reveals nothing but baking powder and a half-full salt container. Nelly puts both in his bag. As we thought, someone's combed these houses for food. Peter opens the refrigerator for a final check, and when we've finished gagging I say, "I thought that was never a good idea."

"We need to keep our losing streak going," Peter says.

"So far, so good. Want to come upstairs with me? Nels and Adam can check the garage."

Upstairs, we steal toothpaste, mouthwash and antacids from the bathroom, and then move into the kids' rooms. The boy's room has jeans and shirts that might work for Hank, and I take a few tiny pieces of unisex clothing out of the drawers in the nursery. I don't want Penny's kid to have to wear frilly pink shirts if it isn't a girl.

"Done," I say.

Peter leans on the crib rail with a rounded back. I know he slept last night because I was up every hour to check on the kids, but he looks haggard. "I wonder what happened to the baby," he says, keeping his eyes trained on the crib mattress.

I picture the baby I put out of its misery in Vermont. I hope this one didn't end up like that. But she probably did—another reason to get Penny to safety. I don't have an answer, so I lean beside him and stare at the yellow and green quilt.

"I never thought I'd have a normal life," he says in a quiet voice. "I mean, I thought it'd be normal—my grandmother's version of normal. A wife I didn't like much, probably. Parties. Kids I'd never see because I'd always be working."

"That sounds terrible."

"I know. Then it all changed, and I was kind of okay with it. It wasn't going to be normal, but it would be different. I'd have all the things I wouldn't have had otherwise. Time. Love. A family."

"You still have a family," I say. "And we all love you."

"I know. I guess I just thought things were going to be a certain way and now they're not. They can't be."

"You'll have the other things again."

He shrugs. "I don't know."

"That's what you said to me after Adrian. Were you lying?"

"No, of course not."

"Good. Because you can't go around spouting off profound things like that and then take them back."

His shoulders jump with a small laugh. "Was I right?"

"Yeah. Well, I can see how it could happen." I don't mention how just when I believed it could happen again it was ripped away. Somehow I don't think that would be helpful. "You, of all people, will get there. Promise."

"Why me of all people?"

"Because you're an optimist. I would've jumped off a ledge by now if you weren't here."

"You'd all keep going," he says. "Just like we're going now."

"It wouldn't be the same." Even with how close we've become, we've only ever joked about our failed relationship. I feel weird bringing it up because there are things I'd rather not remember—how frustrated he made me, how I wasn't always nice to him, all the nights we spent in bed—but I want him to know how important he is. "Remember the night we met?"

"I have a vague recollection," he says. "Wasn't it at a bar or something?"

I elbow him. "When you said that losing people was like having the roof torn off your house?"

"You remember that?"

"Of course I do. You were right, it does feel that way, but now we're all here to shelter you." I drop my head with a groan. "God, that was so corny. It sounded much better in my head. You know what I mean."

"I do. Sorry again I was such a jerk, as long as we're reminiscing."

"I'm sorry, too."

"That I was a jerk?"

"No, that *I* was." I nod when he shakes his head. "I had my moments, Petey. Anyway, maybe we'd keep going now, but who would talk me down off the ledge?"

"Nel?"

"Are you kidding? Nelly would shove me off the ledge. Nope, it's your job, whether you want it or not. The pay sucks, but the benefits are immense. Probably more like immensely annoying, but too bad."

"I'll take it," he says, and puts out a hand to shake on the deal.

"You're hired. I'm always here if you want to talk." I squeeze his arm and start out of the room.

"Cassandra," he says. "Thanks. For saying all that."

I'm gratified to see he has a bit more spark in his eyes. "I meant every word."

T

he next houses are the same in terms of food. I've found a dress for Bits, who may have forsaken Barbies for superheroes but still loves to be fancy, along with some more appropriate attire. I have clean underwear and wool socks. And Penny now has clothes she fits in, with room to grow.

"I can breathe. I swear the heartburn is better already." Penny twirls in her new maternity jeans and blousy shirt. She squeals when Peter hands her the jar of antacids. "Did I ever tell you I love you?" She kisses Peter on the lips and crunches on a few.

"Hey!" James says. "All I had to do was get you Rolaids and a shirt?"

Penny gives James an even bigger kiss and takes a book from the cabinet above the couch. After two ungraceful attempts to get into the cabover bed, I give her butt a push and climb up after. Jamie and Shawn are asleep in the bedroom. I assume they're sleeping, since the RV isn't *a rockin*'. A person or animal covers every inch of floor or seating, except for Nelly and Adam, who keep watch from the roof. I'm trying not to worry that it's been two hours since the others left. There are five gas stations nearby. They might have had to visit a couple before they found fuel.

Ashley strokes her ponytail while she reads a book in the corner. I know her mind must be moving a mile a minute, but she's wearing that teenage nothing-can-touch-me veneer. The same goes for Kyle, who stares out the window from the sofa with Nicki in his lap. I had a personal mission to make him laugh his ass off one day, but the chances of that have gotten slimmer now that there's even less to laugh about.

Bits and Hank have left a sheet of scrap paper up here. I fold it carefully and launch my paper airplane at Kyle, then snort when it hits him in the temple and drop my head.

"Where'd it come from, Daddy?" Nicki asks.

I hear Kyle mumble, but other than quiet voices and the rustle of Bits's and Hank's papers, it's silent. "Cassie," Kyle says. I cringe at his commanding voice; he can't have that little of a sense of humor.

I raise my head and screech when five airplanes come for me, three wielded by Bits, Hank and Ash. I make a decent airplane, but these are sleek and fast enough that I'm going to have a divot in my forehead for the rest of my life. I grab one and admire it, then look down to where Kyle stands with Nicki wearing a broad smile.

"You chose the wrong guy for a paper airplane war," he says.

"These are some fine planes," I say. "But you've won the battle, not the war."

"You think you're going to win with these tired old planes?" Kyle holds up my plane and points to where the tip has bent on impact.

I set his planes in front of me and prop myself on my elbows. "Lesson one in the art of war: Use your enemy's own weapons against them."

I launch them at him one by one until I hear a low chuckle from where he's folded over Nicki. He straightens and shakes his head. "You're crazy."

It wasn't quite laughing his ass off, but I'm getting somewhere. "Just wait. It's gonna get wild up in here."

There's a scraping from the roof and Nelly's voice comes through a skylight. "Zeke and Margaret are running our way."

Kyle's face reverts to its usual hard expression, and I'm on the floor by the time he's opened the door. Zeke's face is red as if on the verge of a heart attack. Margaret breathes easily, although her hair has escaped its ponytail.

"Tony...under the truck...surrounded," Zeke pants.

Nelly looks behind them, his hands gripping his rifle. "Mike and Rohan?"

Zeke bends double, hands on knees, and shakes his head.

"They were at the truck, watching one way," Margaret says. "We were at the other end of the lot. We didn't hear anything until the screaming. They came out of nowhere."

"Could Mike and Rohan be under the truck?" I ask.

"Rohan, maybe. But I saw Mike—" The corners of her mouth arc downward.

The thought of Mike and Rohan being eaten alive makes my stomach lurch, as does the guilty relief that creeps in. Relief that the people I care about most are still alive. Peter and I might have been joking about sticking like glue, but I'm not anymore.

"Let's go," Kyle says.

He has the key turned in the ignition before we're all in. Bits and Hank have abandoned their papers at the sight of Zeke and Margaret. I sit beside Hank and watch Bits across the table, where Peter has seated himself. "We're going to help them," he says. "It's okay, we're safe in here."

In a perfect world, I'd have the kids in another vehicle, fully-gassed and heading out of Winnipeg as fast as was safe, but we can't leave Tony and Rohan. And we need the pump and the pickup's fuel tank. If Tony's under the truck, we'll lead them away and have him follow us. If he's dead, we'll have to get the truck ourselves.

"Is the tank full?" Shawn asks.

"At least half," Zeke replies. His breathing has returned to normal, but he still looks dazed. "It was going for a few minutes before they came."

Kyle follows Margaret's directions onto a wide road littered with bodies. The wind ruffles what's left of the corpses' clothing and swirls plastic bags and wrappers in tiny tornadoes. The gas station is set behind a grassy field at a wide intersection, with a drugstore behind it and a supermarket across the street. It could mean food, and probably does, given that a pod of Lexers streams from the broken glass in front. They may have been trapped in there for over a year with only the noise of the pump, and maybe Mike's screams, giving them enough incentive to break out.

"Jesus," Zeke breathes.

Kyle pulls into the station. The pump lays on the concrete near the ground tank. The pickup's hood is up, with the wires that run the pump still connected to its battery. In order to drive the pickup anywhere, we'll have to disengage the pump and reattach the truck to its battery.

Lexers wander, except for the one who lies tangled in the pump's suction hose; it winds over one leg, then twists around and down the other to the ankle. Even if we get the truck out of here, without the pump we'll be forced to siphon using rubber tubes in deep underground tanks—incredibly time-consuming if not impossible. The hose must be cut if it can't be untangled, but finding a new hose might prove difficult. This particular hose is reinforced to withstand the vacuum of the pump, as well as equipped with some sort of anti-static metal so we don't blow ourselves to hell. We need this one intact.

The Lexers advance on the RV. Barnaby raises his hackles and starts his relentless barking that, for once, isn't unwelcome. We need them to come toward us in order to give Tony a fighting chance. Bits crawls under the table and puts her hands over her ears.

"Tony!" Margaret yells out the window. "We're leading them away. Get in the truck!"

We don't expect an answer, as that would be deadly for him. The one tangled in the hose attempts to rise, the pump rattling along the concrete, and lands near what's left of Mike's body. Mike's abdomen is hollowed out, his face a hole where hands or teeth cut through to brain. Only his pants and the long dark hair make him identifiable. I send this morning's oatmeal back down with a forceful swallow.

We wait until Lexers pound on the RV, but Tony doesn't emerge. The ones from the supermarket have reached the road. They only need two minutes to reach us. Three if we're lucky.

Shawn races into the living area from his vantage point at the bedroom window. "More pods coming. Are the truck keys in the ignition?"

Zeke nods. I join Jamie at the door and hear Bits sob, but I can't think about that right now. Whoever does this has to be fast, and the loads of stupid things I did this summer have made me faster and stronger than ever. I pull out my axe and ignore the sweat dripping down my back.

"We'll get the pump," I say, and point to Peter and Nelly.

Shawn looks to Jamie. "We'll get the battery."

"Let us out behind the pickup," Nelly calls. "Try to block the ones from the street."

Kyle swings around the pickup, where we jump out and keep low while he pulls to the pumps. Between Margaret's calling and Barnaby's howls, the Lexers are focused on the RV.

The zombie in the tubing drags itself forward at our approach. I kneel to unwrap its limbs after Nelly's machete goes through its head. There's no slack where the rubber wraps around his ankle, and the remainder is trapped under his torso. The pickup's hood slams and Jamie's boots pound past. I don't look up; they'll tell me when I need to run. The dead Lexer wears a heavy boot, the knotted lace locked with dried mud. I'll never get the loop wide enough to fit over it. The sound of blades hitting flesh and the meaty thud of bodies hitting the ground nearby tells me that we've become more interesting than the RV. There's no time—this foot has to go. I lift my axe and bring it down on the Lexer's shin with a crunch. Nelly's machete follows my axe, and he flings the severed foot away while I slip the hose free.

"Done!" Nelly calls.

He tosses the pump in the truck bed and jumps in. I use the tire to launch myself after him. Jamie heads for the passenger door and Peter lands beside me just as the few coming our way hit the truck. But that's not all that's coming our way—all the Lexers from the supermarket plus two more pods are closing in—close to a thousand altogether. The RV moves across the grass to the street. Shawn bumps over a body and races after it.

I look down to see the pump inching toward the tailgate. The end of the hose in the ground tank has threaded itself under Mike's body as we passed. All of this, and we're going to lose it anyway. I dive and clutch it to my chest, feet braced against the tailgate, as Mike moves an inch, a foot, and then rolls to the side. The hose whips out of the hole, throwing up droplets of gasoline.

We roll behind the RV, passing stores that must have something in the way of food inside. They might be the only places between here and Alaska that do, and a thousand reasons why they're untouched follow us down the road.

Jamie knocks on the back window and gives us a thumbs up. Nelly returns the gesture and leans against the metal. His cheeks are two spots of pink from exertion. I offer a weak smile and force my fingers to release the pump. There's a momentary high when you've survived something so risky, but I've had enough of that high to last several lifetimes.

Peter puts an arm around my shoulders and I close my eyes while we leave Winnipeg. I'm tired, too tired to look back to where we just left one person dead and two a mystery. We're down to seventeen, and I don't think the Lexers are finished with us yet.

CHAPTER 15

Someone—or *someones*—has beaten us to every gas station two hours northwest of Winnipeg. There's no dearth of stations along the two-lane roads we travel, but they're empty of food, empty of fuel and, thankfully, fairly empty of zombies. The truck's tank is only half full and we've already dipped into it for the RV.

"It has been over a year," James says, although he looks as disappointed as everyone else. "Imagine all the people who left Winnipeg? Most of it was probably gone the first week."

"Which means a trip into more populated territory," Mark says. He flips through the atlas and points to several smaller towns. When I look close, I see they're a lot smaller than Winnipeg but still have enough streets to give me pause.

"We could give Yorkton a try," Mark continues. "There should be enough daylight to find fuel and a stopping place up north. Three hours until Yorkton, wouldn't you say?" James sits opposite Mark at the dinette, and now he turns the atlas his way, studies it for a moment and nods.

No one's spoken of Mike, Rohan and Tony. There's nothing to say, which may seem cold, but the quiet of the RV speaks volumes. I sit on the kitchen floor and braid and re-braid Bits's silky hair. It soothes her, the way it does when Peter rubs her brow after a nightmare. Ashley slides down beside me and sighs.

"Hey, you all right?" I ask.

She gives me her profile. "I'm used to losing people."

Her words are flat. She lost her parents at the beginning of Bornavirus and then Nancy, her surrogate mom, outside of Kingdom Come. I can tell Ash is shutting down, battening down the hatches, and I'm afraid she might never come back if she does. I hope that these kids aren't damaged beyond redemption for what's happened in their formative years.

"I'm not used to it," I say. "No matter how many."

She folds her arms. "You're not crying or anything. Even after Ana and John and—" She stops with her mouth open in apology, but I smile and tuck her hair behind her ear.

"That doesn't mean I'm used to it. I'm choosing to focus on other people. Like you and everyone in here."

"I don't want to be sad."

"Me neither. You know what I've decided?" She shrugs like she couldn't care less and rips a hangnail off her index finger. "I'm not going to cry until I get to Alaska. Then I'm going to let it all out. It's going to be great."

"Sounds amazing."

I ignore her sarcasm. "We'll have a cry party. A sobfest. You can come if you want. We'll have refreshments." I say the last part in a sing-songy voice.

"Cassie's Cry Party?" She turns her head, but the swell of her cheek gives away her smile.

"Only a select few are invited."

"I want to come," Bits says. "Except I don't think I can not cry until Alaska."

"You're still invited. You have to let out the tears or they'll rust your insides. Then we'd have to make you drink motor oil. It wouldn't be pretty." Ash laughs when Bits does, and I turn to her. "Same goes for you."

"How about you?" Ash asks.

"I'm good. I drink a capful of oil every morning."

She rolls her eyes but scoots closer to lift Bits's hair. "You want a fishtail braid, Bits? I can do a really cool one."

"Yes, please," Bits says. "Cassie can only do boring braids."

"Well, excuse me for living," I say. "Ash can be in charge of braids at the party."

Ashley smiles and carefully pulls the brush through Bits's snarls. "Are we having lunch today?" Bits asks.

"Yes. Let's let Ash decide. Should we have rice, rice or rice?"

"I think rice," Ash says, her laugh mixing with Bits's giggles.

I throw on water and measure out enough rice for everyone to have a cup once it's cooked. Ash and Bits declare it movie time after the braid has been admired, and the kids head for the bedroom.

Peter places home-canned chicken stock and a bottle of oil on the counter. "Use these, too."

"Wait, why am I cooking when you're standing right here?" I ask.

He nudges me out of the way. "I'll take over. That was nice of you."

"What? Lunch?"

"No, talking to Ashley. You weren't kidding about not crying, then."

"Nope." I lean against the sink and watch James and Mark trace routes on the atlas. James has found himself a map buddy, which allows Penny to rest rather than listen to him yammer on. Knowing where we're going is interesting, the ratio of paved roads to dirt roads in any given map quadrant is not. "We're going to get there, right?"

He lifts the lid of the pot and sets it back down. "We are. Why, are you on the ledge?"

"No, I just don't want to miss out on a good sobfest," I say. He watches me closely, until I start to squirm and ask, "What?"

"You're a nice person," he says with a shrug.

"Well, if that isn't the pot calling the kettle black." Peter has me beat any day of the week. I get emotional and cranky at the drop of a hat, while he rides along on an even keel 99 percent of the time. But I still feel my cheeks warm from the compliment.

"I don't know that your plan's the healthiest, though. Especially for you."

"Crying's like crack—one taste and I can't stop," I say. "I'm just saying no."

He laughs and dumps in the rice.

Twenty minutes later, we're at the side of the road by a tiny pond eating the extra delicious rice that Peter made. He added some dried fruit, which has plumped up and adds sweetness to the lightly salted rice.

"Why do any of us ever bother cooking when Peter could do it?" Maureen asks me.

"I have no idea." I stick a bit of my rice in Hank's and Bits's bowls and then finish off what's left. "I'm going to wash up." I've added gasoline to my collection of odors and want to use the pond to rinse my gloves and leather jacket.

Nelly hands me his coat and gestures at the pond. "If you would."

"I wouldn't."

He joins me with a grumble. I squat by the edge of the water and squirt dish soap on my gloved hands, then foam them and my coat sleeves. Nelly does the same and lets out a giant sigh.

"Really?" I ask. "All because I wouldn't wash your coat?"

"Not that. Adam doesn't want me to help with the gas in Yorkton."

I heard them speaking in forceful whispers but ignored it because I like to maintain the illusion of privacy. I thought Kingdom Come was bad. Try living in an RV with seventeen people.

"You don't have to," I say, and rinse my sleeves. "We have enough people."

"You have Bits and Hank. They're *kids*. If anyone shouldn't go, it's you, Peter and Kyle."

"We could argue all day about who's most important. I don't like the idea of you going, anyway. I like to keep my eye on you." I raise two dripping fingers to my eyes and then point at him.

Nelly pushes me with his shoulder and brushes the water off his coat. "I just think families should be together."

"We're all family. You and Adam are a family."

"Yeah, but we can't repopulate the Earth if you all die." I burst out laughing, and he rescues me from falling into the pond.

"There's no procreation going on in my neck of the woods, either. He's worried. Just give him this one little thing. Next time I'll stay with the kids and you can go."

I'm scared to go into Yorkton, and I'm scared not to. If I'm there maybe I can stop something terrible from happening. Zombies have given me OCD and made me a control freak. It's another reason to despise them, not that there weren't plenty already.

"You sure you don't mind?" Nelly looks across the field, jaw locked. He's pissed, but I understand why Adam wants him nearby today.

"Mind that *wittle* baby has to stay home 'cause his Mommy won't *wet* him go?"

Nelly attempts his signature icy blue stare, but a laugh escapes the corner of his mouth. "You're such a shithead."

CHAPTER 16

It's the same old story at every gas station we come across, and it doesn't bode well for Yorkton. We stop at every house that doesn't look ransacked, but aside from one can of pineapple chunks, they're empty. The gas tank door of every car has been pried open.

Armed with a phone book and map, Peter, Jamie, Shawn and I prepare to leave the RV parked outside of town. Bits holds Hank's hand and tries not to cry.

"I can stay," I tell her and kneel for a hug. "I will if you want me to." She shakes her head and buries it in my neck. "I promise I'll stay next time, okay?"

I kiss her and Hank's heads, add in one for Ash, and get in the backseat of the pickup with Jamie. Shawn drives and Peter holds a map marked with an X for every gas station. We'll try the ones on the outskirts first and then move into the city if we have to. I think of how resigned Bits looked at the idea we might not come back. I don't want her to get used to losing people. I clench my fists and ask someone—my parents, Adrian, John—or some*thing* to get us back okay.

"Ugh," Jamie says, "didn't these people get tired of looking at the same thing all the time? It's looked the same for over a thousand miles."

"Grass, trees, lake," Shawn says. "Lather, rinse, repeat."

"You guys are from Massachusetts, right?" Peter asks.

"Yeah, right outside of Boston," Jamie says. "We bought a house there."

"Expensive as shit, but we could swing the payments because my lady brought home the bacon," Shawn says.

Jamie was a lawyer in her past life. "Shut up, Shawn," she says.

"You guys know she made close to two hundred thou a year?"

I look at Jamie, whose olive skin has reddened. "So you were a fancy lawyer?"

"Yeah, corporate law."

"You worked for the devil?" I ask, and kick her foot with mine.

She kicks me back. "Yes, yes, I worked for the devil. But I swore I'd only do it until my loans were paid back. Then the house was expensive. We were thinking of selling so I could quit, but..." She points out the window at the new, unimproved world we inhabit.

Shawn says, "The neighborhood had great schoo—"

"So, now you know," Jamie cuts him off in a tight voice. What she used to do isn't a big deal, but something sure seems like it is to her.

"Don't feel bad," I say. "Peter had a lot more money than you. He did evil stuff with lobbyists."

Peter turns in his seat. "It wasn't evil stuff. It was—"

"Did you save people or animals or the environment, or even the country from a foreign threat?" He shakes his head. "Then it was probably evil. Or pointless."

"I'll give you pointless," he says with a laugh.

"Don't worry, we still love you," I say to Jamie. She wraps her arms tight around the knees she's brought up to her rapidly rising chest. "If we can love Peter after that, we can love anyone."

I can tell she doesn't want to have a breakdown right now, if ever, and it looks like she's heading that way. I tousle Peter's hair to let him know I'm kidding. Peter catches sight of Jamie and hangs his head. "It's true."

Jamie gives him a quivery smile and smacks the side of Shawn's head. "No, if we can love *Shawn*, we can love anyone."

✧✧✧

The first gas station comes before we hit the town, just behind a Staples and a garden supply store. It's a no-frills kind of place, with no roof over the pumps or a tiny store, but the expanse of concrete is blessedly empty. I stand in the truck bed and watch for Lexers. I've barely had a chance to get my bearings when Shawn curses. "The tank's already open. Nothing."

We head for the next on the list. It's only a few blocks away, and it takes us three passes before we're sure it doesn't exist any longer. Shawn leans his head on the steering wheel and sighs. "What's left?"

"7-11, which is down this road, or we can try the one that's farther out," Peter says.

"Oh, thank Heaven for 7-11," Shawn says, and rolls down the main drag.

Everything from fast food to medical supply stores line the sidewalks. Most of the buildings were built in the time when people thought square and unornamented were attractive. A few have older brick facades on their second stories, but some genius thought to renovate the business levels to match the newer buildings' complete lack of charm. Inside a small city park, a few Lexers lift their heads at our passing. One takes a couple of steps and trips, which we find endlessly amusing. You have to take your laughs where you can get them.

We cross railroad tracks and hit streets lined with pretty yellow and orange trees. The 7-11 is on the corner of a heavily landscaped residential block, and suddenly I hate trees because they block our view of any lurking zombies.

It doesn't matter anyway, because the tanks are empty. Shawn pulls to a stop at another station down the road. The lot is full of Lexers, none of whom rise at the sound of our engine. They've been dead for months; they're not yet skeletons, but they are shrunken.

The covers to these underground tanks are our favorites—if it's possible to have a favorite underground tank access route—small outer covers with unlocked caps on the pipes. Sometimes it's a large metal disk that has to be pried up. Sometimes they're locked. The keys can often, but not always, be found in the manager's office. A padlock is easy enough with our bolt cutters, but if the keys can't be found for an interior lock, it's a matter of beating the shit out of the cap until it relinquishes its hold.

Jamie and I stand in the bed and leave the grunt work for the guys. They lower the hose and pull it out again. Only the tip is wet with fuel.

"There's some," Shawn says. He brushes the tip of the hose with a square of white paper and inspects the color before sniffing. "Seems okay. Not great."

He drops the paper to the ground and attaches the clips that run the pump to the battery. Shawn is an all-around big guy—tall, broadly built, thick arms, big voice and bigger laugh—but his hands are surprisingly nimble.

"Ready?" Peter asks, nozzle in the truck's tank.

Shawn starts the pump at our nods, and Jamie climbs to the roof of the cab for a better view. The golden arches of McDonald's are in my direct line of vision, and although not a place I frequented much, I'd love to plunk a fifty on the counter and order one of everything on the menu.

A minute into our watch, Jamie knocks on my head. A pack of Lexers is turning off the side street. Shawn looks up at her yell and follows her finger. It's a lot for the four of us, but we need the fuel. The pump quiets and the guys hop in the bed to wait while they close the final ten feet. The one at the head of the pack looks fresher. The gaping hole in her side is still a pinkish-gray, and the small capillaries on her skin are more purple than black. Her clothes don't look new, but they haven't faded to the colorless garments the others wear. She must have survived the winter and possibly most of the summer. And here she is as one of them, cementing the fact that we'll never be safe as long as a single Lexer roams the world.

I kneel to drive the spike end through her eye and stand for the next. The others slash and grunt. The stench of new Lexer mixes with old. I try to keep the splatter off my clothes, but when I bury my axe in one's scalp, my jeans are splattered with pinkish-brown jelly.

There's no time for relaxation after they're down. The pump resumes its buzz just as a new group rounds the corner. This time it's too many: a few dozen, with more behind them. Peter drops the nozzle and runs to Shawn. He shuts off the pump and retrieves the hose, while Peter reconnects the battery and throws our empty gas cans in back. Jamie and I stand in the bed, guns leveled, until Peter and Shawn are safely inside the cab. We sink down as the truck heads back the way we came.

Peter pulls over at the train tracks. "What do you think we got?" he asks Shawn.

"Dunno, maybe thirty gallons altogether. Not enough."

Peter takes the container of antibacterial wipes I hand him and wipes down his hands and the steering wheel. There may be no food or fuel, but no one's made a run on antibacterial wipes. And a year later, as long as they're unopened, they work fine. I wipe black sludge from the edges of the truck bed and then my jeans. Once they're soaked with cleaner, I'm satisfied they're not contagious, but it doesn't improve the aroma all that much.

"How about the one on the other side of the highway?" Jamie asks.

"If those stations were empty, then that one probably is," Peter says. He looks at the map. "But it's our only option, unless you want to head past that group and go deeper in."

None of us does, but thirty gallons is a hundred gallons short of what we were hoping for.

"Let's do it," Shawn says. "What've we got to lose?"

We drive in silence while I calculate how far we'll get on the fuel we have. It's a discouraging thought. I sigh louder than I intended.

"What's up?" Jamie asks.

"Nothing," I say. "It just sucks."

If we're stranded out here for the winter, if we last until then, we're probably dead. I imagine watching Bits starve to death, wasting away in front of my eyes, and a steady beating starts up in my temples.

"We'll find somewhere to stay and scavenge food if we have to," Peter says, reading my mind. "Then we'll go into Winnipeg when they freeze. We have enough gas to get back there."

I'm sure I could find twelve flaws in his plan if I tried, but I want to trust we'll make this work. "Okay."

"Okay?" Peter asks incredulously.

"We'll figure it out." Peter almost looks disappointed. Maybe he likes to convince me as much as I like to be convinced. "See? Right down off the ledge." He laughs, and I want to hug him for being such a good friend when I know he must be miserable. It feels like a month, but Ana's only been gone a matter of days.

We make it into an industrial part of town with no problems. A Walmart sits to our right, and a gas station to our left, surrounded by a few empty car dealerships whose missing cars have been moved into lines to form a passageway that stretches across Walmart's lot to the rear of the gas station.

More cars surround the entirety of the empty gas station. It's a large one, with twelve pumps, a convenience store and two fuel tankers sitting off to the side.

"Wow." Jamie leans her head against the window. "I don't see anyone. They probably would've come out already."

I nod, afraid to jinx it. This is the answer to our prayers. We could take a tanker, if one runs and has fuel, and never have to stop for gas again. Whoever was here seems to be gone, and I hope it wasn't because they ran out of fuel. Shawn opens the doors of the two vehicles not sitting sideways that, if moved, would allow us access to the tanks.

"No keys. No problem." He scoots under the SUV and hums while he works his magic. Jamie has situated herself behind the wheel, and she steers while we push the truck to the side. We freeze at the noise of an engine coming up fast. A pickup veers around the convenience store inside the circle of cars with four men in the bed, and four rifles trained on us.

CHAPTER 17

I sight my pistol on one of the four, a man in his sixties with pouches under his eyes and thick gray hair. There isn't enough time to escape; our only recourse is to make it clear that we can kill them as easily as they can kill us. The truck blocks the opening and the man in my sights yells, "We just want to talk. You can put those down."

"You can put yours down," Jamie calls.

The man rests his rifle on the roof of the truck, but when the others don't lower theirs, neither do we. He hops down and moves to the cars.

"Careful, Bob," one of the other men says.

Bob stops twenty feet away and calls, "We don't want any problems. This is our station. You want fuel, go to the others in town."

"The others are all empty," Peter says.

Bob looks over our truck. "You have anything to trade?"

"What do you need?" Shawn asks.

The three men in the truck have greasy hair and rumpled clothes, but all in all they look like they've done pretty well for themselves this past year. A young one with a beard and snub nose swivels his head between me and Jamie in a way that says he might not have had female companionship in a while. I point my gun at him.

"Why don't you tell us what you have?" Bob asks.

"Let's just go," I mutter. My stomach is in knots. I'll happily spend all winter in Winnipeg. The idea is sounding better by the minute.

"We need the fuel," Peter says quietly. He looks to Bob. "We have ammo. Looks like you have some .22s. We have .22 Long Rifle. We don't want any trouble, either. We're on our way from Vermont to Alaska. If you don't want to barter, we'll leave."

Bob takes in our Vermont license plate and looks us over as if he hadn't believed our story until now. "That's a long drive."

Peter tells Bob our story as succinctly as possible. At the end, the pouches under Bob's eyes hang lower and the men in the truck murmur, but their rifles stay aloft. "South America? Shit. We thought one or two more winters here and we'd be good."

My arms ache from my death grip on my gun. I loosen my fingers one hand at a time while Bob mulls things over. He might not have a lot to do today, but we do, and I'm getting tired of this standoff. They know they have the upper hand.

"How much ammo do you have?" Bob finally asks.

"Enough," I say. I feel Peter's eyes bore into me, but I'm not telling this guy what we have so he can demand it all. "How much gas do you have?"

"Enough," Bob says, and now he half-smiles. "That's the reason you couldn't find any. It takes a lot to run the generator in the store."

So they've taken all the fuel in the surrounding area. I open my mouth and then close it when Peter mumbles, "Will you let me handle this?"

He holsters his gun and calls, "I'm coming to you." Bob nods and Peter strolls toward him like he hasn't a care in the world.

"Peter!" I call. He waves his hand behind him.

"What the fuck is he doing?" Shawn mumbles.

I can't hear what Peter says before they shake hands. His shoulders are squared, but not like he's gearing up for a fight—more like he's confident Bob is going to help. He leans on a car's hood like there's nothing he'd rather do than shoot the shit all day. This is the old Peter, the one who did pointless things with lobbyists. His hair may be longer, with days of stubble and dirty jeans, but I can see he's making headway by the way Bob relaxes and motions to the cars and Walmart as if bragging about his setup. Peter says something and flashes white teeth. A couple of the men in the pickup laugh at whatever he's said.

"What the fuck is he *doing*?" Shawn says again.

The men drop their weapons at a motion from Bob. Peter beckons us over, and although I've holstered my pistol like his nod suggests, I don't drop my hand from the grip. I try to look as self-assured as Peter, but it's all I can do to not trip.

Up close, Bob looks more like he's in his seventies. His teeth are stained brown, and I wonder if dental care isn't high on his list these days. But he appears friendly now that they've reached some sort of agreement.

"Ten rounds of .22 for every gallon," Peter says. "Plus three boxes of .38 and .30-30. We can swing that, right?"

Over a thousand rounds: two large boxes of .22 gone and six precious boxes of the others. I don't see any other choice but to agree. Gas is more important than ammo at the moment. We try not to fire our guns for the most part, but ammunition is finite unless we come across the equipment we need for reloading empty rounds.

"Go 'head and move the truck," Bob says.

Shawn maneuvers our truck through the opening until he's flush with the ground tanks, but I don't move after the others.

"Trust me, it's fine," Peter says in my ear. "They've had some trouble in the past." I nod, but I'm still jumpy. With zombies, you know exactly what they want. People lie.

We use their pump, which is quietly powered by a generator somewhere in the store. I sit in the pickup's bed to keep an eye on our new friends and wave halfheartedly when Peter introduces me. Bearded Guy rests an arm on the side of the pickup. The odor that escapes makes it obvious he hasn't showered recently—not that I should talk, although I'm not in a store with a generator—but his smile confirms that he brushes his teeth.

"You're Cassie?" he asks. I watch Shawn stick a nozzle in the truck's tank and say, "Yeah."

"Chad. It's been a long time since I met anyone new." I give him a friendly nod. I don't want to be rude, but I don't like having my attention diverted. "So, you're heading to Alaska?"

"Yeah."

"Supposed to be nice there. Some of us might like to head there, too. You know, since the Biters are coming up from the south."

I think he just asked to come along. He's nice enough, but I'd noticed that once he found out Jamie and Shawn were married he'd wasted no time in coming my way.

"Anyone who wants to come is welcome," I say truthfully. I would never turn him or anyone looking for safety away. "I have two kids, so we could always use more adults."

"Oh, are you married?"

I wish I could say yes, but if he comes, he'll find out soon enough. "No."

"Boyfriend or anything?"

I'd really like to hide under the truck. If Chad comes because he thinks girls are on the menu, it's going to be awkward. I get it, I do—it's lonely out here. And from the conversations I overhear I know that there are fifty people in the Walmart, most of them families, which doesn't leave much for a single guy. But I am not on the market.

Peter has been behind me talking to Bob, and now he leans over the tailgate for the ammo, but not before squeezing my waist. "This everything, sweetie?"

Chad can't see Peter's wink, and I would laugh if it wouldn't seem out of place. I hand him the boxes and turn back to Chad. "Sorry, what were you saying?"

"Aw, nothing." Chad scrapes at dirt on his wrist. "How many people do you have?"

"Seventeen. Four kids. Some older people. A couple of guys our age, though. You'd like them."

"Yeah," he says. I feel bad at his obvious disappointment. Not bad enough to sleep with him to make up for it, however.

"Well, you're welcome to come." And he is, except for the fact that Peter and I will have to stage a breakup or start sleeping together to keep up the subterfuge. I almost laugh again and smile to cover it.

"I'll probably stay here. We've kind of become a family, you know?"

I think of Bits and Hank, and this time my smile is real. "I do. You couldn't get me to leave, either. The kids aren't really mine, you know, biologically." I point to Peter. "They're kind of our adopted kids."

I'm filled with a rush of gratitude that I don't have to do this alone. I'm surrounded by people I love in a world that doesn't have many people left. I even have a pretend boyfriend to keep unwanted suitors away.

I ask Chad about himself. It turns out he's a year older than I am and has lost everyone he knew, except for a friend who lives in the Walmart. Now that I don't have to fend him off, I listen to him recount everyone he failed to find. When he talks about his younger brother, who was on his way home and never arrived, I tell him about Eric. Sometimes I hate hearing these stories because it rips the gauze off the wound. Sometimes it's cathartic to find everyone else is just trying to staunch the bleeding, too. Today it's the latter.

"I'm the last of my family," he says. "The last of the Bakers. Maybe one day..."

He drifts off when the pump does. We're full, and we're finished here. I pat his arm. "One day for sure. There are people out there, waiting for this to end. One day they'll all come out of their hiding places and there'll be a baby boom."

"I hope so," Chad says. "It was nice to meet you."

It turns out that it was nice. Everyone has a story, and if I hang around long enough to listen, I remember that most of us are just scared and hurt and tired of this. "You, too. I'm sending any single ladies I find your way with orders to look up Chad Baker of Walmart." I give him a big wink.

Chad slaps the truck with a laugh. "I'd appreciate that."

When they're finally gone from sight, I allow myself to exhale. We meet the RV where we left it and in the same condition, fortunately, and after I step out of the truck, Bits rushes into my arms and sends us both to the ground.

"You were supposed to catch me," she says, her nose pressed on mine and eyebrows wiggling.

"When did you get so strong?" I shift to get a rock out from under my shoulder blade but don't get up; I need hugs as much as she. Every time I think of Eric, of Adrian and Ana and everyone else, my second thought is *I have Bits.* It makes it all bearable. "Next time I'm sending you for fuel. You'll come back in five minutes, full up."

She rolls off me and giggles. "While you were gone Barnaby barked at two Lexers in the field and they came over. Zeke killed them."

I don't say anything, but I know Peter can hear what I'm thinking when he gives Barn's head two heavy pats. He tried to get Barnaby to bark this morning so he could teach him to quiet, but Barnaby just stared blankly and wagged his tail. Jamie and Shawn recount the story of our fuel while Peter and I put the extra gas cans in an RV storage compartment.

"Thanks for saving me with Chad," I say.

Peter turns away with tight lips. "Sure."

"What's wrong?"

"Everything. Nothing."

Of course everything is wrong. It could be he's so solid that I forget to treat him like someone in mourning. "I'm sorry."

"For what?" he asks.

"For Ana." I want to say her name. None of us has, and it feels like she's being erased. I don't want to erase all the people who are gone because it hurts too much to remember them. They don't disappear—they haunt you. "I wish she were here."

He brushes his cheek with the back of his hand and makes a sound that's half laugh, half sob. "She probably would've shot Bob."

"Definitely. It would've ended in a bloody firefight, but we would've won."

We smile for a moment before Peter's gaze wanders to Barnaby, who's enthusiastically attempting to cover up his poop by scratching at the asphalt with his back legs. Barn turns, finds the poop uncovered and tries again. Peter shakes his head. "Christ, that dog is so fucking dumb."

I break into laughter. "Well, he's yours now. I'm not taking him back."

"How do you get a dog to be quiet? You've had dogs." He looks desperate for an answer. I don't know if it's some sort of boyhood dog ownership dream or if he doesn't want anything else to be left behind, but either way, I want him to get his wish. A dog shouldn't be too much to ask.

"Not a dog like Barn. We'll figure it out, though, okay? Nice negotiating today. You were cool as a cucumber."

Peter shrugs. "You just have to know how to talk to people."

"Exactly. I don't, not in that way."

"You'd learn."

There's no way I could learn: I can do goofy, angry or nervous to the point of stammering, but definitely not charismatic. I think of our earlier conversation and tap the gas can I hold. "So maybe it wasn't all pointless. Look what it got us today. Doesn't it feel nice to use it for good instead of evil?"

Peter rolls his eyes but his mouth twitches. "Yes, Cassandra, it does."

CHAPTER 18

"We've got to find somewhere to stay, and soon," Zeke says once we've put some distance between us and Yorkton. "We spent so long shitting around for fuel that it'll be dark soon."

I believe Peter's assessment that Bob and his people were trustworthy, but I noticed he'd told them we were taking a different route than the one we'd planned. Unfortunately, the one we planned is not turning out to be the best in terms of finding a house for the night. This was farmland, you can tell by the occasional bale of hay that rises above the grass, sprouting greenery from its rounded top, but there are no farmhouses.

The sun has begun its descent, and it's looking like we'll be in the RV tonight until we see a small, gray two-storied house surrounded by trees. We'd hoped for something more open, but since we haven't seen a Lexer since above Yorkton, it's most likely not an issue. We split into groups to search the trees, which are empty. After crunching sounds from the house, Zeke emerges, trying so hard to look expressionless that I know whatever was inside wasn't pretty.

"They're bringing them out back," he says. "Two of them. Smells pretty ripe in there. We cracked some windows."

The bottom floor of the house is open, with only a half wall separating the kitchen from the living room. Margaret rises from below the kitchen sink with a can of air freshener. She circles the downstairs dispensing a fine mist behind her. Now it smells like Spring Garden and decayed flesh, but it's an improvement.

A rose-colored velveteen couch with two matching chairs makes up the living area. A highchair sits at the dining table to the left of the kitchen. Zeke pauses to rest a hand on it as he walks by, and I know whoever sat in there must have still been in here.

"The upstairs smells better," Zeke says. "The trees are too tall for a decent view even up there, not that we'd see anything come night."

Jamie opens cabinets and plunks a few things on the counter. "Spices. We could use those, right?"

I don't want to play the usual game of how the occupants became zombies, even in my own head, so I climb the stairs to a small landing. One bedroom belonged to someone big enough to have outgrown the highchair, and his many Disney toys are piled in the corner by a toy box. The other room has a queen-sized bed and a crib. I look through the dresser and closet before it's too dark to see, but the woman's clothes are too large, the kind of large that would give a Lexer extra cloth to grab.

Nelly enters and asks, "So, are we calling dibs on beds?"

"You can duke it out with the rest of them. I'll sleep downstairs with Bits and Hank."

He runs his fingers through the box of coins on a dresser by the window. "Maybe we should play poker for the rooms."

"No one is dumb enough to challenge you to poker. But when we get to Alaska you'll find a whole new set of suckers."

Nelly flops on the bed with a squeak of springs. I lie beside him and pull the end of the covers over top. Between Nelly's furnace-like heat and the blankets it's almost warm.

"Think Adam would mind if I slept in the middle?" I ask.

"Does *wittle* baby need snuggles?"

I suck on my thumb and then open my eyes when Adam and Peter enter the room. The kids' voices echo out of the boy's room while they sift through his belongings.

"Well, isn't this cozy?" Adam asks cheerily. His face falls when Nelly ignores him.

"You're welcome to join us," I say. "Nelly said I can sleep in the middle."

"That might be preferable at the moment," Adam says. He moves to the window and stares out.

A tense silence fills the room. The middle of a warm bed would be nice, but I don't want to be in the middle of a lovers' quarrel. I've just eased out of the bed and am heading for Peter and the door when Adam turns to me. "Sorry. Nel's angry at me for making him stay today."

Nelly stares at the ceiling, hands behind his head. He's not big on sharing feelings, although he'll discuss yours all day, and uses humor to brush off any attempt to get inside his brain. I know most of what goes on in there after all these years, but you have to be attuned to every nuance to tell.

"It was fine," I say. "It's not like everyone could go."

"I didn't have a good reason—I just didn't want him to. I know it's not fair. I won't ask again." He runs his fingers through the change the way

Nelly did. The coins drop with tiny plinks in the silence. "I just couldn't lose another..."

His eyes move from me to Peter. I creak across the floorboards to embrace him. "I'm staying next time because Bits wants me to. Nelly understood."

Nelly has closed his eyes as if sleeping, but he's listening for sure. This is the point where he's supposed to jump in and agree, or at least forgive, but Nelly's as stubborn as they come. Without breaking free from Adam's arms, I take a quarter from the change box and chuck it at Nelly. He turns his head and glares at me.

"Last year, when I had to...stop Evan, I swore I wouldn't ever do this again," Adam says. "I thought it would be easy, you know? How many guys could be out there?"

Nelly's face softens from stony to hard, although he keeps his gaze skyward. Adam's eyes are moist when he pulls back. "But it happened anyway. And I love Nel more than...I'm just scared of having to go through that again. To believe in something good and have it taken away."

My throat is so tight I can't swallow. Hours after I believed again, Dan was gone. I imagine him putting his gun to his head, knowing it was his last second of life. That he would miss out on so much. I wonder if he sobbed before he did it or if he looked up at the stars—if he even waited until night—and believed he was going somewhere better.

A tear plops to my cheek. I let it run to my chin. It won't count if I pretend it's not there. Nelly has moved to sit at the edge of the bed and watches the floor with his big hands clasped together. Peter's studying a framed Degas poster as if fascinated, but I know for a fact that Degas is far from Peter's favorite artist.

"If I were as good as all of you are at this stuff, then I'd go with him. But, if I go, I could be the reason he or one of you dies. And I hate that." He draws in a shaky breath. "It's not fair to act like losing Nel is worse than any of you losing someone. That nobody else feels the way I do. We all have to put ourselves on the line."

Nelly looks up, glassy eyes reflecting what's left of the light before he drops his head in his hands. Maybe he's realized that he doesn't have to worry about Adam being sent into harm's way, at least on purpose. He doesn't feel helpless in the same way Adam does.

Tear number two races for my chin. This one isn't for Dan and everyone else who's gone—it's for those of us left here to carry on. Adam says, "I'm sorry I let my fear get in the way."

I wish Nelly could see the love that shines behind the fear in Adam's eyes. It's no small thing to be loved this way, especially now. I hope Nelly knows that.

"There's nothing to be sorry for." I kiss his cheek and walk to the door. "We'll save dinner for you guys."

Just before Peter shuts the door with a gentle click, Nelly rises to take Adam's hand. We walk past the other bedroom and discover Hank surrounded by Lego bricks.

"This kid had a ton of Lego sets," he says. "*Star Wars* and all kinds of stuff. I don't think he even played with most of them. Some are still in their boxes." He raises his hands like that's the craziest thing he's ever heard. If there's one toy Hank still loves, it's Lego.

I sit on the area rug while he explains the features of various plastic brick sculptures. I can barely see the colors in the gloom and ask, "Why don't you bring them downstairs into the light?"

He sets them carefully into the plastic bin. Lego pieces are loud, but Hank doesn't have to be told to keep quiet even though he's quaking with excitement over his newfound treasure.

I cup his chin in my hand. "You're such a great kid. You know that?"

"Yeah," Hank says in his matter-of-fact way. I swallow back a laugh.

"I told your dad I'd take care of you if...anything happened. I want you to know, so you're not worried about what happens next. This is what he wanted."

When we found Bits, she'd thought we were going to leave her. I figure Hank knows better, since he knows us, but sometimes kids get funny ideas if you don't spell things out.

"I wasn't worried," he says quickly, as if he were a little. "But I didn't know if I'd get to live with you and Bits and Peter in Alaska. Bits says we'll be in the same cabin."

I haven't given much thought to living arrangements in Alaska. I should have anticipated that the kids might, especially Hank. All I've envisioned are fences and mountains, and that's been good enough for me. But Hank's with us, whether it's a tent or an igloo or a cabin.

"Of course we will," Peter's voice comes from the doorway at the moment I say the same words. I'm glad Hank has heard it from both of us.

"Okay," Hank says. He stands with the bin and takes the stairs slowly, speeding up when he hits light near the bottom.

I pause at the top of the stairs with Peter. "Every time I think I'm doing a good job with this kid stuff, I realize there were six other things I should've thought of."

"Tell me about it," he says.

"What are you talking about? You're like the perfect dad. It's annoying. Can you mess up every once in a while?"

"I didn't say anything to Hank, either. I just assumed he knew."

"I just want them happy, safe and fed." My stomach growls at the aroma that wafts up the stairs. Dinner must be ready and in from the RV. "Fed isn't going too well, so I'm trying for safe and happy." It sounded like a joke in my head, but when the words make their appearance, it sounds a whole lot gloomier.

"We'll find food." Peter's voice is firm. "Or get there on what we have."

"What do you think it's like there?"

"Probably like Kingdom Come, but a lot colder."

"Great," I say. "So freezing cold and grizzly bears? As if zombies aren't enough."

"Is there anything you can't joke about?" Peter asks.

"Nope." I hear Nelly's voice and don't want them to think we're eavesdropping. "Let's see what's for dinner."

CHAPTER 19

Dinner was pasta, slightly pink with sauce we canned last year. It reminded me of standing in the kitchen with Bits, canning tomatoes, when Peter showed up at Kingdom Come's gate. Out of those of us who left my parents' cabin, he's the last person I would've predicted would be sitting behind where I lie in a tiny living room in Nowhere, Saskatchewan.

Zeke threw a Mad Libs into the bag of books, and the kids are playing in the light of the single lamp on the coffee table.

"I need a verb," Ash says.

"Puke," Hank says.

"Burp," Bits says.

Ash rolls her eyes but laughs. This is how every Mad Libs has gone in the past twenty minutes. "Puke was first. Okay, last one is a noun."

"Jump," Nicki says.

"A noun is a person, place or thing," Bits reminds her. "Try again. Like...bird or car or p—"

"Bits..." Peter says warningly. We both know what the next word out of her mouth will be.

"Poop?" Nicki asks, and the other three lose it.

Ash reads the final product. It's so juvenile and ridiculous, and between Ash's voice cracking and the younger kids in hysterics, it's pretty funny. I turn my head to Peter and poke him with my foot. He's been trying to wean Bits off her obsession with potty words, which is about as likely as teaching Barnaby a trick, but even he's laughing.

It'd been awful to leave Peter to his death in Bennington, but to lose him now would be so much worse. The thought of him hurt or disappointed makes my stomach clench, and I know how much he's hurting right now. I would take it on myself, if I could.

When I turn again, he's still smiling. "Yes?" he asks.

"Just checking."

"Checking on what?"

"You." I give him another poke and jump when he grabs my foot. He rubs it quickly between his hands. A sigh escapes—my feet are icicles, even with two pairs of wool socks. "Thanks. They're freezing."

"They always are." He starts on my other foot, but this one gets a genuine foot massage.

"Foot number one is going to be jealous," I say.

"Tell foot number one she'll get her turn."

I rest my cheek on the rug and close my eyes. This is the most relaxed I've been in what feels like a year, but is only our fourth night on the road. I count to be sure. It seems impossible, but it's right. Our universe has changed dramatically in such a short time—our own personal Big Bang. I drift off with Peter warming my feet and the soft giggles of children hanging in the air.

✵✵✵

I wake with a crick in my neck, what feels like cotton in my mouth and Nelly's voice in my ear. "Wake up, shithead."

I try to roll over, but I'm sandwiched between Bits and Hank on the rug. I accidentally pull Bits's hair when I shimmy out from under the blankets and then step directly on Peter's hand where he sleeps beside Bits. They mumble in their sleep but don't wake.

"You're like a bull in a china shop," Nelly whispers. He watches me in the light of the lantern he holds with his big, white grin.

I stumble to my bag for my toothbrush, toothpaste and water bottle. Nelly lights the way and waits for me to finish brushing at the kitchen sink. After I've spit the last time I say, "You know, I think I prefer Half-pint over shithead. Not that shithead doesn't have a lovely ring to it."

Nelly leans back on the counter. "Consider it done."

"Thanks. So what and where are we watching?"

"There's nothing to see. We're listening."

I use the dry toilet, which is quickly filling up with pee. It's going to smell rank in a day, but by then we'll be gone. Someone sleeps on the couch, and we sit by the window in the chair frames whose cushions were appropriated for beds. Nelly rests his boots on the windowsill. We can't see out because of the closed curtains and sheets we hung to block any light, but we can hear the leaves rustling in the wind through the open glass.

"Did you and Adam eat?"

"Yeah, you were already snoring on the floor."

"I do not snore." I point to where a giant lump in the corner emits a soft noise. We're under orders to poke Zeke if he snores too loudly. "That's snoring."

"I'm just messing with you," Nelly says.

"Give me ten minutes to wake up and then you can damage my psyche all you want. But be nice until then, okay?" My head is fuzzy. I would kill for a cup of tea, loaded with milk and sugar, and a bagel. I take a gulp of water. It's not the same.

We sit for a few minutes, until I've imagined a giant pod of Lexers heading for the house, which wakes me up nicely. I shiver and use one of the house's bath towels to cover myself.

"So, did you and Adam make up?" Nelly grunts, but I'm not letting him get away with that. "Did you or did you not apologize for being an ass, Nels?"

"Yes," he mutters.

"Good. You're lucky I'm not a dude."

"And why is that?"

"I'd steal him out from under you with my masculine wiles." I duck from his punch and say, "Seriously, though, you know how great he is and how much he loves you? I know you don't like to talk about this stuff, but at least tell me you know."

He shifts his gaze away. "I do know."

"Good. I'm done making you talk. Who's on after us?"

"We have two hours and then we wake Jamie and Shawn." He taps his watch. "Oh, look, only an hour and forty-five minutes to go. We're almost there."

We freeze at a noise that isn't the wind. It nears the house, moving too fast to be a Lexer. Nelly covers the lantern with a dishtowel and we sit at the edge of our chairs. I forget the cold and my hunger, forget everything but how to aim and fire my gun. Whatever it is snuffles as it passes. Maybe a raccoon—they can be pretty loud and human-like sometimes. Nelly uncovers the lantern and we resume our listen, both pretending that we didn't just freak out a tiny bit. I'm scared of Lexers, but I'm terrified of humans.

The rest of our shift is quiet. I take another lantern upstairs to find Jamie and Shawn awake and, if not raring to go, then in good spirits. I slip back into my warm spot between the kids, where I curl up and stick my cold feet on Bits. There's no point in having kids if you can't put them to work.

CHAPTER 20

"Unless we want to drive through the center of Prince Albert, which I wouldn't recommend, we're going to have to find an alternate route," Mark says. He and James have been at this since last night, but now that there's better light, they've been poring over the thick atlas at the table. "The North Saskatchewan River only has a few crossings and some are ferries."

"I'm thinking they're probably unmanned at this point," James says. Mark chuckles at his map humor, and James points to a spot with a long finger. "This could work. And here's where there was a Safe Zone a while back. They hadn't made contact since the winter, but I think we should check it out."

"Agreed."

I wander past and give them both a pat on the back. They deserve it. I'm decent with a map, but the atlas is hundreds of pages of miniscule road grids and street names. According to the picture, where we are now looks like a busy network of intersections, when all we saw yesterday was the occasional dirt road branching off the paved one. They weren't kidding about it being a back road atlas.

I find Maureen and Penny in the RV, with the wheat berries that soaked all night already boiling, and remember a prepper tip that I probably heard from my parents, since our basement was full of wheat berries for grinding into flour. "I think you can put wheat berries in a thermos with boiling water and they'll cook overnight." I have no idea from where in my brain I dredged that fact, but I'm sure I'm right. "Maybe it'd work if we insulated a pot with blankets? It would save on fuel."

"We'll do that tonight," Maureen says. She closes her eyes and breathes deep, then turns and stands at the counter as though she's forgotten her next task.

"Let us cook," I say to her. "You don't look well."

"I'm tired, sweetheart."

Sometimes I wonder why we want to keep on living, especially people like Maureen, who have absolute faith in the afterlife. Why they don't give up and go to their reward is a mystery to me.

"I'm okay," she says. "Just having a hard morning."

We insist she sit down. I've brought the cinnamon from the house, and I look over our stock while Penny dumps some in with a bit of sugar. We have seven MREs. Five packs of ramen. Five pounds of flour. A few pounds of sugar. A bottle of oil. Canned pineapple. What's left of the rice and oats. A couple jars of blueberry jam, and green tomatoes from Quebec that show no sign of ripening.

After today, we'll be halfway there. With the wheat berries, it may be enough to feed seventeen people for five days. We'll still look for food, but we haven't yet reached the point where food is worth endangering our lives. It very well may happen—last year, it took us close to a week to make the four-hour drive from Brooklyn to my parents' cabin.

When breakfast is ready, Penny lines up the various containers and scoops out wheat berries. They're brown and somewhat gloppy looking, but they smell good. The bar has been lowered to the point where if it's food, it's tasty. I hand them out the door to Bits and Hank, who take them into the house. James comes into the camper for his, and when Penny turns to the counter, both James and I quickly spoon a bit of ours into her cup.

Penny clears her throat. "Stop. I know what you've been doing, and I want you to stop." We look guiltily to where she stands, hands on hips and lip trembling. "I don't want extra food."

James is silent, so I say, "You need extra food, Pen. We don't."

I wasn't able to sneak her any pasta last night. James might have, but if I'm this hungry, then she must be starving.

"I will not take your food." She enunciates each word before she walks to her cup and scoops out a spoonful. James has hidden his cup behind his back, and she says to him, "Give me your cup. Now."

"No," he says.

"Give it to me."

"You cannot have my fucking cup." He towers over her with narrowed eyes. James usually lets Penny get her way because she doesn't ask for much, but it's obvious it's not happening today.

Penny lowers her eyes to the cup I've covered with my hand. "Please, take it back."

I shake my head. "You may not have to actually eat for two, but you shouldn't be on a diet."

"Neither should you. I swear you're both skinnier, you know that? I don't want to be the reason you starve to death."

"No one's starving to death." James wipes a tear off her cheek with the hand that doesn't hold his cup. If he sets it down she'll throw some in there. "You're eating it. I don't care if I have to hold you down and shove it down your throat for you."

Penny's shoulders slump and she turns to me. "Give your food to Bits and Hank if you have to give it to someone. It's not your fault I'm pregnant."

"It *is* James's fault, though," I say, and point at him accusingly. "I don't want to waste time telling you how babies are made, but I will if I have to."

James laughs. Penny fights to keep her frown in place, loses, and then kicks me.

I clutch my shin. "Ow! You're lucky I don't kick pregnant people!"

"Sorry!" Penny covers her mouth. "I'm sorry. I don't know why I did that."

"Because you were frustrated. But, geez, woman, don't do it again. Go kick a zombie or something."

"Stop giving me food, then." She tries to contain her giggle, but it comes out with her words, and I follow suit until all three of us are gasping.

"Fine, but you have to let James," I say when I've caught my breath. She nods, but it's obviously only to shut me up. "Stop lying or I'll raise my ban on kicking pregnant people. Promise me."

Penny crosses her arms. "Fine. I promise."

"Now eat your food," James says. He spoons his into his mouth without taking his eyes off her.

"Right now?"

"No, tomorrow. Yes, now."

She takes a bite and gives a dramatic swallow. I eat some of my own. It's not bad—chewy and nutty, and the cinnamon makes it taste like breakfast food. I finish it in no time and watch Penny take her final bite.

"Happy?" she asks.

"When did you get so cranky?" I ask. "I thought pregnant people were supposed to be nice."

"You try being pregnant in the zombie apocalypse."

It's supposed to be a joke, but her hand runs along her glasses. It's her tell, as Nelly the poker player would say, and gives away her fear, uncertainty or nervousness every time. I give her a hug and whisper, "Just let him do this for you, okay? He needs to do something."

She nods tearfully when I take her cup and leave. Maureen, who's been sitting on the sofa with downcast eyes, follows me into the house.

"I could stand to lose a few pounds," she says while we wipe out the breakfast dishes, and pats her round hips. On the farm, we never went without. "I'll go back down to two meals a day."

"No, don't you start—"

"Just until we find more food. I don't need extra stamina the way you all do, and I'm pretty sure I'm done growing. Don't argue, Cassie. You won't win this one."

It's nice to have a mother figure until they get all bossy on you.

"Okay," I say, and wonder how many more times I'll have to have this conversation. It's preferable to being surrounded by selfish people, but the fact that we have to have it at all is beginning to wear on me.

CHAPTER 21

Once we're on the road, I lie in the bedroom and watch movies with the kids. Disney movies might not be my first choice, but it's like a vacation to watch anything, to lose myself in a world where I know everything will work out okay. I feel guilty that I get to lounge around in the relatively spacious RV while others ride in the pickup, but I'm not leaving Bits and Hank in a separate vehicle. No one asks me, Peter or Kyle to take a turn, so I guess they understand.

The RV turns onto a bumpy road instead of the smooth asphalt we've been traveling, and I leave for the kitchen. "What's going on?"

"We decided to try some of these houses for food," James says.

A vast expanse of farmland is to our right, a small neighborhood to our left. Modular homes that look to have been well-kept before the grass grew sky-high line the dirt road, although there isn't a tree within a half-mile radius. I go for my gloves, but Kyle stands and lays a hand on them.

"You stay, I'm going."

"But—"

"But nothing," he says, brows so low I can barely see his eyes. "I've been sitting here like a damn fool while you all go for supplies. I should be out there."

"What about Nicki?" I ask quietly.

"I always come back. See no reason that'd change now." He checks his magazine, slides it back into his gun and draws his machete out of its sheath to scrutinize the blade. "I know you'd take care of Nicki if something happened."

I wave a hand at myself. "Hey, Kyle, do I carry around an umbrella?"

Kyle double checks just to be sure. "No."

"Do I have a British accent?"

"No. What the—"

"Good. I was starting to think I was Mary Poppins or something, the way everyone tries to pawn their kids off on me."

I don't know if my joke was funny or if it's the stress needing an outlet, but the laugh that blasts from deep in his belly seems to take even him by surprise. I bounce on my toes, feeling victorious—even if we all end up dead on the side of the road, having failed on our mission to reach Alaska, I'll have accomplished my mission to make him laugh. Nicki runs from the bedroom, probably because her father laughing is not an everyday occurrence. He picks her up in one hand and wipes his eyes with the other. Another chuckle escapes. "I'm going to the houses. Be back in a little while, all right?"

Nicki's brows come down exactly the way Kyle's do. I hold out my arms. "Come here, munchkin. We'll hang out while Daddy goes." I look at Kyle after she's wrapped her legs around my waist. "I've got her, you know."

He knows what I really mean. "I know you do, Mary. But I'll be back." I laugh as he walks out to meet the others.

They're back in thirty minutes with a jar of salsa and expired baby formula, which could be added to our morning glop if necessary.

"It probably took the virus longer to spread this far north," James says. "They had time to eat everything."

Zeke looks around for children, and when he sees none, says, "There were a bunch of bodies in one that had a woodstove, looked like they froze. There wasn't a scrap of wood furniture in any of the houses. They must have cut the trees for fuel. There are stumps under all that grass."

It explains the complete lack of trees, but not the fact that there are still stands of trees along the main road. Maybe they were too weak from starvation or sickness, or it was too snowy to harvest them and bring them back. I'd imagined all the horrors that could happen throughout the winter while I was safe and warm on the farm, and I probably wasn't far off base.

Zeke pulls himself out of whatever vision he still sees. "Well, we'd best hit the road."

We stay well above Saskatoon. As we near the Safe Zone that must have taken in Saskatoon residents, the excitement in the RV is palpable. John and Will used to say that Safe Zones need fuel to radio out, but they don't need fuel to live. They could be safe and sound.

We make our way onto streets with plain but nice houses tucked into conifer trees. At the corner, a fence begins and travels alongside the school-turned-Safe Zone. Nelly stops at the main gate and we stare in silence at the plywood sign that used to read *Safe Zone-All Welcome*. Someone has since spray-painted *UN-* in front of the word *Safe*. Something bumps against the wooden gate, but the doors have been braced with diagonal wooden posts and locked with a chain for good measure.

Kyle opens a window. It lets in cold air and the moans of what's on the other side of the fence. "Maybe we can get in there. At least get to the food."

Shawn reverses the pickup and climbs to its roof. He spends a full minute peering over the top of the fence, while the hisses rise in volume and the gate is battered hard enough to make me fear the posts will give out. He finally turns and shrugs, although his nonchalant veneer has cracked a little. "We'd never make it to the buildings. It's not worth it. Let's go."

Bits runs into the living area and leaps into Peter's arms, the others close behind her. "We're not going in there, are we?" Ash asks. She must think we're even crazier than we are.

"No, honey, we're not," Zeke says. He pulls her to his side, where she huddles under his arm.

If we still had the Command room in Whitefield with its map of the Safe Zones, it'd be another black pin replacing the green. But Whitefield's a black pin now, as are Quebec and Kingdom Come. Maybe we're green pins on Alaska's map, or maybe Alaska's the same as this Safe Zone and the ones we left behind. I have to believe it isn't—otherwise, mustering the courage to travel through this deserted landscape might become harder than it already is.

We pull away, leaving the zombies to their frustration and us to ours.

CHAPTER 22

James was right when he said there likely wasn't much food around. We've wasted time stopping at dust-filled kitchens along the way, but I'm sure the last Safe Zone went on patrol and cleaned out everything within a fifty mile radius. That'd be fine, if what's left of it weren't locked within that fence.

"The bridge should be just down this hill," Mark says. He raises a finger and his eyebrows. "Well, look at that. I didn't think I'd be using the word hill anytime soon."

The tiny lines around his eyes bend and fold with his amusement. Mark has the permanently wind-burned skin of someone who's been outdoors much of his life. He's hiked all over the world, rock climbed when he was younger, and was an archery pro. He's small but strong, with bright eyes and energy that belies his sixty-some years. Sometimes I get the sneaking suspicion he views all of this as one giant adventure—in fact, I think he might view life that way, zombie apocalypse or no.

I stand to look out the windshield. Sure enough, we're heading downhill. It's not a very steep hill, but it's Mount Everest compared to the rest of the topography. The bridge over the muddy, wide river could use repaving. Zeke says as much and Mark replies, "Interesting. I hadn't given it much thought, but we might find the way back east difficult. If we ever do go back."

"Why?" Penny asks from her new home on the cabover bed.

"Bridges need fairly frequent repairs. Roads as well. A few years would be fine, but ten years, twenty years, and people are going to find moving around a lot harder. We won't quite be back to the days of the Oregon Trail, but rivers will have to be forded, roads will need to be cleared."

"We'll have to use wagons like Laura Ingalls did, right?" Bits asks.

"It's certainly possible," Mark replies. "But we know a lot more than they did back then, so we might have it a bit easier. Wagons with struts, at least."

Bits climbs onto the dinette and points at a tree-covered island in the center of the river. "Look at that island, Peter. Is it like the one you stayed on?"

"This one's bigger," Peter says. "Too bad there's not a cabin on it. You could have a big garden and livestock, too."

He watches until it's out of sight. Peter's told us about the island he stayed on with Chuck, Rich and Natalie last summer after we were separated in Bennington. Natalie, Chuck's teenage daughter, had lowered a ladder out a window for him to escape a certain death by zombies, and he'd stayed with them until his hurt ankle healed enough to travel. He'd hoped the three would make their way to Kingdom Come this summer; but whether they were happy on their island or tried to reach us and failed, we'll never know.

"I wonder where they are," he says.

"Probably safe, since they're surrounded by water," I reply. "They can walk out when they freeze and make their way somewhere else."

Peter doesn't remark that the lake could have filled with floating Lexers from the giant pods. Lexers who would've eventually made their way to the island. I'm sure he wants to imagine the three of them safe and sound in their little cabin with their moat of a lake, waiting out the worst of it. I do, and I've never even met them. I'd like to give Nat a big hug one day for saving Peter's life.

"I have a new mission for us," James says. "We're going to need a ton of gas to get to Alaska, and I don't know that one tank's going to do it. This stretch of road—" he runs a finger along the large map from the Yukon into Alaska, "looks pretty empty."

"We'll have just enough to get to Whitehorse if we start from Edmonton with every tank full," Mark adds, "but if we can't stay at the Whitehorse Safe Zone and can't find more fuel, we'll be stuck. We need a larger reserve of fuel than we have. James and I have us going north before Edmonton, but it may be necessary to pay the city a visit."

"Then our first order of business is more fuel containers," Zeke says. "We'll top off everywhere we can and hope to avoid Edmonton. Y'all find the next town and we'll stop there to see what we can find."

Zeke rubs his eyes and leans by the sink. I jump to sit on the counter and put my arm around his bulk. "What's up, sugar?" he asks.

"Nothing. I just wanted to see how my favorite zombie killer's doing."

He smiles, but his usual good cheer is absent. "Tired. Just goddamned tired of this."

I squeeze his shoulder in answer. It seems to be a running theme today.

"I was gonna retire in three years, ever tell you that?" he asks. I shake my head. "Except for Mama's retirement home, I had no bills. Owned my house, my bike and car outright, and had money socked away. Dentistry's a good job and all, but I worked my ass off so I wouldn't have to do it forever. I mean, how many times can you tell patients to floss and have them ignore you before you want to punch them?"

"You'd think they'd listen to you, the big scary dentist."

Zeke lays a meaty hand on my knee with a chuckle. "You'd think. I was going to take a long road trip, maybe a year or so. I'd start out south and work my way up north come summer."

"On the bike?"

"Yup."

"By yourself?"

"There was someone I'd planned to do it with, but she passed away."

I've never heard Zeke's story, not all of it anyway. I know about his travels to Whitefield from Kentucky, but not his life before the LX virus. "I'm sorry. Did it happen on the way—"

"No, she died a few years before that. Breast cancer. I might've preferred this way. Faster. Cancer took two years to get her, but get her it did."

I've always wanted Zeke to find someone. He's kind and funny and has a heart even bigger than his big self. I'm glad to know that he had that kind of love once, even if it didn't last. "She was a lucky lady to have you. What was her name?"

"Julie. Jules." He squeezes my knee. "I was luckier. Can you believe she put up with me for seven years?" Zeke's eyes are bright with amusement or tears, or both.

"Oh, stop. You're the best and it's time you knew it."

"Sugar, I can always count on you for a morale boost."

"I'm only speaking the truth. I'm serious."

"I know you're serious," he says with a show of teeth, "although misguided. That's why it's a morale boost."

I shake my head at his booming laugh, and we watch out the windows until Mark announces the next town is only miles away. "Let's stick to the west side," he says. "There may be a better chance of a fuel barrel around the industrial areas."

We pull off the highway and drive the streets. There are all kinds of businesses, but the few metal barrels we come across either have rusted holes or something that might react with gasoline. We find a couple of gas cans, but they'll only hold ten gallons. After we've given up, we head for the shopping center that houses a gas station, supermarket and Tim Hortons. "Ooh, Tim Hortons," I say.

"What's that?" Hank asks.

"A donut shop. Really good donuts."

He sighs. "Not anymore."

It doesn't look as if anyone has broken into Tim Hortons thus far. I wonder aloud if they have baking mixes in there, and Zeke says, "We'll try everything. Looks pretty quiet."

We save the gas station for last because the pump will attract attention, and once it does we can't hang around to investigate. The two vehicles stop outside the small supermarket whose windows are shattered but doors are locked and fully intact.

I suit up. I've been wearing a thigh or hip holster in order to keep my jacket zipped up tight. I can wear a shoulder holster over my coat in warmer weather, but with the layers under my jacket it's too bulky. I slide in the Ruger .22 I found in the VW and shove the two extra magazines in my pocket. According to John, a .22 will scramble a zombie's brains. That's all that's necessary when it comes down to it, and it's quieter than my revolver. It's still loud as heck, but quieter. By now you'd think I'd be accustomed to being outfitted like this, with a hatchet and knife on my belt and a holster on my thigh, but sometimes I feel as if I'm on my way to a Halloween party.

The parking lot is quiet but for the wind that moans through the broken glass like a Lexer. I stand between Zeke and Peter at the waist-high wall below the windows and peer inside. Empty checkout lanes and a floor littered with empty packaging is all I can see before the murkiness fades to black.

Adam taps the back of his knife on the frame. "Hello?"

We're answered by a moan. I don't know how I could have thought the wind sounded like zombies. Their moans are raspy, almost hisses. The wind is ghostlier, the sound kids make to spook each other. The noises get louder and a figure wades through the debris on the floor. When it reaches the light, the exposed bone of the left half of its face glows.

A few more come into sight, all as decrepit as the first. The black mold grows in patches on every one of them, but they don't appear slowed by it yet. There might come a day when the mold wins. We've seen it happen to a few, so it should only be a matter of time. If we knew how long, if we even had an inkling, it might make this more bearable.

"C'mon, just get your rotten asses over here," Zeke says, which puts a spring in their step, if that can ever be said of zombies.

Mark taps my arm with the compound bow I used on the farm. I'm not anywhere near proficient yet, but I can usually hit somewhere near where I'm aiming.

"What would you say to some target practice?" he asks. He lifts his recurve bow and nocks an arrow. You'd never know how high his draw weight is by the way he pulls it back so effortlessly. When I tried his bow I almost threw out my shoulder.

I nod and take an arrow from his hip quiver. Mark's arrow zips through the air and into the eye of one of the Lexers farthest away. Mark gets another, this time through the mouth. "Your turn, my dear," he says with a small bow.

I curtsy and try to block out the others who I know are watching. In the time it takes me to remember what Mark's taught me about stance, the first Lexer has been impaled with Zeke's spike. I focus on one in back who's walking straight for me. I think mouth, I will it to hit the mouth, but the arrow hits neck. That would be great on a human target, but it does diddly-squat on a zombie. I might as well have asked it nicely not to eat us.

"Try again," Mark says.

This time I don't think so hard. I let it fly and it rams into its mouth with a punching noise. The Lexer's lips move around the shaft before it falls.

"Next one," Mark says.

I ignore the two that are closest. Nelly calls them his way so he and Adam can finish them off. The last Lexer falls when my arrow hits its eye twenty feet from the window. Everyone is suitably impressed, including Hank, who knocks on the RV window excitedly.

"Damn, girl," Zeke says.

"I've never seen someone pick it up so fast," Mark says. "Hitting an eye is something to be proud of."

I consider basking in the glory, but then they'll expect this every time, which is never going to happen. My cheeks are fiery. "It would be, except I was aiming for its mouth."

Peter chuckles and Nelly laughs so loud that he bites his coat sleeve to quiet himself. Mark gives them the teacher evil eye and strokes his beard, which has gotten slightly shaggier the past few days. "No matter. Hitting a head is no small feat."

"Shall we go inside or are we going to laugh at me all day?" I ask Nelly and Peter.

We climb through the windows rather than shatter the glass doors and invite over any nearby Lexers. I shine my windup flashlight down the first aisle's barren shelves. Nelly lifts his light to the sign above our heads. "Noodles, canned soup, crackers. Nope. How about nothing, nothing and nothing?"

It looks as if half the food was consumed in here. Cardboard and plastic litter the floor along with the occasional body. Adam slams into Nelly when Nelly halts and points with a look of horror. The red, white and blue of the torn packaging of a case of Pepsi lies on the tile, surrounded by several dented cans of the same. The sticky brown goop around them attests to the fact that they hadn't been drunk.

"Seriously?" Adam asks. "You scared the shit out of me."

"It's an absolute travesty," Nelly says. "Kill me now. I don't think I can go on."

"Let's finish and get out of here," I say. "Don't you know that stopping to joke in horror movies always gets you killed? Joke later, when we're safe."

"So, never?" Nelly asks. I push him and he walks past his wasted favorite beverage with a dramatic sigh.

The next aisles aren't any better. The cleaning aisle has a wide variety of options, however, and we grab bleach, laundry soap, dish soap and antibacterial wipes. Toilet paper and baby wipes round out our haul.

"Well, it's better than nothing," Peter says as we follow Nelly and Adam to the windows. "That was a good shot before. Sorry I laughed."

"You have met Nelly, right? I think I'm used to being laughed at by now."

"I didn't want you to feel bad."

"I didn't. But thanks, Petey."

One side of Peter's mouth creases the way it does when I call him Petey. He used to tolerate it, but I think he's grown to like his nickname. I hop out the window and turn to say something else, but he's gone. In a second that feels more like a year, I imagine him being pulled back into the store by a Lexer we missed.

Peter reappears at the window holding a ripped bag. "There's food in here. Someone must have dropped it. It was mixed in with all the other garbage." He holds it out and finally takes in the fact that I'm clutching my chest. "What's wrong?"

"You don't just disappear! You gave me a heart attack!"

"I was ten feet away. Getting food. You heard me say this was food?"

"I don't care what's in the bag if you're dead!"

Nelly relieves Peter of the bag so he can exit the store. I know my last statement didn't make total sense, but still I stand, hands on hips, and glare at Peter.

"Calm down, darlin'," Nelly says. "Why are you getting all riled up?"

"Don't tell me to calm down!" I shout at the loudest volume I can get away with out here. "I'll get *all riled up* about whatever the fuck I want to get *all riled up* about."

I stamp to the RV, well aware I'm acting like a teenager. But tears are looming, and I don't want to cry. Anger is easier, although they sneak out when I'm angry, too. Sure enough, they've come by the time I reach the bathroom, where I lock the door and take deep breaths until I've cut them off.

I look in the mirror and regret it immediately. It's been days since I've seen my reflection. Penny might be right about losing weight—my cheekbones and collarbones look sharper, and I have new purplish shadows under my bloodshot eyes, although all three could be from exhaustion. I take down my hair and sigh at the greasy waves. It's not much of an improvement, but it feels good to lose the buns for a bit.

I leave the bathroom as the RV rolls toward the gas station. Bits and Hank pull out the contents of the bag while the others look on: three cans of beans, a bag of frosted cookies, a jar of honey and a jar of olives.

"Can we have some cookies?" Bits asks no one in particular.

I avoid the eyes of everyone but the kids. "Ash's seventeenth birthday is soon. Maybe we should save them if we can. In case we haven't gotten to Alaska yet."

Ashley ducks her head, pleased I've remembered her birthday. I walk to the bedroom and perch on the bed. We have enough people that I can let the others handle the gas station. Peter enters and drops to the bedspread beside me.

"Sorry," I say, and inspect my dry hands. I should've thought to look for lotion in the store. "I didn't mean to flip out."

"I'm sorry I scared you."

I shrug and push down a cuticle. "You were ten feet away. I'm the crazy one here."

"As usual," Peter says, and bumps me with his shoulder. "It's only been a few days since..." He drifts off. I think he was going to say something about Ana and the others. "And Mike, Rohan and Tony—was that yesterday?" I think for a moment and nod, relieved I'm not the only one who can't keep track. "Really? That was yesterday?"

"Yeah."

He scratches his jaw, which is heading from stubble to beard territory. "It feels like two or three days ago, maybe more."

"I know."

I've thought about the three of them today, but not as much as I think I should. I'm so preoccupied with keeping the people I have alive that it's hard to mourn people I didn't know as well. There's a hierarchy of sorts when it comes to losing the people around you, and I'm afraid the next who die will be ones I can't afford to lose.

He rubs his eyes. "I'm sorry I wandered off. I won't do it again."

"You didn't wander off," I say, feeling guilty that he feels guilty. He doesn't need anything else to worry about, especially someone who loses her marbles over nothing. "*I'm* sorry. I got scared. It was stupid."

Peter covers my hand with his. That's something I've always liked about Peter. I touch people all the time—a squeeze, a hug, a punch, especially if it's Nelly—and Peter does, too. "I'll stick like glue from now on."

"Except for the bathroom," I say, and wrinkle my nose.

"Except for the bathroom."

Nelly steps into the bedroom. "Everything settled or are you still yelling at people?"

I sigh. "I'm done. Sorry."

"Glad to hear it. You want to go to Tim Hortons with me, Adam and Kyle while they check on gas? It's totally clear out there."

I look to Peter, who says, "You tell me. I'll go if you are."

"Let's go."

I braid my hair before tucking it into the back of my jacket, find my axe and wait by the door. "Be right back," I say to the kids. "You guys can watch out the window and radio if you need to tell us something. You want to be our lookout?"

Hank scrambles for the radio and whispers, "Hank to Cassie. Over."

"This is Cassie. Over."

"We'll let you know if anything comes." He sets the radio on the table. "Don't worry, I know it's not a toy. We'll only call if we have to."

I nod gravely and once we're outside say, "That kid kills me. He's like a forty year-old in a ten year-old's body."

"He's almost as odd as you," Peter says.

We pass Shawn, who's up to something under a neighboring truck, and circle the Tim Hortons to find the sliding window of the drive-thru has been smashed. Kyle calls through the hole and says, "Nothing, but it looks like it's all gone."

I pull myself through and sit on the counter, ready to vault back outside, but it feels and smells empty. Adam comes in after I drop to the floor. The names of the donuts on the empty glass cases taunt me, and I say them aloud. "Sour cream glazed, honey dip, double chocolate."

Adam groans and points to another. "Toffee glazed? I would sell Nel into slavery for a toffee glazed donut."

"I heard that," Nelly says as he hits the floor.

"You were supposed to," Adam says, tearing his eyes away from the case. "I guess we'll try the back?"

A walk-in freezer and oven take up most of the space. There are no bags of baking mix, not even a dusting on the floor, which seems unlikely since there's plenty of other trash and crumbs stuck in what might be chocolate sauce. The freezer is empty.

"Maybe they didn't bake from a mix," Peter says. He kicks a wrapper on the ground that says 'Apple Fritter.' "Looks like they probably got frozen donuts."

Nelly roots around while I look in the freezer twice more for something to magically appear. I swear, every morsel of food in Canada has been eaten.

"There's coffee and tea," Nelly says. He holds up two bags of coffee and a few boxes of English breakfast tea.

I'd sell Nelly into slavery for tea, especially my favorite kind. There's a box that promises hot chocolate, but it lies. We return to the station to find half of the pickup's cargo on the ground and Shawn bent over the bed. He has smears of grease on his face along with a cocky grin. "We found a fuel container."

"Where?" Kyle asks.

"Where's a good place to store gas?" Shawn asks. We shake our heads. He leans on the truck and crosses his arms. "C'mon, guess."

Nelly raises his eyebrow at me. "If we're not allowed to joke, then we definitely don't have time for riddles."

"Shawn, just tell them your brilliant plan," Jamie says. She returns a bin to the truck. "Or I will."

"So, I'm thinking we need something that won't corrode," Shawn says. "And doesn't have anything in it that would react with or ruin the fuel, right? But that's harder to find than we thought it would be."

Nelly searches the lot, probably hoping for Lexers so that Shawn will get to his point already.

"And how would we clean it out, you know?" Shawn continues. "So it has to be metal or a plastic we know won't react with—"

"Gas tank," Jamie says, and shuts the tailgate. "He took the gas tank off a truck in the lot. It's in the bed."

"Woman!" Shawn shouts.

Jamie tilts her head. "Oh, I'm sorry—did you want to tell them?"

"You're lucky I love you."

"I know that. And you're lucky I don't kill you."

Shawn chortles. "Fair enough. So, is my plan not brilliant? It's big, about forty gallons. James figured out plugs for the holes."

Everyone agrees it's the most brilliant plan ever. And it is pretty ingenious, but as it turns out, the fuel at the station is an unusable sludge.

"We'll have to go into Edmonton," Mark says. "Which once had a population of 800,000." It's an adventure even he'd rather skip, and I pray we find some fuel before it comes to that.

CHAPTER 23

I can tell when we're nearing Edmonton because the abandoned cars, which have been few and far between, grow in number. Doors hang open, and I know that more than a few of the driver's side seats are not stained brown from exposure to the elements. Especially not when what I assume was the driver is still on the asphalt, shredded clothes barely covering the bone and mummified flesh that was left uneaten.

We have a few hours to find gas before we'll stop for the night, and we want to be as far away from the city as possible by nightfall. Our first route is hindered by an accident that involved a tractor trailer and a school bus, and our second by a roadblock. Only one police truck remains in front of lines of cars that stretch as far as the eye can see. And bodies—so many bodies that even though they've been dead over a year, the breeze through the window carries a light putrid scent.

"They must have tried to quarantine, like in New York," I say.

"Except there were no bridges to blow up," Penny says. She's come down from her perch over the cab to start on dinner. We had cold wheat berries for lunch, but the temperature is dropping and something warm might serve to warm us up. It's not bad when the RV is moving, since the vehicle heat is on, but tonight is going to be cold.

"We need a phone book," James says. He leafs through the atlas. "It's too late to start with gas stations now. There were some nice houses back there. We could sleep in one of them tonight."

We choose one based solely on the fact that it's surrounded by a stone fence and follow the long driveway down park-like grounds that have become wildflower meadows. A lake backs the two-story stone and stucco house.

"This place is 6,000 square feet if it's a foot," Zeke says. "Damn."

We enter through double doors into a large foyer with a marble floor and a curved staircase to the second level. A formal living room sits to our left, a formal dining room to our right. In fact, everything about this house is formal, from the furniture to the ten-person table. The woodwork and moldings are exquisite, the windows huge, but it doesn't throw off the vibe that living people once resided here.

The kitchen is the same with its granite counters and steel appliances and empty cabinets. I get the sense that this house didn't have much food in it unless they were throwing a catered party. The den attempts to be inviting with a large TV and leather couch, but it falls short.

"This is fancy," Bits says.

"It is pretty fancy," Peter agrees. He tries the gas fireplace, just in case, and shrugs when no fire bursts forth. "You like it?"

Bits shakes her head. "Me neither," I say. "I feel like I'd have to use a coaster and keep my feet on the floor."

"Coasters aren't the worst thing in the world," Peter says.

"I swore an oath that I would never own anything that would require me to slip coasters under peoples' drinks. Have you ever been to a house like that? It's awful."

"I had coasters," Peter says.

"It's okay to *have* coasters and even use them occasionally. You never made me use them."

"I didn't care."

"Because you didn't want to be the person slipping coasters under peoples' drinks, right? No one likes that person."

He laughs. "You always cleaned up your condensation."

"And you say I'm a slob."

"Was that when Peter was your boyfriend?" Bits asks. "Did you go to his house a lot?"

Bits asks about our lives before Bornavirus like it's a world she's heard of only in stories. Who knows, in twenty years all she might remember clearly are these stories, and Penny's baby will never know that world.

"Yup," I say, and change the subject without looking Peter's way. "Let's go see the upstairs."

The only thing good about being prone to blushing is that it keeps me warm. It's strange to have slept with that Peter and be friends with this one, unless I keep it a distant memory. If there one thing that our relationship didn't lack—and it lacked a lot—it was chemistry. When I didn't want to punch him, and even when I did, I almost always wanted to sleep with him. It was the one time and place where I didn't feel that disconnect.

Our breath fogs as we climb the stairs, Bits and Hank running ahead. I pop each mental image that rises like a bubble—how surprised I was by my desire when we kissed on our first date, his hands on my hips as I moved above him, the way he would hold my gaze steadily, with no trace of fear or hesitation.

Peter catches my arm when I trip on a step. "Graceful as always," I say. "Thanks."

"See you next fall."

I crack up. "I've never heard that one. How can that be?"

"I've been saving it," he says with a grin and makes sure I'm upright before letting go. That guarded look he always wore has been gone for a long time now, and I'm glad that it's a distant memory.

"Five bedrooms!" Bits calls from the top of the stairs.

"And a theater!" Hanks says. "Imagine having a theater in your house?"

"And a full bar in the attic," Nelly says, appearing from the side of the landing. "Except for the alcohol. Which is gone, of course."

"A man cave," Adam says. "Pool table and everything."

The master bedroom is gigantic, with a four-poster king bed and a walk-in closet that boasts more square feet than most studio apartments. The en-suite bathroom has a deep round bathtub set into marble. I drop my axe and step in, then sink down and close my eyes.

"What are you doing?" Bits asks.

"I'm taking a bath. Want to come in? Look at all this room. Let's add more hot water and turn on the jets." Bits steps into the tub, turns the dry faucet and leans back with a sigh.

"I take back everything I said about this house," I say. "This bathtub is perfect. Except for the lack of water."

"A small but very important detail," Nelly says. "Holy crap, are those all jets?"

They're everywhere, in configurations you know would feel amazing on your back and legs. Ashley walks in. "I've always wanted a bathtub like that."

I step out. "Have a turn. I'm going to check out the other rooms."

Two of the bedrooms belonged to children, one of whom appears to have left for college, and there's nothing formal about her room. Her graduation cap tassel still hangs over the corner of her mirror along with a tiny pennant from a university. Photographs of teenage girls with bright smiles are stuck in the mirror's frame. Her name was Aubrey, according to the sign on the wall, which declares *Aubrey's Parking Only*. Magazines, toiletries and jewelry litter the desk and dresser top. Posters of bands featuring cute young boys with earnest expressions are tacked to one wall.

"Oh my God," Ashley says from the doorway. "Look at all this stuff."

She picks up lotion, sniffs it, and then squirts some on her hands. She rubs them together as she takes in the queen-sized bed with its black and white floral bedspread, the window seat behind white gauzy curtains and the state-of-the-art audio system that sits on built-in shelves below a flat screen TV. The closet has some clothes, probably all that Aubrey didn't take to college, and Ashley pushes the empty hangers out of the way to see what's left.

"It's mostly summer stuff," she says, and pulls out a black tank top that's gathered on the sides. "This is nice."

"Take it," I say.

"Do we have room?"

"We'll make room. Find some stuff you want. Think of it as a birthday present."

Ashley wastes no time in opening the drawers. By the time she's finished she has two pairs of jeans, three shirts, a couple of lacy bras and underwear. "Can I take the lotion and stuff?"

"Absolutely."

I sit on the window seat while Ash dumps toiletries into a bag. The corner of an electronic device peeks out from under a pillow. I pull out an e-reader and press the button, thinking it won't work, but it flashes to life. There have to be fifty or more Young Adult books on this thing. I search until I find the USB cord in the nightstand.

"What's that?" Ashley asks. I hand it to her and she scans the screen. "Someone liked vampires, huh?"

"Just a little. I can charge it with my solar charger. Do you want it? I might borrow it if I get desperate for a book."

"I never read the *Twilight* books. I was going to, but my mom said I had to wait and then...you know."

She spins to survey the darkening room. It's time to eat, find our sleeping spots and hunker down for the night.

"I think that's it," she says. "I wanted something, like, nice to wear, you know? It's not like I think there's going to be boys in Alaska or anything. I mean, it'd be nice..."

"I know what you mean." I wave a hand at myself. "It's hard to feel pretty in this getup."

"I always thought you and Ana looked so good." Ashley gives me a quick glance and continues when I smile at the mention of Ana. "Like tough and hot, you know? That's why I wanted to do guard so bad."

"Well, Ana may have felt gorgeous, but all I feel is dirty, bound up in too many layers and tired. And scared." I turn her to the mirror. "Look. If you saw you, what would you think?"

She takes in her boots and tucked-in jeans, the quilted, fitted jacket that ends just above the knife on her belt. Her hair is in a French braid on both sides, accentuating the curves of her unblemished face with its full lips and rounded nose. She looks like a teenage warrior.

"I'd think I looked pretty cool," she admits.

"That's what Colin back in Winnipeg thought." She smiles at the floor. "And so do I. When we get to Alaska, you'll have a bath and dress up in your new clothes. Then we'll go on the prowl for teenage boys. For me, of course."

She giggles. I help carry her stuff and hope there's a teenager of any gender in Alaska. A best friend is even better than a boyfriend, but I'm going to go for broke and hope she finds both.

***

Dinner is the remaining ramen noodles with the last of our wrinkly vegetables and green tomatoes fried in oil. Peter and I give Bits and Hank an extra bite of ours, which leaves us with five bites instead of seven, but I wouldn't be able to enjoy being semi-full if I were full of guilt.

Kyle and Margaret take first watch. I set a lantern and water bottle by one of the sinks in the master bath and hand out floss.

"I like flossing," Hank says, running the string through his teeth.

I gaze at him in the mirror and hold my hand to my heart. "Hank, you are the most awesome human being I've ever met."

"Maybe you should be a dentist like Zeke," Bits says.

"He'd teach you," I say. "He'll need an apprentice one of these days."

"Maybe," Hank says. "I can do electric stuff, too. My dad taught—"

The bathroom is quiet. Peter spits out his toothpaste and puts a hand on Hank's shoulder. Hank leans in briefly, but his natural tendency toward self-control overrides taking any comfort, and he pulls away with a quick nod before he jumps in the king bed. Right before Peter shuts off the lantern, I catch Hank watching the ceiling, looking younger and more vulnerable without his glasses. Hank is so concerned with the details—knowing our route, how much gas and food are left, thinking about future careers—that it's easy to forget he's a kid.

"Hank," I whisper.

"Yeah?"

"I'm glad you're here with us." Silence. I slide an arm under his shoulders. His narrow chest rises quickly and he sniffs a few times. I don't want to make a big deal of his crying, but I want him to know I care. "It's okay to talk about it. I know you miss your dad. We all do."

"I don't know what to say," Hank whispers.

"Say anything. Say you're sad or even angry, say you miss him, say how he was a brave man. He *was* a hero, just like in your comics, you know that?" I feel his head bob. "You don't have to say anything, but I want you to know you can."

" 'Kay."

I hold him until his breathing deepens and his body relaxes against mine.

✷✷✷

Peter wakes me sometime in the night, the lantern on the floor so as not to wake the kids. My arm under Hank has gone completely numb. I extricate myself and clench my teeth as the blood rushes back.

"Our turn for watch," Peter says. "I have toothbrushes."

I sit on the edge of the bed, slip into my boots and rest my head in my hands. I have to get in on the first or last watch shift of the night because this broken sleep every night sucks. "If you said you had donuts it would be much more thrilling."

I force myself to stumble out of the room. I hit my knee against a table on the landing and curse. "Wait a second, will you?" Peter says. "I'm right behind you."

Nelly and Adam rise when we hit the living room, and I don't even have the energy to bother Nelly about the fact that he finally has his own bedroom. I give my teeth a brush and curl up beneath a blanket on the couch. If it's not in the high thirties then it's damn close.

Peter makes sure the thick curtains are closed and sits under his blanket. We don't want anyone to know we're here, whether they're alive or dead. I stare at the curtains and strain my ears for anything moving in the darkness, but even zombies are smart enough to be asleep right now.

"Thanks for talking to Hank," Peter says. "I've tried, but sometimes it's easier to talk to a woman."

I grunt and continue staring at the fireplace. A lit fireplace would be heaven. I would lie in front of it in my blanket and soak in the warmth. I would cook up a hamburger and then make s'mores.

Peter says something, but I'm so busy eating my imaginary feast that I miss it. "What?"

"I said it's usually easier to talk to a woman, except for you, right now."

"Sorry. I'm tired and hungry and blah blah blah. I'm tired of hearing myself."

Peter stretches an arm along the back of the couch. "What do you want to eat?"

"I was thinking about hamburgers and s'mores. How 'bout you?"

"Steak, chicken, more ramen noodles. I don't care."

"If you want ramen noodles, you must be hungry," I say, and he chuffs out a laugh.

"Let's make tea," Peter says after a minute.

"We can't!"

He lifts an eyebrow. "We can. C'mon, there are a lot of tea bags, and we'll reuse them. Your teeth are chattering. You know you want to."

I should object more forcefully, but I follow him to the food bin in the foyer with my mouth watering. The popping of the lid seems as loud as a gunshot. Peter raises a finger to his lips and pulls out a box of tea, then tiptoes dramatically to the single burner camping stove on the entryway table.

He mimes moving the table, and I lift one end so we can walk it to the cracked window, although we leave the curtains closed. It's doubtful the fumes from a tiny stove in a big house will kill us. He takes a lighter from his pocket and lights the stove with a flourish, like they do in fancy restaurants. Peter's not always so silly, except maybe with Bits, and I stifle a giggle.

I hold my hands near the flame. I wish it took longer, but the water boils quickly and my precious heat source is extinguished. Peter drops in a single tea bag while I root out cups. By the time I'm back, the water is a lovely brown. I take a sip from the mug he hands me. It's not the best cup of tea I've ever had, sans milk and sugar, but it has flavor and sends a line of heat down my core. I can pretend it's food. I take another gulp—there's no sense in savoring it if it's going to be cold in five minutes.

I manage to arrange my blanket without spilling any. "Thanks. Think they'll be mad?"

"Why would they be mad? We used one tea bag. It's everyone's tea."

"I guess."

"Stop worrying," Peter says.

"I'm not worrying."

He assesses me over the top of his mug with a smile. "Yes, you are. You have on your worried face. No one will care, and if they do, we'll tell them I drank it all."

"I won't let you take the fall. We'll go down together."

He's right. It's ridiculous to get all bent out of shape about a tea bag. I wouldn't be mad if someone else had a cup. My next sip is a good bit cooler, so I guzzle it down before it will do no good. The warmth lasts a full two minutes before I start to shiver again.

"Let's double up," Peter says.

"You want to play poker? Now?"

"That's double down. And it's blackjack, goofball. Let's double up our blankets."

Peter moves close, then layers our blankets over top before resting his arm on my shoulders. He's so much warmer than me. I wouldn't be surprised if I make people colder. I nestle into his side and bring my feet on the couch. It's not like anyone is here to complain I'll ruin the off-white damask.

"Better?" he asks.

I nod and listen to the nothing outside. Peter's breaths begin to slow. I check to see if he's fallen asleep and whack him with my temple hard enough to make him rub his jaw.

"What was that for?" he asks.

"Sorry, I thought you were asleep. And ouch, that half-beard of yours is sharp."

"I always thought I'd look distinguished with a beard. What do you think so far?"

I pretend to consider but, honestly, Peter would look good in anything. He has high cheekbones, a straight nose and black eyes that match his hair. He was always handsome and well-built, but he's acquired a rough edge that pushes him into swoon-worthy territory.

"Meh," I say.

His head drops back with his laugh. "Thanks."

"Anytime. Sorry about the stench."

"I'm no better."

"I meant you," I say. He pinches me. "Fine, I meant me."

"You have a good smell."

"I have a smell? What kind of smell? It's not like sauerkraut or anything, is it?"

"No, it's—" he thinks for a moment, "like something green."

"Like what kind of green? Frogs? Mold?"

He knows I'm messing with him, and he exhales noisily. "You know what I mean, Cassandra. *Green*. Leaves, cut grass, herbs. But a sweet green."

I make a face even though I'm secretly delighted to be told I smell good. "Well, it's not there now."

"It's your smell. I'm sure it's there now." He leans in and pretends to choke. "Somewhere under there."

"Jerk." I'm becoming accustomed to our stink, which is depressing and cheering at the same time. I pull out my phone to check the time. "Five more minutes. And then two glorious hours of sleep before the sun rises."

James and Penny creak down the stairs a minute later. "Why are you doing watch?" Peter asks Penny.

"I'm pregnant, guys. That doesn't mean I'm incapable of doing things. And, anyway, ever hear of pregnancy insomnia?" We shake our heads. "Yeah, I hadn't either, but I've got it."

"This pregnancy thing gets worse and worse," I say.

"Right?" Penny agrees.

We tell them about our cups of tea and James gets to work while we head upstairs. Bits and Hank have moved to one side of the bed. I fall onto the cold pillow in the middle and move close enough to feel the heat emanating from Peter.

"I'm not trying to get all up in your face or anything," I whisper, "but you're warm."

He grunts in amusement and throws an arm over me, knees fitting into the crook of mine. It isn't awkward like it could be, especially after my little trip down memory lane earlier tonight. That old desire has been replaced by an affection that's almost overwhelming in its intensity. He's Bits's dad, my shrink, the straight man to my one-woman comedy act and, somewhere along the line, he's become my best friend. I catch a whiff of his warm, spicy scent and think about telling him that it's not just me who smells good, but I'm far too tired.

CHAPTER 24

The sky is the bruised purple-gray that comes before the sun makes its appearance. It's time to rise and shine. Peter gets out of bed and puts on his jacket after handing me mine. I want to find something warmer, and I enter the spacious closet once teeth are brushed. The mother of this brood wore nothing but slacks and blouses and expensive ladies' suits. No wonder she's dead. I do find a cute silvery-brown down coat with a furry hood and instantly grow ten degrees warmer when I zip it up. Hank puts on his glasses before bounding out of bed, looking back to normal from last night. I remind myself to not always trust his self-possessed facade and to bring up his dad when it looks as if he needs to talk. Peter did the same for me this summer.

"Nice coat," Peter says. He touches the fur on the hood. "That's real fur, I think. Let me see the tag." He whistles. "This coat was probably two grand."

"I can wear it in the Bentley," I say. "It's so freaking warm."

I didn't wear real fur before, but I'm not planning to take it off ever again. Unlike leather, this coat is comfortable enough to sleep in. And it's pretty. The previous owner would probably die all over again if she knew that it'll be covered in something disgusting soon enough. I head downstairs in my new coat and clean underwear also courtesy of Mom. James and Mark are up to their usual map and phone book tricks, frowning in concentration.

We tried the boiling water method of wheat berries last night, and I unwind the pot's blankets to find it's cooked through and still warm. Maybe I should take the pot to bed with me from now on. I dish it into cups and bowls from the cabinets. There's no reason to dirty our own dishes when there are so many lovely ones here begging to be used and left behind.

"Fancy," Penny says when I hand her a crystal goblet. She takes a bite. "Did you put jam in? It's good."

"Yeah. We could use the energy today."

Penny doesn't complain when James drops a dollop of his breakfast in her glass, although she doesn't look happy about it.

"So," James says, "there were a bunch of gas stations around here. I'm sure they're empty, but we'll check them out on our way north. There's an army base on the northern edge of the city. Maybe someone's there."

"Wouldn't we have heard about a military base?" Penny asks. "They must have radios and generators."

"Yeah, but what the hell, right? You only live once." James runs a finger inside his glass tumbler and sticks it in his mouth. Once he's licked it clean, he lifts it in the air. "Okay, twice, if you count that as living."

Penny bursts out laughing. James rests his hands on what's left of her waist, and I make myself scarce when she lifts her face to his. I summon the others at the front of the house to breakfast.

"Your boot's untied," Bits says. She watches me double knot my lace and asks, "You still use bunny ears, Cassie?"

"Uh-huh," I say, ignoring Nelly and Peter's sniggers while we head for breakfast. "What's wrong with bunny ears?"

"Just that most people graduate from bunny ears at ten," Nelly says.

"I can't do it that other way. I've tried and it doesn't work."

"I thought you knew this kind of stuff," Peter says. "Shouldn't you know how to make knots?"

I turn at the kitchen entrance and raise my hands. "Sorry, people. I missed that class."

"Some survivalist you are," Nelly says. He must have gotten some action last night. It puts him a in a good mood and makes him even more bothersome.

Hank crosses his arms over his chest and glares at them. "Cassie can make a fire from sticks. Can you?"

I pull my tiny protector to my side. "Thank you, Hank. *Someone* appreciates me."

I hand the kids their food and eat mine while I watch through the window as Kyle opens the gate at the rear of the property to allow the RV access to the lake. James has rigged something so that we can pump water into the RV's water tank. We'll have to sanitize before drinking, but we won't die of thirst like Peter almost did on his way to Kingdom Come, until he remembered John and I discussing hot water heaters as a source of emergency drinking water.

I put some of my food onto the kids' china saucers and turn to Peter. "Hey, know why you're alive?"

He stops chewing. "What?"

"Why are you standing here right now?"

"Because we drove here?"

"No." I point my spoon at him. "Because you knew to get water out of a hot water heater. How did you know that?"

Peter feeds Bits a bite of his food and puts a glop on Hank's plate. "You. And John."

"Exactly. Survivalism 101."

He narrows his eyes, but they glint with amusement. "Okay, why are *you* standing here right now?"

"Because you saved all of our lives in a selfless act of love." Peter opens his mouth and shuts it again. He wasn't expecting that answer, even though it's the truth. I turn to Nelly. "I saved you, Peter saved you. You've got some work to do, young man."

Nelly eats his last bite and rubs his stomach. "I'll get you both back one of these days."

I kiss his bristly cheek. Every guy in this group is growing a beard, which I would find more entertaining if I weren't growing armpit and leg hair along with them. "Go find Sparky," I say to Bits. "I'll feed her and Barn in the RV."

Bits runs off to find the cat, who manages to nap in impossible to find places even locked in a room—like inside box springs and on shelves behind clothes. When the RV is back, Barn gulps his food and begs for more.

"Sorry, Barn. That's all you get," I say, and give him a kiss to apologize. He's better fed than we are at this point, although his kibble is less than appetizing. I'll eat it if I have to, but I'm hoping it doesn't come to that.

Maureen finishes closing cabinets and drops on the RV's couch. I sit beside her and watch Bits pet Sparky while she crunches her breakfast.

"You take good care of them," Maureen says. She looks worse than yesterday. I hate to see her like this, almost as if she's giving up.

"You take good care of all of us. Penny's going to need you when the baby's born. She's told me she's counting on having you for a grandma."

A little life comes into her eyes and fades away just as quickly. "I pray for my granddaughter every day. I know she can't be alive, but I still pray like I pray for all of you."

Maureen's first grandchild was born just before the virus hit. I've always wished I could paint her a portrait, but she doesn't have a picture. "It's working so far."

Maureen shrugs. "I prayed for everyone that's gone, too. It's not that I don't think God listens—I just think we can't influence what He'll do by praying. But I do it anyway."

"Just in case?" I have my own kind of prayer, a wish I send out into the ether. It's more a desperate *Please, please let everyone be all right* than anything else. It doesn't seem to be any more successful than Maureen's, but it can't hurt to ask.

"Just in case. Maybe I'd have more influence if I was up there, but I promised John I'd look out for all of you."

I wish John were looking out for us down here. I'd give anything for one more of his bear hugs. I'll cry if I speak, and by her watery blue eyes it appears to be the same for Maureen, so we hug instead. It's almost as comforting as one of John's.

After we've parted, she says, "Thank you, sweetheart."

"No, thank *you*. For being here. We need you here, you know."

Maureen leans close, eyes direct. "I want to be here, honey. I do." She rubs her hands on her thighs and stands. "Well, let's get everything finished up."

"Let the bustling begin!"

"Smart-ass," she says with a laugh.

Once we're loaded, James guides us to the main road and says, "We're just over halfway. Another two thousand miles and we're in Talkeetna. Thirteen hundred to Whitehorse, if we end up staying there."

Whitehorse is fine with me: all I want is a home. If we can fill up down here, we'll make it to Whitehorse with one more stop, maybe two, depending on our route. Cautious relief hangs in the air as we make our way past the expensive homes and toward the gas stations outside the city limits. But that relief begins to ebb when the first two stations are small, with water-damaged signs on the pumps that say *No Gas*.

"There are another two coming up," James says.

He hooks a hand on the cabover bed and watches the six-lane road out the windshield. There are fewer cars than on the main road. The people who made it out of Edmonton must have kept going once they were free of the city.

"There, on the right." James points to two large stations that sit next to each other, where more signs claim that the gas is long gone.

"At least Canadians are nice enough to let you know not to waste your time," I say because if I don't joke, I'll kick something in frustration.

"Now if only we could get some of that free healthcare," James says, and moves back to his map. "Keep going north. Maybe we'll get lucky."

We get lucky-ish at the next one: Fifty gallons of questionable gas in a neighborhood that houses only industrial buildings and auto body shops.

We put this in our new tank so as not to mix it with the fuel we know to be good and pick up a few new gas cans while we're at it.

"If you could see the number of gas stations in the city, you guys would cry," James says. His expression is composed, but he presses his finger to the center of Edmonton hard enough for the tip to blanch. "But I doubt we can get in without killing ourselves."

We've seen a few Lexers going about their zombie business, but I imagine the stations in town are chock-full. Close to a million people, especially with roadblocks in place, must have created a lot of zombies.

We head south because the North Saskatchewan River cuts through Edmonton and the road to the north bridge is blocked. When I swear this stupid river is following us, James shows me how it winds up and down across the map and assures me that this will be the final crossing, after which we'll swing north and east to check out the military base.

The seats are all taken, so I plop myself on Nelly's lap on the couch and fling my arm around his shoulder. "How you doing, darlin'?" he asks.

"Great. Remember how we always wanted to take a cross-country road trip?"

"It's exactly how I envisioned it," Nelly says.

"It might even be better." It's not anything like how we envisioned it, but his presence makes it much better than it would otherwise be.

The trees become numerous as we cross the bridge. The yellows and oranges of the autumn leaves mix with the green of the firs to create a postcard-perfect view. Even so, I'd have been happy never seeing the river again. Maybe third time's the charm.

CHAPTER 25

The closer we get to West Edmonton, the more Lexers we see. A group of twenty watches us go past, their heads turning slowly, mouths agape. Sometimes it's a shock to the system to see them again when we haven't for a few hours. I can pretend we live in an empty world, which is bad enough, until I get a reminder that dead people want to eat us.

We maneuver our way down a wide road that isn't completely clogged and hit an overpass. The highway above is the perfect place to survey the road ahead. Six of us climb the grassy embankment and stand on the guardrail. The lanes are cars, the shoulders are cars, but there isn't anything undead except one Lexer still belted in a hatchback. It scrapes a claw against the window, wisps of long hair covering half its face.

I step from car to car. I'm not taking the chance of living out the childhood nightmare of a hand wrapping around my ankle from a dark space. Peter follows until we're in the center of the overpass on the roof of a green sedan.

"Can I call you Elmer from now on?" I ask, and raise the binoculars to my eyes.

"Why would you want to do that?"

"You know, like Elmer's Glue."

"Have I ever told you that you're weird?" Peter asks.

"I don't think so."

I take in the Edmonton skyline, where I can make out details of the buildings that are miles away, and then focus on the road. These binoculars are the best money can buy, apparently. That's one good thing—you never have to skimp on quality as long as you can get to what you want without being eaten.

What looks like a roadblock is a mile or so ahead, and behind that are zombies. They cover the street and parking lots. A face with one eyeball and a hole where the nose once was fills my lens, and I take an involuntary step back. It looks close enough to eat me.

Peter drops his binoculars with a sigh. "Well, that's out." We make our way back to share the news with the others.

"We'll go north," Mark says. "Then to Grande Prairie. It's possible that if the roadblocks kept people in, there'll be gas up there."

The thought had crossed my mind that we'd get far enough to think we were going to make it and then get no farther. I'd refused to give it credibility because of my new upbeat attitude, but now the possibility begins to eat away at my optimism. I never wanted to be a cheerleader, anyway.

"We only need another hundred gallons," I say, and mentally wave my imaginary pompoms. "We should be able to find that much. Then we're as good as there." Bits believes it even if the others don't.

We waste time and gas, but in the end only have twenty more gallons to show for it. By the time we hit the town that should have taken us three hours of travel, half of the day's sunlight is gone. The brick sign on the town's outskirts welcomes us. The spray-painted sign that says *We shoot thieves* with a skeleton tied to the post beneath doesn't.

"Someone went all medieval," Nelly says.

Our hands move to our weapons. The sign looks old and chances are that if they once would have shot, they might not now or they're out of ammo. And we're not thieves. The first buildings we see—a few hotels, a gas station and a restaurant—are all burnt to the ground.

"Those fires look intentional," Mark says. He rests a finger under his nose and watches the next burned-out building come into view.

We pull to a stop at a roadblock that's abandoned but impassable because of the shells of burnt-out cars that stretch out behind it. Zeke leaves the pickup for a better view and returns with hunched shoulders. "It goes on for a mile. And there's a whole slew of bodies on the other side. I say we get the hell out of here."

"There are two rivers ahead," James says quietly. "We need the bridge."

"More fucking rivers?" Zeke yanks his beard. "I'm beginning to hate Canada."

"We can either go farther north or down south, but both will double our time to Grande Prairie."

"I'd bet the last of our food this bridge is blocked, too, but is there a different way to hit this one?"

"Not without going through the city. Or so far down south that we might as well just go the southern route anyway. And we might as well forget about the military base—we'll never get there."

Zeke balls up a fist and gently rests it on the camper door. It looks like he'd rather punch something. "So we have no fucking choice in the matter, that's what you're telling me?" Zeke's eyes narrow to slits and his jaw works under his beard. Right here is the guy who traveled 1,000 miles to safety in the months after the virus, who used to be a hellraiser, and I, for one, wouldn't want to mess with him.

"Oh, we have choices," James says. "It's just that, as usual, they all suck."

Zeke bellows out a short laugh, good humor restored. "Well, that's better, then."

It takes us half an hour to get to the first of the two bridges that go north, passing a tiny town that can barely be called a town and halting at a bridge that can't be called a bridge, since it no longer connects the two sides of the river. The structure itself still stands, but a stretch of the road has been chipped away as if someone took a jackhammer to it. We walk the asphalt. I want to grab Peter by the back of his coat when he peers over the edge. Nelly follows, but I pull him back.

"What's wrong with you guys?" I ask. "Why would you walk to the edge of a precipice for no good reason?"

Peter faces us and rocks back on his heels, arms whirling to stay upright. I scream—a high-pitched screech that echoes off the water—and rush forward. As I reach him, he plants his feet on the ground and laughs. He actually laughs.

"You're such an asshole!" I yell. I'd shove him if he weren't still six inches from the edge.

Nelly's stupid Texan hoots are louder than my scream. I march past Zeke, who also finds this amusing judging by the way his beard trembles. Jamie rolls her eyes at Shawn and Nelly's high five. I slam the RV's door and flop on the couch. "What is wrong with men? My dad was right when he said they never mentally make it past the age of twelve."

Mark looks up from his map. "A valid theory, and one I won't argue with in most cases."

The others troop into the RV, Peter last and still looking delighted with his prank. He sits and elbows me in the side. I cross my arms and stare out the window. "C'mon, it was a little bit funny," he says. I don't answer and he elbows me harder. "A tad funny?"

"No, it really wasn't. What if Bits or Hank did that?"

"They're kids. I'm thirty-one."

"In actual years, maybe."

"Fine, sorry," Peter says. I give him a sidelong glance to find him not looking sorry at all.

Bits and Hank watch us bicker. In fact, everyone does. I stand. "Who wants to watch a movie?"

I sit and seethe while the TV plays. I might have overreacted in the supermarket, but I don't get why you would pretend to be in trouble when we have plenty as it is. It takes the length of a movie to reach the other bridge, only to find it's the same story. I don't leave the RV; hearing about the Lexers trapped in the steel and concrete supports is enough. I understand why someone destroyed the bridges—the river is a natural barrier to the Lexers—and I suppose if I were north of the bridge, I would think that cutting off access was a fine idea. But on this side it just sucks.

CHAPTER 26

As we drive south, the road rises with mountains that remind me of the rolling hills of Vermont. The sky is darkening with late afternoon storm clouds. I put on the remainder of our rice, dump in a can of pinto beans from the supermarket and politely brush off Peter's offer to help. I've started dishing out the food when I hear a collective gasp.

Everyone's gaze is focused on the windshield. At first I think it's a cloud, but then I make out the very tip of a mountain far in the distance. We're almost at the Rockies. Those mountains I've dreamed of for a week have become a reality. Shawn gives the pickup's horn three long, joyous blasts and giddiness replaces my fatigue.

We pull to the side of the highway to eat. The cold air smells of trees and mountains and moist earth instead of dry, windy prairie. Once I'm outside, I don't want to go back in the RV. I don't want to sit down. I only want to stare at that distant peak until I'm absolutely sure it's not a mirage.

Peter swallows his food in a few bites and turns to me. The coming storm bathes everything in a bright, unearthly light, making the highlights in his hair almost silver. "Forgive me yet?"

"No." I eat a spoonful of rice and watch the mountain. I'm so happy that I want to forgive him immediately, but he still has to make his penance. "That was stupid. What if you fell?"

"I—"

"I wasn't done. Why make danger when there isn't any? Aren't we in enough danger?"

Peter crosses his arms. "Says the girl who went out looking for trouble all summer and almost fell in the quarry."

I open my mouth to argue, but he's right. "Okay, fine. But I was killing zombies. If you're going to do something stupid, can you at least make it have purpose?" I point at him. "Plus, I don't know if you remember, but you promised me. I'm upset that you were willing to take the chance. We're three quarters of the way there."

I can't tell what he's thinking with the way the silver clouds are reflected in his eyes, but he looks sad or serious, or both. I move closer and look up at him. "I want us to live. I want you to live. But do *you* want to live? Tell me the truth. I understand if you don't or if you're not sure, believe me."

A raindrop splatters on my scalp. Lightning flashes where the clouds are darkest. My coat will be close to useless if it gets too wet, as wet down does the opposite of warming you up, but I'm not moving until he answers. I need to know if I should prepare myself to lose him. It might make it easier if I do.

The silver light turns gray and a roll of thunder crashes loud enough to make me jump. Peter's lips are pressed together, gaze bouncing around as if he's afraid to look at me for too long. I know he'll tell me the truth, but now I'm not so sure I want to hear the answer. I wrap my hand around his damp leather sleeve. "And maybe answer before Mother Nature makes the decision for us with a bolt of lightning."

"I want to live."

"You sure?"

A slight smile spreads until his face is alight. "I'm sure."

The lightning moves closer. Every hair on my head rises and every cell in my body zings with the power of the coming storm. We need to find a safe place to sleep, but I wish we could drive all night. The Rockies are so close that I know we're going to get there. Peter wants to live. Bits and Hank are with us. Penny's baby is going to be born. Nelly will torture me for the rest of my life. It makes me want to shout with joy. Or have a dance party. I imagine staging a dance party right here on this lonely stretch of road.

"Why are you smiling?" Peter asks.

"I wish we could have a dance party. But, sadly, we don't have the time."

"I'm heartbroken," Peter says.

"I know you are." I pull out Adrian's phone and wipe away a drop of rain. "Let's get a picture with that mountain."

I take a shot of us before the phone is soaked. Shawn honks. "Really? It's picture time?" he calls out the window.

"It was either that or a dance party," I yell back. I drag Peter toward the RV before we really are struck by lightning now that it flashes directly overhead and the rain has begun in earnest.

"Well, then, I support your decision," Shawn calls.

He revs the pickup's engine and we follow him down the next dip. We lose sight of the mountain, but that's okay. I know it's still there.

CHAPTER 27

I think we'd be able to see the mountains, if they weren't obscured by sheets of rain, while we head toward the town of Hinton. It's far too late to check for fuel, so we exit the highway and end up on a street of large new homes, all different but identical in that planned community way. Every house has been broken into and the cars are either gone or in garages.

"One of these might do for the night," Zeke says from the pickup.

Kyle has insisted on driving the RV all day, and now he stretches his arm above his head and opens the door. The rain has lessened to a drizzle, and the thunder is a distant rumble. We choose a sage green house with a privacy fence and a deadbolt that still clicks into place. It's not fancy like last night's house, but it's spacious and nicely furnished with microfiber couches, Ikea-type furniture and nary a coaster in sight.

The only pictures are of a couple around retirement age posing on beaches and sailboats and what Mark recognizes as Machu Picchu from his travels. The dark kitchen cabinets are empty and the fridge holds a fossilized box of baking soda. The whole place is as cold as a refrigerator. Just once, I'd like to waste the RV's propane and be warm from my toes to the top of my grimy head.

I remind my growling stomach that we've already eaten dinner. I've tried not to think about it or complain, but we've got an hour or so until bedtime, and all I want is something to eat. Going to bed hungry sucks. Waking up hungry sucks. I think about suggesting we eat something else, a couple of MREs maybe, but we should save them.

"Early watch shift for you tonight, sugar," Zeke says, his bulk filling the doorway of the kitchen. "Nothing good, huh?"

"Not a crumb," I say. At least I'll get a full night's sleep instead of waking up to be hungry for two hours during the night. "You must be starving, Zekey."

He spreads his thick arms. "Could do with a meal. But I've got more padding than you. Plenty to live off of for a while."

"Well, you're the first one we'll eat. No point in letting all those good calories waste away."

Zeke guffaws and moves into the kitchen so Nelly can pass. "Who are we eating?" Nelly asks.

"You'd make a decent second course," I say.

I laugh when they flex their muscles and argue about who'd make the better meal. I don't know how I would have gotten this far without them, in both the literal and figurative sense. And I know what I realized a week ago is true—the more people we have in our hearts, the more likely we'll have someone left to help us through.

✳✳✳

After I've set the kids up with Mad Libs, James calls to me from the hallway. I find him in the master bedroom, a conspiratorial look on his face. He wiggles an open pack of cigarettes in the air. "Someone was a closet smoker, for real. I found these on the top shelf in the guy's shoebox."

"Or they were emergency cigarettes. I had emergency cigarettes." I'd tucked a pack under my clothes in my closet in Brooklyn after I quit and forgotten all about them until now.

"Well, this dude must have been eaten right away because if there was ever an emergency, this was it. You in?"

It's not food, but it's something to put in my mouth. "Are you crazy? Of course I'm in. Let me check for clothes first." I open drawers and push hangers aside. When I find a couple pairs of jeans I throw them on the bed along with a sweater that looks cozy.

"James, this guy was tall and skinny. You should try on some of his clothes."

He takes a pair of flannel-lined jeans and some Levis. I hold the woman's jeans up to myself and groan. It may be superficial, but there's no way I can bring myself to put on these high-waisted, pleated jeans that puff at the hips and taper off at what would be way above my ankles. Not unless I was naked and freezing to death, and even then I wouldn't want to be caught dead in them. Nelly strolls in and stops, his trademark smirk appearing at the sight of the jeans.

"It's the pleats that make them, isn't it?" I ask.

"I'd pay good money to see you in those. Try them on for me."

"Not happening. Too bad money isn't worth anything."

"Please?" Nelly clasps his hands together. "Please? Let me take a picture of you in them. I'll give you my dinner."

"No way. And we already ate."

Nelly laughs. "Breakfast and lunch tomorrow, then."

"So you have a picture to hang over my head for the rest of our lives? I'll never be that hungry."

He fingers the denim sadly. "You need clothes. You should bring them just in case."

"Why? So my other jeans can have an unfortunate accident?" I'm down to my last clean outfit, but I'd wash out and wear my slightly stinky jeans before I'd touch these with a ten foot pole.

"You know me too well."

He'll bother me about this all night, but Nelly can always be distracted by mind-altering substances. "James found cigarettes. Want one?"

Nelly perks up, the jeans forgotten, and drags us into the backyard. I sink into one of the chairs on the covered patio and light up. The stale cigarette crackles, but it tastes fine. Nicotine and lack of food give me a head rush that doesn't quite reach the level of nausea, so I help myself to another drag.

Nelly puts his feet up on the table and squints through his smoke. "How many were in there?"

"Six," James says. "Now three."

Zeke comes through the sliding glass door. "Now two, you mean." He settles into a chair and lights up. "Ten years ago I swore I'd never smoke again. It'll send you to an early grave."

"So will zombies," Nelly says.

"True enough."

Peter steps out. Nelly holds his cigarette down by his side. "Narc."

"Are we not past that now? Enjoy." Peter waves at the cloud of smoke that's trapped under the patio roof, then sits in a chair and turns to me. "But I thought you wanted to live."

"This *is* living. You don't know what you're missing."

Peter reaches for my cigarette and I look at him in disbelief. "Really?"

"Hand it over."

We watch Peter take a drag, holding the cigarette awkwardly between his fingers. It's more than I would inhale, even having been a smoker myself. His face goes red and smoke comes out in choking, coughing spurts. I pluck it from his hand and help myself to more while I laugh at him.

"Amateur," Nelly says.

"Why the hell would you want to smoke?" Peter says between gasps. "It's like licking an ashtray."

"A delicious ashtray," I say. "Want to try again?"

"I think I'm good."

"Are you on watch with me?"

"I am."

"Well then, I guess we should get inside." My mouth does taste like an ashtray now that I'm done. "I want to brush my teeth."

Peter stands with his lips quirking. "It's gross, isn't it? Admit it."

"Never," I say.

CHAPTER 28

The next morning, we hit our first service station. Kyle turns off the ignition and rolls down his window. Everyone gearing up for our usual procedure freezes when he sniffs the air and swivels his head. "You smell that?"

I hear them before I see them. The same sound I heard on our last day at Kingdom Come—a droning hum that gets louder by the second. The first few stumble from the wooded area on the south side of the highway and are followed by a whole lot more. They spill out between the businesses down the road to the west.

"Sit down!" Kyle calls.

I hold Nicki in my arms while we screech out of the lot. Voices call from the radio, but I can't hear a thing over Nicki's wails. Nelly turns from the windshield, face pale. "There're more coming. Hold on."

Thankfully, last I saw there weren't many cars on the road. A swerve in a giant box like this RV, at this speed, would surely send us rolling. Peter holds the counter, eyes out the side window, and his face slackens a moment before the rear of the RV is hit from the left. I thud headfirst into the cabinets on the opposite side and Nicki flies out of my arms. When I can focus again, I crawl to her.

Kyle straightens out the shuddering RV. Peter's on the floor, Bits and Hank in his arms and feet braced on a cabinet. I pull myself and Nicki into the short hall between the bedroom and kitchen and do the same. The RV skids to the right and I close my eyes, sure we're going over—and, therefore, sure we're only minutes away from death—either by car crash or the swarm of Lexers.

Kyle makes a sharp right and a minute later calls, "I see the bridge. It's fine."

I don't know what we would have done if it wasn't. The noise from under the tires changes when we hit the bridge's road surface. I move to the bedroom window with Nicki in my arms, since she whimpers and refuses to let go. Dark shapes float in the river, and the Lexers that have washed up on the northern shore struggle to their feet. If that pod was as large as the one in the east, who knows how many thousands will come through here. Some are bound to make it across and up the steep riverbank. I just hope they won't make it over the immense mountains to the west. That hope is the whole reason we started on this trip.

"Everyone okay?" Kyle yells.

We answer in the affirmative, but Nicki yelps and clutches her arm to her middle when I jostle it as I set her on the bed. I sink to the floor. "What's wrong? Are you hurt?"

"My arm," she wails.

"Can I see?"

She yanks out of my reach, fat tears dripping down her cheeks. "No. It hurts."

Maureen has come into the bedroom, and now she sits beside Nicki and says, "We have to look at it to help you, sweetheart."

Maureen coaxes Nicki into her lap and nods my way. It might do more harm than good to raise Nicki's arm to remove her sweater, so I slice my knife through the sleeve and ease it down to find a lump in her forearm where one shouldn't be. I fight a wave of nausea. I can kill zombies without getting ill, but the sight of this little girl with a broken arm makes my saliva thicken.

"We'll get you all fixed up, don't worry," Maureen says. Her voice is relaxed, even as she looks at me with troubled eyes. "Cassie, why don't you go get Daddy for Nicki? And we need Jamie and Zeke."

Jamie was Doc's part-time nurse at Kingdom Come and the closest we have to a doctor besides Zeke. I reach the front on unstable legs and touch Kyle's shoulder. "Nicki's okay, but we think her left arm is broken. Is it safe to stop so we can switch drivers and get Jamie?"

His hands tighten on the wheel and he throws a wild glance over his shoulder, but he doesn't slow. "She's okay?"

"She's scared and it hurts, but she's okay."

"I'll stop in a few miles." He swallows hard and calls, "I'll come back there as soon as I can. Okay, baby?"

"I'm sorry," I say. "I had her, but I dropped her when they hit us."

"Not your fault," he says, but I still feel responsible.

The mountains ahead of us are dark against the light blue of the sky. The pod is behind us, but not far enough behind, in my opinion. The road climbs higher until we have a clear view of the river and surrounding land. I'm not surprised to see figures stumbling north in the clearings.

A few miles later, when the trees are shorter and the grass doesn't reach the height of the grass at lower elevations, Peter takes the wheel.

Jamie and Zeke examine Nicki, who's entered a state of what could be calm or shock in Kyle's lap. He looks as shocked as she. "I know it hurts, baby. Jamie'll fix it."

Jamie nods, but when she moves behind Kyle for the first aid kit the look she throws me is anything but confident. Her hands shake as she fumbles in the bag for gauze. "Cassie, can you get the book?" She looks around. "A splint. What can we use to make a splint?"

I find the medical book and flip to the pages on broken bones. The picture looks just like Nicki's arm, lump included. So far, Jamie's doing everything right.

Zeke looks for splint material while Kyle watches us, breathing deep and murmuring in Nicki's ear. I find her dosage of children's ibuprofen. "This is yummy stuff," I say. "Right, Bits?"

"It's so good, Nicki," Bits says in a singsong voice from where she sits on the table for a better view. "I wish I could have some."

I wink at her and whisper to Nicki, "It's like candy. You'd better take it before she does."

Nicki offers me a wan smile and opens her mouth. Jamie sits with the papers by her knee. "It doesn't look too swollen yet. We have to set it. We should stop while we do that. Zeke, can you hold her upper arm by her side?"

"If only you'd broken a tooth," Zeke says with a smile. "That I could fix up right quick."

Jamie studies the instructions and whispers to herself as the RV slows. "Cassie, come here a sec? Zeke holds, you pull and I'll line up the break." She points to the drawings, which show another set of hands are helpful to be sure the bones line up properly.

"This is probably going to hurt, sweetie. But you can't move your arm, okay?" Nicki's lower lip trembles when she nods. "Okay, Cassie, pull now."

I'm not going to be a baby about this and ask someone else to do it, although I'd really, really like to. I hold the base of Nicki's hand and pull gently. Nicki screams, but if we stop now it'll be even worse to try again. The lump in her arm disappears and Jamie uses her hands to adjust the bones.

"It's okay, it's okay," Jamie murmurs. It might be in answer to Nicki's cries, but I think it's partly for herself, too. "Let go, Cass."

Jamie wraps gauze around Nicki's arm and places the cardboard packaging Nelly has cut and folded underneath. I hold it in place while she wraps an elastic bandage around the whole thing. She looks up from her work when she's secured the end. "I think we're good. There are instructions on making a cast when the swelling goes down, but we're going to need plaster."

Kyle murmurs his thanks and asks, "Does she need a cast? Will it heal on its own?"

"I don't think we should take the chance. I'll stay in here in case Nicki needs me. Let me go tell Shawn." Jamie pulls me out the door and walks up the rocky grass on the roadside, her breaths coming in giant bursts of fog. She stumbles back to where I stand on the asphalt. "Oh my God. I had no idea what I was doing. I think we got it, though."

Her face is pale, eyes perfect circles. She takes her hair out of its messy bun and shakes out the sweat. Now that it's over, mine has turned to ice. "You were great," I say. "I wanted to faint."

"I kept talking just so I didn't. I saw Doc do it last year, but that was before I was his official nurse." She leans on the RV and blows out a breath. "Now we have to go to a hospital for that plaster. We can't let her arm heal wrong."

Hospitals are places to avoid at all costs; they're full of Lexers. But Jamie's right: you can't grow up nowadays with an arm that doesn't work properly. It could be a death sentence.

"How about an art supplies store?" I ask. "They always have those plaster of Paris strips there. I don't know if it's the same thing, but it'll probably work."

"They do?" Jamie asks. "Who knew being an artist would come in handy?"

I think of the painting I made for Dan of Fenway Park. It didn't save his life, but maybe it made him happy for what ended up being his last few hours. And Bits has the locket with the painting of her mother; otherwise, she'd have nothing of her past. Inside my second bag, the one I grabbed when I rescued Sparky, is the box Dan made for me. I took it for the phone charger and other assorted things I'd stored in there, thinking I'd remove them when winter came and we were safe until spring. I'd hoped the giant pods wouldn't make it before the freeze, but I was prepared to be disappointed. I am, after all, my father's daughter.

CHAPTER 29

I want to sob when the mountains become a faded blue as we head northeast to Grande Prairie for fuel and plaster. The mountains here are more like hills in comparison, and even those are flattening out. Everyone either sits unnaturally still or, like Maureen, has busied themselves doing things that don't need doing. Now that it's a certainty we're in a race with the Lexers, we don't have time to waste. James and Mark have informed us that more could very likely be traveling up the highways in British Columbia—and there isn't a wide selection of roads to choose from. Had no one taken out those bridges up north, we would've never gone to Hinton. But that's how it is out here—one thing leads to another until you find yourself on a different course entirely.

It's afternoon by the time we hit the city. We've eaten lunch and given Nicki an MRE dessert, which she ate before falling asleep on Kyle. The other kids refused a taste when she offered, and I plan to reward them by giving them every last dessert when the MREs are finally cracked open.

The first barren gas station we hit has a phone book. We find a wide, empty crossroads south of the city for the RV to wait while the pickup goes for fuel and plaster. We'll have to hit the busy sections of town, where there's a better chance of fuel and there's definitely a craft store. Or I should say *they'll* have to hit it, given that I've promised Bits I wouldn't go—a promise I already regret. Heading out with a purpose is better than waiting.

Everyone is packed inside the RV, mapping out gas stations or making sure blades are sharp and guns are loaded. "I'd like to stay with Nicki, if no one minds," Kyle says.

"And I should stay in case she needs something," Jamie adds. I know, like me, she'd rather go. Shawn blinks a few times. They're always together, and he's not fond of the idea at all.

"I'll go, Shawn," James says. He touches Penny's shoulder when she pales. "I practically have the map memorized."

"All right," Zeke says. "Me, James, Nel, Margaret and Mark are going."

"You could use six people," Peter says. "Two for the pump and four to watch. I'll go." My mouth drops. This is not what I'd call sticking like glue. But I notice Bits's anxious expression and bite my tongue.

They fill the RV with all the fuel it will hold before tossing the empty containers in the pickup. I stand on the road beside Bits and smooth down the flyaway hair that the never-ending wind has pulled from her braid.

"Be good," Peter says to Bits. He lifts her above his head and then pretends to drop her while she cackles. She still hasn't grown tired of their game, and she's still small enough to do it at almost nine years old. "Love you, baby girl. More than all the stars in the sky."

"Love you infinity," Bits says once she's on the ground, and then she runs off to hug the others.

Peter turns to me. I haven't said a word, but it's obvious he knows how I feel by the way he sucks in his cheeks. "They could use the help. We don't want what happened to Mike and—"

"I know." I watch the grass bend in the wind. I'd thought we left the stupid prairie behind us, but here we are yet again.

"You're not mad?"

I drag my eyes to his. "No. I'm scared." Now it's Peter's turn to stare at the stupid prairie and run a hand through his hair. I clear my throat. "Just come back."

He pulls me into a hug. I grab the back of his coat and consider refusing to let go. I could throw a little tantrum right here and maybe get my way, but I won't. We all have to put ourselves on the line; it's just that I want Peter's life to be on the line when I'm there, too.

"I will. Promise." I step back with a shake of my head. Peter can't promise something like that, and he knows I'm a stickler for promises. He pulls me close, jaw set and eyes ink-black. "*I promise.*"

It shouldn't make me feel better, but it does. I'm beginning to think Peter could make me believe anything at all. "I'm holding you to that. If you break your promise, I swear I'll kill you."

Peter's teeth flash. "Deal."

✫✫✫

Dinner has grown cold and the sun is setting. They were supposed to be back by nightfall. I never thought that people actually wring their hands, but Penny and I have become masters at it. I spent my watch shift on the RV's roof staring down the road for the red pickup. I kept thinking I heard it, only to have my heart plummet when it was once again the sound of the wind rushing over the grass and through the few trees.

"They might have to stay the night somewhere," Penny says. "Or they're heading back right now. It's just taking longer than they thought. What if they have to leave the city by the north and make their way down? There could be cars to move and..."

She trails off. It's not the first time she's listed all the things that could be happening, but there's one she leaves out and it's the most likely of all. We can travel 400 or so miles on the fuel we have, enough to get out of here and find gas someplace else. It won't be easy with a hand-pumped siphon and only a few of us who can fight.

We've agreed to leave if they haven't returned by mid-morning tomorrow. When they get close, they'll call on the radio. The radios have a decent range on flat terrain, but all we've heard so far is static. I take out my buns so I can lie down comfortably but leave on my coat and boots because I want to be ready to help if need be. Maybe all they need is help. I refuse to contemplate any other outcome.

Shawn and Adam leave for their watch shift on the roof. The others are lying down, Maureen and Ashley resting upright on the couch. I sit at the table and study the map by the light of the single lantern; their destinations don't leave them many ways to get south to us again. It's possible that they took a circuitous route or had to stop for some reason. I shake my head—I'm running Penny's speech through my mind now that she's asleep in the cabover bed with the kids.

It's dark and quiet outside but for the scuffling of boots up above. And it's freezing, but warmer in here out of the wind. I wrap my blanket tighter, rest my forehead in my hand and stare at the map, praying it will lead them home.

CHAPTER 30

The rumble of an engine wakes me with my forehead still in my hand and wrist bent in an unnatural position. I pull out my phone to check the time—it's late but not yet tomorrow. Barnaby trots to the door, nails clicking on the kitchen floor. Bits is out of the bed like a shot with Hank close behind. Now that they're back we'll have to squeeze into the RV to sleep, but I'm positive not a single person minds. Especially Penny, who grins at me from the top bunk and begins to work her way down in awkward pregnant-lady fashion.

A car door slams. Bits freezes at a growl from Barn, who stares at the door with raised hackles before the boom of a single gunshot sends him into a frenzy of barking. At first I think it's Lexers, but it's followed by more booms and the sound of feet running on the roof. A bullet hits the side of the RV with a thud. I shove Bits and Hank to the floor and follow them down. This isn't zombies—it's voices I don't recognize. Jamie races from the bedroom, hair and eyes wild.

Kyle isn't far behind, gun already drawn. "Lock the doors!"

I crawl to the main door and lock it. A volley of shots mixes with Barnaby's piercing barks. Ashley scrambles for the doors of the cab and sinks between the seats when a bullet smashes the passenger's side window.

Jamie runs to her while I drag Bits and Hank into the bedroom and cram them alongside the bed with Nicki. I return to the kitchen at a long, pained scream. Ash is huddled in the passenger's seat, a man's hand wrapped around her braid and the other holding a pistol to her head. Jamie crouches behind the seat, out of eyeshot, but there's nothing to do that won't get Ash killed.

"Put your guns down and call off your dog!" a man's voice yells.

Heat rises off Kyle, only inches away. He snarls and lowers his gun to the dinette, and I place mine next to his. We both know we don't have a choice.

"They're down," Kyle calls.

Ash shrieks as she's dragged outside through the cab's open door. It's followed by the sound of a hand smacking flesh. The RV's main door rattles. "Open the door," another voice commands.

"Cassie!" Bits screams from the bedroom. Penny moves in that direction, but I point her to the cabover bed and motion Maureen to the back. Penny shakes her head, and I hiss, "Hide. Now."

I wish the kids had never come down from there. These men might never know they're here if they were well-hidden behind the jumble of blankets. Kyle unlocks the door and steps back, hands fisted at his sides. I hold Barn's collar as he strains, looking fierce with white fangs and a low growl vibrating in his throat. Ash is shoved in first. Finger-shaped spots flare on her cheek. The man holding Ash is followed in by five others, the last being supported by two of them as if hurt. They wear stained winter coats and short, unkempt beards. I think they were once average guys, but now they're gaunt, with watery eyes and rough, broken skin. None are older than fifty, and one appears to be in his twenties, although it's hard to tell with the hair and dirt.

"Close the door, Whit," the man who holds Ash says to the youngest. "Get that dog out first."

He's the oldest, with a gray-brown scraggly beard, rotted teeth, and an authoritative manner that the others defer to. All of them look sick and desperate, but the worst part is the stench. We might smell bad, but we smell like people. These men smell like Lexers. And not just how you smell when you've gotten into a scrape with zombies, but like they *are* zombies. It fills the camper so that I gag.

I can barely hear over Barnaby's barks, can barely make sense of what's happening. I've gone from relief to terror in seconds and the adrenaline outpaces my brain. My heart is attempting to escape my chest. The men's shouts become distant echoes while I try to think of a way out of this situation and come up blank.

Barnaby squeals when a boot connects with his side. "Take him out!" the boss orders me.

Barn's feet skid along the smooth surface of the kitchen floor as I drag him to the door and grope for the handle. The night air is cold and holds who knows how many terrors, but I could slip out and run. I'd love to run, to feel my feet pound the ground as I fly away. Not that I would ever leave. I give Barnaby's behind a shove. He hits the ground and scrambles back up the steps. Whit, the youngest one, slams the door in his face.

Barnaby scratches at the door. I will him to run away, to slink off and be frightened the way he always is, but he howls until an auburn-haired man fires out the front door into the night. There's the sound of paws scrabbling on metal and then nothing.

I stand beside Kyle, whose tense body is waiting to spring. But they aren't stupid. They don't take their eyes off us or lower their guns for a second. One swings his pistol with a hiss when Jamie moves.

"Shawn!" she yells toward the ceiling. She turns to the men. "Where are they?"

Another man with a scraggly beard and an eye that twitches constantly says, "You mean the ones bleeding out on the road?"

A vein pulses in Jamie's neck before she launches herself at the twitchy-eyed one like a rabid animal. The boss knees her in the stomach and she falls at Twitch's feet with a gasp. I bend to help her and am rewarded with the barrel of a gun at my ear.

"Sit," Twitch says.

I help Jamie to the couch, Kyle beside me, and Twitch pushes Ash to the floor by our feet. She clasps her knees to her chest and drops her head. I stroke her hair and keep my eyes down, afraid that anything will set them off. They don't know about the kids in the bedroom. Maybe we can keep it that way, give them what they want and get out of this relatively unharmed. I won't believe that Shawn and Adam are dead. They could be hurt or devising a plan to help us.

"Let's get some lights and heat in here." The boss turns to the controls built into the wall and the lantern is drowned out by bright light.

"Put Jay in the bedroom," Boss says.

I dig my nails into my palms at the shrill cries when they enter the back. After much yelling, Maureen falls through the short passageway to the kitchen with the kids clustered around her.

"Leave them alone!" Maureen yells.

"Get on the couch," Boss commands. Bits runs for my lap and I set Hank between my feet, but Nicki clings to Maureen's leg and sobs.

"Her arm's broken," Kyle says, voice hoarse and body rigid. "Nicki! Baby! Just come here."

Twitch tugs on her bad arm. Nicki screams, locking her legs around Maureen, and he slaps the back of her head, teeth bared. "Shut up!"

Kyle is off the couch and makes it three feet before a rifle butt slams him in the temple. He doubles over, droplets of blood splattering on the laminate floor. It's a terrible blow, one I likely wouldn't survive, but Kyle raises his head and takes another step before he's hit once more. He goes down like a felled tree.

"Nicki," Jamie says in a quiet voice. "Nicki, come to me."

Twitch tosses Nicki by her shirt into Jamie's lap. Maureen sits at the table as ordered, lips thin and eyes murderous. It looks out of place on the face that's always pleasant. They drag Kyle to drop him between the front seats. His chest rises. I thought he was dead.

"Food, fellas." Twitch pulls everything in the cabinets to the counter. The other men stare at the bounty as though it's a fully-stocked supermarket.

"These are good," Whit says, holding up an MRE. "We used to take them hunting." A man with dark hair and a giant sore on his cheek slices one open and dumps the contents on the stove.

"You can take it all. Take it and leave," I say, and hate how weak and begging my voice sounds.

No one answers. They don't bother with the heating pouches, just spoon food into their mouths with open-mouthed chewing. Cracker crumbs hit the counter and floor. An MRE contains a lot of food, but it takes no more than minutes for them to finish them off.

"We're not leaving," Boss says when he's done. "But we will take the food."

"You can have the RV," Maureen says. She holds her trembling chin high. "Just drive away with it all."

"Don't worry, we will," Twitch says.

And now, with their stomachs full, they focus on us. Every one of them looks sick. Months of starvation, maybe, or some sort of illness. One of them hacks up something with a deep cough and spits into the sink.

"We haven't had real food in a week," Auburn says. I catch a glimpse of bloody gums when he pops in the last bite of his dessert. Not *his* dessert—the dessert I was saving for the kids. "Know what we've been eating?"

The answer hits my brain and gag reflex at the same time. There's no way they'd smell this terrible otherwise. You can change clothes, take a cold bath with soap, brush your teeth. You might still reek, but this is more than a dusting of Lexer innards on clothing.

They've been eating Lexers.

None of us speaks, although the appalled looks on the others' faces tells me they've come to the same conclusion. I didn't think it was possible without getting sick. But they *are* sick. You can see it in their eyes, in their almost feral expressions. They're still human, but only because they're not dead. It could be something similar to mad cow disease, or it could be that having to choke that down drives you insane.

"If you cook them you don't get infected," Boss says with a rotten smile. He motions to Ashley and when she doesn't move, yanks her to her feet. "Take off your coat."

Ash unzips her coat with jerky movements. Her chest jumps as he inspects her long-sleeved shirt and jeans, then spasms with quiet sobs when he runs a hand down her side. The breathing of the other men speeds up. I'd hoped they were too sick or hungry to think about anything but food and maybe showers, but he looks at her the same way he did the MREs.

I shove Bits behind me when I bolt to my feet. It's doubtless a mistake, but I can't watch this. "Get your fucking hands off her!"

Boss's mean eyes slither my way. "Or what?"

I don't have an answer. I would rip off his head, disembowel him with my fingers if I could. He works his tongue around his mouth and spits a chunk of food to the floor. "You volunteering?"

He leaves no doubt as to what he means with the way his eyes slink down my body. If this is what it takes to get his hands off of Ashley, I'll do it. She's a virgin. I won't let this be her first experience with a man. I attempt a breath, but the RV suddenly feels as tiny and stifling as a closet.

"If you leave her alone," I whisper. He nods and shoves Ash into the kitchen, where she hits the refrigerator with a moan.

Auburn's rifle rises at a gasp from the cabover bed. "Get down here," he says.

Penny hits the floor and stands with her shoulders back and lip curled. The only part of her that doesn't resemble her sister is the hand curled protectively over her belly.

Boss crooks a finger at me. "Come here."

I trip over Hank to get there. The creases of Boss's face are filled with grime and his hands are filthy. I shudder when I imagine them on me. He leans close, and there's nothing in his washed-out eyes but a whole lot of crazy. "You fight, you die."

CHAPTER 31

I thought they'd do whatever they're going to do with me right away. Instead, Boss has shoved me into the dinette across from Maureen while they pick through our food and argue over who gets what.

They discuss Jay, the man in the bedroom, who's dying of a gunshot wound. Shawn and Adam got one of them, at least. They must be dead—I know they'd do anything to stop this if they weren't. I don't want to see Nelly's face when he hears about Adam, but I probably won't be here to see anything. I just need to keep Boss and his friends busy long enough for the others to get here.

Boss's eyes land on Nicki's arm. "Who did that? You said she has a broken arm. Who bandaged her up?"

We're silent. Finally, just as he looks about to explode, Jamie speaks. "I did."

"Go and look at Jay. One of your men shot him." It's accusatory, as if they'd been out for a leisurely walk when we opened fire.

"If you let me check on the ones outside," Jamie says.

"You think you can make a deal?" Twitch asks with a harsh laugh. He's the first one I'd kill. I'd love to shove a knife through his thin lips. "You'll look at him if we tell you to."

"Let her see her dead men," Boss says with a shrug. "When she's done."

Jamie sets Nicki on the couch with Penny and the kids. They're only feet away, and I want to hold them so badly that it might be worth dying for if I wasn't already doing the one thing that might keep them alive.

Twitch herds Jamie to the bedroom with his gun in her back. The handheld radio crackles softly from somewhere on the table. If they call when they're close, these men will be waiting and they won't stand a chance. I scan the surface and spot the short black antenna peeking out from under a map. I slip the walkie-talkie down by my thigh and lower the volume when the can opener grinds on a can of beans. Maureen watches with round eyes and sags when I succeed without anyone noticing.

They've opened our honey. They chew on uncooked oatmeal. Crumbs fall as they dig into Ashley's birthday cookies. The kids' faces are blank. I know they don't care, but I do. There's so little left to celebrate, so few presents to give, and these men are taking every single thing we have—Shawn, Adam, and even our fucking cookies.

I wedge the radio between the seat cushion and wall, looking down quickly to make sure the button is depressed. Maybe they'll hear us when they get close. But no matter how much they call, the men won't hear them.

Boss grabs my arm and bashes my side on the table when he drags me clear. It'll leave a bruise, but I barely feel it. This is it. "Time to go. Where're you taking her?" he asks Whit. "Bedroom?"

Whit looks like the most normal of the bunch, although that's not saying much. He has most of his teeth, at least. I'd love to curse him, to stand my ground, but I'm scared. Scared of what's going to happen, scared they'll hurt someone else.

Whit grimaces. "Jay's in there."

"So?"

"The truck."

My stomach heaves. I've talked myself into believing I can let them take whatever they want of my body and leave my mind intact, but now I'm not so sure.

"I'll keep watch," Auburn says.

"Remember what I said," Boss says to me. My head nods of its own accord. "You don't want to die, do you?"

I'm probably going to die, anyway. I don't know why he's bothering to pretend. I stumble when Bits calls my name. She breaks free of Penny's arms, face a blotchy mess. She knows exactly what's happening; she's lived through this before. This could be the thing that destroys her forever, but I think she's stronger than that.

Whit's fingers dig into my arm and I turn with a scowl. "Let me talk to her."

He backs off. I take in Bits's sweet face, from her small nose to every last freckle. I wonder if her mother wiped her tears away or lied the way I'm about to. "It'll be all right, sweetie. Listen to Penny and Maureen, okay?"

They'll protect the kids to their dying breaths, of that I'm sure. It's just that their dying breaths might only be minutes away.

Bits's head shakes wildly. "Don't leave!"

I try to remember every detail of how she feels in my arms and look into her eyes. This has to count. "I love you so much. More than all the stars in the sky."

Bits fights when I peel her fingers off my coat, and I fear they'll hurt her if she doesn't stop.

"Stop, Bits!" She jumps, startled. I hate that it's the last thing she'll ever hear from me. "I have to go. I'm sorry."

Her hands drop and her eyes dull. She does an about-face and walks to Penny as if I'm already gone. I know she's doing it to protect herself, but it hurts. And I wonder if she'll ever come back if I don't.

CHAPTER 32

Auburn stands on the RV steps while Whit pushes me to the pickup that's parked forty feet away. It's no surprise Adam and Shawn were fooled. What are the chances another pickup was going to pull up when we've barely seen anyone for thousands of miles?

Between the low moon and the light spilling from the RV windows, I make out a dark lump at the end of the RV. I stop with my hand to my mouth. Shawn really is dead. Whit jabs his gun into my back and I trip to the truck. He lowers the tailgate and points to boxes in the truck's bed. "Take those out."

I pull the two wooden crates to the ground, followed by a cardboard box that clanks when I drop it. Whit's lantern illuminates two bows and a jumble of arrows at the bottom. If only I could grab this and run. Hide somewhere in the grass and shoot them from afar.

"Get in," he says.

It takes me two tries, shaking so hard my bones rattle. I'm not going to fight, like I promised, but I'm not going to help either. He sets the lantern on the ground and climbs up after me, knife out.

"Take this off." He yanks my coat zipper, and I let it fall. Jesus, it's cold out here. I'm going to die in the cold. "Shirt."

I pull it over my head and point to my tank top. My teeth chatter from fear as much as the temperature. "C-can I leave it on?"

He pushes me to the truck's metal bed in answer. Cold soaks into my bare arms and shoulders and through the thin fabric of my shirt. There are so many stars out tonight. The prairie is a giant bowl of sky. Maybe it's not such a bad place to die—here, looking up at the stars.

Whit straddles me, knife hand pinning my shoulder to the steel. He paws beneath my bra and fumbles with his pants. I bite my tongue so hard I taste blood. I refuse to scream—I'll force myself to concentrate on that velvety black bowl twinkling with lights. I find Cassiopeia, who was hung in the sky as punishment for her vanity. She might have deserved it, but there's plenty of punishment in this world for people who don't deserve any.

This close, his odor is unbearable and, when he coughs, even the food he's eaten doesn't cover the smell on his breath. It makes me wonder where the Lexers are. Where are they when you need them? I would welcome a pod right now. It'd be preferable to die that way, but it wouldn't do us any good. How you die does matter, and I'll die doing my best to protect the people I love. I find the Big and Little Dippers—the easy ones—and stare at the north star. Sometimes Pegasus is hard to see, but not with the way the stars gleam tonight. I follow Whit's instructions to undo my belt and jeans but don't pull them down. He'll have to figure this out alone.

I clench my fists by my side when his hands lower. I can taste the stench coming off him. I think I'd rather die than choke down that so-called food. I know I'd rather die than turn into something sick like these men, if there's any possibility that's what made them this way.

I look for the stars that make up Cetus, the sea monster, and don't resist when Whit yanks at my jeans one-handed. I'm tired of fighting. Tired of being optimistic. Tired of losing people and living in a world that, quite frankly, doesn't seem to want us here. I don't want to worry anymore. If there is a Heaven, we can meet there. Even if there's not, I won't have to worry about anything ever again. And I don't want there to be a Heaven at this moment—I don't want my mother and father and brother and Adrian to be watching me at my most helpless, unable to come to my aid.

I find the Andromeda constellation. She was the daughter of Cassiopeia, punished for sins that weren't her own. Chained to a rock and left to be eaten by the sea monster. Helpless, like me, until she was rescued by Perseus. But Perseus isn't coming.

I let my last bit of hope float up to the stars. It's not so bad. I don't know why I didn't give up a year ago, a few months ago. Next world or not, I'm done with this one. I'm done with this body that has always been mine to give and no longer feels like it belongs to me.

He grunts something I barely register. A scream comes from the RV, loud enough to pierce through the haze I've worked so hard to create. I think dimly that they're supposed to be okay. That's why I'm allowing something every cell in my body revolts against.

Whit gets my jeans to my ankles before he loses patience. "Take your boots off."

It could be the first time he's done this. He's clumsy and unsure, but by the way he breathes I know he has no intention of stopping.

Ashley howls. Maureen scolds. A faint anger ripples through me. When the chorus of screaming begins and I'm sure that Boss has broken his word, the anger swells to rage. As far as Bits is concerned—as far as I'm concerned—I'm already gone. But I could come back. I just have to figure out how. I take a final look at Andromeda before I sit up. I'm not chained like that poor girl. The sea monster is breathing down my neck, but maybe I can fight him off myself.

I glance into the shadows for a weapon. He has a gun, but I don't know where it is. The screams from the RV cut off and my head clears in the silence that follows. I can do this. I can work with what I have. I untie my left boot and then use my left hand to unlace it completely while I work on my right. He can't see what I'm doing in the dark. I ball the shoelace in my hand and work off my jeans.

I gasp when my bare legs hit metal. Whit pushes me to my back and my collarbone creaks under the weight of his hand. Now that I've returned from the stars I feel every degree of cold, every centimeter of his skin on mine. He growls when he finds that I still wear my new underwear. I'm not making this easy—this is my only chance. I'm going to take it, and I'm going to take it before he gets what he came for.

"Stupid bitch!" He moves to the side, knocking over something in the process. I kneel as if doing what I'm told and take each end of the shoelace in my shaking hands.

"Everything all right?" Auburn calls.

"Fine," Whit calls back. "Just keep watch."

I use the moment his head is turned to loop my bootlace around his neck. He freezes in surprise, which gives me time to pull it into a half knot—the way one begins to tie their shoes, bunny ears or no. His fists flail backward, punching at my ribs hard enough to take my breath away and keeping me from pulling the lace as tight as it needs to be. I need to get him down. I need more leverage.

Die, I want to scream, *Fucking die already*. When he doubles over with the effort of drawing a breath, I push him to the metal and scramble onto his back. He kicks his legs, but his feet hang over the edge of the truck's bed and hardly make a sound. I can see Auburn standing with his lantern forty feet away on the RV steps. If the low noises Whit makes carry that far, I hope he thinks they're grunts and thumps of pleasure.

Whit's knife has landed above his head, just out of his reach as well as mine. It would be a better weapon, but he could get to it first if I let go. And I'm not letting go. I pull until there's enough slack to wrap the lace around my hands. The deeper it digs into my flesh, the deeper it digs into the soft skin of his neck.

He jolts under me. I press my knees into his spine. It's taking so long, or maybe it just feels that way—such a quiet yet violent battle. It's sweaty and desperate and more horrible than I thought to hold a man down while he struggles for his life. But it's his or mine.

Help me, I beg my mom and dad. *Help me live. Help me kill him.* Maybe a prayer for murder is the wrong kind of prayer, but I don't give a shit.

It could take another minute, and I can hold on for as long as it takes. There's a loud snap and my hands fly out, each holding an end of my broken bootlace. Whit takes a shuddering gasp of air. He'll be stronger than me in no time. I plant my knees in his shoulder blades and lunge for his knife.

I've sunk a blade into the back of a skull countless times by now. He's not a Lexer, though, and it glances off the side of his head when he rolls out from under me. He gags and smashes a fist into my cheek. I fall to my side—eye tearing, cheekbone on fire—and scramble to my knees. I clasp the knife over his exposed neck and bring it down two-handed with more force than I'd need to get through skull. And then I do it again.

I'm used to the grinding of bone and the crackling of gristle, but the blood is new and it's everywhere. It sprays my arms and body, which are only inches away. The tangy, metallic smell overpowers his rot. My knees skid in its warmth and I topple beside him, blood oozing under me.

"Hey, Whit," Auburn calls. "You like it rough?" He laughs at his own joke. After a moment, he calls, "Whit?"

I get on my hands and knees. He has a gun and I have a knife; it's no mystery who'll win that contest. I need his gun for when I go back into the RV. I slip off the edge of the truck and remember the bows when my feet hit the box. I don't know if I'm strong enough to use them. I drag my slippery palm along my blood-soaked shirt and get enough of a grip to nock the arrow and test the bow. It might be hard to draw under normal circumstances, but it pulls back as easily as a child's toy in my adrenalized arms.

I hide behind the tailgate. They may be crazy, but right now I'm crazier. I'm going to take back the things I love. No one's going to stop me. Auburn is twenty feet away and closing in with a gun and lantern that allows me to see my target. And I need to see. I have to hit his neck or mouth or eye. I can't give him time to make noise.

I draw the bow and let the arrow fly. I will it to his throat—at the soft V below his Adam's apple—because my getting any kind of head shot is unlikely. The lantern clatters to the ground when my arrow hits its mark. Auburn's eyes widen and his hand goes to his neck, but he doesn't stop coming. Something low and fast streaks past and I catch a glimpse of golden fur in the rolling lantern before Barnaby hits him head-on and takes him down.

I run to finish him off, but Auburn is motionless. Barn raises his head from the dead man and whines into the dark. I spin at the quiet call of my name. The moon is higher now, bright enough to dim some of the stars and to see the whites of Peter's eyes all around when he grips my arms. "Are you okay? What's going on?"

"More inside." My teeth clack together. "Four more. One's hurt."

"Is everyone okay?" Zeke asks.

I shake my head and don't look at Nelly. He'll know if I do. Zeke opens his mouth and closes it. We're behind the truck's cab, but it's only a matter of time before someone checks on Auburn and Whit. I grab Zeke's coat when he spins for the RV. If they rush in there, someone's bound to get hurt. "Give me a gun. I'll say there are zombies and try to send them out. If they don't, you come in."

Somewhere I'm aware of how wild I must seem, standing in my underwear and a tank top with blood freezing on my skin, but right now all that matters is that every last one of these men die.

"You can't kill..." Zeke says. He looks me up and down and hands me his gun.

✵✵✵

I scream for help and fall through the RV's door. The plan is to send at least one of them outside to help their friends, but my script deserts me at the sight of Maureen on the kitchen floor in a spreading pool of blood. The tips of her fingers lay limp in the crimson lake. Her eyes are open and an icy, dead blue.

On the couch, Nicki's head is buried in Penny's side. Bits and Hank look almost as terrified of me as they do of the men. Ash and Jamie are missing, as is Twitch. We had a deal, me and Boss: I didn't fight and he didn't hurt anyone else. My part of the bargain is null and void.

"What the fuck is going on?" Boss asks when he sees me. The dark-haired man looks up from the dinette, hand on his gun.

I keep my arm behind my back, where I've tucked the gun in my underwear, and meet Penny's eyes. *"La familia es fuera."* The family is outside. It's the best I can do, since I cut Spanish class more than I went.

Boss and Dark-hair look to her in confusion. I could pull my gun and have him lay down his, but it's going to end with a bullet to his head either way. And I've seen enough movies to know that when you give the bad guy a second chance, he takes it.

The shot is deafening. It's loaded with .38 instead of .357, thankfully, or we might never hear again. Boss's head explodes out the other side, bathing the dinette and Dark-hair in brain and blood. Dark-hair points his gun my way, but Penny's already behind him. She tangles her fingers in his hair and slams his head sideways into the window frame. He has no time to react before she does it again. This time the crack is loud enough to hear over the ringing in my ears.

The RV door flies open just as Twitch enters from the bedroom. When he sees Nelly and Peter, he drops his gun at their command. Dark-hair lifts his hands in a daze. Penny's knuckles are white, her glasses askew, chest heaving. Her eyes spark with more fury than I thought she had in her. She unclenches her hands reluctantly when James reaches her side. I think she wants to finish the job.

CHAPTER 33

Adam is alive. He was shot through the shoulder and ended up under the RV. He's unconscious but stable, and they bring him into the RV after Mark drags Jay, now dead of his wound, from the bedroom. Shawn isn't as lucky. I find Jamie weeping on the road with Shawn's head in her lap. She gently lowers it to the ground and insists on seeing to Adam and Kyle over our protests.

I still clutch Zeke's gun and wear the blanket Margaret wrapped around my shoulders after she made sure Ash was all right. Ashley's shirt was cut open, but her jeans were on and belt still buckled. I couldn't hug her with my covering of blood when she burst into tears at the sight of me.

Peter drags the four dead men to the side of the road while Mark and James keep watch where Twitch and Dark-hair kneel on the asphalt. I don't know why they're still alive. I stalk toward them and duck away when Peter tries to head me off with a hand on my shoulder. I don't want anyone to touch me. I want to be left alone, but first I want these men to be erased from the face of the Earth.

"Go inside," Peter says. "Get cleaned up."

My hair has formed into long, blood-thickened ropes that remind me of Medusa's head of snakes. It was Medusa's head that Perseus used to kill the sea monster and free Andromeda. Seems fitting. I strangle the wild laugh that bubbles up in my throat. Dan would understand, but no one else would get my sick joke.

"Not until they're dead," I say.

Twitch glares at me in the lantern light. "Just finish it," he hisses.

If that's what he wants, I'm happy to oblige. I drop my blanket and raise Zeke's gun, but Peter pushes my arm down. "Go inside. Please."

"Not until they're dead," I say again. Dark-hair recoils, but Twitch only twitches.

"Fine." Peter's voice is scarily calm. He tucks the blanket around me like he's swaddling a baby, then drops his coat and walks forward, rolling up his sleeves on the way.

His machete *chings* when he pulls it from his side. He runs it across Twitch's neck without taking his eyes from mine, as though an offering to appease a bloodthirsty monster. I even feel like Medusa—cold and vengeful and full of death, protector of virgins and hater of men. The blood splatter almost hits my feet, but I stay put. It's not like any more will make a difference.

I don't feel a lick of pity when Dark-hair begs. Shawn didn't get the chance to beg. Maureen might have begged, but she's still dead, body in a blanket shroud by the RV steps. Peter's blade whips deep before Dark-hair can finish his plea, and he has to brace his foot on Dark-hair's shoulder to draw it out. He drops his machete beside the body and strides my way while James and Mark gape in astonishment.

"Now, please, go inside," Peter says.

The shadows on his face would be frightening if I didn't know him better. Any second now he'll snap out of it, I think, but he waits for my answer with no change of expression. I pivot and walk up the RV steps. There's no space in the tiny bedroom where they've moved Kyle and Adam. Zeke tells me they're okay so far. I return to the kitchen that's soaked with Maureen's blood and Boss's head cavity, where the smell of Lexer and bodily fluids make me woozy.

I sink to a clean part of the floor and rest my head on my knees. There's no victory here—only shock and sorrow and violation. If I sit long enough, I'll cry, and the tight feeling of someone else's blood on my skin will send me over the edge. I need to get it off. I lean at the kitchen sink and start on my arms. The water is warm—maybe it turned on along with the heat. I fill a bowl to conserve water and scrape at my knuckles with a fingernail. Peter steps in and watches me. I keep my eyes on my chore and wait for him to say something. I'm not sure what I want him to say, but somehow he always knows what I need to hear.

"You should get in the shower," he finally says, which falls way short of what I was hoping for.

"I don't have any clean...I was going to wash out my other jeans tomorrow. I'll see if Maureen has—" *Had*, I remind myself. *Had*.

"I'll find clothes and put them in the bathroom. Just go."

I look up. Peter is already on his way to the cabinets. I think about calling him back because I no longer want to be left alone, but I'm afraid the dam holding back my tears might give out if I let so much as a trickle through. I murmur thanks and walk to the shower.

***

I'm covered with streaks of reddish-brown that remind me of how Eric and I would paint ourselves with ground-up river rocks when we were kids. I scrub until the soap's lather turns from pink to white, but it isn't enough. I check every speck of skin to be sure no trace remains and then quickly scrub again. Zeke said to use all the water I needed because we're getting a new vehicle tomorrow, and then he touched my bloody shoulder.

"I'm glad you're okay, sugar," he'd said. I nodded and closed the bathroom door before I admitted I wasn't.

I step out of the shower and run a hand along the fogged mirror. Now that the blood is gone, I'm able to see the large pink welt under my eye and the bruises forming on my sides. The finger marks above and below my collarbone won't wash off. I shiver although the bathroom is a sauna. I got off lucky, I know I did, but I still want to scream. I hum tonelessly to distract myself from the thoughts that creep in.

I freeze when I reach for the bag Peter's left—Ana's bag—and sit on the toilet lid with it in my lap. Her scent rushes out when I unzip the top, and I close my eyes against the onslaught of memories. God, I loved that girl. She was bananas, for sure, but I think I loved her *because* she was bananas. I smile at the leather pants and bottle of hair conditioner. Her jeans are a little short but they'll tuck into my boots just fine. Peter left those in here, too. My left boot has a new red lace to replace the broken one, and they're cleaner than they've been in a year. I take out underwear and a bra, tank top, shirt and cozy hoodie I can wear under my leather coat since my new coat is destroyed.

I find a tiny baby dress wrapped in tissue paper—fancy French linen embroidered with a delicate pattern of flowers and adorable forest animals. Ana had loved this dress when she found it at that boutique in Stowe. I don't know that there will ever be suitable weather in Alaska, but I promise Ana her niece will wear it, even if I have to jam it over a baby-sized parka. Even if she's a boy.

A jewelry box at the very bottom holds a pair of small silver hoops with a blue bead in the center. Of course Ana packed earrings. But then I realize they weren't for Ana. They're the kind of earrings you get at a piercing shop, made of titanium or something similar. We'd promised to pierce Bits's ears for her ninth birthday, and the beads match Bits's eyes. Ana must have put them in here so we'd have them wherever we were.

I clutch the box so hard it dents. I want to tear this fucking bathroom apart, to smash the mirror and kick in the shower door. I want Ana to be here. I want Maureen to have been able to keep her promise to John. I wanted Ash to have birthday cookies. The MRE desserts that I'd wanted to surprise the kids with are gone. Shawn, who always had a joke, who loved Jamie with all his heart, is gone. So many people are gone that I can't even mourn them properly. It would take every hour of every day to do it. I want to hold on to them, to think of them, but I would never get any living done if I gave them all the time they deserve. Especially now, when we're barely living as it is—barely surviving.

I hug Ana's bag to my chest and sob. I cry over the things in my dead friend's bag and for all the things we've lost so far. I don't know why I thought saving my tears for Alaska was a good idea. It was stupid as fuck. There's no point in saving things for later if later never comes.

CHAPTER 34

The sun rises over blood-stained asphalt and two holes dug by the side of the road. It's too dangerous to find a new vehicle in the dark, so we used the night to dig these graves. Maureen and Shawn are lowered in while Mark says some fitting, eloquent words. I watch Zeke throw the first shovelful of dirt over Maureen's body, and then I can't watch anymore. Jamie stands over Shawn's grave, face swollen. She spent all night with Kyle and Adam, insisting she had to do something. We made Nicki's cast, which turned out serviceable if somewhat lumpy.

The force of the bullet that passed through Adam's shoulder knocked him off the roof, and he'd managed to roll under the RV before losing consciousness. He's pale and in pain, but Jamie and Zeke think he'll be okay. They think Kyle will be okay, too, although he still hasn't fully woken.

"For whatever the opinion of a dentist is worth," Zeke had said, but he'd smiled.

He's not smiling now. My knuckles are smashed from Bits's grip on my hand, but I don't mind. I don't mind when Hank leans into me so hard that I stumble. I held them for hours last night in the pickup, until Bits no longer looked at me as if I'd abandoned her. Until the color returned to her face and she would smile at one of my jokes.

Once the graves are filled, we walk to the vehicles. We're heading around Grande Prairie to a used car lot that sold RVs, according to the phone book, because we have two people who need to lie down. Whether or not we find one, I won't set foot in this one ever again. I'll ride in the pickup's bed before I do that.

I hug Ash to me. She says she's okay, but she isn't. Twitch had barely had time to touch her, but Jamie says he said plenty of things a sixteen year-old shouldn't hear. After I'd dug out one of her new tank tops and gave her a shirt of Ana's, she asked for another. I scrounged up one of

Maureen's, and she put the layers on one by one, zipped her jacket and wrapped her arms around her waist like a shield.

We check Boss's pickup for anything useful we might have missed in the dark. Peter accidentally knocks the lid off a cooler and steps back with a gag. I catch a glimpse of a blackened arm and the smell of the men before I rush to the side of the road and throw up my tiny breakfast. Another thing they've stolen from me. I may not be hungry, but I'm livid that they're dead and still taking our food.

I flinch when Peter touches my back. He dug graves and cleaned up all night, barely speaking to anyone except Barnaby, who stayed by his side. Everyone gave him a wide berth; the set of his face and shoulders made it clear he wanted us to.

"Are you okay?" he asks.

I wipe my mouth and keep my eyes on my breakfast. "I'm fine. Thanks for the clothes and my red shoelace." I kick out my boot. "I think I'm going to start a new trend."

It's the wrong answer, I can tell by his harsh exhalation. I look up to find him squinting at me in the early morning light. He lifts his hand and lowers it, then splays his clenched fingers by his thigh. If I tell him how angry I am, how I can't shake the powerless feeling from last night, it'll make him worse. I need Peter, not this angry person I barely know.

"I'm clean," I say, and force a smile. "Cleaner than all of you. I know you're jealous."

Peter watches me with a frown. "What did he—"

"He didn't get far. I don't want to talk about it." What I want is a hug, but I don't want to have to ask for it. "I'm fine."

He chews his cheek and turns away. "We should go," he says over his shoulder.

I watch him walk to the pickup. If he looks back, I'll muster the courage to tell him everything. I'll ask him to hold me for a minute before we go. But he doesn't.

***

We find an RV north of Grande Prairie, in amongst a couple newer RVs we can't get running no matter what we try. No one says that Shawn would be able to, but Jamie stands with her hand on his toolbox and tears in her eyes. The RV that does start is almost thirty years old, with fake wood grain cabinets and brown-striped upholstery. It has a full propane tank and needs water, but water hasn't been a problem so far. The fluorescent numbers on its windshield that advertise a "Low, Low Price!" don't make me confident in its ability to take us the last thousand miles.

They'd found enough gas last night to get us to Whitehorse and were on their way back when they heard voices on the radio. They thought they were picking up other survivors until they heard Penny's voice and found Barnaby limping along the road, possibly following their earlier trail. They parked as close as they dared and ran the rest of the way on foot, Barn straining on his rope leash until Peter let him go to take down Auburn.

I ride in the pickup. I don't like the idea of sitting in any RV right now, no matter how different. James drives, with Penny riding shotgun and Peter in back with me and the kids. Penny put on a shoulder holster this morning after breakfast, and I saw her slide one of the men's knives into her pack before she'd zipped it up.

We tire of playing I Spy and start on a round of Twenty Questions. I'm doing my best to be cheerful for the kids, but Peter doesn't bother to pretend. His voice is flat and he curses loud enough to make Bits bury her face in my side when we have to spend an hour backtracking. He stands watch at a pit stop, and when I offer him coffee in lieu of lunch he waves it and me away.

We stop at a Walmart in Dawson Creek. We have no choice but to risk our lives for food now. Besides what they ate, the wheat berries were soaked in Maureen's blood on the floor. It's left us with salsa and tiny amounts of rice, flour and pasta. It's astounding how much food those men consumed in so little time.

I step into the parking lot. Peter walks to my side and says, "Stay in the truck."

"Why?" I don't ask why he thinks he's in charge, although I'd like to. I cross my arms when he doesn't answer. "I don't want to stay."

"Do what you want." He shrugs and walks to where Zeke and Mark stand blinking in the sunlight.

I join the group and try to catch his eye, but he studiously avoids my gaze. Margaret puts a hand on my arm—I don't think Margaret has ever touched me. I've spent the day acting normal in response to all the troubled looks. We all had a bad night. Maureen is dead. Jamie lost her husband. Adam has a bullet wound. I'm not going to complain when I'm still alive and practically untouched.

"What's the plan?" I ask, and pat Margaret's hand with a big smile.

"We'll look for food and then skedaddle," Zeke says. "C'mon, sugar, you can be my partner."

"I've been waiting a year and a half to hear those words," I say. Zeke's chest rumbles with a laugh and he takes my arm as we near the doors.

The Walmart has skylights; it's nice to not have to peer into complete darkness for once. The food section is full of debris from the fights that must have ensued when people got desperate. Freezer doors hang open and one aisle's shelves are on their side. Everything edible is gone, including pet food and birdseed, but we do find some overlooked fuel stabilizer.

We decide to try the hotel across the street whose sign touts a deluxe continental breakfast, as it's the first hotel we've seen with undamaged doors and windows. Peering through our cupped hands on the glass reveals a lobby that's untouched except for the ten Lexers that wander around the check-in counter and couches. The day's newspapers sit on a table with a sign that says they're free for the taking. Carafes of coffee also advertise themselves as complimentary.

A Lexer moves to the door, stumbling over the body of one who didn't make it past thawing. The others follow suit until the doors rattle with their fists and faces. More enter from the hall, but we can take them if we let them out slowly.

"I'll pry the doors," Zeke says over the pounding. "Y'all want to get them?"

He leaves and returns with a crowbar. I'll take zombies over living people any day. They have no interest in our flesh besides eating it.

Three come out at Zeke's first heave. Peter jumps in front of me and takes out mine so quickly that I almost hack him in the back. I move near Mark, but Peter does it again with the next few that emerge.

"You're in my way," I say to him after Zeke lets the doors shut.

He ignores me. I change position and get close to the entrance when he tries to follow. If he wants to block me, he's going to get eaten. He steps to the side with a scowl. I want to kill something, and God help me, it will be Peter if he tries that again. I can't tell if he's trying to protect me or infuriate me, but I can protect myself just fine.

The doors stick open with Zeke's next grunt, and then there are too many for Peter to concern himself with my whereabouts. I drive my spiked end into the eye of a hotel employee still wearing a nametag that says *Jackie*. I turn to the next one, grab the back of its hair and dig into the base of its skull, like I tried to do to Whit. A man with a bathrobe still knotted around his waist gets the blade in his forehead. I push him to the side and look for another, but they're all down.

My breath is easy. I feel like I've barely moved a muscle and almost wish there were more, but I'm not crazy enough to really want it to be so. I grin at Zeke, who crinkles his eyes like a biker Santa Claus and says, "Normally I'd say ladies first, but you'll pardon my manners this time."

There have to be others in the building, but so far the coast is clear. The breakfast area has a wall of windows and counters that hold cereal dispensers and drink machines. Margaret throws open the door to the storage room.

The packaged pastries are green fuzz, but there are five-pound bags of waffle mix in the low cabinets. Small containers of syrup. Mini boxes of cereals full of sugar and loaded with vitamins to make up for it. Hot chocolate mix, tea bags and coffee. Packets of oatmeal and sugar and even powdered creamer. I jump up and down silently at the treasure trove.

"I'll go get the bins," Peter says. "Cassie, you want to help?"

I startle at the sound of him addressing me. He follows me past Mark, who's keeping an eye out in the hall. I give Penny and the kids a thumbs up as I jump in the truck's bed and hand empty bins down to Peter.

"We have it," he says. "Stay out here."

I lean on the edge of the pickup and narrow my eyes. "Why are you trying to get rid of me?"

"I'm not trying to *get rid of you*, Cassandra. You're not needed in there, so why go?"

I'm not arguing in the middle of zombie-infested territory, so I take a page from his book and ignore him. "Do you want me to take a bin?"

"No."

I stride ahead into the lobby and stop short at Mark's holler and the clatter of plastic bins hitting the floor behind me. Two Lexers have come from the manager's office, although everything in there looked dead when we checked it. One knocks Peter to his back and the other drops to its knees. I run and kick one so hard that it slides along the slick tile. I puncture the other in its forehead and turn to the first, but Peter's already up, machete smashing its skull. We stare at each other, wheezing, and I think this is where he'll stop being angry at me or the world or whatever it is he's pissed at, but his shoulders harden. "You could have died."

The tears come, but I turn away before he can see. "You're welcome," I say, glad he can't hear them in my voice.

CHAPTER 35

I watch a small factory milling with Lexers until it's out of sight of our vehicles. Even up here, with nothing for miles around, they've taken over. We won't make it past Fort St. John today, so, well before the city, we stop at a house hidden from the road by shrubbery. It has a *For Sale* sign and is furnished just enough to give potential buyers an impression of the rooms' purposes. The fridge is clean and kitchen spotless.

Inside the RV, Nelly sits on the couch and smiles through the worry evident in every line on his face. "Adam's sleeping, but he's okay. I made him drink some syrup and oatmeal soup," he says before I can ask.

I smooch him on the lips. He rubs it off, but his eyes sparkle. "You look a damn sight better than last night. You okay, darlin'?"

I wave away his question. It's embarrassing to think about what I must've looked like, barely dressed and bloody, which makes me angry that I feel any shame at all. The only people who should feel ashamed are lying on the side of the road with their throats sliced. "How's Kyle?" I ask.

"He woke up for a few minutes. He was babbling and didn't make any sense. Nicki's sleeping next to him."

The only thing we know to do with head trauma is leave it alone and hope it sorts itself out. Jamie sits at the dinette with her head in her hands. It's a different kind of head trauma for her, but the treatment is the same. I touch her shoulder. "I'm going to make dinner. The house is all clear if you want to lie down."

"I'll sleep in here so I'm close to Kyle and Adam," she says, head down. "They need heat."

I hug her even though she might want to be left alone. She squeezes my arm before she nods and lets go. The kitchen in the RV is different, but I get a vision of Maureen's dull eyes and pale skin, the kids in a terrified pile on the couch, Boss's brains scattering across where Jamie sits. My hand shakes when I dump waffle mix into a bowl.

"Maybe I should use the camping stove," I say. "Since you need the heat tonight." I rush out the door and drop onto the RV's steps. I'll go back once I've collected myself.

"Want help?" Margaret asks. She never helps with the cooking, preferring to sharpen blades or clean guns.

"I'm going to cook outside. I just have to get the pans and waffle mix."

"I'll get it." She puts her hand on my shoulder as she steps past.

I set up the stove on the house's front porch and add filtered water to the mix. My breathing has returned to normal by the time Bits and Hank hover over me. "We're having wafflecakes," I say. "These are gonna be the best wafflecakes you've ever tasted right here."

"And the only," Hank says, but he laughs along with Bits.

"Will we get a big one?" Bits asks. "With syrup?"

"Not one," I say. "You're going to eat as many wafflecakes as your little hearts desire. And you can drown them in syrup. We'll fill up a tub with syrup and you can get in and eat your wafflecakes while you swim in it."

Peter is in the pickup's bed arranging things, head cocked as if listening. I pour batter into the pan. The smell of browning flour and sugar is so wonderful that I want to cry.

Hank hesitates and then asks, "Shouldn't we save it?"

I can see how badly he doesn't want to, and I want to do anything that might bring an ounce of pleasure into these kids' lives. "Not today. There's plenty and we all need a big meal. I'm tired of saving things for later."

"Me, too," Bits says, and swings on the porch rail. "I'm going to eat five."

"Ten," Hank says.

"Well, I'm going to eat twenty-seven," I say. "How many are you going to eat, Peter?"

Peter glances over. "I'm not very hungry."

I flip the wafflecake and consider throwing my pan at him, but instead I say to the kids, "More for us, right?"

✳✳✳

Penny is my partner for the first cold watch shift of the night. But we had the presence of mind to take a couple of carafes from the hotel and now we have copious amounts of hot coffee and hot water in which to brew tea. I've only allowed myself creamer and sugar in one cup, but as long as it's warm, I'm happy.

Penny pours herself coffee number two and pats her stomach before she gets back under our blankets. "Sorry, kid, but you'll have to deal."

"She'll be fine," I say. "Maybe a little hyper, but fine."

"Maybe it'll make her run fast. That's what you want with zombies, right?" Penny's joking about zombies. Penny never jokes about zombies. I watch her carefully, but she takes another sip of coffee and leans back, eyes closed. "You'll teach her what she needs to know."

"Of course."

Penny's eyes open. "And you'll teach *me* this winter. Maybe I didn't have to learn on the farm, but I don't ever want to be caught out again. You've seen how terrible I am at this stuff."

"I saw you last night. That wasn't terrible. He might've shot me if it weren't for you."

Penny's cup trembles in her hand, but she looks pleased to have had a part in bringing them down. "I don't know what I was thinking. I didn't even think—I just jumped him. It was really stupid."

"It's only stupid if it doesn't work," I say with a grin. "Otherwise, it's genius."

"You sound like my sister." Penny takes an extra long sip of coffee after the words slip out.

"That's not so bad, is it?"

"No, it's not. I do know what I was thinking last night," Penny says slowly. "It was *what would Ana do*? And then I did it."

"W.W.A.D?"

"She'd love that, wouldn't she? Me asking myself that and then actually following the advice?" She'd looked on the verge of tears a moment ago, but now she rolls her eyes in a loving sort of way.

"Except the acronym is *wad*. I don't think she'd be into that."

Penny's laugh has changed—another weird pregnancy side effect—to a throatier, louder belly laugh that might attract Lexers but is so contagious I join in. James lifts his head from where he's camped out on the house's living room floor. "Trying to sleep here. What's so funny?"

There's no way to explain, and, anyway, we can't stop. Penny grabs her stomach. "Ow!" James leaps up, but she waves him away, tears running down her cheeks. "It's just round ligament pain."

One side of James's hair sticks straight out as he dances around her like a frantic daddy long legs. I point at him and say, "That's the father of your child right there."

Penny and I lose it. My bruises throb less than they did a minute ago. They've spent all day reminding me of where I was held down, trapped and defeated, but now, if only for a little while, I revel in the fact that I'm free.

CHAPTER 36

Kyle woke again and was able to carry on a conversation before he lapsed back into sleep. After my shift, I get into bed next to Hank instead of the space by Peter, who ate plenty of wafflecakes but didn't say another word the entire night. It takes me forty minutes of shivering to fall asleep, even with Barnaby stretched along my legs. He couldn't believe his luck when I invited him up, but as far as I'm concerned he's earned a place in my bed and our group even if he never learns to shut up. If Auburn hadn't gone down from my arrow, Barnaby's attack would've given me and the others time to get to Auburn before he killed me.

My sleep is fitful and loaded with dreams that wake me up in a panic, until I wake to a hand on my shoulder where Whit pinned me down. I know it can't be him, but my brain neglects to tell my arm that fact before my fist connects with Peter's face.

"Jesus!" he says, and holds a hand over his cheek.

I sit up in the morning light and reach for him. "Oh my God, sorry! Peter, I'm really sorry."

"It's fine," he says, and backs out of the bedroom.

He has to know I didn't want to punch him. Or maybe that I didn't *mean* to, because with the way he's been acting I'm kind of glad I got one in. I help Penny with breakfast in the RV's kitchen without losing my mental faculties, which I take as a good sign, although Maureen's absence looms large. She might be whispering directly into God's ear at this very moment, but I'd take her comfort over any special favors. We have enough people up there to look out for us.

Ash reads at the table. Instead of her usual chattiness about vampire relationships, she lifts her head to stare into space every few minutes. I remember the hope on her face as we stood in Aubrey's bedroom. I'd told her that she could have all the trappings of a normal life, or as normal as it gets nowadays. I'm as bad as Peter, promising things I'm not sure I can deliver. My hand tightens around the flimsy spatula so hard that it bends.

I take breakfast to our patients in the back of the RV. Nicki perches alongside her dad on his twin bed, face still sticky with last night's syrup.

Kyle dives into his food and I head back to the kitchen for more. He didn't eat yesterday, so they'll be gone in seconds. I don't think I'll ever get tired of wafflecakes with syrup, although we did put a cap on our intake this morning.

"How are the folks in the sick bay?" I ask after I've deposited three more on Kyle's plate.

"Fine," Kyle says. "I'll be up later today and I'll get—"

"You're not getting anywhere," Jamie says, wagging a finger. "Except to the bathroom and back into bed. And you should thank me for not giving you a bedpan. The last time you stood up, you fell down. Nicki, you're in charge of keeping your dad in bed."

Kyle mutters, face dark and lips pursed. Nicki wags her finger in imitation of Jamie. "Daddy, I'll bring you stuff. Like Mama did when I was sick. Don't yell at Jamie."

"You're right, baby," Kyle says. He turns to Jamie. "Thanks for taking care of her while I was out. And me."

"You're the absolute worst patient I've ever had. You were much better unconscious," Jamie says, to which Kyle grunts. She turns to Adam in the other bed. "And how's my best patient?"

Adam resettles himself like an old man and struggles to eat with his left hand, but he's pleasant as always. "I took my morning meds, so I should be feeling better soon. I only took half of the Percocet. I don't think I need it all."

He's on antibiotics and painkillers. We learned our lesson last year with Nelly's arm infection and packed all different types and dosages of antibiotics. I hate to think of what will happen when all the drugs are gone or way past their expiration date. We'll die of the infections that killed people a hundred years ago.

Nelly looks up from where he sits on the nightstand. "I'll take that Percocet off your hands if you don't want it. I think I have a pain somewhere."

"You *are* a pain," Adam says.

"How are your bruises?" Jamie asks me. "Let me see."

I raise the side of my shirt and get a chorus of *oohs* at the purple-black smudges under my ribs. "You might want some Percocet," Jamie says.

"I'm fine." I don't want anything that will dull my senses. Actually, there's nothing I want more than to dull my senses, but not at the expense of staying alive.

"Yes, she wants one," Nelly says, hand out. "I'll hold onto it for her."

"Thank God Nelly's okay," I say. "I had him as a patient last year. You don't even want to know what that was like."

I take my breakfast and find Peter in the house's kitchen with his wafflecakes. Determined to make him my friend again, I point to the pink welt my fist left under his eye and then my own face with a smile. "Hey, look! We're twins."

He slams his plate on the counter. "This is funny?"

I set down my plate next to his and sigh. "I'm sorry. Do you really think I meant to punch you? I'm *sorry*."

"Not every fucking thing in this world is a joke."

"Thanks, Humor Police. I know that. I was just—"

"Then act like it," he says. "Stop pretending you're fine."

"I *am* fine!"

He leans forward. "You wake up throwing punches, but you're fine? A man held you down and tried to rape you, but you're fine? Aren't you angry? Aren't you something besides *fine*?"

The rage builds in my chest and when it reaches my arms I grip the counter to stop myself from punching him, on purpose this time. It doesn't help, so I fling my wafflecakes at the wall, where they leave streaks of syrup before they drop to the carpet.

"You're not giving me a chance to be angry!" I try not to shout, but I want to, can imagine the release as the screams rip my throat raw. "You've taken every fucking bit of anger like you own it all. Why the fuck are *you* angry?"

"I have every right to be angry. So do you."

"Well, you don't have to be such a dick about it." I swallow multiple times and dig my nails into my palms. My bruises throb in time with my heart. "And maybe I don't want to be angry. Maybe I wanted—forget it."

His fighting stance melts before I flee into the yard, where I sit on the bench and breathe deep. Footsteps swish through the grass. I'm surprised when Margaret lowers herself beside me.

"It's nice out here," she says, eyes straight ahead. "I overheard you and Peter. I hope you don't mind, but I wanted to talk to you."

"I don't mind. Everyone overhears everything. It's like one big soap opera on wheels."

She dips her head with a snicker. "When I was eighteen, I was at a bar with some friends." Her voice is soft, different from her usual no-nonsense Northeastern twang. "I'll spare you the details, but I ended up being raped in the parking lot."

She rubs her hands together and nods at my shock. "I was angry at everything. I blamed myself for letting it happen, for not fighting harder. I played the violin, was good enough to get into music school, but after that I stopped. It was a long time before I forgave myself for doing what I needed to do to survive. I was angry for years. My father was angrier. Not at me—he was angry he couldn't protect me. He'd always liked his drink, but he hit the bottle hard after that."

"I..." I say. "I'm sorry that happened to you."

Margaret shrugs. "It was a long time ago. But sometimes the people who love us can't bear to see us hurting. They get all wrapped up in their own hurt. I just wanted to say I know a bit about how you feel. What it's like to be at someone else's mercy."

"Nothing really happened," I say quickly. "He didn't—I would never compare it to what happened to you."

"Honey," she says with a sober laugh, "it's no contest. And if it is, I don't want to win, that's for sure."

I can see the pretty girl she must have been. The years haven't been kind to her, or maybe she hasn't been kind to herself. Right now, with her gentle smile and warm hazel eyes, she's an attractive older woman. Maybe the stern face and standoffish manner are protection against what she ran up against all those years ago and whatever's happened in the years since.

"All right. Gotta get ready to go."

"Thanks, Margaret."

She pats my arm and leaves for the house. That was more than I've ever heard her say, but I guess she chooses her words wisely.

Peter steps out as she goes in. I watch my feet until he sits and says, "I'm sorry. I was just tired of hearing you say you were fine."

I brush away a tear. It seems the waterworks are back on now that I've called off the crying party. "Okay. But you're acting like you're mad at me."

"Hey, I'm not mad at you." I don't look up, and he lowers his face to mine until I do. "The last thing I am is mad at *you*. I was just...really fucking angry." He chews his lip, looking more remorseful than the situation warrants.

"I don't know if you forgot, but you're not supposed to be the angry one," I say. "You're the calm, level-headed one who listens to me blather on about stuff and tells me to stop when I do stupid shit."

"Sorry, I didn't get that memo," Peter says. I sniff at his joke. "I was worried about you."

"You were so worried that you wouldn't talk to me? That makes no sense. Why do men act like idiots when they're worried?"

"Because we're idiots." Peter gives me a rueful smile. He's annoyingly handsome and affable, even with the dark hollows below his cheekbones and under his eyes.

"Stop being charming. I'm mad at you."

"You know I can't help it. It comes naturally." I roll my eyes at his wink. His expression grows serious as he drags a boot through the grass. "I thought we were too late when we got there. I left you when I was supposed to stick like glue."

"I'm glad you were safe." I'd relive the whole experience, and even worse, before I'd take the chance that Peter die.

"I'm not glad. I could have protected—"

"I don't need protecting." It's not strictly true—we've all needed protecting at some point during the past year, but I can take care of myself most of the time. And, as much as I took care of myself the other night, I would've liked some protection. Not only do we women have to worry about marauders and Lexers, but we also get rapists—the post-apocalyptic trifecta.

"I know that," he says, as if it's a slightly irritating quality instead of a kick-ass one. "I know you'd fight to your last breath." I shake my head and he says, "You did."

"I didn't. And when he—in the truck, I decided to stop fighting altogether. I gave up. And it didn't even work. Maureen is...." Her death hangs around my neck like an albatross. It feels as though it was someone else who lay in the back of the truck and surrendered. Someone I don't like very much. Those moments when I welcomed death play on a loop in my head. I swore I wouldn't let this world get the best of me again, but it did.

Peter's eyes darken. "What you're forgetting is that Ashley is okay, and so are Bits and Hank and lots of other people. You were willing to do that for them. You were strong, just not in the way you thought you should be. Okay?"

I nod and try to believe that my momentary lapse was just that. Maybe I would've fought no matter what, or maybe I fought the only way possible in that situation. Shadows flit across Peter's face, reminding me of how he killed Twitch and Dark-hair. Peter does what's necessary and never utters a word about it, but he's so kind that I fear it affects him.

"I don't know if you feel bad about killing those—"

"Not in the least. When I saw one had his fucking hands on y—I'm glad you killed him, but I wish I had." He seems unaware of the way his hand grasps his machete's hilt, knuckles white, and I take it in mine until it releases.

I have no qualms about killing those men. I'm sure I'll have nightmares, but I have no qualms. I stare at my red shoelace. I think it might belong to one of them, but I don't want to ask. Instead of letting it creep me out, I decide to see it as a battle trophy—a head on a pike, a scalp on my belt.

"What I said before, in the kitchen?" I say. "It's not true. You're allowed to be as angry as you want. It's not your job to make me feel better."

Peter lets out a long-suffering sigh. "Yes, Cassandra, it is. You hired me for that job a few days ago."

I remember our conversation in the nursery and knock on my head. "I totally forgot!"

"I knew working for you would be a pain in the ass." Peter catches my incoming fist and turns it over in his hands. "You mean a lot to me, you know. That's why I was so angry. I don't know what I'd do if I lost you, too."

I can't put into words what he means to me without it being corny as all get out, so I simply say, "You're my best friend."

"You're mine. How'd that happen?"

"I have no idea. But we're gonna need one of those best friend necklaces where we each get half a heart and when we put it together it's whole."

Peter's laugh helps to fill the hole that's been in my chest since Grande Prairie, since Adrian. My heart's gotten used to feeling like one of those necklaces. I know it's on the mend, though I wish it would repair itself a little faster.

"Sometimes it feels like I only have half a heart," I say. "Sometimes it hurts so much you can barely stand it. But just when you think it won't ever be whole again, it starts to regenerate. I didn't believe John when he said that, but it's true."

"I know," he says. I think he must—he's lived the majority of his life with a broken heart—but I want him to know I understand.

I use my free hand to pick at a string on my jeans—Ana's jeans. I wonder if it's hard for him to see me in them or if they're just a regular old pair of jeans to him. "It's like a lizard's tail."

"What is *what*?" Peter asks.

"The heart. It's like a lizard's tail. I read once that when the tail regenerates it's never an exact replica, but it's a tail nonetheless."

"You do realize you get a tiny bit weirder every day?" Peter asks. "The heart is like a lizard's tail? It's very poetic."

"So I should give up painting and become a poet?"

"I wouldn't quit your day job just yet."

His anger has been swapped for crinkly eyes and a light voice. That I might have had something to do with it fills that hole a little more.

"We're all packed," Penny sticks her head into the yard and calls.

Peter spreads his arms when we stand and I bury my face in his coat. "You smell clean," he says before he lets me go.

"Jealous?" I sniff my armpit. "It's one of the many perks to being held down in the back of a pickup truck against your will."

Peter's lips clamp but a laugh escapes. "I can't believe you went there."

"I'll go wherever I need to go for a laugh. You know you love it—that's why you're my BFF."

"It's part of it," Peter says. "An infinitesimal part that's so small it's almost nonexistent."

"You're pretty funny when you're not being a party pooper." My cheek hurts from smiling, and I raise my hand to it with a wince. "Ouch. No more jokes."

Peter points to his own cheek and then takes my arm. "Hurts, huh? A taste of your own medicine. Let's go, weirdo."

CHAPTER 37

Fort St. John had a Safe Zone back when this all began. It became a black pin on Whitefield's map when zombies took over, and we don't want to go anywhere near it now. We don't know exactly where the Safe Zone was. Some Safe Zones were named for their exact locations and some for nearby cities. I'd check on the paper map we brought from Vermont, but it was destroyed by the contents of Boss's skull.

I'm in the RV, which has prompted only a few moments of residual panic. Peter drives and I sit in the passenger's seat with Bits on my lap and Hank on the floor between us. They're often drawing or reading or whispering, but since the other night I'm glad they've stuck close.

"We're going to have to go through the bottom of the city," James says. "It's just a few miles. It should be quick, if all goes as planned."

"And when does that ever happen?" Nelly calls. He has the perfect vantage point from the nightstand between the two beds in the back, allowing him to sit with Adam and toss out smart-ass comments at the same time.

James lifts his eyes to the ceiling. "Never. Thanks for the reminder."

But the few miles of wide, paved lanes and empty businesses are quiet. Once we're past the city, we come across the Safe Zone at the lake where we'd planned to fill the water tanks. Whether a giant pod has reached this place or every zombie in Fort St. John is here, I don't know, but the Safe Zone sign that hangs from a telephone pole would be laughable if it wasn't so terrifying, hanging as it is over a giant mass of Lexers.

"Keep going," Zeke's voice comes over the radio. "Go on through."

Whatever's kept them focused on the lake and woods is not as appealing as us. We zip by and watch them spill onto the road in our wake. I tighten my arms around Bits when twenty or so appear around a bend. The last thing we need is a kid going through a windshield. I slide off the seat with her in my lap. "Hank, get in the seat and buckle."

I've given up on trying to keep myself and them buckled in, especially in this older RV, but the chance of an accident has just multiplied. Hank's up and belted in immediately. He'll make a good patroller one day, although I pray we have no need for patrols. Small isn't an issue—as long as he's strong and fast and as quick-witted as he is now.

"Where do we turn?" Zeke's voice breaks through the silence. James flips pages and curses without answering.

"We need that west road," Zeke's voice comes again.

"There is no fucking west road!" James yells. "We passed it at the lake. There's another up ahead."

I relay his response into the radio sans cursing and brace myself for a collision. Just when I think we're out of the woods and regular breathing has resumed, the RV slows.

"Jesus," Peter breathes. "James, you're sure there's not another road?"

James peers out the windshield. "That *is* the other road."

I stand and snap up the binoculars. The crossroads ahead is filled with Lexers that feed from the west onto the Alaska Highway. They're hundreds of feet deep and who knows how many more are waiting to make the turn. Of course they'd follow the roads up here; it's the path of least resistance.

Zeke reverses the pickup and hangs out the window. "Can you see how far they go? Can we get through?" I pass him the binoculars. He raises them briefly and lets them fall to his lap. "God-fucking-damn it."

"There were houses down that incline toward the lake," Mark says. "Let's head there before they spot us."

We reverse slowly to avoid drawing their attention and follow the pickup to a string of lakefront homes tucked in the trees. A three-story house with a lakeside deck and two balconies looks promising if we have to stay for the night, as it's built into a hill and surrounded by a chain-link fence. Mark closes the gate after we're through and Nelly busts a window to open the door. We file in silently, quickly, and I sense everyone feels the dread that's overtaken the lingering trauma from the other night. Everyone except Sparky, that is, who naps on a windowsill in the RV.

Penny bolts the door and sinks to the white couch. The whole interior is white with turquoise accents, as if the owners had wished they lived by the sea. Hank stands at the sliding door to the balcony and watches the floating bodies that dot the lake. "I know they can't swim, but can they still get to us?"

"We'll see them if they do," Mark says. The house isn't fenced at the waterline, so we'll have to watch in case they're not too bloated to come ashore.

"Are those islands?" Bits asks. I follow her finger to the dark, distant masses of Lexers in the water. She realizes her mistake and shudders before I say a word.

Jamie and I distract the kids with a tour of the house while James and Mark study the maps for an escape route. We end up in a walk-out basement rec room. Bits and Hank don't ask to play ping pong when they see the table, but Nicki practically begs.

"It's too loud," Jamie says. "We're playing a fun game right now. It's called *Who Can Be the Quietest?*"

"That's the game you play when you can't play anything," Nicki says, lip jutted and on the verge of a tantrum. I can't blame her as she's four, broke her arm and almost lost her dad in the past two days. I'd have a tantrum too if I could get away with it.

"I'm going to win," Bits says, sounding smug. "I'm really, really good at that game."

"No, you're not!" Nicki says, ping pong forgotten. The nice thing about four year-olds is that they're easily distracted. "Listen to how quiet I can do this!"

She tiptoes up the stairs, and I wink at Bits and Hank when they follow. Jamie leans on the banister with her eyes on the lake. "I'll be okay," she says when I touch her hand. "Last year was worse. It's just that he was all I had left."

I think of how devastated I was after Adrian died—how I still have to work at not dwelling on how different things would be if he were here—which makes me wonder how last year was worse for her. I'm about to ask, but Nelly's voice comes down the stairs. "Y'all had better come up here."

We crowd around the table while James shows us the lake on the map. "Here's where we are." He points to spots at the north and south ends of the water. "Here are the pods."

There's not a single road west. To our east is lake. We're well and truly trapped. The only thing to be thankful for is that we didn't hit them at night. We would have been eaten, not trapped, had we not seen them in time.

"If we were on the east side of the lake we could drive around." He traces a line that heads north and circles to the Alaska Highway. "We'd hit the Alcan forty miles north of here."

"What about crossing the lake in boats and finding some cars?" Kyle asks with eyes closed due to his pounding headache. His only concession to Jamie's badgering was that he agreed to sit in an overstuffed chair instead of lying in a bed like she ordered. He might be worse than Nelly.

"If we're going to do it, we have to move now," Mark says. "We have, at best, thirty-five hours to meet up with the highway before the monsters get there, if they haven't already."

"Are there any other roads in case we're cut off again?" Peter asks.

"There's one," James says, and flips to a new page that's almost unmarked by roads except for a few lonely lines. "This would put us 150 miles farther north on the highway, but even if we beat them, we'd be out of gas long before Whitehorse."

"How long is that route?" Zeke asks.

"A thousand miles," Mark says. There's a collective moan—that's all the gas we have. "We could head north to Yellowknife, but no one's heard from them since last year."

James blows out a breath. "So, our choices are either we cross the lake and find something that'll take us to Whitehorse or stay here for the winter."

CHAPTER 38

There's a third choice, too—the death wish choice of trying to drive our way through a pod of Lexers. We've all seen how that goes, so we settle on hunting down boats. Zeke, Peter, Nelly and I walk down to the lake's edge and find a rowboat under a tarp. It's an easy climb to the next yard and the next, where we find a canoe.

"See that boathouse?" Zeke asks, pointing to where the shore bends out. A sprawling house is set back on an overgrown lawn with a tiny version of itself suspended over the water at the shore. "People store their boats full of gas and disconnect the battery for the winter. We could do with a motorboat, noise be damned—I don't see how we'll get our gear across without one. Those fuel tanks are heavy."

At the fourth house, we find another rowboat and an electric motor in the shed. It works for thirty seconds before it dies. "We'll use the battery in the RV," Zeke says. "How 'bout a ride to the house down the way?"

With four of us, three of them good-sized men, the boat sits low in the water. "You want to row, sugar?" Zeke pulls at the oars and winks.

"Biggest one rows. That's the rule. I'm not dragging you giant people around."

"That's not a rule," Nelly says.

"Well, it should be," I say. "So it is. Therefore, I'm going in a boat with one of the three of you every time."

It's quiet on the lake. I sit in the stern with Peter and watch Zeke pull the oars through the water like he was born rowing. He's got a bit of a belly from all the good eating at Whitefield once the summer crops were in, but underneath is all muscle.

"You're good at this," I say. "I'm in your boat."

Zeke chuckles. "Spent a lot of time out on lakes as a kid. There wasn't much quiet in my head, except when I was on the water. It's peaceful."

"It is." I watch the Lexer islands bob a half mile away. "Or it could be."

The two Lexers we pass are bloated, but not as bloated as I think they should be according to the absolute nothing I know about the subject. One does the dead man's float and the other lifts an arm as we go past. It spins face first into the water, where it flounders for a moment before going still.

"Well, they can't swim worth a damn," Zeke says. "If we can get between those islands we'll be good."

A few minutes later, Nelly ties the frayed rope to the dock at the boathouse. The structure is silent but for the sound of water lapping at its posts and has a door that's quietly jimmied open by Zeke. "Another thing I was good at," he says.

"You're a mysterious man, Zeke," I say. "Dentist, boater, felon. One day you'll have to tell me your story."

"One day I will." Inside, Zeke pulls the cover off a glossy white motorboat that's suspended in midair by a pulley system. "Let's get her down."

Peter examines the control box. "I don't see a hand crank."

Zeke sighs. "Christ on a crutch, is nothing ever simple?"

Cutting through the steel cables that suspend the boat isn't an option—the boat won't fall evenly and the crash would destroy it. I move to the edge of the floor that runs the perimeter of the room and back away when a white, almost featureless, face rises from the water. There are many horror movie moments these days, but this thing, with its wide, dark mouth and white expanse of swollen flesh, might be the creepiest thing I've ever seen.

Nelly kneels across from me and looks up with a grimace. "That thing must die," he says. We can't reach it, though, and we watch it wade under the boat in fascination. "It can't see us with no eyes. And the lack of a nose isn't helping any. My hypothesis is that it hears us." He knocks on the wood floor and the thing turns. "Yup, hears us."

"I think I found something," Peter says. We look up from Nelly's science project. "I need an allen wrench."

He pulls out toolbox drawers until he finds a few, then fits one into the back of the motor and cranks. "Keep going," Zeke says. "It's working."

Every turn brings the boat down a centimeter. An electric drill would speed things along, but that'd be asking for the moon. Peter spins until the boat is halfway down and then shakes out his hand when Nelly takes over.

"Look at you, figuring it out," I say to Peter.

"Is that so surprising?"

"I guess all your yachting experience paid off. Aren't those what you richies use for your regattas?"

Zeke chuckles and Peter lifts a boot to kick me in the rear. I hop away and teeter on the edge of the boathouse floor. Thankfully, the boat's now low enough to catch myself before I visit our horror movie friend underneath.

Peter points a finger. "That's what you get for ridiculing my enormous wealth."

"I almost died right here and you make jokes. Nice, Petey."

"You're rubbing off on me."

"It's about freaking time," I say.

We may be standing in a boathouse on a lake full of zombies, clock counting down the hours until we're stuck for the winter, but I can't stop smiling. It occurs to me that I do know why I don't give up: Bits and Hank and Peter and everyone else. I don't want to leave them, even if it is hard and discouraging. I want to see the kind of life we build when we make it to the end of this mess. The lines on Peter's face smooth away when he beams back. I have an urge to throw myself at him for a hug but restrain myself with a punch to his arm.

"What's that for?" he asks.

"It's a love punch."

He chucks me under the chin. "Right back atcha."

I stifle my laugh, but only because we have to be quiet. I'm happy and I'm not going to talk myself out of it. No more saving things for later.

We startle at the sound of Nelly clearing his throat. "Grab those batteries, y'all. We're down."

The boat starts without a hitch—something is actually simple, for once. Nelly stabs the bloated Lexer as we pull out of the boathouse towing the rowboat. A few Lexers wade into the water and the floaters wave as we pass, but the trip is short enough that it doesn't gather a pod.

At the house, Hank's amassed himself a real estate empire in the game of Monopoly the kids play with James and Penny. When I say I'm impressed, he says, "I have a system. But I can't tell you what it is."

"My favorite's Baltic Avenue," I say.

He tucks his money under the edge of the board. "Baltic's a waste of time. I'll teach you one day. But only you."

"I'm honored."

"So, I'll go across to look for vehicles," Zeke says. "Let's say three of us?"

"I'll join you," Mark says. "I can get an arrow into anything on shore before we reach it."

Nelly agrees to be third and leaves to tell Adam. I wander over to where Mark fits his arrows into his quiver.

"Thanks for teaching me to use a bow," I say. "You saved my life the other night."

"I might have given you the skills, but that, my dear, was all you. I had my bow up once we were close enough, but you beat me to it." His eyes twinkle like the elf he resembles. "Were you aiming for somewhere else or did you hit your target?"

I laugh, and somewhere I think I should feel bad we're joking about killing another human, but I don't. "Bull's-eye."

"Excellent."

Margaret and James empty the hot water heater while the rest of us pack the essentials we'll take across the lake. I sit in the RV's bedroom with my two bags that must be winnowed down to one and realize I haven't seen Adrian's phone since checking the time when Boss showed up. I can't remember if I left it on the table or returned it to my coat pocket—the coat that's drenched with blood in the back of a pickup.

I paw through my stuff. There are plenty of phones in the world that could be charged, but only one has pictures of everyone who's gone. Adrian's in there, Ana, John and Dan, too. But that's not all—I have pictures of Henry for Hank, of all the other people at Kingdom Come, the farmhouse, the garden in full bloom, the lake in Quebec. It's every song I've ever loved, ever listened to with Adrian. It's a piece of everything and everybody.

I dump out my bags, hoping that someone stuck it in without telling me. The box Dan carved hits the rumpled blankets and the unicorn inside rattles. I put the tiny figurine in my pocket. Dan had started on a unicorn family for Bits's birthday that she'll never get. I'll give her mine. I can stand losing the box if I have to, but not the unicorn. I stare at the pile as if the phone will appear out of thin air and can't even cry when it doesn't. It's the dog shit icing on the fucked up cake of this week.

Peter grabs his pack and sits on the bed across from me. "My God, that's a mess."

"My phone is gone." I separate my stuff into two piles and finally remember how I slipped it into my coat pocket.

"I have it. It's broken, but we can fix it." He pulls it from a compartment of his bag. The front has been taped so that the gazillion pieces of cracked screen stay where they should. I turn it on and can just barely make out the icons.

"James is almost positive everything is still in there," Peter says. "He can switch out the screens when we find a new one. I wanted to do it before you noticed." He shrugs. "I cleaned it as well as I could."

Blood has settled into a few of the cracks beneath the tape, but the rest is spotless. I think about Peter going through the mess of the truck to find this for me. Scrubbing off the blood until almost no trace remained, even in the cracks. It must have taken forever. The whole time I thought he was mad at me he was doing this. He might have been an idiot, but he was a thoughtful idiot.

"Don't cry," Peter says when I sniffle. He pats my knee awkwardly. "I know how much it means to you. We'll fix it."

"It's not that. I'm crying because you cleaned it."

"I'm sorry. I had to—"

I burst out laughing. Peter looks around for someone to save him from the crazy laughing-crying person on the bed, and my laughter wins out. "Really? I'm such a slob that I'd be *mad* you cleaned *blood* off my phone?"

A corner of his mouth rises. "You never know."

"Thank you. I was trying to say thank you."

"That would have been much clearer. I thought you weren't going to cry until we got there."

"You were right, it was a stupid plan. I don't want to deny myself things and then kick myself when it's too late. Not that crying is so spectacular, but I don't want to miss out on anything, you know?"

"I do."

I grab him by the shoulders and draw him close enough that our noses almost touch. "So let's not save anything! Let's eat all the food. You and me, right now."

"I should've known it was an excuse to eat." I let him go with a cackle. He goes back to his bag, removes the mini espresso maker and throws it to the side.

"You brought it?" I ask.

"It was so small, and I didn't think I'd find another any time soon. Dumb, huh?"

"Not at all. You should keep it."

I want him to have something that's impractical, that makes him happy, but he shakes his head. "There's no decent coffee. Or milk. What's the point?"

"Because there might be? Because you like it? Because I really want a latte?"

He smiles but leaves it on the bed. I can tell it's a lost cause. I zip the phone in my bag, and when he's not looking I take the leather pants, baby dress and earrings from Ana's bag. I leave her big bottle of fancy conditioner, although she would've deemed it necessary, give her bag a goodbye pat and pack the stuff with Dan's box and the phone. My small pack holds useful things—ammo, poncho, dental care supplies, et cetera— but it's quite possibly the least useful assortment of survival items ever. But that's only if you're thinking about food, water and zombies instead of people.

CHAPTER 39

Our three scouts radioed when they reached the other shore and then made their hourly check-in, but it's been over an hour since then. One hour and eight minutes after the first check-in, which I keep track of by asking Peter for the time so often that he finally strips off his watch and hands it to me, they call again.

"Plan *We're All Gonna Die* is a go," Nelly says, voice crackling. "Coming back now."

Our wafflecake lunch is made and supplies sit at the water's edge by the time they step out of the boat looking tired, dirty and extremely satisfied. "We got ourselves a pickup," Zeke says. "There wasn't much to choose from, and it's going to be a cold ride in the back. We'll bring the batteries in case we find something else."

"We'll use less gas this way," Mark says brightly. He's one of those people who thinks it's refreshingly brisk when I'm curled in a ball, shivering.

Most of us will be rowing because of the Lexers across the water; we can only use the speed boat once if we don't want to be surrounded. I watch the men bring the truck as close to the boat as possible and then grunt and curse while they remove the in-bed gas tank. They follow it with the tank that Shawn took from the abandoned pickup. They must weigh hundreds of pounds.

"Sometimes I like being a girl," Jamie says. She's trying extra hard to be normal, but whenever she's silent her face loses all animation.

"Except when it's time to pee in the woods," I say.

"I got my period behind a tree the day before yesterday," Jamie says. Penny and I groan. "Yep, pretty fun."

"That's something I'm not missing about now," Penny says. "Running faster than a snail, yes. Alcohol, yes."

"Yeah, too bad for you," I say. "You're missing all those wild alcohol parties we've been having after you go to sleep."

Nelly, James and Peter walk toward us. "Y'all going to do any work today?" Nelly asks.

"We were just discussing how sexy you all look doing manly things," Penny says. "We couldn't tear ourselves away."

"Well, then, carry on."

We pile the food bins and extra bags on the tanks and set Sparky's box in a safe spot. Zeke, Kyle, Nicki and Adam will cross in the motorboat once we've made it ashore. That way we'll limit the amount of time we give anything over there to eat us, although there are far fewer on the east side. We assign spots in the other boats, leaving Peter, the kids, Barnaby and me in a rowboat.

"Guess you're rowing, huh?" I ask Peter.

"You *are* the biggest," Bits says.

Peter looks at me. "I had nothing to do with that," I say. "See? It's just common sense."

Peter swings Bits and Hank into the boat. I've locked them in lifejackets and offered to tie them to the boat, but they weren't keen on that idea. I sit in the stern and face Peter, keeping an eye on how far they lean over in the bow. The other rowboat needs a lookout so the motor doesn't get tangled in Lexer hair and clothing, and they've insisted we need one as well.

It should take about thirty minutes to reach the other side of the wide lake. It's nearing late afternoon, but we won't stop for night. What's heading north on the highway is just as bad as or worse than anything we'd meet up with on a back road. The canoe skims across the water, leaving us in the dust, and the rowboat with the motor putts alongside for a moment before pulling ahead.

"We should've gotten a head start," I say. Peter nods and pulls the oars. "I will take a turn, you know."

"I'm fine," Peter says. He stops and pulls off his coat and long-sleeved shirt. "Hold these?"

I put them in my lap and watch the floating Lexers on the still water in the distance. We're lucky today is a lovely fall day with almost no breeze to make rowing more difficult. The sun is warm, the trees colorful, and the lake a mirror reflecting the blue sky—where it's not a mass of dead bodies. I'd trail my hand in the water if it wouldn't get chewed off.

"Cassie," Hank says in a stage whisper and points. "Look."

A Lexer floats face up, mouth opening and closing. Barnaby, who sits in front of Hank and Bits, lets out a low growl. "Quiet," Peter says in a firm voice. Barnaby stops.

I look from Barn's tilted head to Peter. "That's impossible. Tell me that was just a fluke."

"It didn't take that long. He figured it out the other night."

I shake my head when he shrugs. "This is a big deal. You taught our dumb old dog a new trick. I never thought I'd see the day anyone would teach him anything."

I want to hug Peter for taking the time to save Barnaby. Not that I didn't love Barn before, but he'll forever have my gratitude and any extra food I can scrounge up in Alaska.

Bits scratches his neck. "You're a good boy."

Barn spins around, nails sliding on the metal, and the rowboat rocks until Hank tackles him. Barnaby may try to save lives, but he also tries to kill us on a daily basis.

"Barn, sit," I say. He plants his butt on the boat and I raise my eyebrows at Peter, who grins.

"Good boy," I say, and he resumes his prancing. "I think the problem lies with *good boy*. Whenever you say *good boy*, he totally freaks out."

"Well, who doesn't like to be told he's a good boy?" Peter asks. He's hauling ass across this lake. The muscles in his arms ripple with every stroke and his t-shirt is already soaked. I'd be bitching up a storm, but like I've said, Peter does what's necessary and never complains about it.

I pat Peter's head. "You're a good boy. Who's a good boy? Huh?"

Peter doesn't stop rowing as he barks out a laugh. A few minutes pass in silence, then Bits says, "Cassie, look."

The canoe and rowboat have just reached the two islands of Lexers we'll have to pass between. As they weave their way through, the gentle splashing becomes a wild thrashing that reminds me of a school of piranhas eating their prey.

Peter watches me for instructions. "You're good," I say. "Keep straight."

The water gets choppier. Twenty feet away, a tangle of clothing and bodies and hair moves. It's impossible to tell where one ends and the next begins. The rowboat dips in a way that would make me seasick if I weren't so anxious. Drops of water spray through the air. I keep my mouth closed against the onslaught while Peter rows like a madman. Bits grabs Hank when one rises from the water, peeling hands gripping an oar. I raise my axe, but Peter shakes it off and it sinks into the darkness of the lake, fingers flexing.

I grip the bench with one hand and order the kids to hold on. Tiny waves break on the sides of the boat. The smell of dead things mixed with the wet decay of lake weeds is everywhere. Peter keeps his eyes on me, trusting me to tell him which way to go, which makes me terrified I'll fuck it up somehow.

"To your right," I say. Peter dips an oar until I say, "Straight!"

The Lexers' movement has narrowed the channel we have to pass through. I order Bits and Hank to the bottom of the boat as we near the entrance, and Barnaby begins a chorus of barks that echoes over the water.

"Quiet!" I scream.

Barn drops and looks at me with wounded eyes. I'll feel bad about that later. I pull my poncho from my pack and call for Hank to catch it. He spreads it over himself and Bits like a fort. Peter must be worn out, but he pulls faster when the splashing becomes a downpour. I throw his jacket over his head and use the hand not holding my axe to cup over my eyes. Water streams down my face and over my lips. The boat rocks at a perilous angle when a hand grips the edge, and Peter leans to the opposite side so I can kill the Lexer without sinking us.

A few more strokes and we're through. Peter's jacket has fallen to the bottom of the boat and he pulls like he was captain of the rowing team at Harvard. Who knows, maybe he was. Now that we're in calm water, I can hear his breaths with every stroke of the oars. Water soaks my hair and runs under my jacket into every spot that was clean an hour ago. Peter's as drenched as me, but the kids are dry.

I panic at the thought of what's running down my back into my underwear, what has probably hit the mucous membranes of my eyes and lips. I snatch my mouthwash from my bag and gargle a small mouthful. The alcohol will kill any germs. I pour it in my gloved hands and rub them together and then pour more onto my bare hands to smooth over my face, neck and hair.

Between fifty-degree temperatures, water and now Refreshing Mint, I'm freezing. I dump out more and rub Peter's face. I rake some through his hair and then get his bare arms.

"What are you doing?" he asks, screwing an eye shut. "That shit stings!"

"Sting or die," I say.

He stops mid-row and stares at me in wonder. And not the good kind of wonder, either. "You are out of your mind," he says, enunciating each word.

I'm hit with the absurdity of the moment. I'm kneeling in zombie water in a rowboat in British Columbia rubbing mouthwash on Peter. I'm minty and burning and sweating and freezing all at the same time. I collapse to the bottom of the boat and laugh until my stomach hurts.

"I really am," I gasp. "Holy crap, I really am."

CHAPTER 40

I change into Ana's leather pants and spare bra, underwear and shirt, but only after rubbing myself down with the antibacterial gel that was in the speed boat. This is it—my final outfit. And the most uncomfortable of the bunch.

Nelly smirks when I walk outside. "Why are you walking like that?"

"Like what?"

"Like you have something up your butt."

"Well, you would know."

Nelly chortles and wraps an arm around me. "Good one, darlin'. You should've taken those mom jeans while you had the chance."

"I'd rather be dead than have you see me in those."

"And I'd gladly die for a chance to see you in them." He takes a long sniff of my head. "You and Peter are minty fresh."

"Don't ever do that. There's mint in my bones. I'll never be warm again."

"Maybe you should ride up front first."

The kids, Kyle and Adam will ride in the truck's cab while the rest of us switch between the bed and cab. We're down to twenty-some hours to reach our intersection point. Mileage-wise, it's four hours of driving, but we know how little that means. It's evening by the time we leave. Peter drives and I cram in with Kyle, Penny, the kids and Jamie, while Ash shares Adam's front seat at his insistence.

"You don't need to take a turn in the back," I say to Penny, as James has said repeatedly in the past hour.

"I'm hot and pregnant. I'll be fine. Stop talking about it or I'll kick you."

"Geez. Sorry for caring about the welfare of your unborn child and stuff."

Penny laughs and wrinkles her nose. "You guys stink."

Peter runs a hand through his crunchy hair while he sighs for the millionth time. Dried mouthwash acts like hair gel, we've recently found, but I don't care that I'm sticky and crispy. We'd probably be feeling sick by now if we were infected, so I'm going to pretend that mouthwash saved the day.

The road starts out paved but quickly turns to dirt. Hank is on my lap and there's not a centimeter in which to shift with the bags under my feet, but when I look out the back window at Nelly and the rest bundled in blankets and squished among our supplies, I'm okay with the lack of space.

Hank rests his head on my shoulder and murmurs, "I think you smell good. I wish we had gum."

For all his maturity, he's also a little kid who longs for gum, and I want so desperately to shield him from the hurt so he can stay that way. I hold him close and wake up when the truck stops at what could be the same road and trees of an hour ago. Hank is so used to sleeping in strange places that he remains in a seated position with his head hanging when I slide out from under him.

"I'll be in the back," I say to Bits, who nods sleepily.

They've cleared out a space by tying things down and stacking bins. I climb into the truck's bed with the others and James, who refuses to take his turn in the cab without Penny. "Besides," he says, "Nelly and Kyle are big dudes. Margaret'll be squashed enough."

"I like it out here," Mark says, which only solidifies my belief that he's off his rocker in some harmless way.

At first I think it won't be so bad—I'll fall asleep wrapped in my blanket and ride out the cold. It starts slowly, like when you think a breeze is a bit chilly, and then builds until I'm not sure I'm still wearing my gloves and wool socks. The leather pants are better than wet jeans, but now that my sweater is soaked, all I have is the hoodie and my leather coat. I brought a wooden box and baby dress and earrings instead of an extra pair of jeans, but I still don't regret it, even an hour into the ride when my limbs have frozen into the fetal position. An hour after that, when I'm about to die of full-body frostbite, the pickup slows.

Nelly steps out. "We've got a tree up ahead."

A tree over two feet in diameter stretches across the road. James asks Nelly for our mileage so far and shivers over the atlas with his flashlight. "Nope, there's no other way around this now. We're in the home stretch."

The tree sits ten feet into the woods on either side, and the only way past is to cut through in two spots and roll out a section wide enough for the truck. Zeke starts on one end with my tomahawk and Nelly on the other with our one axe. Hitting a tree repeatedly is not a quiet activity, and it's only a few minutes before the first Lexer shows up. Jamie runs it through and we lean on the truck to wait for more while the axes pound. Penny stands with us, long knife in hand. We're not going to let her kill anything, but it appears she was serious about helping out.

"Ow," she says. "Nice kick, baby."

"What's she doing in there?" I ask. "That must feel so weird."

"How about when they kick your bladder?" Jamie asks. "I can't tell you how many times I almost peed my—"

She stops, and it all clicks into place in the stunned silence that follows. Why Jamie has said she wouldn't have kids until this was over, never talks about her life before, and how last year could have possibly been worse than losing her husband.

"Oh, Jamie, I'm so sorry," I say. Penny says something equally as lame.

"She was five, going to start kindergarten in the fall," Jamie says in a tight voice. I put an arm around her and find her shoulders even tighter. "She was with my mom while I worked late. I made it home before they closed off the city, but when Shawn and I got there they were already gone. I didn't want to tell anyone. Shawn agreed not to. Because I didn't want this—this fucking silence. I really am happy for you, Pen. Don't treat me weird now, please."

Penny sniffs. "I promise I won't. What was her name?"

"Holly, after my grandma. She had big brown eyes like Nicki's."

I can only imagine losing Bits for a split second before I'm engulfed in despair and on the verge of tears. I wonder if when you lose a child you almost wish they'd never been born so as to have avoided the devastation. Not that you'd really wish it, but almost. I don't ever want to find out for sure.

I walk forward to stab another Lexer coming up the road. These monsters have taken so much from us—little girls with big brown eyes, brothers who could climb mountains, lovers who appreciated the little things about us. They left parents childless and children parentless. After the Lexer falls, I want to kick it. I want to beat the shit out of it until it's nothing but a wet pile of bones and flesh. But it would be pointless; they have no idea what they've done. We might have been punished, but so were they.

I walk back. I can't see Jamie's face, but her voice is even. "...two hours of pushing. I had the hugest hemorrhoid after. Shawn called it The Other Baby. He'd pinch my butt and say, 'How's it hanging?' "

I can't help it when I giggle. I miss Shawn's obnoxious but good-natured comments. The two of them join in, Jamie's laugh the loudest.

"I wanted to tell you both, but it got harder the more time passed," Jamie says. "It started to feel like a dream. Then when you got pregnant I thought you'd be afraid to talk about it in front of me."

"No," Penny says. "Believe me, any tips you want to share, I want to hear."

"I will," Jamie says.

"Good. All I've got is Cassie, and she doesn't know shit about this."

"Hey!" I say. "I read those books you gave me. Birth is going to be orgasmic and wonderful. You'll be a lotus flower opening to the sun or a river flowing to the mouth of the sea or something."

"I read those books," Jamie says with a snort. "It's amazing, but the only flower I felt like was one that was having its petals torn off."

"Oh, God," Penny says, and rests her head on the truck.

"It won't seem so bad once it's over. And I'm sure it won't be as long as mine. Don't worry."

This is why we need a Safe Zone. I'm sure we could figure out childbirth if all goes as it's supposed to, but Jamie heard Doc talk of a midwife in Talkeetna, and we know for sure there's a medic. We need to be safe in the spring, when the Lexers thaw and the baby cries.

Peter comes bearing hot beverages and then leaves to relieve Nelly. Jamie takes a sip of her coffee and says, "He remembered how I like it. He's awesome."

"He is. I have to pee again," Penny says, and takes James into the dark with her.

"The girls are going to be all over Peter in Alaska," Jamie says.

My stomach flops. I don't want someone new who might disrupt our little family, who won't love the kids the way we do, and I know it's completely selfish of me to feel that way. I'm still searching for an appropriate reply when Jamie says, "Thanks."

"For what?"

"For being...I don't know, a good friend."

"I love you, dummy," I say. "You can always talk to me."

"I don't want to pretend she didn't exist anymore. I've wanted to ask you for a favor for a while. I only have one picture of her and it's getting all crumpled..."

"Of course I'll paint her. And when my phone is fixed we'll take a picture of the picture." My fingers itch to get started. I don't want her to lose the only memento she has of Holly. I'll look at it in the light tomorrow so I can try to commit it to memory in case it's lost.

"Thanks." Jamie takes a deep breath and holds it before exhaling.

It's quiet until Zeke hoots in triumph. "All right, let's give it a go."

With the truck pulling and us pushing, the giant log rolls. The kids have slept through the entire experience and continue to sleep when we move on, although I'm wide awake. We're almost at the Alaska Highway and what we find will determine our fate.

CHAPTER 41

What we find is nothing but open road bathed in early morning light. It's only when we've gone twenty miles north—another day's walk for the Lexers—that we stop to switch places and eat, although I consume my wafflecake with much less enthusiasm than previously.

"I thought you'd never get tired of wafflecakes," Peter says, and chases his last bite with water.

"I need savory. This has been too much syrup in too little time."

"What do you want?"

"Spanakopita."

"What's that?" Bits asks.

"Like a spinach pie with cheese and onions," Peter says. "It's good, if sort of random."

"In five seconds it'll be something else," I say. There's a revolving carousel of food running through my mind every second of the day.

"How about now?" Peter asks.

"Everything bagel with cream cheese and tomato."

Bits grins. "Now?"

"Salami on Italian bread with oil and vinegar and banana peppers."

"Now?" Hank asks.

"Steak. I could do this all day, you know."

Bits and Hank play the game while I help to put away sticky dishes. There's only enough water to drink, not wash. I sit in the truck bed and hope that the coming sun means a warmer ride than last night.

✳✳✳

It doesn't. Maybe we're at a higher altitude or winter is one day closer, but whatever it is, my jaw aches from chattering teeth. Peter pokes his head into my blanket burrow. "Come sit with me."

My hair whips out of my buns when I climb between his knees. I put my blanket over my head and lean into his warmth. I'm in no danger of overheating, but it's better. His stubble scratches my neck when he leans in to say, "How can you see the beautiful scenery with a blanket on your head?"

"You've seen one tree, you've seen 'em all."

He must laugh because there are a few warm gusts of air on my ear. "I'll tell you about it. The clouds are huge and the sky is the same color as Bits's eyes. The trees are all evergreens, with the road the only thing to break them up. It looks like a painting. You'd be able to do it justice."

It's tempting, but I keep my head covered and say, "Pretty."

I've been lulled into a place somewhere between waking and sleeping when he says, "You have to look now."

I peek out. The mountains are close enough to see the variations in browns that make up their craggy peaks. I find Peter's hand under the blanket and squeeze rather than ruin the moment by shouting something that won't match my level of happiness at the sight of salvation.

"Okay, you can hide again," he says, but I wait until trees have blocked the view.

✷✷✷

Zeke coasts to the side of the road at a crystal blue lake. "Water fill up."

I pick my way through sparse fir trees to the turquoise water. Bits dips her hands in the water and pulls back. "It's freezing!"

"Want to go for a swim?" I ask. "I'll toss you in."

"No way!" she says and sneezes. She wipes her nose with her sleeve.

I hand her a handkerchief. "Yuck, booger arm. Hey, I just remembered another joke." She and Hank look up expectantly. "How do you make a tissue dance? Put a little boogie in it."

Bits groans and coughs into the handkerchief. I don't like the deep, ragged sound and press my lips to her forehead even though she says she feels fine. Her cheeks are a deep pink, but she has no fever. I drop the water filter tube into the lake and pump to fill a container.

Bits looks to the clouds tinged gold with afternoon light. "I miss looking at the stars."

"I do, too, but once we're in Alaska we'll watch all the time. And we'll probably see the Northern Lights."

"I really want to see them. They sound so cool."

"I saw them once, when I was a little older than you."

Peter crouches by the water's edge and fills a container to be treated later. "You did?"

"One summer, way up at the top of New York State," I say. "We were camping on a lake. They were kind of like yellow-green clouds made of light." We'd stood on the shore, my father's arm around my shoulders, until the magical colors had faded away.

"Dan told me all about them," Bits says.

I concentrate on pumping the filter. "Yeah?"

"What'd he say?" Peter asks when I don't ask any more.

"That you'd be granted any wish in the world the first time you saw them because they were made of fairy dust. Did you make a wish, Cassie?"

"No, I didn't know I should." I smile; Dan would've told Bits something silly like that while wearing an absolutely serious expression.

"I think you still can, even if it's not the first time you've seen them. Since you didn't make one before. I mean, it's not like you knew."

"Dan was kidding," Hank says, and pushes his glasses up the way he does before a lecture. "They're particles from the sun hitting the Earth's atmosphere. That's the simple version, anyway. The Earth's magnetic field—"

"He told me that, too," Bits says. "But it's fun to pretend."

Hank thinks about it and then nods when he's decided pretending is an acceptable activity. Sometimes he's just too darn serious.

"You can see them all the time in the winter, apparently," Peter says. "We'll have our wishes soon enough."

Hank looks down the road we have left to travel. "I wish we had them now."

"Me, too," I say.

CHAPTER 42

It may be foolish to stop with less than a day of driving to reach Whitehorse, but Adam's shoulder weeps blood and Kyle has puked four times from carsickness. We also don't want to show up at Whitehorse in the dark with no idea of what will be there to greet us, or run into a pod on the road, although we haven't seen a zombie for hours. We've seen animals, though—moose, elk and what looked like a bear before it lumbered off the road—and hitting one of them at night could destroy the truck and kill anyone not buckled in.

We pass on staying the night in a small cabin full of dried blood and body parts. Now that we're in the mountains, I can't stop staring at the golden grasses, low red bushes and white trunks of what look to be birch trees, their leaves as bright a yellow as I've ever seen. I thought I was surrounded by mountains at Kingdom Come, but these tall, rocky peaks are the real deal.

A sign advertises a hot springs ahead and another promises hotel rooms. I look longingly down the road that leads past a ranger station to the hot springs; to be warm and clean would be indescribably wonderful. Just past the springs is a lodge-type hotel with a few cars in a gravel lot out front. My legs are creaky from sitting in a truck for twenty hours, and between that and my pants I walk like a malfunctioning robot.

"What is wrong with you?" Nelly asks.

I don't want to bitch about Ana's pants in front of Peter, so I shrug and then freeze at footsteps from the side of the building. It's a lot of crunching, maybe a pod. We edge toward the pickup just as five large animals with shaggy brown beards, humped shoulders and thick fur covering their forelegs round the corner. They stop but don't look half as shocked as we.

"Well, I'll be damned," Zeke says. "Bison."

They look us over briefly and head for the opposite corner of the lot to poke around in the grass. Usually animals fear Lexers, possibly because of the smell, and their calm is a good sign. Barnaby watches them with round eyes from the truck but doesn't make so much as a whimper. He knows when something's out of his league.

"Let's go in," Nelly says.

"You said you were shooting the next animal you saw," I say. "And there they are, ripe for the taking."

"We'll be in Whitehorse tomorrow. What would we do with five hundred pounds of meat?"

"Eat it? Bring the rest as a present?"

He shakes his head as we step into a lobby that smells of mildew and decay, but it's an old decay that's barely there. The place looks like it could have used a major renovation before zombies, with the battered tables in the restaurant and fuzz-covered upholstery on the lobby furniture. Pots are scattered willy-nilly in the kitchen, some with dried food crusted to their sides. The upstairs guest rooms are empty as well.

Zeke pats the woodstove in the lobby and says, "We'll sleep down here. Let's get everyone inside and bring down mattresses."

I help bring in wood from the pile outside for Peter to start a fire. Nelly sits in a chair with a brochure about the hot springs, driving me bonkers with talk of deliciously hot water and boreal forests. Once the fire's roaring, Nelly asks, "How about we take a dip?"

"We probably shouldn't," I say. We've spent the past year trying not to do anything too dumb, and I don't want to start now.

"We could drive over," Peter says. I look at the floor to keep from laughing when his hand goes to his hair.

"It should be safe enough," Mark says.

"I've never been," Margaret says, eyes aglow. "I say we go." Heads nod all around.

"Please, please, please," Bits says. She folds her hands under her chin. "Please? We never get to swim. I'll do anything you want forever."

I tickle her side. "Stop with the drama already. Everyone's agreed to go."

Hank is excited enough to jump up and down with Bits, which makes me glad we've said yes. Who knows when they'll go swimming next? Definitely not during an Alaskan winter.

We drive past the ranger cabin to a boardwalk that passes through a warm water swamp. Even walking softly, fifteen pairs of feet are loud on the wooden planks that wind through the autumn woods, but I don't let myself get crazy about it. I'm not going to pass up this chance and hope we get back one day. Besides, we've grown pretty good at feeling out an area, and with the way the birds call and little rodents scamper in the underbrush, it seems we're the only living or undead humans here.

The boardwalk becomes a bridge where we get our first glimpse of a long pool surrounded by a riot of red and orange bushes. Tendrils of steam rise into the cool air and yellow leaves float on the surface. Several staircases lead into the water from a roofed wooden deck that houses changing rooms and cubbies for clothes.

"Ladies first," Zeke says. "We'll get in once y'all are in the water."

We strip down, me to nothing and the others to their spare underwear. I've brought my zombie-water clothes in order to wash them, but I don't want to wear them until they're disinfected. I take the soap, shampoo and conditioner and shiver my way to the steps.

"Oh. My. God," Jamie says when she hits the water. "This is amazing."

I sink into the hot water, every muscle crying in joy, then sit on the wooden benches built at the sides of the pool to scrub Ana's clothes with a bar of soap. I slip on the bra and underwear once they're rinsed.

"Get over here with that rat's nest," I say to Bits. She swims over, spitting out water, and I drag the brush through her snarls while she acts as if I'm murdering her. Now I wish I *had* taken Ana's conditioner instead of a small bottle of cheap stuff.

Bits hangs on Peter's back like a monkey when he comes up from dunking himself, hair freshly shampooed. "All aboard," he says, and brings her to the opposite end and back again.

"You're nice and clean," I say. "Sorry about the mouthwash debacle."

"You were trying to keep me alive. How mouthwash was going to do that, I don't know, but it's the thought that counts." I splash him and stand to cool down.

"Your cup runneth over," Nelly says, eyes on my chest.

I look down. Ana's bra is a bit too small, hardly inappropriate, but I turn a few degrees hotter than the water anyway. Peter glances down and away just as quickly. It's a basic black bra, but he might recognize it as hers. I sink into the water and glare at Nelly.

"Let's live here forever," I say because we need an immediate subject change. "We'll eat moose and bison and drink pine needle tea so we don't get scurvy."

"Pine needles have vitamin C?" Peter asks.

"Doesn't everyone know that?"

"I didn't," Adam says.

"I did," James says, and we high five.

Margaret is on a bench, eyes closed, looking younger and more relaxed than I've ever seen. "I knew."

"See?" I say. "So we'll be set."

Kyle sits on the steps, dipping Nicki in the water by her armpits so her cast stays dry. He looks less ashen now that we've stopped for over ten minutes. "I'm down. I'm tired of puking in the truck."

The peacefulness of the water soaks into me along with the minerals the brochure raved about. I float on my back and listen to the sounds of merriment, then swim to where Peter sits staring into the forest. "Hey. We're almost there."

"We are."

He doesn't look happy to be almost there. I sit beside him, run my hands through the water and blurt out, "I'm sorry I have to wear Ana's clothes."

"They're just clothes."

"I don't want it to upset you." This is probably where I should stop, but my mouth keeps going. "I wouldn't, except I didn't have underwear or a bra. I didn't think I'd be wearing it in front of people or I would've washed my old one. It doesn't fit that well, but running without a bra is, you know...Well, I guess you don't *know*, but—" I finally get my mouth to shut and watch a leaf float by.

"I didn't know it wasn't yours," he says.

"Great. So I've made it worse."

"You haven't made it anything. I told you, it's fine." There's a long silence in which I decide that drowning myself will be the best way to never have to look at Peter again.

"How's your side?" he asks. "Those bruises look like they hurt."

I don't want to think about the bruises, have barely looked at them. "Only to touch. How's your cheek?"

"Better than yours." His has faded to a pink mark, while mine is a lovely purple-black.

"I'll have to practice my punching, then. I guess it's almost time to get out."

I rise off the bench. I haven't looked at him since schooling him in the hazards of running without a bra, and he takes my arm. "I'm fine. I was just thinking."

"Sorry I interrupted with the insanity of how my underclothes don't fit properly."

I'm relieved that he wears his half-amused by my antics expression. "I'm used to your insanity. And you look nice—" He stops with his lips pressed together.

I'm not sure how to respond to being told I look nice in a bra by someone who isn't unfastening it or selling it to me, and I stare at him for a few seconds before a giant laugh escapes. I think his ears might be pinker.

"I have no idea why I said that. I didn't mean—"

"It was the automatic you-look-nice reflex," I say, and pat his shoulder. "You look nice in your underwear, too. There, now we're even."

Bits swims between us and comes up with a splash. "Cassie, quick, what do you want to eat?"

"Vanilla milkshake with French fries for dipping."

"Really?" Bits asks. "That's gross."

I widen my eyes at Peter. "Oh, no, she's never dipped fries in ice cream. This is not okay."

"It's delicious," Peter says. "I thought it was gross until Cassie made me try it."

"Then I want to try it," Bits says. "Maybe we can in Alaska?"

"I'll do my best," Peter says. "All we need are potatoes and cows. They're a dime a dozen."

Peter winks, but I know he'll move Heaven and Earth to get that cow and potatoes. The little things that make life sweet, like milkshakes, are rare these days. The big things, like people who'll do their damnedest to get those milkshakes, are even harder to find. But I'm surrounded by them.

CHAPTER 43

The warmth of the woodstove dries my hair to its soft brown self and my jeans will be dry by morning. I feel almost normal. We've brought mattresses down to the lobby and enjoyed our famous wafflecakes in celebration of our last night of traveling. None of us says it's our last night because no one wants to jinx it, but everyone settles on their mattresses in better spirits than since we started this journey.

I toss and turn all night with worries about Whitehorse and nightmares about Whit, who wins our battle in sleep if not in real life, and wake up feeling as tired as I did before bed. They've managed to get a rusty VW in the lot working, thanks to Miss Vera's battery, and Peter's at the wheel when the sun pokes up its head.

"Bye, hot springs," I say from the passenger's seat. "I'll miss you."

"Bye, Cassie," Peter says in a deep voice. I crack up, and he says, "I figured one of these times the inanimate object should talk back."

"And that's the hot springs' voice?"

"Hey, it was pretty good."

"It was great. Although it did sound a bit like Scooby Doo," I say, and dodge his retaliatory pinch.

Everyone left of last summer is in the VW. It magnifies the people we're missing, but I take comfort in the fact that anyone is left at all. I poke around in the Grateful Dead-stickered glove compartment and find a CD case. This VW is nowhere near as nice as Miss Vera; the only upgrade is in the aftermarket CD player.

I flip through the case. "Let's see—Grateful Dead, Grateful Dead and surprise, surprise, Grateful Dead. Well, we've got all the concerts that are highly admired in the Deadhead community." Nelly groans and flops back on the bed next to Adam.

"How do you know they're highly admired?" James asks from the floor near Penny's feet. Hank is crammed by the gearshift, head resting on my thigh.

"The daughter of Patrick and Abigail Forrest knows her spacejams. Even if, according to them, she doesn't appreciate their genius."

I flip until I find a few that aren't The Grateful Dead, and one of them couldn't be more perfect. "This one goes out to Peter Spencer," I say in a radio announcer voice. "For talking me down off the ledge."

"What is it?" he asks.

"You'll see."

I stick in the CD, find the track and turn up the volume. This stretch of road is empty, the windows are rolled up, and I want to drive with music blasting one more time in my life. Just for this song, I'll pretend that everything is normal and sane. I glance at Peter when "Don't Worry Baby" begins. He looks away as though embarrassed, and I tug his non-crunchy hair until he cracks a smile.

The Beach Boys' harmony fills the car and tells us in the loveliest way possible that everything will be all right. That it'll all work out in the end. We travel through lush, colorful forest and wind our way past a deserted car as the song fades away.

"Again," Hank whispers.

Peter rests his hand on Hank's head before bringing it back to the wheel. I press the button and wipe my eyes. I notice I'm not the only one who does.

✧✧✧

We've passed through one other town on our way to Whitehorse, which was empty but for the requisite Lexers. Our cheer at the Whitehorse city limits wakes Bits, who's asleep on my lap. "Are we here?" she asks.

"We are, baby girl," Peter says.

She presses her face to Hank's. "We're here, Hank!"

"I know that," he says matter-of-factly, but his smile is dazzling.

"Why would they want the Safe Zone in the middle of everything?" I ask. Whitehorse is one of the Safe Zones in the middle of a city, or as city as it gets in the Yukon. If I've learned anything, it's that the more populated a place before zombies, the more zombies there are now.

"Look here," James says. I spin for a view of his map. He points out a ridge that runs along one side of the downtown, with the river on the other side. "John said they dug out the ridge to make a wall so they only had to close off two directions. He wished we had something like that."

And I wish John were here to see it. The road's sides have been dug away, leaving only a bridge of asphalt to the first gate—the open first gate. It's not a good sign, and I tighten my arms around Bits when she slumps. The road dips and makes a sharp left at a wall of concrete and rebar. We travel its length until we hit another wall. Mark and Zeke leave the pickup to knock on the giant wooden doors.

"Hello?" Zeke booms. No one answers. Peter pulls close for a view over the barrier and we climb to the roof.

I can see why they chose this area: The large metal buildings offer plenty of housing, and a wide expanse of field to the north appears to have been gardens. And I can see why they left: The field is mostly empty, but the rest of the Safe Zone is inhabited by Lexers. They walk and stand and crawl in and out of the buildings. Windows are shattered. Clothes and everything from lanterns to furniture are strewn on the streets.

Nelly rests his head on the wall. "Of course. Why did we think it would be any different?"

I rub his back before he jumps down. Zeke tries to smile when our eyes meet, but he looks as dispirited as I feel. The only thing that's been keeping me sane after a long night of nightmares has been this moment. It was going to be a dream come true. I look over the wall one more time. This Safe Zone is ugly and flat and rocky, so far removed from Vermont and its pretty green mountains and farmhouse and fields. I tell myself I wouldn't want to live here, that I wanted to be in Alaska anyway, but I'm lying to myself. All I really want is to be safe.

CHAPTER 44

We have to spend the night near Whitehorse, since it's afternoon, but we'll do it farther north. We don't want to wake up surrounded. It only takes ten minutes to be clear of the city—ten minutes in which no one speaks, except for James to say that we have enough gas to get two vehicles to Talkeetna. We've just passed a few homes when we hear a yell and turn to see a thin woman with short dark hair running up the street waving her arms.

James slams on the brakes. The woman nears and he says, "Dude, is that *Liz*?"

I gasp. It *is* Liz, our friend and fellow patroller from Kingdom Come, who was in one of the first trucks to leave when the giant pod arrived. We'd assumed they'd been stuck in the giant pod and had met the same fate as everyone else. We throw open the doors and she stops with her legs spread and arms thrown in the air.

"Holy shit!" she screams. "Holy motherfucking shit!"

I don't know who starts crying first, but by the time we've reached each other we're both in tears. "I can't believe this." Liz uses her sleeve to wipe her face. "You're here, right? I haven't gone nuts?"

"Nope," Zeke says. "If you're nuts, then we are too."

"Holy. Motherfucking. Shit." She gives us all back-clapping hugs and steps back. "Is this...everyone?" We nod and her eyes flicker around the group, cataloging all the missing people. Her mouth thins.

"Who's with you?" Nelly asks. "Why are you still here?"

"Mikayla, Ben and Jasmine," she says. "We're out of gas."

✷✷✷

She directs us to a fenced-in house with a metal roof. Liz closes the chain-link gate behind us and kicks it with her boot. "Not that it'd do dick against a pod, but it's better than nothing."

Zeke laughs and tugs his beard. "Why are you here, then?"

"We were hoping someone would drive by and give us a ride." She shakes her head in disbelief and punches Nelly, which is much more a Liz-type show of emotion than crying, then opens the door and calls, "You'll never guess who I found."

We walk into a living room with couch and kitchen table on one side and mattresses on the other. A large woodstove graces the back of the room. Mikayla drops her spoon when she sees us and brings her hand to her chest. She runs forward, screaming, "Ben!"

Her ringlets are greasy and there are streaks of dirt on her clothes, but her golden-brown skin glows and her eyes are bright. Ben enters in a panic and stops, eyes bulging. His compact, muscular frame is as limp as the curly mop of brown hair that lays flat on his head. He's one of those still-waters-run-deep kind of guys, but when I throw my arms around him he almost breaks my ribs.

Half an hour later, we're eating boiled potatoes and listening to the end of their story. It's similar to ours, except they drove across the top of the United States and southern Canada. It wasn't so bad after they reached the Dakotas, narrowly escaping the pods we'd last heard were in Iowa.

They'd managed to save eight year-old Jasmine from the school bus by waiting out the zombies for two days before driving back to look for survivors. Jasmine answered their calls from under the seats, blocked in by bags where her mother had stashed her, and they had to kill a lot of good friends to get in. Liz tells me quietly that Henry was taken care of, but they didn't check the roof of the ambulance. I'd like some closure, but I know there's no surviving a zombie bite. Dan is gone either way. She tears up at mention of John.

"I would've looked at the bodies if I'd known he was there, Cass," Liz says.

"I know." I squeeze her arm and resign myself to never knowing what's become of him.

Jasmine inherited the doe eyes and serious demeanor of her mother, but when she saw Bits she dragged her to the floor in ecstasy.

Ben rubs his eyes. "So we're all that's left."

Everyone stares into space until Mikayla says, "Nineteen is better than four, right?"

It's hard to dismiss her optimism because she believes it wholeheartedly. And she's right, nineteen is better than fifteen and most definitely better than four. Ben wraps an arm around her shoulder. They still have each other. I'm glad someone does, and I'm happy that I'm finally able to feel glad instead of bitter.

Jamie stands, eyes averted. "I'll go check on the kids." We sent them to another room to play with Jasmine's scavenged toys while we spoke.

"How is she?" Mikayla asks once she's gone.

"Better than you'd think," I say.

"So what's the plan?" Ben asks. "Talkeetna?"

Kyle nods. "What else is there? Can't stay here."

"What were you planning to do for the winter?" Mark asks.

"We've been stockpiling as much as we could," Ben says. "There's a back way down into the potato fields at the Safe Zone. We used the last of our gas to load up the truck and now we've been going by bike. We fill up bike trailers and bring them back."

"We were going to be pretty sick of potatoes by spring," Mikayla says with a soft smile. "But we thought we'd move into the Safe Zone once they froze. It looks like the survivors left quickly. I'm sure they left behind food, like we did."

"There's got to be fuel in there, too," Ben says. "The rest of the city is dry."

"And ammo, for hunting," Liz says. "We tried to get in there once. I'm not trying that again without an army. Or at least not without Zeke."

Zeke bellows. He and Liz have always been friends who admire each other's badassery. "Well, we think we've got enough gas to get two vehicles to Talkeetna," Zeke says. "We don't want to hit Anchorage in the dark, so we'll take two nights to get there."

As the sun goes down, we light the lanterns, close the drapes and I ready my toothbrush. "You have any mouthwash left?" Nelly asks, and proceeds to tell the others about my dousing Peter in mouthwash. By the time he kneels and mimes my panic, they're in tears.

Sorry, I mouth to Peter and wiggle what's left of the bottle. He answers with a shake of his head and upturned mouth. I'm lucky he finds me amusing most of the time, since he's stuck with me for as long as we have the kids. Actually, I'm lucky just to have him at all.

CHAPTER 45

I sit to play with Bits's hair on our mattress while they go over tomorrow's route one more time. It's damp with sweat. I press my lips to her cheek and call Peter over. "She has a fever."

He kneels with his hand on her neck. "You feel okay, baby girl?"

"Not so much," she says. "My chest hurts and my throat is sore."

I know it's probably a run-of-the-mill fever, but I remember the runny eyes and coughing of Boss's men. It could have been from their diet, or a cold, the flu or even something worse. The fact that I can't name what it was scares me. I tend to overreact when it comes to Bits, but I can feel the reach of those men hundreds of miles away. If they manage to kill her too, I might lose my mind. "Let's give her some antibiotics."

"They won't work if it's a virus," Peter says.

"I know, but..." I don't want to alarm her, but I'm going to pump her full of everything we've got just in case. Peter acquiesces and helps Jamie figure out a dosage.

Bits swallows a pill, takes her ibuprofen and asks, "Do I have to brush my teeth?"

"No, sweetie," I say. "Just curl up with me."

She's asleep immediately. I brush her hair away from her face and hope the medicine does its job. Peter lies on Bits's other side and I whisper, "Why don't you sleep with Hank? You don't want to catch this."

"Neither do you," he says, and stays put.

Bits kicks off blankets and coughs all night, and I give up on sleep to watch her by lantern light. Before dawn, Peter sits up like he's been shocked out of sleep.

"Bad dream?" I ask.

He runs a hand down his face. "Yeah. What are you doing?"

"I can't sleep."

"It's just a fever." Peter leans against the wall, shoulder touching mine. "She'll be fine, I promise."

"You can't promise things like that," I say, angrier than I ought to be. "You promised you'd come back before, when there was no way to be sure."

"But I did come back."

"It doesn't matter. You can't promise—"

Bits coughs, a deep sound full of phlegm, and sits up choking. Peter holds her while she gags and throws up last night's dinner. I run to the kitchen for a bowl, but by the time I'm back she's asleep on Peter's chest. The next coughing spell wracks her body until even Peter looks alarmed.

The thermometer reads almost 105 degrees. I look to Jamie, who's been woken by the coughing along with everyone else. "Can I give her more ibuprofen?" She nods and brings me the bottle. It wasn't full to begin with, and now it's less so.

I measure out the dose and hold the cup to where her head lolls on Peter's arm. "Bits, wake up. You have to take some medicine. It's the good stuff."

Bits rouses enough to swallow and sinks back into sleep. Jamie takes the cup and says, "It's okay. She probably just has the flu." I think but don't say that people die from the flu every year.

We load up early, and I tuck Bits next to Adam on the VW's bed. "I'm sorry, Adam. I know you don't need any germs on top of a bullet hole."

He squeezes me with his good arm. "Don't worry about that. Just take care of Bitsy for us."

"I had the flu one time, Cassie," Hank says. I half wanted him to ride in the truck so he doesn't catch this, but I kept him with me in case we get separated. "I was so sick it was crazy, but they just said to drink lots of water and juice." He thinks for a moment. "Well, we don't have juice, but we can give her water."

I kiss his cheek. I want juice for Bits—juice and doctors and my mother here to tell me that I was sick like this too, once, and everything turned out fine.

The mountains in the distance are the same brown peaks as yesterday. A few hours in, we stop at a rocky beach on an immense blue lake. I make a compress using the icy water, careful to filter it first, and rub Bits's skin to cool her down. She mumbles in her sleep and kicks at me in a foggy, mindless way. But this is what the book says to do, so this is what I'm doing even if she pummels the shit out of me. I murmur softly and take her temperature again—the medicine has barely made a dent.

The previous group who rode in the pickup bed has raw noses and looks desperate for warmth, which means my time has come. "I'll go first," I say to Peter. "She can have more medicine in a half hour. Rub her with the cold water even if she yells at you, okay?"

"Let me go," he says.

"I just want to get it over with."

"I'll do yours so you can stay with Bits."

It's too long to be out in this weather, which has taken a turn for the worse and looks like rain. I almost take him up on his offer, but he doesn't want to spend hours away wondering about Bits any more than I do. "That's okay, thanks."

Adam kicks Nelly, who's perched at the end of the bed, hard enough to make him grunt. "I'll take your turn," Nelly says with a sigh.

"You already went. You don't have to take mine for me."

"I'll never hear the end of it if I don't," Nelly says. He raises an eyebrow at Adam, who nods and pats the bed for me to stay.

"I'd do it if I could," Adam says. "So think of it as my turn. And you can't say no to me. I've been shot."

"Thank you, Nels," I say. "And Adam, of course." Nelly grumbles and rubs my head as he leaves. Of course he rubs it harder than he needs to, but it's a friendly noogie.

"These mountains are amazing," Adam says once we're rolling.

I have to crane my neck to see the cloudy sky now that we're surrounded by mountains. The two-lane road barely fits in the space between peaks and lake. It's absolutely stunning, but it also feels secure to be encircled by mountains this enormous.

"It's like a giant bear hug from nature," I say.

"That was one of the stranger things you've ever said," Peter says over his shoulder with a laugh. "But it does."

He turns on the wipers to clear the drops of rain that have begun to hit the windshield. "Poor Nelly," I say.

Adam waves off my concern. "He's fine. He would've offered anyway. And if he didn't, he would've ruminated on it until he felt so guilty that he stopped us to switch."

"You know him well. He's the best pain in the ass ever."

"He is." Adam rests back on his pillow with a suppressed wince. He doesn't complain, but a bullet in the shoulder must hurt like crazy.

"You're good for him. You're what he was looking for all along. It just took the zombie apocalypse to make it happen."

I think of what Dan once said—that maybe this happened so the people who belonged together would find each other. I don't really believe it—not after losing Adrian—but it makes for a nice story when people like Nelly and Adam find true love.

"We're good for each other," he says.

"The way it should be. Now get some rest while your boyfriend freezes his butt off."

Liz, Zeke and Margaret sit in varying levels of comfort on the floor and seats. Except for Hank, no children, parents of children or pregnant people are allowed in the sick bus. I watch the passengers in the pickup's bed fight a losing battle to keep the tarp they use for shelter out of the wind's grip. It must be miserable out there. Everyone in our nice warm bus exclaims when the rain changes to snow flurries and the fat, white and, in all probability, cold flakes spiral through the air and under the flapping tarp.

I put my hand to my mouth. Nelly is never going to speak to me again.

CHAPTER 46

W e've gone farther than we'd anticipated due to our early start. This part of Alaska is so empty that it seems we could drive all night safely, but the icy rain coming down could cause hypothermia and we'd hit Wasilla before dawn. The suburb of Anchorage is probably infested and therefore better traversed in daylight.

We slow at two mailboxes, the only sign of life we've seen for miles after the tiny town an hour back. The long dirt driveway ends at two hunting camps, one of logs and the other red clapboard. The doors are unlocked, nothing of value inside. Each has an old woodstove, a scuffed dining set and empty bed frames. A cord of wood sits out back with an outhouse.

"What do you say we split up tonight?" Zeke asks the assembled crowd. "Same as the vehicles."

"As long as I get out of this rain, I'm good," Nelly says. His cheeks are raw and his hair has gone crazy, but he winks when I blow him a kiss. He'd insisted on staying in the truck for Peter's turn and wouldn't budge when Peter argued. He stands over the stove while I build a fire in the log cabin. "How's Bits?"

"The same," I say. The dry kindling lights immediately, as do the logs, and in a few minutes the heat begins pushing out the cold. I stare into the flames and think of all the things that could go wrong with a sick little girl.

"Hey, Half-Pint," Nelly says in a firm voice. I look up, and he says, "Stop stressing."

"Sometimes I think if I consider every bad thing that *could* happen, it won't come true. Like the opposite of jinxing."

"Reverse jinxing? I'll have to try that. How's it working so far?"

"It's got about a fifty percent success rate, if I'm lucky. So not at all, I guess."

He pats my head. "That's what I figured."

It's tight with nine people in our cabin, but cozy with the roaring fire and lantern and giant cup of tea. I sit at the bottom of the bed frame and cringe whenever Bits coughs in her sleep. She'll be warm tonight—that's got to be better for her than cold, damp air.

We eat boiled potatoes with the jar of salsa, which is better than the plan we had to mix the baby formula into mashed potatoes. One sniff of the vitamin-saturated powder made us decide to save it for when we're really desperate. I mix some with hot cocoa mix and manage to get a few sips down Bits's throat, but she's so unresponsive I give up or risk choking her. Hank drinks his down and proclaims it a little weird but chocolaty.

Mikayla refastens her short ponytail and sinks against Ben. "I wish we'd gone to the hot springs. You guys are so clean."

I'd rather have made it across the country without losing five people along the way, but I know she doesn't mean it that way. "Tomorrow you'll get a shower, maybe. They have to have some way of washing."

"Less than a full day's drive," Zeke says from his chair. "Might get a little dicey in Wasilla, but we'll go around as much as possible."

"There's not another way to Talkeetna?" Ben asks.

"There is, but it's a gravel road," Peter says. He sits on the floor with coffee in one hand and the other on Bits. "It would add hundreds of miles and we don't have enough gas."

Liz shoots out a sinewy arm. "We'll blast our way through Wasilla. We've made it this far, right?"

"Famous last words," Peter says, and barely smiles when the others laugh. He doesn't feel like laughing any more than I do, I guess.

I find it hard to be anxious about tomorrow when my thoughts are consumed by Bits's rumbling chest. We've given her a child's dose of cough medicine, but her coughing continues unabated.

Our beverages consumed, we get in bed. I squeeze in with Bits and Peter sleeps on the floor with Hank. Just before the lantern is extinguished, Peter reaches for my hand. I hold tight, our hands resting on Bits, and pray into the darkness that somewhere up there someone gives enough of a crap to not punish us by taking her away.

☆☆*☆*

I insist on taking my turn in the pickup and go first to get it over with. Bits drank a little of the hot cocoa this morning before passing out, but her fever is still set to broil instead of bake. Nelly sits with his arm around me as we yell over the wind. The rain and flurries have cleared up, thankfully.

"Look at those," Nelly says. White-capped mountains stretch south and east and west of us under a bright blue sky. Nothing's getting past them without a whole lot of trouble, and Lexers don't go in for a whole lot of trouble unless they see people.

"You know what I keep thinking?" I ask.

"What?"

"Adrian and I wanted to drive to Alaska. He would've had a heart attack at all of this." I wave my arm at the scenery. Nelly nods—he knows how fanatical Adrian was about mountains. "He would've been pointing and almost running off the road. I would've driven him crazy pumping the imaginary brake on the passenger's side, until I finally flipped out and demanded the keys."

Nelly laughs so loud that everyone in the truck looks our way. "That is totally how it would have gone."

"I know. But it still would've been amazing."

Nelly hugs me to his side. I miss what could have been, but it's the gentle ache I've grown used to. Most of all, I miss having him to hold on to when it feels like everything is collapsing around me. And with Bits sick, that's exactly how I feel.

My shift over, I get in the VW. Bits wakes coughing and I clean the horrible-looking stuff she brings up. I've never seen someone so limp with fever, and I cross my fingers that by the end of today we have a doctor to see to her.

The houses and businesses are spread out when we slow at what was to be our turnoff onto a less traveled road. It looks like half of Anchorage used this road as a getaway route, and most of the cars are still here although the bodies have wandered away. We luck out at the main road, where someone has taken advantage of its width and the parallel train tracks to create a travel lane. Last year's bodies hang out of cars and lie on the road, along with the ones that are milling about. Not a ton, but it's more than we've seen since Whitehorse.

Hank raises a shaky finger to his glasses when we pass a large group of Lexers. I'm glad Bits can't see them. Let her think we made the trip just fine and that there's nothing below us when we get to Talkeetna. I can see there's a lot below us, even if the winter did kill off half of them, and there will be plenty next summer.

"This map sucks," James says via radio from the truck. "We're going to have to stay on this road."

We pass strip malls and dead traffic lights. An ice cream shack and motel. As long as we keep moving, the Lexers can't get close. They converge on the road behind us, a slow-moving swarm of bodies and grunts, and I wonder how long they'll follow before they forget we were here. I breathe a sigh of relief when the businesses become fewer and farther between.

"Seems like there should've been more," Zeke says. "Where'd they all go?"

CHAPTER 47

His question is answered on a semi-rural stretch of highway, where a whole bunch of undead Wasilla waits around a bend. Zeke manages to swerve around the pickup rather than hit it when it skids to a stop.

"Where do we go?" Peter yells into the radio.

I hear James's curse through the truck windows. He points back, the obvious choice, and Zeke reverses to an access road. We take it a quarter mile west, paralleling the highway, and stop when it hits a gravel road that dead ends fifty feet to our right.

"Christ!" Zeke says. He spins the VW around.

Lexers make their way onto the road from the woods. All that separates us from that pod on the highway is a few hundred feet of trees. I hold Bits in place while Zeke slams on the gas and trails the truck up a steep driveway to a house built into the hill. The garage doors are at ground level but, thankfully, the front door is on the second level and can only be reached by stairs. Peter gathers Bits in his arms and Hank drags Sparky from under a seat. I grab the closest bag and race up the stairs. Zeke and Nelly open the door with a splintering of wood and enter with their weapons out. It's empty.

I look out before the door slams. The Lexers are at the base of the driveway and moving up the hill. Once everyone's in, James severs the cords that attach the stereo and TV to the wall and he and Mark drag the entertainment center to the door.

Ben looks out the window. "They're coming, but I don't think they know where we went."

Footsteps close in. As long as we're quiet, they might leave. It could take days, but it's possible they'll go. I won't think about the fact that most everything we need is outside—water, food, extra ammo. Jamie raises a finger to her lips and Jasmine nods, eyes two dark orbs. Nelly leads Adam to a chair and stands over him. We're all on alert, heads cocked. Even Barnaby doesn't need to be told to be quiet.

Bits lets out a cough that must be heard outside because the moans grow in volume. Peter hugs her to his chest to muffle the sound and nods when I point to what I think is the basement staircase in the foyer. This level of the house is the kitchen and living room, with a hallway that might lead to bedrooms. We pass the garage door landing into an unfinished basement. A couple of high windows at ground level let in enough light, even through overgrown grass, to see boxes, bikes and tools.

Peter sits on the concrete floor and cradles Bits in his arms. She's stopped coughing for the moment. Her next doses of medicine are in the VW with everything else. I sit with my head on my arms and wait for the next round of coughing or the breaking glass that'll mean they're coming in. Peter nods when I look up, like everything will be all right, but this is not all right. Not at all.

Twenty minutes later, Penny pads down the stairs and kneels by my ear. "They're still out there, but they don't know where we are."

As if on cue, Bits coughs for a minute straight. Her clothes are soaked and her body shakes with chills. I take off my coat for a blanket. Penny disappears upstairs and returns with blankets stripped from the house's beds. I sit under them next to Bits and Peter, staring at the box labels I can't read in the dim. After what seems like forever, Nelly and James come down with a mattress they set on the floor. Peter tucks the covers around Bits and props her head on a pillow. Everything is done silently—the most important game of *Who Can Be the Quietest* we've ever played.

I return to the main level. The house is from the seventies and the furniture isn't far from that decade, either. Margaret's in the kitchen, gingerly opening and closing cabinets. She points to the counter, where a few cans of soup, the end of a bag of bleached flour and four boxes of macaroni and cheese sit. The few bags that made it in add some small boxes of cereal and two old protein bars to our larder.

The others move around the house, gathering blankets and pillows from the bedrooms and setting them on the shag carpeting. I visit the smoked-mirror bathroom, use the dry toilet and search for anything vaguely medicinal. I come up with expired cough medicine and Tylenol. I can crush the pills, maybe, to bring Bits's fever down. It's what I'd been doing with her antibiotics once she found it too difficult to swallow. I have to hope that they're still in her system, if indeed they're doing anything at all.

Back in the basement, I grind a pill with a hammer. Peter opens Bits's mouth for me to dump it in. I follow it with the cough medicine and coerce a bit of water down after. I find a lantern, some citronella candles, two sleeping bags and a camping stove in a box labeled *camping*, but no propane. I leave one sleeping bag and candle and bring the rest upstairs.

Sheets are hung over the blinds with thumbtacks, making the room and its plaid furniture a ghostly blue. The steady drone of Lexers seeps through the closed window. I lift a corner of fabric to find it's worse than I thought—well over a hundred roaming around the driveway and sniffing at the vehicles, with who knows how many on the road. The backyard is no better. One bumps into the swing set's glider, which hits another in the behind and knocks it to its knees. It would be funny if the situation wasn't so bleak.

But I won't be hopeless. They aren't banging in the doors. Right now they're hanging around and are bound to move at some point. Or they'll freeze, maybe soon, with the way the weather's been. I can hear Bits coughing, but it's almost inaudible if I weren't listening for it.

Kyle gives every weapon we have a once-over and lines them up on the kitchen table. Thankfully, we all wear our guns, my tomahawk is on my waist and Mark had the presence of mind to grab his bow. I grab every decent-sized knife out of the wooden block on the counter and set them with the rest. Kyle nods and returns to his work, Nicki crouched at his feet.

I kiss the top of Hank's head before I follow Jamie and Liz to the basement, where they work on getting water from the water heater. Jamie leaves behind a container for us and brings the rest upstairs.

"What's happening?" Peter whispers from where he lies next to Bits on the mattress.

I crouch next to him. "They're everywhere but not trying to get in yet."

"What's the plan?"

"Wait it out."

Peter lifts the blankets. I crawl in and turn on my side. "Bits kicks whenever I touch her," he whispers in my ear. "So stay on this side."

It's not as loud down here, nor is it as cold, although there's only a few degrees difference. I listen to the distant hum of the dead people on the lawn, and when evening comes I find three good-sized rags, hang them on the window frames and light the candle with the lighter I keep in my pocket. Dan's unicorn is in there, too, the same way I carried the ring from Adrian last summer. It's still on my right ring finger, the silver star shining gold in the candlelight. The thought that I'm forever meant to carry reminders of people I've left behind makes me weary. But the unicorn is for Bits, and I'll be damned if she isn't going to get it.

I crush another pill and ready her cough syrup. Her forehead may be a tiny bit cooler. She gags on her medicine and rolls away gasping for air. I pound her back with cupped hands the way my mother did when I had a chest cold, but it's too loud. If I had access to heat, I'd boil water so she could breathe in the steam. It seems there's always a reason we can't get what we need or do what would be best, and I'm so sick of it I want to scream.

Her coughing tapers off to a whimper and rattling chest. I lie down next to Peter, so tired I can hardly breathe myself, and fall asleep.

CHAPTER 48

Another full day passes with even more Lexers holding a semi-silent vigil. Barnaby visits us throughout the day, as do some of the others, but I barely listen to their hushed voices. I put cut newspaper in a bin for Sparky's litter box. She doesn't leave Bits's side and neither do we. Bits's chest is a symphony of noises now. A low, deep moan, a high-pitched wheeze and a slight rattle. The rattle scares me most of all.

There may not be much food to eat, but I'm not hungry and send it up to Penny and Hank. I don't know how long we can live without food, how long before we'll be too weak to fight our way out if we have to. But all of that is a distant concern. I hold Bits when she coughs and watch her breathe when she's still. She's so still.

I think about her dying. I'm not sure I would care if the Lexers found a way in after that. I'm completely embroiled in a game of reverse jinxing when Peter lights the candle and says, "You should sleep."

"*You* should sleep," I say.

"You first."

"No. What if she stops—" I may reverse jinx in my head, but saying it out loud is too real.

"We'll take turns." He must see something in my face because he says, "You know I'll watch her just as carefully."

I trust Peter with my life and even more so with Bits's, but I can't relinquish control over this situation. "You sleep. I'll wake you."

"No," Peter says. "Because I know you won't."

"She wants to look at the stars. That's not so much to ask—just to want to see the fucking stars, is it?" Peter shakes his head, candlelight reflecting in his damp eyes. I'm torturing him the way I'm torturing myself. "I'm sorry."

"She'll be all right," Peter says.

"Promise?" I shouldn't ask, but I want so desperately for it to be true.

"Promise."

Peter sits at the head of the bed and pulls me to him, arms around my waist. We watch Bits, my hand resting lightly on her chest. Neither of us suggests sleep. His chest rises when Bits's does, as though he's taken on the role of breathing for her. I'm doing it too, and I'm light-headed, which could mean she isn't getting enough oxygen. We sit until the basement windows are gray with morning light and I no longer think it's my imagination that her breathing is less labored.

The pounding starts just after dawn. Peter runs upstairs and returns a few terrifying minutes later. "Something fell," he whispers. "They should stop soon."

Bits croaks, "Cassie?"

I cover her mouth, although I've never been happier to hear someone say my name. "Shh, they're outside."

"Water?" she whispers. I hold the bottle to her mouth and she drinks, watching me with round eyes.

"Are you hungry?" I ask. She opens her mouth but thinks better of it and nods.

"Feeling better, Freckles?" Peter asks.

She nods again and her cracked lips rise. I want to shout my thanks, but I kiss her and go upstairs, where everyone's listening to the havoc outside. I mime a spoon to the mouth and whisper, "Her fever's gone."

I'm flashed sixteen silent but huge smiles, of which Hank's is the largest. I squeeze his shoulder and open the can of chicken noodle soup Penny's pointed out. It sits on the counter next to macaroni and cheese noodles soaking in a pot of cold water. I add water to some of the soup to create an unappetizing mixture of clumps of congealed broth and noodles.

Back in the basement Bits is propped up, a tiny shadow with even darker shadows under her eyes. She takes a sip off the spoon I hold and grimaces. It may not be delicious, but the smell of the soup has reminded me of how hungry I am—hungry enough to want cold, not fully uncondensed soup. Peter relights the candle and holds the bowl over the flame until it's a little warmer than ice. She finishes the bowl and is asleep in seconds. It's a healing sleep, though, not the restless one of the past days. Peter and I watch her breathe, this time in relief.

***

By nighttime, I'm starving. Two boxes of macaroni and cheese spread between nineteen people is little more than a tease. And macaroni soaked in cold water with powdered cheese on top is a chewy, disgusting tease. Baby formula has begun to seem appealing.

The Lexers are still outside. We've lived in silence for so long that part of me wants to shout just to be sure I still can. I've strained my eyes reading a crime thriller and taken Barnaby for his walk to one of the bedrooms, where he guiltily pooped on the floor. I didn't dare tell him he was a good boy, just gave him lots of quiet love when he was finished.

Before dark, the pounding starts again. I hear glass shatter and run upstairs to find it was a garage door window, but it would take a lot more agility than Lexers possess to get through those high windows. Bits is asleep, still coughing but bouncing back quickly. Nelly sits with me and Peter now that Adam's asleep. He's not afraid of catching whatever it is Bits has; he says he's immune to everything. And barring that infection last year, I've never seen him so much as sniffle. The only good thing—and I mean only good thing—about the pounding is that we can speak quietly in the basement where our voices are muffled. Nelly deals himself in on solitaire while Peter sits with his chin in his hand and a far-off look on his face.

"Whatcha thinking about?" I ask.

"Food," Peter says. "And how much I want some."

Nelly groans. "Could we not talk about food?"

"Okay," I say. "Let's talk about other things we want."

"What could you possibly want besides food?" Peter asks.

"A pair of comfy pajamas and—"

"Like those ugly pajama pants you always wore?" Nelly asks, and slaps one card over another. "Those were sexy."

"The blue ones?" Peter asks.

"God, they were hideous," Nelly says.

"Can you guys let me have my fantasy here?" I ask. "When it comes to pajama pants, comfort trumps sexy any day. Anyway, I want to get in my *unsexy* pajama pants and watch a movie. You can come if you don't make fun of my pajamas."

Peter stretches and cracks his knuckles. "What movie?"

"We're watching *Groundhog Day* or *The Big Lebowski*. Or a romantic comedy."

"You're incapable of watching a movie without eating."

"So make me some food. What's it gonna be?" I ask. "We'll hang out at your place with your big-ass TV."

Peter's eyes light up. "I'll grill steak on the terrace."

"Stop," Nelly says.

Peter cooked me a lot of food, steak included, and nothing he ever made was bad. "With those green beans?"

"The sautéed ones?"

I drop my head back in ecstasy. "Yes. And I'll bake bread because my bread kicks your bread's ass."

"True," Peter says. "I'll get that Irish butter with the sea salt."

"Why are you doing this?" Nelly asks. "Really, why?"

Peter watches me with a half-smile. I wink and say, "Popcorn dripping with butter. Gummy worms."

"You're pure evil," Nelly says.

"And Pepsi for you, Nels." Nelly sighs. "And croissants for breakfast?"

Nelly looks up from his cards, light flickering on his leer. "Oh, are you staying the night?"

Nelly should know better than to allude to things like that, and his grin says he's getting a kick out of it. I stare at him until he gives me an innocent shrug and continues his game. Thankfully, Peter looks untroubled by Nelly's remark.

I sink back, stomach growling. "My stomach is eating itself. Nelly's right. Game over."

After I've yawned twenty times, Nelly stacks his cards. "Are you trying to tell me something? Okay kids, I'm heading to bed."

Once he's climbed the stairs and we're in bed, I ask Peter, "Do you think they'll ever stop out there?"

"Oh, they'll stop at some point. Maybe when they freeze and we're long dead, but they'll stop." I elbow him. He reaches across me to rest a hand on Bits. "You're shivering."

"I don't know if you noticed, but it is late autumn in Alaska, which is probably more like early winter everywhere else."

Peter turns on his side so I can fit into him. After a minute he says, "I'm eating your hair."

I choose to ignore the fact that my hair must smell vile and say, "Well, it's better than that macaroni and cheese. Want me to tie it back?"

He twists my hair loosely and tucks it between us, then brushes it back from my temple. "No, it's fine. Leave it down."

Peter used to like my hair. He'd curl a wave around his finger and let it pop back into place, tug on it when I walked ahead of him, and stroke it as we fell asleep like he's doing now. Maybe it's Nelly's comment, or the fact that Ana should be here instead of me, that makes me feel a bit guilty for finding his touch so soothing, for wanting Peter close by. I close my eyes and think about how I slept with Nelly almost all of last spring and summer. This is no different. Our past doesn't mean we can't take comfort from each other.

CHAPTER 49

"There are fewer Lexers outside," Peter says in my ear. I wake with a start and headbutt him.

"Jesus!" he whispers, hand to his forehead while Bits giggles quietly.

"Shit, sorry. Have you not learned your lesson about waking me yet?"

"I'm using a pole next time. Kyle wants to scout out the road. I said I'd go, but only if you did. Liz is going."

"I'll go," I say. I don't see any other choice. We need to eat. We need to get to Talkeetna before it snows. Bits needs warmth and food to recover for good. I turn to her. "How's my sweetie-pie?"

"Good," she says. "But the water tastes like spiders."

Peter raises his hands. "I asked her how that's possible. It's old, but other than that it tastes fine to me. Taste it."

I swish around a sip from my bottle. It's not terrible, but it definitely has a musty aftertaste. "It tastes like basements and old ladies. I totally see what she means."

"Of course you do," Peter says. "Why did I even bother asking?"

I giggle along with Bits and bring her bathroom bucket upstairs to dump in the toilet tank. The two toilets stink, even with the bathroom doors closed. Another reason to get out of here—we're using pee to flush down what's in the bowl. I leave as quickly as possible, but there's no way to feel clean after that experience. I give everyone an update on Bits and find out that today's menu is just as lacking as the previous.

My stomach growls to the point of nausea when I think of the wafflecake mix and little boxes of Frosted Flakes that sit twenty feet from the door. Penny bustles around like she does when nervous, except that the cute little pregnant lady is lining up sharp knives and guns instead of knitting baby booties.

"Can I see Bits?" Hank whispers.

"I don't want you getting sick," I whisper. It's likely she was most contagious a few days ago, but having to watch another kid struggle to breathe would be more than I can take. "She can't wait, believe me." He wraps his arms around my waist. It may be the first real hug he's ever initiated with me, and I don't let go until he does.

I peek out the window. The light makes my eyes water after days of semi-darkness. Fifty or so Lexers are scattered around the house, with trees blocking our view of who knows how many on the road. I let the sheet fall and sit on the couch with Kyle. He'd had a befuddled look in his eyes for a while, but his gaze is sharp once again.

"So, what's the plan?" I ask.

"We'll go through the woods to that dirt road," Kyle says. "James says there's train tracks on the map that go right alongside. Maybe we can get out that way." He watches Nicki cut pictures from an old catalog with her good arm and rubs his face.

"We'll get her somewhere safe," I say. His jaw bulges when he nods. "You're such a good dad."

"She's my light," he says with a shrug, as if there's no other way to be. But not every father is like him. Mine was. Peter is. Not everyone is as lucky.

There's a thump from outside and then what sounds like a door rattling along with zombie noises. "We've got to get out of here," Kyle says. "Or else I'm gonna go *dinky dau.*"

"You're gonna go what?"

"My dad was in 'Nam. *Dinky dau* is what they called crazy over there. If I have to hear that sound," he gestures to the window, "for another twenty-four hours, I'm going to go crazy."

"I like that," I say. It even sounds crazy. "I don't blame you. It's not as bad in the basement."

Kyle crosses his arms over his wide chest. "They don't fucking stop."

"Well, you know what they say: Ain't no party like a zombie party, 'cause a zombie party—"

"Don't stop," Kyle finishes. His laugh is quiet, but it still catches Nicki's attention.

Nicki climbs on his lap. "What's funny, Daddy?"

"Oh, just something Cassie said, baby." He returns the kiss she bestows upon him with a smack of his lips.

"Cassie's funny," Nicki says.

"Cassie's *dinky dau,*" Kyle says. I punch him in his rock-hard side, which hurts my knuckles but doesn't make him flinch.

"*Dinky dau,*" Nicki repeats under her breath. "Cassie's *Dinky dau.*"

"Thanks," I say to Kyle.

"If the shoe fits," he says. I'd punch him again, but I'm going to need my hands later.

***

The clouds threaten rain, which would help to cover our noises in the woods. As long as it's not snow. We know from last year that snow alone isn't enough to freeze Lexers—you need days of temperatures where it consistently dips below freezing before they fully succumb. Snow and warmer temperatures will only make driving difficult or impossible.

I put on Ana's leather pants for warmth and protection, then layer as much as possible without restricting my movement. It's a delicate balance, which is why I spend half my life freezing my ass off. I give Nelly medication instructions and tell him to take care of Bits.

"Always," he says, and tweaks her nose. He'd tried to volunteer, but he's not quiet in the woods the way we are.

I hug Bits. "Be back soon, honey. Love you."

Bits nods and tightens her lips. I want to stay, but I'm sure-footed in the woods, if nowhere else. If the Lexers discover we're here, their moans will call back any who've left.

"Love you," Bits says.

"More than all the poop in the toilet?" I ask.

Peter heaves a sigh. But you've got to play to your audience, and my audience is amused by potty words. It sends her into a coughing spell, but she's smiling. I wanted that to be the last thing I saw.

"There's a whole lot of it," Nelly says. "If you're good, I'll take you up to see it later."

"Gross," she chokes out.

Peter says goodbye without being vulgar and we head upstairs to a side window close to the trees. Kyle cuts the screen rather than pop it out and attract attention. Liz does a quick check before saying, "Lexers to our left down the driveway. Stay low and head straight."

Liz drops to the crunchy grass and hurries into the trees. Kyle soundlessly follows, more agile than one would think. I check for any new threats before I meet them at the base of a tree. The leaves on the forest floor would be crunchy but for a recent rain that's made them a softer covering of mulch.

Peter moves to my side, takes my arm and moves his finger between us. I nod that I'll stay close. I roll my feet as we inch through the trees. Short, fast moves are sometimes better because they mimic animals, but animals don't hang around with zombies, so we use slow shuffles, although it's hard to go slow when your body is yearning to run. And although I'm worn-out and ravenous from the past couple of days, that's exactly what my feet want to do.

We avoid a few who linger by a tree to our right. Everyone freezes when a twig cracks under someone's foot and continues when there's no reaction. The moans are louder out here, more so as we near the road. Another twig cracks and a Lexer appears. I sink behind some brush and wait for it to pass, Peter's hand on my back.

Now that there are fewer trees between us and the road, we can see a few dozen Lexers near the base of the driveway about a hundred feet down. We could drive through those no problem. But it's a different story farther down the road, where it's packed with zombies in varying stages of decay—from riddled with mold to freshly-turned this summer. They haven't moved the way pods do, unless this isn't really a pod.

The days we've spent trapped have given us plenty of time to ponder why the road was blocked in Wasilla. The highway could have been cleared by survivors from Whitehorse, which would've attracted all the lone zombies to the area. For all the time I've spent around them, Lexers are still a mystery. Why some form into moving pods and some don't, how long the mold will take to kill them, and how the hell they exist in the first place are questions no one knows the answer to. No one I know, anyway.

Liz raises her eyebrows and points to the end of the road. The walk may be 500 feet, but it takes us twenty minutes of tiptoeing and skirting around Lexers to make it to where the gravel road begins. We saw the dead end the other day, but in our haste to turn around we hadn't seen the clearing that provides access to the train tracks but for a lone tree. The trunk is four inches in diameter, thick enough to damage a vehicle if it isn't cut down. But before we tackle the tree we need to take out the few Lexers between us and the tracks. And the only way to do that is to cross the road in plain sight.

It doesn't take them long to notice us once we leave the safety of the trees, and their noises seem to echo for miles. I bring the spike of my axe into one still wearing a coat and one thin glove and get the next with a side swing through its ear. When they're down, we sink into the trees along the tracks. Peter drops and creeps forward until he's resting on a railroad tie. He looks one way and then the other before crawling back.

He points east with a shake of his head and then says, "But west isn't bad. Maybe twenty. Spread out."

Kyle's head bobs. "Now how about that tree?"

We stare at the tree as if it might just suddenly up and move of its own accord. I hold up my axe in answer, but the impossible part is going to be chopping down a tree without bringing everything in a mile this way.

"Distraction," Liz says, and points to the woods that separate us from the highway. If someone made noise in there it would cover up the chopping. My axe is sharp; it shouldn't take that many blows to get the tree down, especially if Peter or Kyle wields it.

I point east. "It'll get them off the road, too."

"And surround whoever's in there," Kyle says.

"I'll go," Peter offers.

"Chop it fast and they won't have time to surround us," I say because I'm going with him. I hand Kyle my axe and stare Peter down. He's the one who volunteered for the job after telling me to stick close. Besides, if I stayed to chop down the tree, I'd probably cut off my own fingers. "We'll give you a few minutes before we circle north to the house."

Kyle passes me his machete. It weighs a ton and I'm more likely to drop it on my foot than lift it into a zombie's head. I hand it back and pull the knife from my belt. It'll have to do.

"Ready?" I ask Peter in a voice that sounds a lot less scared than I am. I've never purposely walked into the middle of a pod. Unless you count the quarry, which was in an ambulance and a completely insane idea.

Peter nods. "When you hear the first shot, start cutting."

We cross for the woods. Fifty feet in, Lexers stand singly and in groups. Some cross the forest floor while others sway with limp arms, waiting for something to interest them. They'll get it soon enough.

This side of the woods is noisier—leaves rustle underfoot and moans filter through the air—so we don't have to be as quiet. Still, we scurry from tree to tree and make a wide arc around a few dozen who wander in circles. I try not to count them, but I can't help it. We want to draw as many as possible our way, but every one we pass is one more we'll have to fight through to get back to the house.

It reminds me of being trapped in the woods with Adrian and Marcus, and I don't want to be the only one who makes it out this time. We crouch at a wide trunk and Peter points to a clump of trees on a small rise 400 feet east. We'll have to skirt around a lot of Lexers to get there, but it's far enough in that Kyle should have the time he needs.

Footsteps near. We press ourselves against the bark, barely breathing. Tattered jeans and the back of a head of matted, blond hair come into view. It stops for a moment and raises its head before continuing on.

Peter whispers, "Once they start coming, we run."

His heartbeat pulses in his neck, but he looks focused. Adrian was focused, right before he took off to save me. Peter wouldn't hesitate to do the same, and the thought of him running off is more terrifying than zombies.

"Together," I whisper. "Don't leave."

Peter grips my arm and leans close. "Never."

We dodge from tree to tree and slam through bushes when we're close. At the top of the rise, it becomes apparent just how many there are, and they all start toward us at Peter's yell. We space out our shots to keep their attention away from the distant hatchet thuds I think I hear.

They've closed in enough to cause panic, for me if not for Peter, and we run for a clear area of forest away from Kyle and Liz. I fire into the crowd, not caring if I hit, only that I make enough noise to keep them coming.

"Behind you!" Peter yells, and grabs my hand before I have time to fully take in the new group coming our way.

We run in the direction of the road, zigzagging through trees and over logs until we come upon a solid line of Lexers that blocks escape—a search party combing the woods. Peter drags me straight toward them. He's planning to hit them head-on. The Lexers move into thicker formation, but Peter doesn't stop and neither do I, although in a perfect world I'd sit him down for a discussion of what exactly doing something stupid entails. When we're five feet away, Peter yanks me down the line to an opening that wasn't there before, and we're through.

We slide through a muddy ditch and cross the road into the north woods. Lexers march down the gravel and struggle up the incline behind us, but the forest is clear except for a few buzzing around that we don't bother to kill. The cold air burns my lungs as we climb higher into the trees. The house is built on a hill; if we move up and to the west, we'll eventually find it below.

From our vantage point, we see that though many of them walk east to where Peter and I disappeared, plenty remain. The train tracks are still our best bet. We stop to catch our breath on a steep ridge. Peter's smile is bright against his smudged face. "We did it."

I don't want to count our chickens before they hatch, but this should be the easy part. Of course, that could be said about almost everything else in the past week. "We did it," I repeat with an answering grin. "Although I thought you'd lost your mind there for a minute. Thanks for pulling me through."

After I say it, I realize I could be thanking him for any number of things. He pulled me through Bennington, through Adrian's death, through thinking I was a horrible mother, through the four thousand miles of this trip, through the night when I thought for sure Bits was lost. Every time I come up against a wall, Peter opens a door.

"Not that you needed me to."

"I did," I say, and I mean it. "Let's get out of here."

We walk slowly, both to keep quiet and because my muscles aren't capable of much more. Strenuous exercise and the lack of food are taking their toll. I have a tickle in my throat which I want desperately to clear. We spot the house and pick our way down to the side window where Nelly's golden hair shines in the gloom. Only two Lexers remain at the base of the driveway.

Nelly hooks his hands under my arms when I struggle through the bedroom window. Once we're in he says, "The tree's down. We're ready to leave."

I collapse on the edge of the twin bed. It's afternoon, but as far as my joints are concerned it's bedtime. The mattress has been moved to the living room, but I could happily curl up on the box spring for a week.

"You okay?" Peter asks.

"I'm just tired." He furrows his brow when I stand and stagger. "C'mon, let's go."

CHAPTER 50

It's so easy it's mind-boggling. By the time we're in the vehicles and down the driveway, they've only just noticed us. We kick up gravel as we round the bend and bump onto the train tracks. I offered to ride in the pickup bed, and now my skull is about to crack open from the jouncing. It still might be better than the VW, which bounces along at a slant beside the tracks so it doesn't bottom out.

It's only a few hours to Talkeetna, and I can take a few hours of anything if the end means food and warmth and safety. I eat my mini box of Fruit Loops with my eyes closed and try to ignore the way my throat hurts when I swallow. My plan is to sleep for two days when we get there, after I eat some real food.

The bouncing ceases. I hear a cheer from inside the truck when we reach the highway and my head cheers by reducing its banging to bearable. I nestle in my blanket and sleep until Nelly's elbow hits my side. "Wake up, darlin'. We're turning onto the Talkeetna road."

We count down the distance. The town is fourteen miles from the turn, but we're bound to hit a fence sooner. I wish everyone were here for this moment. I've been plowing through, trying not to think about anything but making it here, and now all the losses press down on me. I've cried along the way, but I feel a doozy coming on once I'm through their gates.

We hit a guard house at a crossroads—a cabin high above the ground, same as ours at Kingdom Come. Two men and two women stand on its walkway and watch Zeke step from the truck.

"How are y'all?" he asks. "We're here from Vermont and Whitefield, New Hampshire."

The other two above wave while a man and woman climb down the ladder to stand in the road. The woman slings her rifle on her shoulder and sticks out a hand.

"I'm Patricia," she says. She's a couple of years older than me, with shoulder-length platinum hair and features that would be delicate if they hadn't just turned slightly bitchy. She looks us over, a line forming between her eyebrows.

The man is late thirties, with dark, almond-shaped eyes and dark hair tied in a short ponytail. He gives Zeke's hand a rough shake and says, "Terry. Glad to have you here." Patricia shoots him a look. He points two fingers up the road. "The gate's a mile ahead. They'll meet you up there."

He waves when we pull away. Patricia stands with her hands on her hips, mouth moving a mile a minute in Terry's face. I try to figure out what's wrong with us, but come up with nothing.

"She was nice," Nelly says.

We pass houses and a sign for an airport before we reach the chain-link gate with a log wall on either side. It heads west down a dirt road and ends at the railroad tracks a few hundred feet to our east. A thin man with a hook nose and a friendly expression swings open the gate. "Hey there. I'm Clark, but everyone calls me Eagle. Frank will meet you down at the brewery. Make a left on Main. You'll see the sign."

The two-lane street has wide shoulders that serve as sidewalks. Wooden houses that were once businesses now look more like living quarters. We're the only vehicles on the street, and the people walking stop to watch us pass. A few raise their hands.

We turn left at a small village green. Main Street is lined with everything from log cabins to larger wooden buildings, many with slightly rusted tin roofs. It could look dreary, but the overall impression is of a quirky, welcoming village.

A man waits outside a blue two-story building whose sign says *Talkeetna Brewery*. Rooms, a few the color of freshly sawed wood, grow off it in all directions. The man's skin is tough like he's been around a lot of Alaskan winters; he could be anywhere in his forties to sixties. He folds his arms as we step out. I take Bits's hand. She still looks ill, and I'm worried they'll accuse us of bringing Bornavirus to their Safe Zone.

"I'm Frank," the man says. "How many are you and were you wanting to stay?"

"Nineteen," Mark says in a friendly tone, as if the man's question hadn't been curt and bordering on rude. "And, yes, I believe you spoke to John at Kingdom Come and told us we'd be welcome? The Vermont and New Hampshire Safe Zones were both compromised by the large pods—you must have heard of them."

"We've heard of them," Frank says. "But we have a problem. Why don't you send whoever's in charge inside so we can talk?"

We look around for the person in charge until finally Zeke says, "Why don't you tell us your problem?" He crosses his arms in a mirror of Frank's stance, mouth a line under his beard.

"We can't take in anyone else. We've got a lot of the Whitehorse Safe Zone here."

James draws himself up to his full height. He's thinner than usual, but he manages to loom over Frank, and he most definitely isn't calm. "Are you fucking kidding me?"

Bits whimpers and begins to cough. Frank tries to speak over her coughing but finally gives up and waits it out with a blank expression.

"There's no room?" Peter asks, hand on Bits's shoulder.

"There's room," Frank says. I'm thinking he could look a little more apologetic about the fact that we've driven 4,000 miles to get here and are being told we can't stay. I'm also thinking I'd like to punch him. "There's not enough food. We're short food for forty of our people. Add in another nineteen and we'd be cutting it too close."

Penny steps forward. "We have seeds, and potatoes that could be used for seed."

"That's all fine and good come the spring." Frank speaks quickly as a man and a woman exit the restaurant and walk to his side. "But it won't do us much good in March when we're starving."

"Well, we don't have food, but we have a dentist." Mikayla gestures at Zeke and then points to James with her smile that's never failed to make a friend. "And he's an expert with solar. We can set up greenhouses. Ben knows farming and the rest of us have been doing this for a year. We're not here to just eat your food. We'll work..." She trails off when he shakes his head.

"There are houses on the other side of the fence," Frank says. "You're more than welcome to stay there and hunt for your food, set up however you want. But we can't help you. I'm sorry."

I drag Bits toward the VW. I'm not going to beg to live in this stupid town. We'll walk to Anchorage if we have to, where we can winter over and find supplies after the Lexers freeze.

"Cassie, where are you going?" Peter asks.

I spin around. "We're leaving. Fuck this shitty little town." Frank looks at me with raised eyebrows. I glare at him. "If you'd shown up in Vermont we would've taken you in. We would've figured it out."

"We sure as shit wouldn't have told you not to let the gate hit you in the ass," Zeke says.

The woman to Frank's left tries to speak, but I cut her off. "You don't know what we went through to get here. We lost people. We couldn't save them, but this—" I wave my hand at the kids, "*this* will be on you."

I suppose I've just effectively killed any chance we have of living here, but I enjoyed seeing Frank blanch like I'd hexed him. I set Bits in the VW. She closes her eyes, pale and drawn. She needs to be warm and fed. I'm so angry I want to kill everyone here and take over the place myself. Hank follows, then Peter and Penny. Zeke opens the truck's door and Liz hops in the bed. We should've gone to northern Canada, where we'd probably already be dead, but at least we would have died with people who gave a shit we were dying.

The woman comes forward, hands fluttering. "Whoa, whoa, whoa, slow down." She has soft wrinkles around her eyes—true laugh lines—and short gray hair tucked behind her ears. "Let's talk about this. We're a Safe Zone, Frank. And we're not a Safe Zone if we refuse to keep people safe."

"We don't have—" Frank begins.

"Shut up, Frank." She stretches a hand through the open door of the VW. It takes me a second to realize she's reaching for me. "My name's Glory. Please come inside and talk."

CHAPTER 51

It would've been stupid to refuse, which is how we've found ourselves inside what was once a brewing company and restaurant. The main room is full of booths and wooden dining tables, and the rooms beyond it look to be the same. It still smells of hops and something's cooking somewhere. My stomach growls when I perch on a barstool.

"Would you like something to eat?" Glory asks.

"The kids would," I say.

I would too, more than she'd believe, but I'm not taking anything from these people. I guess the others feel the same because no one takes her up on her offer. If they say we can stay, I'll have to for Bits's and Hank's sakes, but after Frank's greeting it's going to take quite a large gulp of my pride.

Glory walks into the kitchen area and returns. "They'll bring some food outside."

"Thanks," I mumble.

She removes her coat, under which she wears a long tie-dyed tunic and jeans. Her earrings jingle when her head swivels around the six of us who've come inside. My mom would've loved her, and I feel myself soften a bit at the kindness on her face. She perches on one of the tables next to the bar and leans forward. Frank and the other man, an older guy with a white moustache and bushy white brows, seat themselves at a table farther back.

"I just want to talk," Glory says. "We three don't make all the decisions, but we're the counsel for Talkeetna. I'm sorry that we started off on the wrong foot. Frank's our hotheaded one." Frank mutters, and she flaps a hand behind her without looking back. "Oh, Frank, you know I'm right. I'm the soft-hearted hippie." She points to the white mustachioed man. "And Bernie's the voice of reason." Bernie nods impassively and inspects us over his steepled hands.

"So talk," says Kyle, who looks more pissed than I am.

Glory walks behind the bar and raises a pitcher. She fills glasses and pushes one in front of me, Peter, Kyle, Zeke, James and Liz, then moves around the bar to her table. "At least have some water. We don't have enough food for the winter, but that's something that can be worked out."

"How about hunting and fishing?" Zeke asks.

Bernie speaks up. "We still get infected from Fairbanks and Anchorage. This summer we had several pods north and south of us. They scare away the game. We're hoping they come back when the snow starts or that we can get to the herds, but we can't count on it. The river was full of floaters and we're just now catching up on our fishing. There hasn't been a problem with eating the fish so far, but..."

"We met people who ate zombies," I say. Glory gasps and the men look sickened. "As long as they were cooked they didn't infect them."

"But it might've made them crazy," Kyle says with a glance at me. "They weren't right in the head."

"*Dinky-dau*," I say, to which Kyle snorts. He's getting the hang of this humor thing.

Zeke clears his throat. "Fish are fine as long as they're cooked."

"Good to know," Frank says, but he doesn't get up to embrace us.

"Let's come up with a plan," Glory says. "I know I won't send anyone away. And I know that Frank won't either. Right, Frank?" She rolls her eyes when he doesn't answer.

"There's a grocery store distribution center in Anchorage," Bernie says. "People lived in there last year, but a month or two later they were attacked by a pod. Most of them turned. It's full of food. We've been trying to get some more volunteers to go down before the snow—"

"The last group didn't make it back, except Terry and Patricia," Frank says. "It's impossible. No one's voluntee—"

"We lost a lot of good people," Bernie says. "And we don't want a repeat of that. We have the food divvied up, but we could factor you in for the next two months. If hunting doesn't pick up and food runs low enough that we don't think we can feed you through the winter, we might have to ask you to leave."

"I'd never ask you to leave," Glory says.

"It's only fair," Frank says.

"Why not wait until they freeze?" Zeke asks.

"It took a long time for them to freeze last year," Bernie says. "And once they did, we had too much snow on the ground. What we would have done was snowmachined down and killed them frozen, then hit the place in the spring, but we didn't know about it 'til this summer."

"And if we volunteered to go down there?" Zeke asks. "Would that give us some stake here?"

I'm not the only one who glances at Zeke in surprise. If we're going to do it, we should keep it all for ourselves. But we still wouldn't have a doctor or a safe place for the winter and, more importantly, spring.

"With that, we'd have enough through the winter and more," Bernie says with a nod. "No matter what, we'd take in your kids and the pregnant woman for good. But give it a lot of thought. It might be less risky to see what happens with the hunting." He stands. "I'm going to call Terry up from the guard house. He can fill you in."

In the ten minutes that we wait, a platter of bowls leaves through the front door—enough to feed everyone out there, I'm pleased to see.

"When is your friend due?" Glory asks.

"December," James says.

"I'm a midwife. I'd love to speak with her."

James sags against the bar, and I know this has clinched it—he's on board with whatever we'll have to do as long as it means Penny's safe. "We heard there was a midwife. The baby's moving fine, but we want to make sure everything's okay. She hasn't had much to eat in a couple of weeks."

"Are you Dad?" she asks, and gives a warm smile when he nods. "Well, she looks healthy. I'll take you both to my office after you get settled in?"

"That'd be great," James says.

Terry steps into the restaurant, hands in his pockets. "What's up? They said you wanted me."

Terry nods after Glory explains. "I was in the second group that went, and I knew one of the guys who'd lived there and managed to get out. I can tell you what to expect."

"Can you draw a map of what you remember?" James asks.

"Sure. I don't think it'll help much, but sure."

"We'd need gas," Zeke says.

"You'll need a truck, too," Terry says. "We have tractor-trailers, you have anyone that can drive one?"

"I can if you refresh my memory," Zeke says. "I used to spend a lot of time in one. Never drove it but once."

"No problem."

"How do we know you'll take care of the kids?" I ask Glory.

"I can only give you my word. We'll take care of your children, I promise. We'd never let them go hungry."

Frank strides to the restaurant door and slams it behind him. The three Talkeetna residents watch him go before Glory turns to us. "His son was in the second group."

"People are scared," Terry says. "Not even the food shortage scares them enough to volunteer."

Bernie strokes his mustache. "This would create some goodwill. Some residents won't be happy to find out you've arrived."

"But a lot of people will," Glory says. "Even if they won't join you, they'll be glad you're here. We want you here. Don't let Frank put you off."

Bernie nods. "When would you want to leave? We got a radio call from one of the islands that a storm is coming in. Either you should go tomorrow or wait a few days, up to you."

Kyle stands, hand on his machete, and faces us. "Tomorrow? I say we get it over and done."

I nod along with the others. Anticipation isn't going to make it any easier. Plus, my sore throat seems like it may be here to stay. If I'm getting sick, I won't be in any condition to help in a few days.

"Glory will show you the empty cabins," Bernie says. "I'll make sure everyone knows you've volunteered. You can still back out, no hard feelings."

There's silence while we look to each other. Liz shrugs. "Do we have a choice?" she asks us. "I mean, really?"

We do, but as usual the other option sucks. Zeke sticks out a hand and Bernie rises to grasp it.

✻✻✻

Glory gives us a short tour of the village and then directs us to where honey-colored log cabins sit in a grassy lot bordered by trees, with a sign that says *Denali Vacation Cabins*. "A few of these aren't occupied. They don't have running water, but you can use well or river water to flush to the septic." She laughs. "Most of the time. Otherwise, we have outhouses and composting toilets."

Bits and Hank scamper to the door of a small cabin that will hold the four of us, a dog and a cat. The decor is hotel rustic and has a comfortable couch, two easy chairs and a four-person table. A kitchenette sits to the right, with a downstairs bedroom to the left and a loft above.

"We could put ice in this in the winter, right? Like they used to?" Bits says of the little refrigerator. She dismisses the electric stove and microwave out of hand and points to the small woodstove. "And we can cook on there."

She's so thrilled that she's forgotten she's sick. It's what she'd envisioned, but she doesn't know what we have to do to keep it. She and

Hank run through the door off the living room, where a king-size bed is covered with a colorful quilt.

"Big bed!" Hank yells. They emerge and climb a ladder to the loft. Bits hangs her head over the rails and coughs up a storm before saying, "Two beds! This is where I want to sleep."

Hank bends over, finger on his glasses so they don't drop. "Me, too. This is cool."

I climb the ladder. Two twin beds are tucked under the eaves, each with nightstand and dresser. "We'll work it out," I say, and wish I could take pleasure in their excitement. "Let's talk for a minute."

They flop on the couch. Peter sits heavily in one of the chairs and leans forward, elbows on knees. "We have to go back to Anchorage for food because there isn't enough for winter. We leave tomorrow morning, and you two will stay here with Penny and Adam until we get back."

Hank's feet halt their tapping on the floor. "You mean they won't let us stay unless we get more food?"

"They will, but we'll have to leave if the food runs out," I say. "Whether or not we're here, we'll need that food to get through the winter." And I've been assured of the kids' survival. That alone makes it worth it.

"I don't want you to go," Bits says. The whites of her eyes are already pink. "Can't we go somewhere else?"

"There's nowhere else," Peter says. "We're almost out of gas. They're giving us enough to get to Anchorage and back."

"But you might not come b—" Bits begins before she starts to cry.

Hank lays a hand on her shoulder. "They'll be back. Don't worry, Bits."

"It'll be okay, Bitsy." I take her in my arms and try to think of something that won't be a lie. "Hey, we get a real dinner tonight. And we'll watch the stars—" I bite my lip; I almost said *one last time.*

✻✻✻

The last few hours have been spent mapping the route to the warehouse in the living room of one of the larger cabins. Under Terry's direction, I've sketched as much of the inside as he's seen or heard about from the man who had lived there and died on the first attempt at entry.

There's a row of loading bay doors that stretches the length of the building and approximately twenty aisles of shelves with a few skylights above. The residents moved pallets around to make private rooms in the open space between the doors and shelving, where the grocery stores' orders were assembled before being loaded onto trucks, back when there were things like orders and grocery stores. A fence of dismantled metal shelving was erected between the living quarters and shelves to keep the supplies from being pilfered. Apparently, the people who controlled the distribution center ruled with guns and demanded favors for extra food. When I think of what life must have been like in a dark, cavernous space filled with food and supposed safety, but where one was still in danger of death and starvation, I know I'd rather take my chances on the outside.

Terry picks up the drawing. "This is really good."

"Thanks," I say.

"Cassie's a painter," Nelly says.

"Yeah?" Terry asks. "There were a bunch of artists here. I know there are a lot of art supplies around. I could find some for you."

"That'd be great," I say. "If I'm alive to use them." Terry grimaces and looks away. I'd apologize, but I don't feel like apologizing. The only thing I feel like doing is going to sleep.

"So, if that's all you need from me, I'll get going," Terry says. "Dinner's in a half hour. I'll see you there."

We study the building for a few more minutes. We have no earth-shattering ideas. Basically, it's get inside, open the loading doors and kill them as they come into the parking lot, then finish off the ones trapped behind the fence.

The living room of this four-bedroom cabin is high-ceilinged, with comfy couches and a long dining table just off the full kitchen. One wall is made entirely of glass, but with its enormous area rug and muted colors it feels as cozy as my little cabin. I walk to a window. The grass courtyard between the houses isn't mown, but it's not overgrown, probably due to the goats I saw wandering when we came in. Talkeetna is the kind of town in which I'd want to live, full of cute, interesting houses tucked into the trees, but I don't want to like it here. I know I already do, and it pisses me off that I want to be somewhere I may not be wanted.

"If we can't get in, we'll figure out something else," Peter says. "We're not dying for these people."

"Fucking right," Zeke says. "We'll die for us, not them."

These are the people worth dying for. After four thousand miles, we've become an even larger family than I had before. I trust every single person here, and I know they trust me. And the faintest glimmer of faith pushes through the discouragement. We can do this.

CHAPTER 52

We head to the brewery for dinner. Terry told us that Talkeetna's population is close to 300 with the refugees from Whitehorse, and they need an overflow restaurant to serve all the residents. People on the streets watch us go past. A few say hello, but many look away. I'm irritated until it dawns on me that they might feel guilty for not volunteering. After all, this food will feed them, too. I can't blame them, as much as I want to be angry at somebody. I might not leave if I didn't have to.

Inside the brewery, the wood walls and festive atmosphere remind me of Kingdom Come, but the way the voices cease when we walk in doesn't give off the same vibe. Glory rises from a bench near the door. "Let's get you some food."

The food is set up on the bar and nearby tables. I take a plate and follow Bits and Hank, who chat happily, unaware of the stares or pretending they are. I slow at Patricia's glare from a nearby table.

"Calm down," Penny says from behind me, but she sucks her teeth in Patricia's direction.

"Hand me the Vaseline," I say, and pretend to tie my hair in a ponytail. "I'm about to go Brooklyn on someone." Penny shushes me while she laughs.

"What the hell are you two talking about?" Nelly asks.

"The older girls in our neighborhood would rub Vaseline on their faces, take out their earrings and tie their hair back so it wouldn't get pulled during a fight," Penny says.

"This I've got to see," Nelly says. "Go challenge someone to a duel."

We swordfight with our forks until he gets me in the side and I've forgotten about the people staring, most of whom have gone back to their meals. I head straight for a pot of soup, anticipating how good it'll feel on my throat, which is worsening by the second. Anytime after tomorrow is fine, but getting sick now would be the world's worst timing.

"Try the cornbread," Glory says. "We still have some cornmeal left. We tried growing corn this summer, but it's tricky up here. We saved seed for next year. Those greenhouses your friend mentioned would come in handy."

I want to tell her that we'd be happy to help out if we weren't dying tomorrow, but I know she means well. And my mother always said I'm notoriously cranky when I'm sick. The only thing keeping me from crying or yelling is that I refuse to show anyone in here how scared I am.

I grab a piece of cornbread and some butter. "You have cows?"

"Four, and two bulls. They came from Homer Safe Zone last year."

"Homer's still going?" My brain begins to hatch a plan of taking us all there in the gassed up vehicles tomorrow.

"They've moved off the coast now. I'm sorry—we're all that's left besides some people out in the bush that we trade with. And the islands, but getting there is next to impossible."

"Where should we sit?" Bits asks, eyes scanning the room.

"I saw some tables in the back room," I say. "This place is nice, right? And look at all that food!"

My tone sounds false to me, but she walks carefully past all the tables with a smile that most people return. Hank glances at me before we follow. "I'll take care of Bits, Cassie. Don't worry."

I can't swallow, and it's not because of my throat. I'd hug him if I wouldn't scald him with my soup. "I know you will, sweetie. But I want to take care of *you*, too."

His downturned face is hidden by his glasses, but a tear plops from his chin. The nearby tables have gone quiet. I set my meal on one of them and wrap him in my arms. "And if I can't, Penny and Adam will. You're not alone. I promise you're not alone, okay?"

He nods against my neck. I can feel the eyes of the diners on me when I retrieve my food, but none meets my gaze when I look up. I stand there for a second and walk away shaking my head. I don't expect them to come, but it'd be nice not to be treated like we're already dead.

I pull out the chair Peter's saved for me and sit facing the room, teeth gritted. "I see you've already made some friends," Nelly says.

I burst out laughing and the rest of the table joins in. You can always count on Nelly to bust up a perfectly good moment of rage. I taste the soup, which is so much better than the cold, uncondensed kind, and close my eyes at the warmth sliding down my throat. It makes swallowing worth it; otherwise, it's become agony. I attempt the cornbread but don't think I can get it down.

"Good luck tomorrow," Terry stops to say. He points to the couple behind him, both in their early thirties. "This is Tara and Philip."

The man is brown-haired and scruffy, with a friendly face and an upturned nose. The female counterpart is tall and willowy, with long, auburn hair and full lips. "Hi," she says. "We just wanted to say welcome."

Philip surveys the room, then turns back with his eyebrows up. "They're usually not like this, don't take it personally. We were in Whitehorse on holiday last year from Ontario. I guess we still are. But we hope you'll come around for a beer when you get back. I've got some put away."

We murmur how that'd be great. "They were nice," Peter says once they're gone.

"That's because they're Canadian," I say to make him laugh.

We finish our meals and are almost out the door when a voice booms, "Peter?"

A man stands at a table, hand on the head of a teenage girl with chin-length blond hair. Everything about him is square, from his broad shoulders and barrel chest to his head. But his formidable presence is canceled out by the friendly grin under his trim beard. I can count the number of times Peter has been flabbergasted on one hand, but whoever this is has made his mouth drop. He spreads his arms when the teenage girl launches herself into them and then swings her around.

"How did you end up here?" Peter asks after he's put her down and hugged the man. Another guy as square as the first, but with blond hair rather than brown, waits for his turn, looking just as delighted.

I think I know who they are, but it's unbelievable that we'd meet up with them on the other side of the country. Peter steps back from the trio. "This is Chuck, Rich and Nat. The people I stayed with in Vermont."

"The island people?" Bits asks.

"Uh-huh," Nat says, her small, pretty features alight. "And I know who you are—you're Bits, right?"

Bits nods, eyes huge. Nat laughs, a tinkling laugh that matches her little self completely, and says, "I've seen you before, you know. You just didn't see me." She bites her lip after her eyes scan the group—maybe she can see who's missing.

I feel a bit under scrutiny when Peter introduces me, but I move close to Nat. For once in this world, I'm going to get to do something I was sure would never happen. "I smell horrible," I say, "but I've been waiting a year to give you a hug for saving Peter's life."

She flings herself my way. "I feel like I'm meeting celebrities or something! I know all about you! Peter said you like to read. I have tons of books you can borrow."

I smile over her shoulder at Peter. He was right when he said she was nutty in a good way. Chuck elbows Peter. "Peter knows all about those books. Don't you, Pete?"

Peter laughs, completely at ease. I see him through their eyes, people who didn't know Peter before the world ended, and can tell how happy they are to be around him. He'd already changed before we parted in Bennington, but by the time he'd arrived at Kingdom Come his metamorphosis had been complete. Maybe finding that people liked him for nothing other than being himself had been the final stage.

"Wait a minute," Chuck says, brow wrinkled. "You're not the new arrivals who volunteered to go to the warehouse?"

Peter shrugs like it's no big deal, but I know the nuances of his body language well enough to see that his shoulders are weighted down with worry.

"Jesus." Chuck shakes his head slowly. "Come on back to our place. We need to catch up."

✳✳✳

Chuck, Rich and Nat live in a small log cabin with a green metal roof only a few blocks away. The furnishings are nicer than I expected—an overstuffed sage green couch with an expensive coffee table flanked by striped chairs. I remember what Peter told me about Rich's propensity for decorating and direct my comment to him. "Nice place."

Rich scratches his chin. "Thanks."

After they've lighted the lanterns, we sit and sip water. Rich offers us something stronger, but we decline because we don't need hangovers tomorrow. Ash has come with us, and she, Bits and Hank follow Nat to the loft, where the giggling is nonstop.

"So, tell me what's going on," Chuck says. He stands, arms folded and face impassive while Peter explains the deal we made. He reminds me of John, soaking in information quietly before passing judgment. Then he curses, which is all the judgment we need to know we're screwed. The surety that we'll be able to complete this job evaporates.

"From what I hear, it's next to impossible," Chuck says. "We've been here since the end of August. The first group went down on a lark, as I understand it, since they didn't need the food. Then when the people from Whitehorse came, they tried again. Sent down the youngest and strongest, which is why they didn't let me go. I offered."

Rich mumbles something I can't hear.

"Yeah," Chuck says, "this is bad timing. Crops weren't too bad this year, but the hunting and salmon catch weren't good. Once everything freezes, I think we'll get in some good hunting." He pushes out his lips and stares at the ceiling. "I'm coming with you."

"No," Peter says. "I won't ask you to do that."

"You're not asking, I'm telling."

"But you have Na—"

"And why do I have her? You saved Nat's life and almost broke your ankle for it. You put off your trip north to make sure we were set for winter, Pete. You were willing to take her with you if we didn't come back. Now I'm going to help make sure you're set for winter."

Peter nods at the floor. Nelly, Penny and James straighten, as bewildered as I am. Peter never mentioned those parts. He'd only said he hurt his ankle and had to recuperate. It's no wonder they love him. I thought I knew how kind and selfless Peter could be, but it's even more than that. He's a beautiful soul, as my mother would say. I give him a *what-am-I-going-to-do-with-you* head shake. He shrugs but returns my smile before looking away.

"I'm going," Rich says. We wait for more, but that's all we get.

"They won't like that," Chuck says. "Rich is the nurse here—we have a medic, nurse and midwife."

"Too bad," Rich replies.

"You're taking a truck, I guess?" Chuck asks. We tell him about Zeke's limited skills. "I'll drive. I drove a truck years ago. That's how we got out here."

"How did you end up here?" Peter asks, looking relieved that we haven't pressed Chuck for more details of his stay. He's not getting off the hook so easily, but I'll bother him about it later.

"We left the island just past midsummer," Chuck says, "We were coming to your place, Pete. Nat insisted, not that she had to, but she said it would be like never getting to the end of a book if she didn't know what had happened. 'Like if *Breaking Dawn* had never been written,' she kept saying."

Peter snorts. *Breaking Dawn* is the last of the *Twilight* books. He'd said Nat was obsessed with them.

"Anyway, we set out in the G-class, which you should've taken when you had your chance. Rode like a dream." Chuck winks. "We ended up south of Albany, between blocked roads and a pod of zombies, and bumped into a group from Mexico. They told us the giant pods really were coming. We'd listened to the radios and thought Alaska was the safest bet, so we took off straight from there. We thought if we waited, we might never get cross country. Found a tanker half-full of diesel and made it here three weeks later. We hitched up a trailer for supply runs once we got here."

He makes it sound easy when it couldn't have been. But either he doesn't want to go into detail or is saving them for another day. Peter tells him a similar story of our travels and glances at his watch when he's finished. "It's ten. We should get some rest."

Chuck gives a long whistle. Natalie pops her head out of the loft a moment later and rolls her eyes at us. "He thinks I'm a dog. Yes, master?"

"Time for your friends to go. We have an early start tomorrow. I'll explain what's going on later."

She comes down, followed by the others. "We were listening. Ash and I think we should be able to help."

"And just how were you planning to do that?" Chuck asks.

"Help kill zombies, Dad. How else?"

"Not happening."

"When I'm eighteen, you won't be able to stop me."

"Too bad you're not eighteen," he says.

Ash doesn't look disappointed. I think she's had enough adventure for one year and knows we'd never let her go, anyway.

"You guys can help by babysitting the kids while we're gone," I say. Nat groans. "It's not so bad. We'll pay you in stuff we find. You can have first dibs."

"Seriously?" Nat asks. "Okay." She grabs Ash's arm and her eyes widen at the thought of all the goodies that might be available this time tomorrow. It looks like Ash might have found a candidate for best friend.

"See you bright and early," Chuck says. He holds the door while we file out and stops me with a hand on my arm. "Good thinking with that babysitting gig. Pete told Nat you were smart."

"I'm afraid to know what else he said," I say lightly, but I can feel the flames in my cheeks.

"It's all good," Chuck says. "Don't worry."

"Well, he said you were all great, and he was right. Thank you. I know you don't have to do this."

"I couldn't live with myself if I didn't."

CHAPTER 53

Peter takes my elbow when I stumble on the way back to our cabin. "You're tired," he says. "You should go to bed."

He has no inkling of how tired I am. If I could sink down on the street and sleep, I would. I try to remember how long it took Bits before she was incapacitated; I should have at least a day. I flop on the couch when we reach the cabin. This one is much nicer than our cabin at Kingdom Come and would be even more improved with the cheesy moose paintings that decorate a few walls taken down. Or, better yet, painted over. Bits and Hank feed Sparky and Barnaby the tidbits of food they saved from dinner.

"Are we watching the stars?" Bits asks.

"Of course," I say. I haul myself up for ibuprofen and then half-sleep, half-listen to their noises. Peter pokes around in the kitchen drawers and organizes things. I can't imagine what it is he's organizing since we have almost nothing, and I come to the conclusion that I'm doomed to forever be roommates with neat people.

"Do you want to put your stuff away?" he asks.

"Why bother?" I say without opening my eyes and am answered by a heavy sigh, but I'd rather he think I'm in a bad mood than sick.

We head into the night and lie on the grass. The stars are just as vibrant as the other night. I try not to think about Whit's hands, the knife, the blood. I'll add it to the list of terrible things I've had to see and do, acknowledge it, and let it go—my mom always said that the best way to move on was to go straight through. I won't let it ruin my love for the night sky, especially for nights like this, when it looks as though there are more stars than space. There are so many suns, maybe so many worlds—worlds that might not be as fucked up as ours. I decide not to share that cheerful thought and say, "Tell me what you see."

Bits points out the Big Dipper and moves around the sky. Whatever she falters on, Hank's encyclopedic mind fills in.

"There's Canis Major," Bits says. "The good dog. We should call that constellation Barnaby, since he's a good watchdog now."

"Who's a good boy?" Hank asks. Barnaby wags his butt and spins around.

"Who *is* a good boy?" Peter asks. "I heard there was a *good boy* around here." Barnaby lets out an ear-splitting bark, races twenty feet away and then back, barking the whole time.

"Okay, okay. Quiet!" Peter says. Barnaby stops and pants happily when Peter puts an arm around his neck and points to Canis Major. "It's really bright."

"It's Sirius," I say. "They call it the Dog Star sometimes. It's the brightest star in the sky. At least in our sky."

"I wish I knew what I was looking at," Peter says.

"Cassie knows almost all of them by heart now," Bits says. "We'll teach..." No one speaks when she trails off, and dread weighs down what was a light moment.

"Look, it's the Arrow," Hank says. "It must be a good omen. Like, for killing zombies." It's so unlike him to make something like that up that we agree emphatically.

We brush our teeth with the jug of water Glory left. Bits and Hank stand in the living room, dead on their feet, but they don't attempt to climb to the loft. It feels so far away, and although I know they're safe up there, I'm not ready to be in a separate bed from them, Peter included.

They eagerly agree to cram in the big bed. I give them both kisses and by the time I get in my spot between them, they're sound asleep. Peter looks over the duplicate drawing I made of the warehouse. "See you in the morning," I whisper.

He reaches across Bits to pat my head. "Goodnight."

Sickness beats out worry, and I fall asleep quickly only to wake from a dream involving buildings with no escape. Hank throws an arm over me. Bits's rear is jammed in my side. Peter still pores over the map. My throat is raw and every breath I take feels like a stab in the lungs. I guzzle half my water bottle and ask, "How long have I been asleep?"

"About fifteen minutes."

"That's all?" I'm overcome by a rush of heat that forces me to struggle out of the blankets and stand at the side of the bed. Peter looks alarmed at my dramatic escape. "I was hot."

"You don't say."

The heat turns to chills as only a fever can. I pretend I'm cold and rub my arms. "I'll go upstairs."

Peter sets the map on the nightstand and folds back the covers. "You don't want to sleep up there."

I don't at all. He flaps the blankets. I climb in and close my eyes, hoping to fall asleep as quickly as before, but I'm wide awake. Peter hasn't yet shut off the lamp, and I roll over to find him staring at the ceiling. "What are you doing?"

"Staring," he says.

"I got that part. You'll never fall asleep with the light on."

"I don't want to be in the dark."

"Literally or figuratively?" I ask.

"Both."

I nod and tuck my hands under my cheek. Now I'm hot and dry like the desert. I stretch to relieve the ache that's sprung up in my hips.

"I don't want to die," I whisper. My voice sounds so wretched that I want to take it back. But I *don't* want to die, and if there's anyone to whom I can admit how scared I am, it's Peter.

He faces me, looking so miserable I would take his hand if I didn't think he would feel my fever. "Me neither."

"So let's not die, then. Why didn't we think of this before?" I clamp down my urge to giggle. Hysteria lurks underneath, vying for a chance to run free.

He forces a chuckle at my terrible joke. "Don't leave my side tomorrow."

"I'll stick like glue, Elmer."

"Good."

"Why didn't you tell us about Nat?" I ask, since neither of us appears to be going to sleep.

"It wasn't important."

"What? You saved someone's life in a heroic manner. You should be screaming it from the rooftops and trying to work it into every conversation."

"Like, 'Oh, mashed potatoes for dinner? That reminds me of the time I saved Nat's life.' "

"How about 'That shirt reminds me of the time I saved your asses in Bennington?' " I say. "You go around saving people's lives, don't you?"

"You saved mine."

"With the water heater? I was just being silly."

"That's not what I meant," Peter says.

"The mouthwash? You can't forget that one."

His lips twitch. "I wish I could."

"Ha ha. So how did I save your life? I need to know so I can work it into a conversation."

"Nothing, it's stupid." Peter rolls to the nightstand to check his watch. "It's late. We need to get some sleep."

"No way. You can't say something like that and then tell me to forget it." I poke his back until he faces me again, head propped on a hand and eyes on the wall. "What did you mean?"

"If I hadn't been with you when this all started, I'd be dead. And I have you to thank for it."

"You don't know that for sure."

"Yeah, I do," he says softly.

"Oh." It's all I can think to say. I once thought that Peter was the only good thing to come out of the end of the world. That he thinks I had something to do with it makes a non-feverish warmth spread to my toes and the tips of my fingers. I draw a shaky breath and try to hold back the subsequent cough, but it's impossible. I try not to suffocate on the crap in my lungs while Peter looks on suspiciously and puts a hand to my forehead.

"You have a fever!" he says, and cuts off any response with a glare that manages to convey concern. His fingers graze my cheek while he assesses my temperature. I close my eyes at the painful chills they leave in their wake. No wonder Bits couldn't stand it. "And when were you planning to say something?"

"I think I'm getting what Bits had. But I'm fine."

"No, you're not fine." I don't have to see his face to know he's furious. "How long has it been?"

"Just before."

He huffs and leaves for the living room. "Take these," he says upon his return.

I open my eyes and dutifully swallow the pills he hands me with water. "Thanks."

"Let me take your temperature." He holds out a thermometer and practically growls when I shake my head. "Really? You're not going to let me?"

"It's just a number," I say with a wave of my hand. "I know how I feel. I'm fine."

He stares like I'm from another planet. "I can't believe y—You know, I wondered why all you ate was soup. You never say no to cornbread. You didn't *just* get sick, Cassandra. You're staying here tomorrow."

I sit up and cross my arms. "Don't even try it. I'm going."

"You can't go with a fever."

"Why? Do the zombies have a rule that you have to be fever-free for twenty-four hours before you can visit?"

"Jesus Christ, make a fucking joke about it. If you're sick, you might get hurt. I'm not fighting about this. You're staying with the kids."

A large part of me wants to acquiesce, to not leave Bits and Hank behind. Glory said she wouldn't kick us out mid-winter, but I don't know how much say she has in the matter. A town full of hungry people wouldn't hesitate to send me packing, and possibly the kids, too, no matter what they've promised. We've seen what hunger can do to people firsthand. This is the only way to ensure that Bits and Hank will be safe and fed for the foreseeable future.

"At least you'd be here if we don't come—" Peter begins.

"You don't know that! They'll kick me out if they run low on food, even if they let the kids stay. I'd rather die trying than freeze to death by myself."

"You're one person. They won't kick you out."

"Can you guarantee me that?" I ask. Peter doesn't answer. He knows he can't guarantee me anything. "Frank would probably murder me in my sleep. You think everyone's going to want to give us the food out of their kids' mouths? They're not."

Peter crosses his arms. I wish I could stay, but he's going and so is Kyle. It wouldn't be fair—they have just as much to lose as I do. The only legitimate reason would be if I was at death's door, and I'm not. One extra person could be the difference between coming back fully-stocked and not coming back at all.

"I'm not sitting here when I could be helping," I say. "You might need me."

Peter's eyes flash. "Right, maybe you can cough the zombies to death. Obviously, you *are* going to fight. If that's the way you want it, then—"

"I'm not fighting." I try a placating smile and wonder what his ultimatum was going to be. "I just need sleep. If I'm worse in the morning, I'll stay here."

Peter studies my face. He doesn't believe me, and rightly so, because there's no way in hell I'm staying here when one of the most important patrols we've ever done goes on without me.

"Promise?" he asks.

I stare at him, working up the nerve to lie, and finally answer, "No."

He breathes through his nose. "You know what? Fine."

"Fine."

I turn on my side and stare at Bits's peaceful features. The thought of not being the person who raises her makes my chest heavier. I don't want to fight with Peter on top of this. He must feel the same because he turns off the light and puts his arm around me. I hug it to me like a teddy bear.

"I just want you safe," he whispers.

"We're safest together," I whisper into the dark. "Please don't ask me to stay." The thought of never knowing what's happened to him and the others is agonizing. The thought of never knowing if the kids are okay is devastating. The only option is to get that food and come back. If there was ever a time to believe it'll be all right, it'd be now—and I'm going to believe.

Peter is silent until our breathing has slowed, then he finally says, "Okay."

CHAPTER 54

Something wakes me before the sun is up. It could be the achiness, the fever that may be a degree or two warmer, or the tight burning in my lungs that makes breathing a chore. It could be nerves, but I'm almost as nervous that Peter will try to make me stay as I am about heading to Anchorage.

I rummage through the medicine bag. I take cold and cough capsules, followed by ibuprofen and Tylenol, and top it off with a Vicodin for my throat. It's a cocktail that has to get me through the day and then I swear I'll heed any and all sickbed advice this afternoon. I put extras in my pockets and pop another Sudafed because it says you can take two. Of course, they probably weren't taking into consideration that the cough syrup has some in it.

"Fooled ya," I say to the directions on the box and then realize how crazy it is that I'm talking to a box of medicine. Crazier than usual, at any rate.

Maybe it's the fever, which should go down soon. But today's agenda would make anyone loony, so I blame it on that and wait for the meds to kick in on the couch. Sparky climbs on my chest and Barnaby stares woefully until I invite him up. Once the sky has lightened, I feel somewhat better. There's the low-level buzz of pseudoephedrine, the pain-relieving cushion of Vicodin and the fever-reducing effect of ibuprofen. I give a tentative cough. The rumble in my chest sounds no better than it did, but the pressure has lessened. I'm good to go—or at least as good as I'm gonna get.

Peter stumbles out of the bedroom and stops when he sees me. "Oh, I wanted to make sure you were okay." He runs a hand through his hair and scratches his scruffy cheek absently, then hitches up the wrinkled jeans he threw on.

"You're very rumpled this morning," I say.

"Have you seen your hair?"

I can feel the frizz before my hand is two inches from my scalp. Sweaty, fevered sleeping has not improved my morning look. I didn't glance at myself when I brushed my teeth; I was too concerned with taking medicine before Peter caught me. I would smooth it down if I had the energy to care.

"How do you feel?" Peter asks.

"Dirty," I say. I'd like to die clean, but no one offered us a shower or whatever it is they have here.

"You know what I mean."

"Better." I may be sicker, but I feel better thanks to the miracle of modern medicine, so it's not a total lie.

Peter feels my forehead. "You are cool."

"What, did you think I was lying?"

"Of course I did," he says, his laugh a bit strained. In fact, all of him is strained, from his anxious expression to his rigid stance.

I'm bordering on petrified, but I concentrate on that tiny kernel of faith from last night. I can still feel it—a glimmer of peace and quiet amidst the noisy fear. Of course, that could be the Vicodin. But, whatever the case, it looks like Peter needs a dose of faith—it was his to begin with, after all. I take his hand for a moment before letting him move toward the bathroom. "It'll be all right, Petey."

Even rumpled and half-grouchy, the smile he flashes me before he closes the door is radiant—white teeth, black stubble, shining eyes. I pull on Ana's leather pants, my boots and a black shirt. I load the extra magazines for the .22 and hang my axe off my belt. I've just finished winding up my hair when Nelly strolls in looking handsome and ready to kick ass in his work boots, leather coat and machete.

"Glory brought breakfast to the big cabin," he says. He opens the kitchenette drawers, inspects the pictures and flips through the Alaska tourism magazines on the coffee table. "Nice place. Tell me you're ditching those moose paintings."

I take in the sarcastic curve of his lips. I've made it this far with him by my side. We might be dead later today, but I'll always be thankful that we were together to the end. "Why are you looking at me like that?" he asks.

"I just love you. I really, really love you, Nels." I want to say all the things that need to be said. The only thing worse than dying is not saying what you should've said before doing so.

Nelly purses his lips. "Oh, God, really? Don't start with that shit." I choke on my laugh and end up doubled over with the force of the contractions in my chest. Peter comes to stand beside me and shakes his head.

"You okay, darlin'?" Nelly asks. "You sound like you're dying."

"She's sick," Peter says, "but she won't stay here."

"She's even more stubborn when she's sick. You really think that pain in the ass would stay here?" Nelly may be calling me names, but he's on my side.

"I can hear you," I sputter between coughs.

"We know," they both say. I give them the finger and spit the coughed-up phlegm into the garbage can.

"Attractive," Nelly says.

"Thanks," I say. He's jesting as usual, but he has circles under his eyes from worry and lack of sleep. "It's all going to be fine."

Nelly opens his mouth just as Bits and Hank appear. We wait for them to wash up and head for breakfast. "Why are you so happy?" Nelly asks me on our way through the damp grass.

"Nothing's going to bother me today. Well, except zombies."

"Just that one small thing."

"An itty-bitty detail."

Nelly pulls me to his side with a chuckle. "I love you, too, Half-pint."

"I know."

Everyone is ready in order to leave after we've eaten. The mood isn't as somber as I'd feared—we're all trying to make the best of it. I force myself to eat eggs and a piece of jerky under Doctor Peter's watchful gaze. What I'd like is buttered toast, but Glory has told us flour's saved for special occasions. Unlike Vermont, they haven't been able to grow wheat. There's probably a ton in that warehouse, though.

I motion Penny into one of the bedrooms and pull some things out of my pack. Penny stands by the window and watches a woman walk a dog with a baby in a carrier on her back. At Kingdom Come there was no escaping the feeling that it was a Safe Zone—no matter how much I loved the place—but this could be the same town it was before the apocalypse.

"It's nice here," I say. "I'm sure everyone's still in each others' business, but at least there's room to spread out."

She ekes out a pale-lipped smile. "I don't care where we live. Just come back."

"We'll do our best. We'd have to do this anyway, even if we weren't here. Right?" She nods and wipes under her glasses.

"I have some things for you," I say, and open the jewelry box. "Earrings for Bits's birthday. You'll have to pierce her ears for her. Just don't do what you did when we were fifteen." She'd tried to give me a fourth hole in my ear, but she'd jammed the needle in at such an angle that it never came out the other side.

"You're going to bring that up now?" Penny shoves me and laughs through her tears.

"Just putting it out there," I say, and have to stop for a few deep breaths when I imagine not being here for Bits's ninth birthday. No, I *will* be here. "The constellation book is for Hank. I don't want to give it to him before I go because it seems...I know he wants it." I pull the unicorn from my pocket. "This is for Bits, too."

I set them all on the windowsill and lay the tissue-wrapped baby dress in her hands. "This is for the baby. From Ana. She found it in Stowe."

She folds the edge of the tissue then smoothes it back into place, whispering, "I'll wait."

I hold her as close as possible with the baby in the way and then rest my hand on her belly. I'm going to meet this baby, too. I'll be here for its birth day, and all the birthdays thereafter. But, just in case, I say, "Don't take shit from them. You don't either, baby."

"Don't worry. No one's giving me shit. I'll cut those bitches." I can see she means it, but I laugh anyway. It's so much better than crying.

"I'll take care of Bits and Hank," Penny says, eyes fierce. I nod. Of that I have no doubt, but a tear still works its way out as we hug one last time.

The tension mounts as plates are cleared, and my symptoms return with a vengeance. I pull a handful of pills from my pocket and take a few on the short walk to the first gate, where we pulled our vehicles once they'd been unpacked.

I hug Adam gingerly. "I'll see you in a while," he says.

"Yes, you will."

"I wish I were coming."

"I know," I say, and think that Adam's hunched shoulders and obvious distress are another reason why I don't want to stay behind.

I hug the others, including Nat, who's chewed her nails down to the quick. Her expression lightens when Chuck speaks softly in her ear. She may be seventeen, but she still thinks her dad is invincible. I know I did. I hope he is this time, too.

I almost fall from the force of Bits's hug. I'm not going to drag this out. If I don't do it quick, I'll never let her go, and I don't want her to see my worry. "I love you so much, Bitsy. More than anything, ever. I'll see you later, okay?"

She nods and steps back with a swallow. "I love you. And I'll see *you* later."

I expected tears and pleading but other than her bloodshot eyes, her face is set. Maybe she believes we'll always come back, that Peter and I are invincible. I can see she'll be all right if we don't, but that doesn't mean I'm going to prove her wrong.

When I whisper the same words in Hank's ear so as not to embarrass him, he clings before he lets me go. The kids wave as James pulls the VW through the gate between the pickup and semi. There's a roar over the sound of Chuck's engine and another semi pulls across the railroad tracks.

Terry jumps out and makes his way to us. "We're coming. We can bring back more that way. Frank, Patricia, Tara and Philip are in the truck. We'll lead you down there. We know a better way to go." He grins and ambles back to the truck.

"Well, look at that," Nelly says from the passenger's seat.

I cross my arms. "So the two people who most don't want us here—Frank and Patricia—are coming to *help*? I don't like it."

"Me neither," Jamie says. "It's like they want to be sure they get their shit no matter what."

"Maybe they felt bad," Peter says from beside me on the bench seat. "And Tara and Philip are *Canadian*. I thought that was enough for you. Why don't we give them the benefit of the doubt?"

"Okay, you do that, and I'll be ready to shoot them." It's going to be a long ride and I already need a nap. I close my eyes, but the zinging in my gut won't let it happen. I open them again to find Peter eyeing me.

"What?" I ask.

"I promised I wouldn't ask, but—"

"So don't ask. I'm fine."

"She's sick," Peter explains to Jamie, "and she won't stay home."

"We don't have a home," I remind him.

"I wouldn't," Jamie says.

I give her a Girl Power thumbs up and hold back a cough. The old medicine is wearing off, but the new should be here shortly. Peter sighs. He sighs at me a lot.

"You have control issues," I say to him.

"What are you talking about?"

"You're constantly sighing at me when I don't do things your way."

His eyebrows come down. "*I* have control issues? The person who has a fever and should be in bed but refuses to do so because she's going to change the entire day's outcome by herself thinks *I* have control issues?"

"Well, you do." My red shoelace is undone and I bend to double-knot it. "It doesn't mean I don't."

"At least I know how to tie my shoes like a grownup."

I look up open-mouthed. "That was a low blow, Petey."

Peter laughs. We hit the highway and turn south. I watch the scenery and only realize I've been drumming my fingers on my leg when Peter stills my hand with his. He laces his gloved fingers through mine and stares out the window. Forested highway becomes occasional houses and businesses. I close my eyes, even though I know sleep is a lost cause, and practically leap through the roof in fright when James stops the VW with a holler. Terry screeches to a halt ahead, as does everyone behind.

James grins while he points at a grouping of fireworks stands. "John was always on the lookout for fireworks to use if we were trapped. They might come in handy."

"He said, 'Light 'em, throw 'em, then take off the other way.' We have to check," I say, and send John silent thanks for still looking after us. Now if only there's something left inside.

We step into the gravel parking lot and explain the plan to the others, all of whom agree it's worth a shot.

"Good old John," Zeke says. He kicks in a door, not bothering to use his cat burglar skills, and our flashlights illuminate shelves that have enough inventory for a whole lot of distraction.

Back in the VW, we rip open boxes and choose the fireworks that look least likely to trap us in a blazing inferno. "Look at this," Jamie says. She holds up one called Death's Door. "Fitting."

Nelly calls out names as he separates them. "Mother Lode, Civil War, Blown Away."

Peter opens a box labeled Zombie Zingers and a few green paper balls spill into his hand. "I'm kind of partial to these."

"Lemme get some of those," James says.

We avoid the main highway until we're forced to pick it up thirty minutes later in order to reach Anchorage. The foliage is a frosty brown and the mountains are tipped with solid white, as if winter's come overnight. We eventually turn onto the city streets due to stopped traffic, where taller buildings are interspersed between fast food chains and strip malls. Following the Talkeetnans' semi, we drive a network of side streets to easily avoid blockages. Lexers hit the empty sidewalks as we pass; the engines call out everything within shouting distance. I'm not sure how far we would've gotten without Terry's help. Maybe I should give them the benefit of the doubt, like Peter said.

We pass warehouses, including a beer warehouse that makes Nelly drool, until we come upon a concrete building the length of a city block. It's flat and squat, with at least a dozen loading bay doors along the street side. Rows of trailers line the back of the lot in which a few zombies ramble.

"Dude, this place is gigantic," James says after he's pulled to a stop. He tucks his hair behind his ear and his legs pump up and down.

"No wonder no one wanted to come back," Jamie mutters.

I can imagine the nooks and crannies hiding Lexers in a building this large. We'll only venture into half of it; the food on the cold storage side is definitely past its sell-by date. Terry pulls past the guard house and around the building. There are the standard-issue Lexers who lay on the concrete, finally dead, and those who begin the excruciatingly slow task of coming to devour us.

"Sometimes I wish they were just a mite faster," I say. Everyone but Peter laughs, and I nudge him. "Joking."

He nudges me back. "Oh, was that what that was?"

"Let's meet them halfway," Nelly says. "We don't have all day to wait for ten dumbass zombies."

It feels good to stretch my legs; every muscle has tightened upon seeing this place. The Lexers' groans are louder than our footfalls in the quiet. I'm used to the silence by now, especially in the woods, but sometimes it's still strange in places with dead machinery, trucks and buildings that used to have such noisy purpose.

Once the Lexers are down, we inspect the lot. Whoever said a storm is coming must be right; the temperature has dropped in the past hour. Frank rubs his eyes. He stayed behind to examine the bodies we dropped, maybe looking for his son, and I grow more sympathetic toward him even though he hasn't become any nicer to us. "The others are all in there?" he asks.

Terry nods. Tara and Philip shift on their feet, and I wonder how many times they've done something like this. By the way she holds her knife, as if she's going to slice carrots instead of stab through bone, I'm thinking not many. But I like Tara, so I sidle close. "You should hold your knife like *Psycho*," I say.

She bites her lip. "What?"

"You know, Ee-ee-ee." I hold up a fist and pretend to stab what's-her-name in the shower.

"Right." She turns it in her hand and says, "Thanks."

Patricia rolls her eyes and swings her machete. Tara throws her a dirty look. Now I'm certain that I love Tara.

"So, let's get the first ones out," Zeke says. "Then we'll go in and get the loading doors up."

After a futile attempt to raise the loading bay doors from outside, some of us wait in the pickup's bed while Nelly opens the employee door and comes running. Over a dozen Lexers emerge from the gloom, shuffling along until they fall headfirst down the stairs. They rise up, answer our calls with hisses and walk our way. I lift my axe and spike one before pushing it as far away as possible to leave room for the next.

A woman with the remnants of tattoos under her rotten skin throws herself against the pickup. I bury the spike in her forehead and she slides to the ground before I can move her. Peter shoves his machete under the chin of a tall one and then uses the blade to toss him away.

"Impressive," I say. He glances at me in amusement and tosses another.

"Now you're just showing off," I say, which elicits a real laugh.

We wait for the stragglers to make their way across the lot. The last one is moldy, with a single tuft of hair and exposed ribs, but it gets back on its feet every time it trips. It's the epitome of zombies—no matter how dead they should be, somehow they keep going. I guess you could say the same about us. It lands face-first into another body on the ground, rises covered in brown gore, and then slips again.

All the others are dead and, as Nelly said, we don't have all day, so I jump to the ground and cover the five feet. Its hand scrabbles for my ankle as I bury the axe blade. I spin around, slam into Peter and squeak in surprise.

"Glue," he says, and steadies me by my shoulders. "You sure you can do this? You look awful."

I don't argue; I made the mistake of looking in the mirror before we left. "Yeah, I can."

Nelly grimaces at the gray sky. "Today is a shitty day to die."

"We've already decided we're not dying," I say. "Right, Peter?" Peter nods, jaw tight.

Jamie's flushed face is surrounded by a halo of black frizz that's escaped from her bun. She looks like the Jamie of two weeks ago, small and bursting with energy instead of tired and beaten down. "I'm not dying."

Nelly gives a firm nod. "Let's do it."

An orchestra of groans filters through the open door. A far-off clatter comes from somewhere inside. I can't tell if it's as bad as it sounds or if the vast space amplifies the noises, but even with that factored in, it sounds like somewhere I don't want to be.

I put extra magazines in one coat pocket and fireworks in the other. I have my axe in my hand, a spare knife on my belt and the reality that I might be about to die hanging over my head. I take a deep breath and immediately regret it when my lungs seize. I'm as ready as I'll ever be.

CHAPTER 55

We enter through the door marked Receiving Office on the far end of the long building. This is one of what I'm sure will be many tricky parts—how to see without being seen for as long as possible. Zeke and Liz enter first, followed by me and Peter. Zeke's flashlight illuminates the remains of what were once beds and are now twisted piles of blankets, sleeping bags and cardboard. There's a rudimentary woodstove made out of a metal barrel, daylight seeping in around the stovepipe that feeds through a hacked-out hole in the wall. The air smells strongly of zombies and faintly of burnt plastic and shit and spoiled food.

Zeke covers the flashlight beam with his hand and motions us to the windows that face the warehouse's main floor. The few skylights make what could be pitch black a shadowy gray. The light is brightest at the top of the shelves, which run in long rows to the rear of the building. There are empty spaces on the shelving, but the majority is pallets of plastic-wrapped boxes as far as the eye can see. We suck in our breath. No matter what they'd said, I don't think any of us believed there could still be this much stuff left anywhere in the world, much less a city. It's akin to finding the dragon's treasure, but there's still the dragon to contend with.

Lexers move in the light that filters to the floor. More Lexers than we bargained for. They don't know we're here, but they will soon enough. The plan is to raise the loading doors, both to let in light and let out the zombies, and then kill them in relative safety from the vehicles outside.

Once Nelly, Chuck, Rich and James have joined us, Zeke presses his flashlight to the glass. To our right is a single loading door and a small office built into the corner. He turns the beam left, to where the remainder of the warehouse stretches for hundreds of feet. The loading area in front of the first few doors is cleared and past that are the pallet rooms Terry mentioned, as well as jumbles of debris too shadowed to make out. It looks like all hell broke loose.

The five foot high fence is made of strips of metal and runs from the wall to our right into the darkness. It looks secure enough to hold back the hundreds of zombies behind it. In places, boxes are piled against the fence.

In the places where they aren't, Lexers strain against the metal, arms groping through the wide spaces. It's taken us thirty seconds to get the lay of the land, which is also enough time for everything in here to have noticed us. The ones on this side of the fence lurch toward the office with dumb, ravenous faces.

"You ready?" Zeke asks. "Head to the first two doors after the fireworks."

Nelly and I lob our lit Zombie Zingers to the right, away from the main area. The tiny flames arc into the dark. A few moments later, when the groans have reached a crescendo, the room is filled with loud cracks. The Lexers turn toward them, lit by the flashes of light.

We jump the ramp and make for the loading doors. I flick on my headlamp—there's no choice in the matter if we want to avoid tripping. Nelly tosses more fireworks well away from the first. The last thing we need is to start a fire or make zombie torches. Using fireworks indoors is already risky enough.

Peter and I stand sentry while Chuck and Rich get to work. Nelly and James guard Liz and Zeke. I hand Nelly more fireworks to throw. He played football in high school. I flunked softball. He's the obvious choice.

Daylight shoots across the floor when our door rises two inches, but it goes no higher. Chuck yanks on something with a curse, and Zeke and Liz aren't having any better luck. Three Lexers approach, skin bleached and blood black in my LED light. James hits one with his machete and then lunges for another. He didn't have much practice on the farm, and he kills them as if he's been waiting a year to do it. Peter gets the other and returns to my side.

More Lexers limp toward us. The rattling and light have attracted them, and Nelly's added fireworks do nothing to dissuade them. The door cranks up another few inches, although not enough to escape. I try to focus on what's in front of me and not panic that more Lexers have cut off our route to the office. At this point, it's either into the fray or out the door. Rattling comes from behind, and then the front of the warehouse is light enough to see that every Lexer this side of the fence is on its way.

"Cassie!" Peter yells.

I turn, heart hammering, to see the door not much farther from the floor than when I last looked. The smallest of us—me and Liz—might be able to fit through. Liz flattens herself to the floor and slides out feet first. Peter motions for me to do the same. I want to be sure they're safe. I want to get out of here. It feels wrong to leave and stupid to stay.

Nelly shoves me to my stomach when I hesitate, waits for me to feed my feet through the opening, and hacks at the oncoming bodies. Peter pushes at my shoulders while someone pulls my ankles from outside. I wince as the edge of the door scrapes along my back. Peter looks the same as he did a year ago when he thought he was as good as dead—black eyes and pale skin and resigned expression. I won't let it end this way, with him saving my life one last time. I kick the hands off my feet and try to gain purchase on the floor, but he gives me a final shove that sends me to the concrete outside.

I peer through the opening, my eyes adjusted to the dark enough to see Peter fighting his way deeper into the building, toward the shelves, with the others just ahead of him.

"We'll come back in!" I yell. Too many people have been left behind, too many people are a mystery, and I will not tell Bits I've left her father behind unless I have no other choice. And I promised Adam and Penny I'd do my best.

Peter lifts a hand. I watch him disappear into the dark until a putrid face sinks to the opening and forces me to back away.

Liz's chest heaves. "The doors should lift by the chain once you've pulled a release cord on the electric controls, but someone's fixed them so they won't go up. It looks like wire's threaded through the links. We need something to cut them. We can't force them any higher."

Ben runs to the truck for our bolt cutter and a pair of wire cutters and meets us at the office door. "Stay out here," he says to Mikayla. She shakes her head stiffly, terrified but unyielding. I don't know what she had to do on the way here, but at the farm she was always in the kitchen and never at the fence.

"Who has the radio?" Kyle asks.

Liz unclips the radio from her belt and holds it up without a word. We stare at the only link to those inside. But if they've made it to the shelves, they'll be safe for a while.

"Wait out here," Kyle says to the Talkeetnans. "We'll get the door open. You start on them after they're out."

They nod, either completely willing or too frightened by the snarl on his face not to heed his command. Liz and I lead the others inside to the office windows. A couple of shadowy figures stand on the second tier of shelves behind the fence. I wish I could tell who they are, but I'm also afraid to know.

The Lexers are so focused on the shelves that they don't notice when Kyle runs his Maglite along the glass. A light flashes from the shelves.

Three short bursts, three long bursts, three short bursts. Then again. We all know the Morse code SOS signal. Kyle answers with three short, one long, one short. *Understood.*

"I'm at the door with Liz," Kyle says. "The rest of you keep them away as long as you can."

We hop over the ramp and to the floor, retracing our earlier route. Kyle boosts Liz to his shoulders to work on the chain while the rest of us fan out. There's not many to kill because whoever is on the shelves is purposely making enough noise to keep their attention.

Light floods in behind me, illuminating garbage, discarded clothing, bodies, five gallon buckets-turned-toilets that spilled their contents long ago, and Lexers that have begun the short shuffle toward us.

We hop off the ledge and run to the pickup while Lexers drop off the loading dock. It's a parade of open sores and exposed bones and ragged clothing, and when they hit the truck it rocks hard enough that I grip the side. I hack into brains and eyes and anything else I can reach. The faster this is finished, the sooner I'll know who's alive. The Talkeetnans hang out the back of the semi's trailer and kill their fair share.

Peter. Nelly. James. Zeke. My axe beats with every name. I don't know Chuck and Rich, but Peter loves them and that's enough for me. The bodies pile around the pickup until they become a wall too high for the next ones to climb. I sight down my pistol. The .22 scrambles their brains just like John said.

And then it's done. We jump to the ground in the sudden quiet. It's impossible to avoid stepping on the bodies, and I destroy all of Peter's boot-scrubbing when I sink ankle-deep into what I think is empty space but is actually a torso under two corpses. We move the trucks so we have space to kill the remaining Lexers before we take down that fence and lead them outside.

Inside, the quiet is swapped for moaning. The fence rattles at our approach. There must be two hundred, maybe more.

Liz swings a flashlight and yells, "Who's up there?"

"All of us," Zeke's deep drawl rings out. "You gonna let them out the door or what?"

I droop in relief while Liz whoops and yells, "Simmer down, Z.K. You'll be out in a few."

We mull over killing them while standing on the boxes along the fence, but the stacks look too unstable to hold our weight. The fence is bolted and welded, with a gate near the open loading bay door.

"Let's check the fence line to make sure this gate will let them all out," Kyle says. "Then we'll do it."

Half of us follow the metal toward the rooms of pallets. The fence sways but holds, although I wouldn't spend too long teasing the Lexers behind it. We turn to make our way back and see Frank stabbing through the fence down in the light of the open bay. In the few seconds that it takes me to wonder what he's up to, he steps on a lower rail and leans over, dragging a Lexer up and over the top.

"What the f—" Kyle begins before we take off in Frank's direction.

Between zombies pushing and Frank yanking, the fence gives way with a loud pop. We stop dead; we'll never make it to the exit now that Lexers pour into our safe area, killing our surefire plan. I will them to head for the light, but they don't. They head for us.

We scatter. I race between two pallets and find myself in one of the makeshift rooms. I turn for the entrance, where a preteen girl with long hair and an eyeball that's oozed from its socket knocks me to the floor and comes down after me. Her mouth opens in slow motion, teeth gleaming in my headlamp. I scramble to my feet, but more are in the entry, and I back away until I hit the rear wall of boxes almost as tall as me. Preteen zombie is on her feet. Five Lexers are closing in. I'm fucked.

✲✲✲

My brother climbed mountains. Eric always said there was nothing better than the rush of reaching a peak, that he thought no drug could come close. Why he would want to climb to somewhere cold—to risk his life for a thrill—was beyond me, but I'd listen to his stories with awe. And one always stuck out in my mind.

He'd been on the top of some mountain or other, making his way up the ice, when he'd started to slide. Not just a little slide, but one that took him over the edge of a cliff of ice. Eric didn't panic, although the story alone, told by the woodstove in my parents' cabin, was enough to make my heart race and mouth go dry. He said the scene played out in slow motion. That he felt as if he had all the time in the world to think about his next move. Just in time, he sank the spike of his axe into the sheet of ice as far back as he could reach and used the handle to pull himself up and over.

And that's what I hope will save me now. I kick at the first two zombies and slam my axe into the top of the pallet wall. I pull to check it's secure and use the handle to climb, my feet scrambling on the side. When I reach the top, I sink to my knees and struggle to breathe through the muck in my lungs.

There's so much noise that I can't think, but I'm grateful to still be breathing, such as it is. I wave in the blinding beam of a flashlight from the shelves before it moves to search for others and then turn off my headlamp so it doesn't act as a zombie beacon. I rise to my feet and stumble when a hand catches my boot from behind. They're on both sides now, and I don't have enough clearance to escape a two-sided attack.

The boxes shake and shift. The cardboard beneath my feet sinks an inch, then another. It's going to collapse. I leap for the pallets that make up the side wall of the room and know instantly that I've overshot the distance. I teeter on the edge before plummeting hand-first to the concrete floor. I'll feel this in my wrists tomorrow, but right now I don't feel anything but sheer terror mixed with relief that I've landed on the other side instead of into their waiting arms. An empty can skitters past, kicked by something coming my way, and I raise my hand. My axe-less hand.

This is how it happens: one small mistake, one tiny stroke of bad luck—they grow exponentially and then you're dead. I unsnap my knife. Something moves through my path of escape. Whoever created this labyrinth of boxes may have been thinking in terms of privacy for the occupants, but it's what's going to kill me now. I press on my headlamp to better see my target and grunt with the effort of bringing knife through bone. I use both hands, but it won't come out no matter how I tug.

A sharp pain blossoms in my calf. My throat clenches in agony when I scream at the sight of the one-legged zombie with its jaw practically unhinged, teeth grinding on my leg. I fire my pistol point blank and turn to flee, in what direction I have no idea. The shelves. I'll go to the shelves.

I'm no longer thinking straight, consumed as I am by the fear I've been bitten. Either Ana's leather pants have saved my life or they haven't. I think it's sweat that courses down my leg in warm streams, but it could just as easily be blood. My foot hits something and my axe spins on the concrete before it thuds into a dark corner. Maybe I shouldn't take the time to stop, but I need more than just my gun. My ammo will run out sooner or later. All of our ammo will. The boxes we traded for fuel were a large chunk of what we had.

I retrieve my axe, hack my way to the fence and practically fly over the top. Nothing can catch me in my wild state.

"Cassie!" Peter's light switches on ten feet up and two aisles over. I ignore the closer shelves and run for him. I don't want to die alone. I don't want to have to do what Dan did. And then Peter's on the floor in front of me, tossing a body out of the way and boosting me up the diagonal metal braces on the end of each aisle.

He follows me onto the shelf. I stumble on open boxes of cans and send them crashing to the floor. I hear his voice, but the roar of dread in my head drowns out his words as I rip off my light and shine it on my calf. I check again and again to be sure, but there's no rip, no tear. I sink to the open boxes and for a moment forget what surrounds us. I'm by no means safe, but there's still a chance I'll live.

Peter crouches. "What's wrong?"

"I thought one bit through."

Peter looks over the wet, gory leather and pulls me close. The Lexers bang and the shelving vibrates, but these shelves are bolted to the floor, made to hold a lot more than us. I want to stay up here forever, but I let Peter go and take out my pistol. We can't reach their heads from this shelf without longer blades. Guns are going to be loud and messy, but I'll take loud and messy over dead.

We lean over the shelf's edge. The Lexers follow our every move, hands lifted and bodies bent our way like ardent lovers—sick, twisted lovers who'll swallow you whole if given the chance. We're not the only ones who've opened fire. The reports are so loud that I tilt my ear to my shoulder to save at least one eardrum. Even this close, we miss when the Lexers shift and fall. I have another fifteen rounds and I blow through them quickly, saving a few for an emergency.

Peter and I are farthest away from the majority of Lexers, who've gathered in the daylight that illuminates the others on the shelves and where Jamie, Kyle, Mikayla, Ben and the Talkeetnans stand on a long row of pallets along the fence.

"I think we can get them out the door," Peter says.

I nod. We've thinned out the nearby Lexers to the point where we might make it to the loading door if we keep low. We climb to the floor and are over the fence and halfway there when we have to duck behind a pile of garbage to avoid a passing group.

A shout comes from the row of pallets by the fence. One end has crumpled to the floor, and Jamie, Kyle and the others kick at the Lexers' hands on what remains. They can't let down their guard for a second, and they stab and jab, out of ammo by now. What was supposed to be the easiest part has turned into a complete and total fuckshow.

Ben stands at a gap leading to a wider grouping of pallets that would keep them out of reach of groping hands. He pushes Mikayla behind him and takes three quick steps before he's airborne. I'm certain he has it until a Lexer bumps him in midair and sends him crashing to the floor, Lexers following.

Ben's frenzied screaming is pain and despair rolled into one. It mixes with Mikayla's wails to pierce through the dullness in my ears. Mikayla drops to hang off the pallets when his shouting grows hoarse, her shoulder-length curls loose of her ponytail, and I want to drag her to her feet. I know I tend to be overcautious—hair tightly wound, gloves on, mouth closed against splatter—but it's because any tiny thing can, and often does, go wrong.

Mikayla rips at the hands that tangle in her curls with high-pitched shrieks. She's dragged forward a few inches. Jamie and Kyle yank at her legs and fight to keep her out of the zombies' reach. A corner of their platform crumples, her torso slides into contact with waiting teeth, and they finally allow her to slide headfirst off the boxes. The shrieking ends, which chills me more than the shrieking itself.

The group of Lexers that forced us to stop has moved for the pallets. Peter and I could run to the door, but we wait, needing no discussion to agree that we'll detour from our original plan in order to help Jamie and the others if necessary. Jamie leaps across the gap while the Lexers are busy with Mikayla. She's followed by everyone but Tara and Philip, who are last in line and trapped by a new wave drawn by the blood and screaming.

The boxes under their feet bend. Tara's knife plunges viciously, but the skull isn't easy to crack. And from her vantage point, with a knife, all she has to work with are the tops of skulls—the hardest spot as well as the spot most likely to be intact. She dances like a boxer to keep out of the Lexers' reach until her feet are yanked out from under her and she goes down. Philip struggles to rise from his knees.

I look to the loading bay. There aren't many Lexers in the way. We could make it. Tara and Philip are closer to where we crouch, yet in the opposite direction. But I can't watch them die—I can't *listen* to them die— like Mikayla and Ben, and there's no way those Lexers will leave them behind to come for the door. I nod when Peter tilts his head their way. We run and climb up the collapsed end of the pallets. I leap over Philip because I know Peter has him, and Tara is in worse shape. Lexers hang from her ankles that jut over the pallet's edge. Her mouth is open with the effort of bucking to keep her skin out of the reach of teeth. Hands are twisted in her hair.

I start with the Lexers at her feet. Black sludge flies when I slice through wrists, and the stumps continue to wave wildly when the hands loosen and drop. Tara brings her legs under her, head still pinned to the cardboard. I stand astride her and bring down my axe. I don't care what I hit as long as they let go, and when they have, I yank her to her feet. My arm aches and my lungs are on fire, but I pound away until we can push through the remainder and make it to the door.

Tara and Philip follow when Peter and I leap to the floor. I wouldn't be surprised if they ran all the way back to Talkeetna without a glance behind them, but they halt at the loading bay and call the Lexers along with us. When we have a large following, we race to the pickup's bed while the first drop off the ledge. I grip the roof of the cab to steady myself. Every cough is a sharp spasm. Phlegm fills my throat.

"You okay?" Peter asks.

I nod and point in the direction of the zombies that are only feet away. I help when I can breathe again, but my arm is weaker and it takes several strikes to finish each one. Thuds and yells ring out of the warehouse. It isn't long before the truck sits in the middle of a mound of zombies and Nelly and James appear at the loading bay with tired but triumphant faces. I try to find my second—or maybe fourth—wind, but Peter has to help me out of the truck and up into the building. I throw my arms around them both and watch the others move toward us.

"We're all okay," Nelly says. Everyone except Mikayla and Ben, that is, but I don't say it and neither does he.

Another door rattles up, and I look around in amazement that any of us is okay. Bodies are everywhere. What look to be entrails are stuck to the floor along with other unknown and revolting substances. I might have run through it, crawled through it, and I'm glad I didn't know at the time. Nelly surveys the room and then peers at the sole of his boot before wiping it on a blanket that doesn't look much better. "I don't want to hear shit about having to take short showers when we get back."

"Hey, sugar," Zeke says from behind me. I fall into his arms. "Thought you got rid of me, did you?"

"Oh, well. Next time."

He releases me with a laugh. "Liz kicked some righteous ass back there, but there may be a few more in the back. Let's finish this."

I give Liz's arm a weak punch. She punches me back, eyes aglow. "Ready to kick some more ass?" she asks. I nod, although I don't think I could kick at the air right now.

"You look like shit," Nelly says. "You sure nothing bit you?"

"You don't know the half of it," I say. If I weren't already sick I'd be terrified that I'm infected.

Peter takes my arm and says, "Sit this one out."

I want to refuse, but I feel worse with each passing second. There's not a scrap of adrenaline left. My two-pound axe feels like it weighs fifty. Peter strips off a glove and presses his hand to my forehead, then leads me to the receiving office and rolls out a chair from the corner.

"Sit," he says. "Please. I'll have Rich come look at you."

I use my feet to roll it to the window and press my forehead against the cool glass. "Keep the door open?"

He nods, hands me a water bottle, and leaves down the ramp. There are still pills in my pocket but standing to reach them and then uncapping the bottle is too Herculean a task. I'm done for, as Zeke would say.

Rich walks into the office a few minutes later. "Not feeling well?"

"Not really."

"Peter says you're playing it down." He sets a first aid kit on a desk and rubs antibacterial gel on his hands. His cheeks are ruddy from all the exertion, but he wears a gentle smile. Peter's told me how Rich had to kill his daughter and wife, and that he's been a man of few words ever since.

I shrug. "He's overprotective."

"He took great care of Nat. It's a good thing." I open my mouth for the thermometer and Rich raises his eyebrows at the display when it beeps. He has me remove my jacket for the stethoscope. I start to shiver the moment it's off. "Just a minute and you can put your coat on. Take a deep breath."

I choke when I do, and he makes me choke several more times before he pulls the stethoscope from his ears. "You have a lot of congestion. High fever. Bits had this?"

"Yeah. We gave her antibiotics in case it wasn't viral."

"Good call. We'll get you on some when we're back. For now, I want you to rest." I shake my head and point to all the boxes that need to be moved into the trucks. "Nurse's orders. We should have you on a nebulizer and in bed."

Rich has me take a few of my pills and suggests I lie down. I take in the rubbish-strewn floor. "I'll sit."

Rich chuckles. "Don't blame you. I'm going to help out. I'll stay close in case you need me."

***

I wake from sleep, head against the window, when Terry says, "We can't find Frank. Have you seen him?"

I shield my eyes from the light—a few more doors have been raised. My head throbs unrelentingly, and through the haze I remember that Frank's the reason Mikayla and Ben are dead. Something I'm trying not to think about. "No. Why did he come if he couldn't be trusted? He almost got us all killed."

Terry opens his mouth, but Patricia comes out from behind him and says, "We came for ourselves, in case *you* couldn't be trusted. Not to keep you alive."

She shakes off Terry's hand when he shushes her, and he throws me an apologetic glance. I peer out the window. Tara and Philip move bodies while Rich works on dismantling the fence, but I don't see Nelly or Peter or anyone else. "Where is everyone?" I ask Terry.

"They're in the back doing a sweep." Terry points to the rear corner of the warehouse. "They're almost done."

I want to lie down. I want someone to tuck me into a bed with cool, clean sheets. My body is numb and fuzzy. My ears are clogged. Terry smiles before he leaves and Patricia follows after she scowls. My hand tightens into a feeble fist; I'll have to save punching Patricia for another day. The thought cheers me as I watch her head to the small office in the corner.

She pulls on the door handle, and I think dazedly that she wouldn't be stupid enough to open a door unless she was absolutely sure of what was behind it. I'm wrong. Once cracked, a Lexer with brown hair and a flannel shirt shoves its way out. Patricia turns, slips on flattened cardboard, and falls to the floor with the Lexer on top.

There's no one else nearby, and as much as I think she's a bitch, she doesn't deserve to die for it. I pick up the axe by my feet and run as fast as I can manage. Patricia, who doesn't have the sense not to open mysterious doors but at least has the sense to wear gloves and leather, holds its snapping teeth inches from her throat. Frank appears from the office and races toward her. The Lexer is recently turned, his skin still plump by zombie standards, and probably good-looking before he began to rot away. I skid to a stop and raise my axe.

"No!" Frank yells.

I bring it down. It crunches into the Lexer's skull and he lands on Patricia, who stares up at me with wide eyes. I hold out a hand. "Are you—"

Frank's palms slam into my chest. I'm barely standing as it is, and it doesn't take much to send me down on my ass. He advances on me with a snarl when I scramble back, gasping at the knife-like pain in my lungs. I grab my gun, wondering how Frank turned so quickly.

"You stupid bitch!" he says. He's not turned—just turned on me. I struggle to my feet and feel the cold muzzle of his pistol on my temple. "Drop your gun."

I'm tired. I'm sick. I'm sick and tired of this. Of fighting zombies and having nowhere to live, of course, but most of all I'm tired of people who think they can call me a stupid bitch. I press my gun to his chest and raise my eyes to his. "Fuck you."

"Frank! What are you doing?" Rich yells from behind me.

"She was bitten," Frank says. I swear he's smiling in a tight-lipped way.

"No I wasn't," I try to yell, but the words are insubstantial.

"She's sick, Frank. That's all."

"She was just bitten," Frank says. "I saw it." Terry, Tara and Philip have joined us, and now they back up. I must look infected, feverish and struggling for breath.

"Frank, put the gun down," Rich says.

"She was bit!" Frank screams, face purple.

I point to Patricia, who looks up from the body of the Lexer without expression. She's letting this happen after I came out here to save her. I should've let the bitch die. "Tell them it's not true," I say hoarsely.

Patricia motions to the Lexer. "She's fine. She killed…it's Corey. He didn't bite her. Frank had him in the office." Terry takes a closer look and moves toward Frank, but stops at Frank's warning shout.

"Frank," Rich says quietly. He puts a hand on the arm that presses the gun to my temple, and I pray Frank's finger isn't resting on the trigger. "She saved Patricia, Frank."

"She killed him." Frank's voice cracks. "She killed Corey."

"She had to. Did you want Corey to kill Patricia?"

"I don't fucking care!" Frank says. The gun shifts on my temple. "She's not coming back with us. None of them are."

"I had to kill my daughter, Frank," Rich says quietly. "My own daughter. You know it had to be done. Don't take it out on her."

The pressure on my temple vanishes. Frank sinks to his hands and knees with a moan, but I still don't trust him, even after Rich has eased the gun from his hand. I don't trust any of them. I shouldn't have given them the benefit of the doubt—they used us to get the supplies in hand, and now our usefulness has ended.

I don't know what to do next. I draw in air to clear my head, but I can't get enough oxygen. I need to sit, to pass out. I need help. This is a time when I could use some protection. Patricia moves toward me, gun in hand. I pull Frank to kneeling by his hair and press my pistol to his head. He doesn't fight. He hardly seems to notice. Patricia freezes and the others stand stock still.

"I wasn't…" Patricia sets her gun on the floor. "I was already holding it."

My friends are probably dead. Frank will find a way to kill me, too. He said as much. "Where...is everyone?" I ask in short breaths.

"In the back," Terry says.

"I don't...believe you. Get them."

"Chuck's back there, Cassie," Rich says. "He wouldn't hurt them."

"You were going...to kill us." My hands shake. Blackness encroaches. I focus on breathing and keeping the gun that weighs a thousand pounds to Frank's head, where the back of his neck is scratched and bloody.

"Cassie, I promise no one is going to hurt you," Rich says.

I stare at Frank's neck. Deep gouges run below his shirt collar. The skin around them is raised and turning purple before my eyes. Beads of sweat race down from his hairline. He has nothing to lose. He'd be happy if I died along with him.

"He's infected," I say. Five sets of eyes drop to Frank.

"I got scratched, not bitten," Frank says. He raises a hand and licks his lips. "If I am, let me come back and say goodbye."

He was going to kill me, and I can see by their sympathetic expressions they're going to capitulate to his plea. What will stop him from killing me once he's free? Footsteps sound. Nelly, Jamie and Peter halt at the end of the closest aisle and raise their guns before moving closer. My muscles weaken in relief, but I don't let go of Frank.

"What's going on?" Peter asks. He circles around until he's beside me, keeping his pistol on Terry.

"It's a misunderstanding," Terry says.

"Frank said...none of us were going back," I say. Now that they're here, I can give in to the cough that's been trying to work itself out. My chest hurts more than I thought possible.

"I swear that's not happening," Terry says. "Frank's infected. He's not thinking straight." He points to the body. "That's his son over there."

"Rich?" Peter asks.

"No, Pete," Rich says. "We all go back together."

"I don't know what Frank's talking about," Tara says. "I want you to come back."

She looks honest enough, but so do most people who lie. "They're not Canadian," I mumble. "They said that so we'd trust them."

Tara and Philip glance at each other in bewilderment. Peter's mouth works in a way that makes it clear he thinks I've gone round the bend. The moment I try to explain, I realize how insane it is to think that they would masquerade as Canadians so they could kill us. I shake my head to clear the half-formed and befuddled thoughts swimming around.

"It's all right." Peter lowers his gun and puts his hand over mine. "We're all right."

I'm sinking fast. I'm going to have to believe him—it hasn't failed me so far. "Promise?"

"Promise."

I don't want to kill anyone else. Any*thing* else. I just want to ensure the safety of the people I love. I want to give them what they need as well as all the little things they want. And this place is full of the little things they want.

"We get the candy," I gasp out. "And espresso beans. Tea. Pepsi." Nelly chokes on a laugh from behind me.

"It's yours," Terry says with a nod.

I holster my gun. My chest groans with every inhalation and the edges of my vision grow dark. I manage to hold it together until my knees buckle in the parking lot. Peter and Rich carry me the rest of the way to the VW, where I willingly surrender to the blackness.

CHAPTER 56

I have fuzzy memories of the last few days: an all-encompassing heat, coughing until I puke, a hand on my hair and voices—Nelly, Rich and Jamie—but Peter's voice was ever-present, so I'm not surprised to come to and find him on the other side of the king bed in our cabin. Even in sleep, he looks exhausted.

He sits up when I do, rubbing his eyes. "What's wrong?"

"Nothing," I say, and try not to choke to death on the first word I've spoken in days. I lean back. I think someone's stolen one of my lungs. "No, maybe I'm dying."

"Glad to have you back," Peter says. He pushes my hair off my temple and says something more, but I close my eyes.

I wake again what could be an hour or a day later. Peter's still there, but now he's engrossed in a book and shoveling something into his mouth. He hands me a glass of water and rests the back of his hand on my cheek. "Drink. How are you feeling?"

"Like I'm breathing underwater."

"You have pneumonia. Your lung collapsed."

"Seriously?"

Peter shuts his book and points it at me. "I *told* you to stay here."

"You know what I like about you, Petey? You never say I told you so."

He gives me a half smile and frowns when I shiver. "There's a fire in the living room. Are you hungry? You need to eat."

"What are you eating over there?" He holds up a package of Oreos. "*You're* eating Oreos? Do you know what's in them? High fructose corn syrup, for a start. They'll kill you."

He closes his eyes while he chews. "Have another cigarette, why don't you? I don't care what's in them. Oreos are delicious."

I laugh-cough. I like to see Peter scarf down Oreos with abandon, attempt giant drags of cigarettes even though he despises them and make snarky comments. Light floods in the two windows of the bedroom. Peter's nightstand is cluttered with pill bottles, while mine holds Dan's box and my repaired phone. I reach for it and scroll through the last of the pictures:

The mountains. Miss Vera by the side of the road, beaten to shit. Peter driving, knuckles raw from punching Oliver. It seems like a year ago. I lay it back on the nightstand, not ready to relive all the losses that got us here.

"Thanks for fixing it," I say.

"James did it. He found a few phones and brought them back. Bits and Hank won't stop playing Angry Birds."

"Is she better?"

Peter swallows the last of his cookie. "Bits is fine, besides wanting to see you. They're at Nel and Adam's cabin. We didn't want them to get sick. Penny, either. Everyone's fine."

We're here. If I didn't think I'd collapse, I'd jump for joy. Instead, I celebrate by easing my feet to the floor and admiring my new fuzzy pajama pants. "So, are you sharing those Oreos?"

"I'll share after you eat something real."

"And brush my teeth. And pee. It's been—how long has it been?"

"Three days."

"Have you slept in three days?"

He rushes to take my arm when I stand and says, "Some."

"I like my pants. Thanks for taking care of me."

"I didn't do anything. Rich took care of you."

I remember enough from the past few days to know that's not true, but I don't argue. He helps me with the first few wobbly steps until I stop at the bedroom door. "I think I'm okay to walk."

"Good, because you're on your own when you pee."

I smile and follow him into the toasty living room. He tells me the toilet flushes, which I also remember, although I prefer not to recall whoever brought me to the bathroom. Thank God I didn't have dysentery. I use the pitcher of water to brush my teeth and find that the toilet does indeed flush. A pail of water sits in the corner for filling the tank, but one try tells me I don't have the strength to lift it.

"Don't lift that bucket!" Peter calls.

"Wouldn't dream of it," I say.

I cast a longing look at the dry shower and avoid the mirror. Some things are better left unseen, and the knotted greasy strands of hair that hang around my head are enough for me. I let Peter lead me to the couch; brushing my teeth has taken the wind out of my sails. He stirs a pot on the woodstove, looking clean and shiny with only the usual trace of stubble.

"You shaved," I say.

"Well, someone did tell me my beard looked *meh*." He ladles soup into a bowl and sets it in my lap, then sits in a chair across from me.

"I don't know, I kind of liked traveling around with a bunch of fledgling Amish."

Peter waves his hand for me to eat. I don't feel hungry, but once I take a sip of soup I can't stop. I want to hook up a soup I.V. and dump in a gallon, even if it is canned and probably expired. I slurp it down without a spoon, chewing like a cow, and hand him the bowl for more.

I'm on my third bowl, which Peter has insisted be only broth, when Nelly walks through the front door. "There she is! How are you, Half-pint?" He kisses my cheek and perches on the coffee table bursting with disturbing good humor.

"I'm okay," I say cautiously. Now that my bowl's empty, I finally take in the boxes that are stacked in the kitchenette and peek out from the loft. "What's with all the boxes?"

Peter coughs into his fist. Nelly leans forward and cracks his knuckles with glee. "It's your share."

"My share of what?"

"The candy, tea, coffee, and hmm, let's see," he rustles in the bag he's set on the floor, pulls out a can of soda and pops the top, "Pepsi."

Oh, no. I hadn't forgotten—the memory is clear as day—but I hadn't yet remembered demanding all of that. Frank and my gun and Tara and Philip. I cover my face and whisper through my hands, "I said they weren't really Canadian."

They roar with laughter. Peter claps Nelly's back when he chokes on his Pepsi, and I pull the blanket over my head. "I can't ever leave this cabin. You guys will bring me stuff, right?"

"You are in dire need of a bath." Nelly yanks the blanket down, enjoying every second of my mortification. "And we all have to work. So, no."

Peter was right. I should've stayed here, if only so I didn't make a complete idiot of myself. At the time it had seemed so logical. "I had one lung! And lots of medicine. I didn't really want all this stuff, I was pissed off. Oh my God, everyone must hate me."

"Well, they might, but we all love you," Nelly says. "Our cabins are all full of this crap. Glory and Bernie said it was the least they could do, since we didn't have to come back at all after what happened."

I moan. Nelly pats my head. "There's plenty of junk in circulation right now. We emptied out that place and there was even more than they thought. We're set."

"We have to give most of it back." I won't give away the espresso for Peter or Christmas candy for the kids, but this is overkill.

"Peter said you'd say that. I say we keep it. We didn't take it all even though we could've."

"You can keep your Pepsi."

He finishes his drink and belches. "Don't worry, I will. Two cans a week. I'm good for two years. Thanks for being crazy, by the way."

I smile despite myself. "Merry Christmas."

Now that the torture portion of the afternoon is over, Nelly sits on the couch and drapes an arm around my shoulder. "Penny will take you to the baths later. If you're up for it."

"I am so up for it. Can I see Bits?" I want to hear Bits and Hank's goofy arguments. I want to see the relief of their faces after weeks of strain and worry.

"She's in school," Peter says. "But we'll get her when you go to the baths."

"Geez, those two can talk," Nelly says. "Adam and I have a cabin with a loft, and they spend all night yapping up there. They might not want to come back, as long as I come over here every day and get them candy."

It hurts to laugh, but I'm overjoyed to be sitting with two of my most favorite people in the world. I pray this was the last time we'll have to run, but as long as I have them it'll be all right wherever we end up. The happiness dampens when I remember Mikayla and Ben, and I say their names aloud.

"We buried them," Peter says. "There's a graveyard outside of town. They buried Frank and his son there, too."

I blink, afraid of what crying will do to my breathing capacity.

"Tara and Patricia told everyone what Frank did," Nelly says. "No one hates you. They're kind of scared of you, actually."

I make a face, glad to be thinking of something besides Mikayla. "Yeah, I'm real scary."

"You certainly look scary." Nelly lumbers off the couch. "I'll tell Penny you've joined the ranks of the living. And then I've got work."

"What kind of work?"

"James is running solar and hydroelectric power or some shit. I just do what he tells me."

"Have fun. Hate you."

He tickles under my chin. "Hate you, darlin'. I'm glad you're better."

Cool air circulates when he closes the door behind him. I tuck my blanket around me. "It's already freezing out there."

"It snowed the other day," Peter says. "It didn't stick, though."

"So I should be happy my lung collapsed and I didn't have to go outside."

Peter doesn't crack a smile at my joke. "You were really sick, much worse than Bits. They had to stick a needle in your chest to draw out the air."

"Aha! That would be why I feel like someone punctured my chest with a needle." I run my fingers along a tender spot on the side of my ribs. I can feel my ribs. I need more soup.

Peter chews his cheek. He does that when he's upset, and obviously he's too upset to enjoy my witty remarks. I pat the couch until he sits next to me. He closes his eyes and his chest hitches.

"Hey, everything's fine," I say. "We're all right."

He cries in the quiet way I've only seen a few times. He held it together the whole way here—after he'd lost Ana, while he sliced men's throats, when he feared losing Bits and, I guess, me. He's one of the most resilient people I've ever known, but this is a lot to come back from in a matter of weeks. Still, for all of that, it's not much of a cry.

He wipes his face and shrugs. "Sorry."

"If we have to start apologizing for crying I'm going to be writing apology notes for the rest of my life."

"True."

I jab him with a finger and rest my head on his chest. I've gotten used to being this close, to sleeping in the same bed as him. What would've been weird even a month ago feels normal and safe.

"You suck at crying, anyway," I say. "Five tears and you're done? I could've stretched that out for twenty minutes, at least."

His chest jumps with his laugh. "I'll try harder next time. You can have some more soup if you want."

I would like more, but I don't want to move. "Not yet."

"Just tell me when and I'll get it for you," he mumbles. His breaths deepen, arms twitching in sleep. I rub his shoulder when he mumbles in a way that sounds distressed. I'll watch over him for once. God knows he's done it enough for me.

CHAPTER 57

I'm winded and freezing by the time we arrive at the bathhouse, even though I have on a parka that's more suitable for arctic exploration than the high thirties. Penny hasn't told me what to expect, only that it's a surprise. On the way to the rectangular wooden building, she'd waved at a million people and several of them stopped to talk. There was Glory, who warned me to take it easy, an older hippie with dreadlocks who repeatedly said *right on*, a harried mother, two little children clinging to her sides, who asked Penny if she'd want in on the babysitting co-op when the time came, and a young guy asking for James's whereabouts. It was a relief to find they didn't seem to hate me and none of them were scared—exaggeration is Nelly's favorite sport. I would breathe a little easier except for the fact that I can't breathe all that well.

Penny leads me into a small room with a sign-in desk. Apparently, I have a towel coin, once known as a silver half-dollar, which Penny hands to the lady at the desk along with hers in exchange for two towels. We undress in a changing room full of wooden cubbies and wisps of fog that drift past every so often. Bits races in, followed by Jamie, Margaret, Liz and Jasmine. I have to sit on a bench when we hug, but it's the best hug I've had in a long while.

"Hank wanted to come, but since he has to go to the boys' side he had to stay at school," Bits says. She looks down at the floor. "Sorry I got you sick."

I pinch her cheek. "It's not your fault. It's the germs' fault."

"Stupid germs," she says, to which I agree wholeheartedly.

I hug the others, complimenting Margaret when I see her hair has lost its auburn ends to become a flattering shoulder-length brown. She shrugs but gives me an extra squeeze.

The next room is warmer, with showerheads spaced between partitions and pump handles instead of faucet knobs. "This is like the YMCA," I say. "Or summer camp. How is this a surprise?"

"The water's kind of on the cool side," Penny says, ignoring me, "so be prepared."

I take my towel off the hook and wrap it around me. "Pneumonia, remember? No way."

"It's worth it afterwards," Jamie says. "Just do it fast." She grabs shampoo and conditioner from a wooden rack and puts them on the ledge between two showerheads.

I step next to her with a sigh, then crank the pump and wash myself as fast as possible in the lukewarm water that falls. I give a few cursory swipes with a razor, but I don't have enough stamina to finish the job. When my hair is clean I wait, shivering in my towel.

Jamie stands beside me. "Jaz, don't forget the conditioner," she says to Jasmine. She turns to me. "I swear her hair was matted this morning."

"Are you two sharing a room?"

"Yeah. We're in the big cabin with Kyle and Nicki, Margaret, Zeke and Liz. I kind of checked with everyone to see if anyone minded if I take care of her." She gnaws on her lip. "Is that cool?"

"She's all yours. I have more than enough kids."

She pushes me with a laugh. "Thanks."

"Next stop," Penny says cheerfully.

I grumble while I follow her into a foggy room, suspecting she's trying to finish me off until I see the two large, rectangular wooden tubs that sit against opposite walls, each with its own stovepipe that rises through the roof. I climb into the water and sink to a bench. My parents always wanted a wood-fired hot tub, and now I know it's every bit as marvelous as they'd said.

"So, now what do you think?" Penny asks. "You can take unlimited lukewarm showers, pretty much, but you can sign up for two baths a week. Or drop in and see if anything's open."

"This is heaven." The steam makes me cough, but it's worth it. It's even worth a cool shower. "What's it like here?"

Everyone seems at home after only a few days. Days I wish I hadn't spent passed out because I feel as if I'm late to the party and might never fit in.

"It's so great." Bits wiggles her toes above the water. "There are lots of kids. Jaz, Hank and I are making comics to sell. We're going to trade them for stuff. And our teacher, Joe, is funny. Adam's teaching the older kids math. Ash and Nat are in his class. There's a girl named Peony. Isn't that a funny name? But I like it. We're putting on a play. It's like *The Wizard of Oz* but different, and I'm helping with the set."

I blink at the torrent of information and listen to more before she finally fizzles out. "Was I out for a month? How did so much happen?" I ask, and she giggles. "I'm glad you like it here."

Margaret squints through the steam with a small smile. "You will, too. Don't worry." A few days here seems to have done wonders for her. Or maybe it was the journey here.

Jamie has been playing Safe Zone nurse again, as well as doing guard and taking care of Jasmine. She tells me that they have a ranking system— First Guard, Second Guard and Third Guard. First Guard does patrol along with the usual guard duties.

"We're all on First Guard," Liz says. "No test needed. We told Bernie that you probably wanted to do guard and kitchen when you're better." She leans her head against the tub's edge and sighs. "Guard's cool, but there's no action. The Lexers to the north are frozen and we've only had a few at the fence."

"That's fine with me," I say. "I've had enough action to last me a lifetime."

People enter for the other tub, Tara and Patricia among them. I flash a quick smile instead of sinking under the water the way I'd like. Tara comes to the edge of our tub, her auburn hair piled on her head. "Cassie, you're up. That's great! Philip and I have been waiting to visit you."

"Sorry if I was, um, a little..." I'm not sure what I was. Crazy? Weird? Out of my flipping mind?

"You and Peter saved me and Philip. With a collapsed lung, no less. No worries! We owe you a ton of beers when you're up to it."

She walks to her tub, leaving Patricia standing with her arms behind her back and eyes on the wall. "Sorry I was...not very nice."

I get the feeling Patricia doesn't like to apologize for anything, so this is probably a huge deal. "That's okay."

She raises a slim shoulder. "No, it's not. I was looking for Corey the whole time, and when I saw him I...sort of lost it. He was a good friend. I'm usually better than that when we're outside. I'm on First Guard."

She's more concerned I might think she can't fight zombies than I might dislike her, which reminds me of Ana. They might've been friends, which would've been very interesting for the rest of us.

"I could tell," I say. "Before that, I mean."

"I like your tomahawk, by the way. Oh, and thanks for helping me out with...Corey."

"Sure." I hide my amusement that the last part was added as an afterthought. But it's not that big of a deal. That's what we do, and why having people you trust is so important. I've saved people, and I've been saved plenty.

"If you ever want to practice or whatever, that'd be cool. I run every morning if you want to come. When you're feeling better."

"I might," I say out loud while thinking *I might never.*

Penny waits until Patricia's in her tub facing the other way before she shakes her head. "How do they find you?" she whispers. "You're like the crazy person den mother."

"It's a gift," I say. "You know how cats flock to people who don't like them? The ones who love exercise always find me."

"They know you're a sucker," Liz says. I splash her.

"You mean lollipop," Bits says to Liz. "Oh, Cassie, I wanted to ask if there are any lollipops at the cabin. Nelly said he couldn't find them and we ate all of his."

"Why don't you come look? Rich says you and Hank should sleep at Nelly's for a while longer in case there are germs lingering, but you can visit. There's a lot of candy to sort through."

Bits licks her lips. "I love you."

"Are you talking to me or the candy?"

"Both," she says, and dunks herself before I can splash her.

CHAPTER 58

I'm on my fourth day in the cabin. Rich says he let me out for a bath as a morale boost, which might have been a nice way of saying I stank, but now I'm back on bed rest. I'm allowed visitors, though, and there's been a steady stream of people who must be so bored they stop by to hang out. I've met almost everyone, and I've sent them all home with something from the boxes. That's probably why they visit.

There's a knock at the door and Peter opens it on Terry, who lugs in a big box and sets it on the floor next to the couch. "There's more, but I picked the stuff that looked the newest."

I don't try to contain my excitement as I pick through the art supplies. The tubes of paint are like old friends and the brushes are the highest quality—the kind I would splurge on when I had the money. "Thank you so much. I love it all."

"No problem."

As much as I'm tired of sitting on the couch, I don't yet have the energy to do much else. The painting of Holly will have to wait or it'll be terrible. I point at the boxes that still litter the room. I made Nelly hide most of the coffee at his house, and now I only need to find a stovetop espresso maker for Peter's Christmas present to be complete. "Will you take this stuff back already?"

"I hear you keep giving it away. You could trade for it."

"I'm a terrible capitalist." I think of Dan saying those very words, and I laugh when Terry does. "They'll stop coming once I'm out of the good stuff."

"You'd be surprised. People here love to visit, especially when the dark and snow set in. Well, I should go." He puts his hands in his pockets but doesn't move. "Did Patricia apologize?"

"She did," I say, and grin when I remember how foreign the whole process seemed to her. "Why, did you make her?"

"Sometimes she has a little difficulty with...feelings. I didn't make her, though. Anyway, she wants to be friends, but she'd never ask."

He tugs at his dark ponytail and keeps his eyes on a moose painting, which I've just renamed Painting Project Number Two. I think he wants everyone to like Patricia as much as he does, and I'm beginning to think he might *like* like her a whole lot.

"Of course," I say, and pray this doesn't mean I have to take up running.

"I'm sorry about Frank. I just wanted you to know we all don't feel the way he did."

"I know. No hard feelings."

"All right, good. Feel better and get some rest."

Peter closes the door behind him. I keep telling Peter to go do something, but he's a worse mother hen than Penny. He crushes a few empty boxes and says, "Terry's a nice guy."

"He seems it. He has a thing for Patricia."

"How do you know?"

"You know I know these things. That's going to be a tough one, but I think I can make it happen."

"You're already trying to pair people off and you've only left the cabin once," Peter says.

"People like to be paired off, and I like to pair them. It's win-win. I'll live vicariously through them."

"What do you mean?"

I was trying to keep the conversation light, but I've blown it. "Just that I'm not looking...I don't want to lose—"

I break off at his grimace. In the past days, all the loss has hit him full on. Blindsided him, really. Maybe he thought he'd already mourned enough for one lifetime, but it seems there's always more to mourn.

"Yeah," he says. "I'm going out for a bit. Will you be okay?"

I have nothing profound to say, so I go with silly: "I'll be fine. Run free like the wind!"

To call what he gives me a smile would be a stretch. I watch him leave, my heart breaking for him. I feel all the losses, but I haven't fallen apart as I thought I would. What Peter needs is time, something we seem to have plenty of right now. Time may heal you, but it also gives you space to think about the things that hurt the most.

***

Peter comes through the door two hours later looking much better than when he left. He sets a bag on the counter and holds up a canning jar of white liquid. "I got potatoes and carrots. And cream. I'll make soup tonight."

"You could get food from the brewery. You don't have to cook."

He picks out the vegetables and slams them to the counter one by one. "I like to cook."

"I'm not complaining," I say softly. "I just don't want you to go to all that trouble." I pick up my book and try to reread the same line twenty times. I've been trying hard to tiptoe around his feelings and I'm not sure what I've done wrong.

He sinks to the couch and puts a hand on my knee. "It's not trouble, that's all I meant. I'm sorry."

I take his hand. It's rough and still cool from the outdoors. "What's wrong?" he asks. I'm sure my eyes are pink, making it obvious I'm trying not to cry.

"Talk to me," I whisper.

"About what?"

"Anything. Everything."

His eyes dart around the room. "I'm okay. This is—it's hard to go from survival mode back to normal. Or our new normal, I guess."

"I know. I miss her, too."

"She loved you," he says. "Quite possibly more than she loved me."

I laugh through my tears. Ana was my little sister, my friend and my partner in crime. There's a gaping hole where she once cajoled me into running and watched over me in her brusque and bossy way.

"She brought out the crazy in me," I say. "I liked being with her, even when she drove me bonkers. She let me be whatever I needed to be that day, no questions asked."

"She was good at that."

"This isn't what we expected," I say, and wave my hand at our cabin. "But maybe months or years from now we'll realize that we're exactly where we want to be."

"I know. It's the getting there that sucks."

"It does. Big time."

Peter squeezes my knee again before he heads for the kitchen, where he picks up a vegetable peeler and says, "Thanks."

"Remember how you would talk about Adrian even when I didn't want to? Because you knew I needed to. It's a taste of your own medicine. But it's good medicine. It makes it easier."

Peter nods and runs the peeler down a potato. I'm tired of watching him be productive while I sit on my butt. Enforced laziness loses all its fun by day four. "I'm not an invalid. Will you let me help?"

"You want to cut the carrots?"

"Sure."

Peter adds our chopped vegetables to the broth, and it's not long before we're eating the best creamy potato-carrot soup I've ever tasted. "Do you have some sort of magic that you sprinkle in your food? Is it in your fingers?" I ask. "It's crazy how good this is."

"And you wanted to eat someone else's food."

"I'd never want to eat there again, but they're planning to steal you away the second I'm well. I've seen them pacing around outside, peering in the windows, so I cough a few times to get them to back off. I can't keep it up forever."

"Where do you get these ideas? Eat your soup."

I don't need to be told twice. The fire crackles and in the soft glow of the lantern Peter almost looks happy. He has me in tears when he mimics all the people he's seen skulking past Zeke because they don't want to visit the dentist. Maybe this isn't what I was expecting, but right now I can't think of a single place left in the world I'd rather be.

CHAPTER 59

We've been in Talkeetna for almost three weeks when I pull my first guard shift. They've kept me in the kitchen thus far, and although I love it, I've been looking forward to guard. I said I'd had enough action, and it's still true, but guard makes me feel as if I have some control over my surroundings, however mistaken that notion may be. This extended absence from the fence line has made me uneasy.

I'm leaving breakfast shift when the lunch shift comes in. We're conserving the food that's harder to find and using what's fresh. That means salmon or some other fish has been on the menu every lunch and dinner. I may love food, but I hate seafood, and I've been doing breakfast to avoid being anywhere near the smell.

Peter, who's been co-opted by the kitchen just like I'd predicted, inspects the catch of the day. "Are you going to try my salmon later?"

"Not a chance," I say.

"Just a taste. It has birch syrup and garlic and all kinds of good stuff."

"That sounds lovely. I'll be sure to check it out."

"Stop humoring me," Peter says. "That is what you're doing, no?"

"I'm sticking to reindeer sausage. Or moose or bear or whatever it is. Sorry."

He pulls an evil-looking knife from a rack and begins to gut a silvery, slimy specimen. "I thought I had magic in my fingers."

"There's not enough magic in the world, let alone your fingers, to make fish taste good." I hold my nose as he scrapes out the innards. "You shower today, right?"

"Nope, and I'm going to wipe my hands all over your pillow when I get home."

I laugh and follow Nelly out the kitchen door onto Main Street. We wave to James, who's doing something to the greenhouses they're building beside the train tracks close to the river. The plan is to harness some power for the greenhouse lights, amongst other things. What they'll do when the light bulbs die, I don't know. James will probably figure out how to make them.

"Speaking of pillows," Nelly says as we turn for the gate, "where is your pillow these days?"

"What?"

"Your pillow. Is it still in the same bed as Peter's?"

I take in his smirk and slow to a stop. "Really? You're going there? I have my own side. Bits and Hank wanted the loft."

I'm blushing. I know I am. They begged for the loft, in fact, and we gave in. And then neither Peter nor I suggested looking for two twin beds to replace the big one. It would be weird to sleep in separate beds in the same room. Like we'd be saying we're afraid we might jump each other in our sleep. And we're not.

He pulls me along by my arm. "It was just a question."

"It's never *just* a question. Barnaby sleeps in the middle. It's not like we spoon all night or anything."

"Oh, just at the beginning of the night? Or in the morning?"

I shove him. "Neither. You and I slept in the same bed for months. Stop trying to make it something it's not. Why does everyone have to try to hook two people up all the time?"

"*You*, of all people, did not just ask me that."

"We're just friends. Please don't say anything in front of Peter and make it weird."

"Fine, fine," he says, but I know I haven't heard the end of this.

I don't have nightmares every night, but the ones I do have are doozies. If Peter wasn't there to pull me close in his sleep, I'd wander the cabin for hours trying to shake off my dream of John as a zombie or the back of a pickup in the middle of dark prairie; it's what I've done the two nights he's been on guard. And I can usually quiet him before he wakes so he doesn't remember what a bad night he had. I can't explain it to Nelly, who wouldn't believe that it can be intimate and innocent at the same time.

The weapons are kept in the long row of buildings, once gift shops, that sits fifty feet from the main gate. Talkeetna is so spread out that most people wear their weapons in case they happen to be in an area when an alarm sounds. I haven't yet heard the alarm, but I know which section of the fence to go to depending on the number of bells. It was all in the manual that was, unsurprisingly, penned by Patricia.

A green clapboard cabin sits beside the gate, smoke billowing from the stovepipe. It takes a lot of wood to warm Talkeetna in the winter; they cut it somewhere north and bring it downriver. They've lucked out here—the rivers and the Alaska Range serve as natural barriers. Glory has told me that at first it was all bloodshed and zombies, but she, Bernie and Frank managed to clear it of Lexers with the help of those who survived. I haven't asked how or when they took care of Frank. I want to hate him for wanting us dead, but I know it's easy to lose your way, or your mind, from grief.

The guardhouse interior contains a desk with a logbook and radio, several desk chairs and a couch next to the woodstove. Terry stands when we enter. "Hi, Cass. I thought I'd walk you around the fences today so you can get your bearings."

Patricia sits on the couch next to Clark, the man who opened the gate our first day here. He's good at spotting Lexers, which is why they call him Eagle. He even looks like one.

"She's already walked the boundary twice," Patricia says. She folds her arms over her chest and nods in satisfaction at herself for noticing or me for doing so.

"I missed the tour when I was sick. But I'd like a real tour, too." I walked the fence line to get a feel for what we were up against. It's impossible to sit in the center of town and be told I'm safe without seeing it for myself.

"Let's do it," Terry says, and throws on a thin coat. These people are crazy—it's barely above freezing and the nights dip well below. I'm still wearing my parka and positive I'm going to be living in it until next summer.

Nelly stays behind. The fence is much like Kingdom Come, made of whatever they had available—chain link, wood, corrugated metal—and parallels the dirt road to the river. Houses, some tiny and others a bit larger, sit just inside the fence. Terry explains that in order to live in one you have to be a guard.

"They have their benefits, though," he says. "Like running water."

"Before the pipes freeze, anyway," Patricia says.

Terry looks to Patricia with a smile. "Patty and I are neighbors."

"Patty?" I ask.

Patricia scowls but glances at Terry with something like adoration, which I find interesting. We hit the end of the road and follow the fence around the edge of a field. Leafy stalks stick out of mounded dirt in a few long rows, along with the lacy leaves of carrots. The rest of the field is dug up, but the overall size is impressive.

"That's a lot of potatoes and carrots," I say. "Glory said they grow well here."

"You know your plants," Terry says. "We'll dig up the rest of them this week. They can overwinter, but now that we have that root cellar we'll use that."

We pass a guard post cabin that flanks the fence by a wide river. Something that could be an arm or a small log floats past.

"Nothing really stops at this part of the river," Patricia says. "Unless they're washed ashore, they're usually stuck in the current and end up by Anchorage."

There's another guard post before the fence turns at the confluence of the three rivers that border Talkeetna. Chuck and Rich sit out front and stand as we approach.

"First guard today?" Chuck asks.

I pull Rich's sleeve. "Now that this one's finally cleared me for duty, I'm getting the tour." Rich smiles but doesn't speak. I've gotten used to his quiet, although it makes me fill in the silence with random thoughts. I point to the gate in the fence. "So that's Exit Three?"

"Yep, wanna come through? It's time to check if anything's washed ashore anyway."

Here, the river is broken up by narrow islands. It seems slow and shallow, although Terry says that changes during breakup in the spring, when it thaws. The riverbank is sandier than I expected, almost like the ocean.

"Glacial silt," Terry says.

The tall grasses on the silt islands resemble a marsh at the edge of the ocean. But unlike the ocean, beyond the water there's a sea of green that ends at the Alaska Range. I stop in awe at the spectacle. The days have been overcast and the weather here fluctuates wildly, so I haven't yet seen Denali, the tallest peak in North America.

"Beautiful, right?" Patricia asks. She tucks a strand of platinum hair behind her ear and shrugs like she's said too much. This girl needs to learn how to share her feelings.

I've seen mountains, and ones closer than Denali is to where we stand, but the way the white-capped range rises like a solid, jagged wall is something I've never seen. John would have taken it as further evidence of God and Adrian would have dropped to the ground in wonder.

"This is why people come to Alaska and never leave," I murmur.

"That's what I did," Terry says. "Came up when I was twenty, went home, packed and never looked back. I flew tourists to the glacier. We still have planes and some fuel in the airport across the tracks."

I keep my eyes glued to the mountains while we continue on. I've seen the advertisements for those glacier tours in the Alaska guidebooks in our cabin. Landing on a glacier smack dab in the middle of the range must be gorgeous and grand and safe and quiet. And freaking cold.

Chuck catches my arm when I stumble and says, "I think everyone who comes here on a clear day doesn't look where they're going."

I laugh and pay attention to the trail. "It's distracting."

"It sure is. How's Pete doing? He seems better."

I pat his arm. "He is. I'm glad you're here. He's always happy when he comes back from your place."

"Ah, we just shoot the shit, nothing special. Get in a few rounds of cards, maybe. He's improved. I whipped his ass last summer, but he's giving me a run for my money now."

"That'd be Nelly's tutoring," I say. "Well, whatever you guys do, it helps."

"I wouldn't say it's just me."

"Time. It takes time."

"He thinks highly of you, you know. Says you're strong."

I know I'm strong, but when I contemplate all the times I haven't been, it seems like a whole lot. "I wish I were stronger."

"Don't we all?" Chuck asks. "Looks like they found something up ahead. Things tend to wash up right around there."

The others have stopped at what looks like driftwood but, upon closer inspection, are two bodies. They're naked and white, limbs made formless by water. They're the same as the one in the boathouse—swollen to where the subtle bump of a nose is the only indication you're looking at a face. But even with being so far gone, one's mouth opens like a hungry baby bird.

I kneel beside the body, pull my knife out of its sheath and gently press it where an eye should be. The mouth closes once more and then gapes open forever. The anger or terror or hate I usually feel is absent. I don't have to run in fear that there are others, so I silently say a few words for these now harmless creatures. I'm sorry for the way their lives have played out.

Rich bows his head for a moment. I think he understands why I did it this way—they were people, like his own daughter, like Adrian and Ana and countless others. Patricia turns away, blinking quickly, and I suspect that she yearns for someone to crack her tough exterior—don't we all?

I take in the mountains, the grasses waving above the silvery river, and the bodies on the ground. I'm surrounded by beauty and horror and suffering and love. I was before the virus, but they were never quite so present and closely intertwined.

There are so many things I wish hadn't happened. I can't change the past, but I can strive to not live in fear they'll happen again. I can believe that if they do, I'll make it all right. A lightness expands in my chest until

I'm filled with something I haven't felt in a while—joy. Joy that I'm here to carry on when so much has been lost.

I wipe my knife in the long grass and take Patricia's arm in mine before we move on.

CHAPTER 60

By November, the ground is white, the roofs are white and, if you stand still long enough, you're white. Our cabin is delightfully warm as long as the fire's going, which has become my top priority. I stomp off my boots and step into the thoroughly domestic scene of two kids doing work at the table while Dad turns a screwdriver on a metal box of some sort. The fire crackles and something smells good. Once the snow flies, many people take their rations of food and cook in their homes during the dark dinner hours. Breakfast and lunch are still noisy affairs, and we often eat those meals at the brewery to confirm that the rest of the world hasn't frozen to death.

"Did you know that so far this is the snowiest winter they've had in twenty years?" I ask, and take off my coat, scarf, hat and mittens. The snow hasn't let up since it started. The zombies are officially popsicles, and even if they weren't, they wouldn't be able to get through the drifts.

"Of course it is, because you're here," Peter says.

He goes back to his screw and the kids go back to their papers. Evidently, no one is as appalled as I am by this news. I listen to their chatting as I pull on pajama pants and a clean shirt. I've managed to avoid laundry shifts, being classified as First Guard, but when the zombies are frozen we all get our turn with the poop wash.

"I see you've dressed for dinner," Peter says when I reenter the living room.

"I'm sorry, were we dressing for dinner? Is the president on his way, or was that the queen tonight?"

"The potluck, goofball."

It means I have to go out into the cold again, but it's only across the clearing to one of the big cabins, and there's no one there I feel the need to impress. "Right. I'm dressed, then."

The first thing I do when we arrive is make a beeline for Penny. "So? Anything?"

She rests her hands on the stomach I mistakenly thought couldn't get any rounder. "Oh my God, would you stop asking me that twelve times a day? You know Glory said most first babies are late. Start asking in mid-December, when I'm actually due. Unless you're trying to torture me?"

"Fine, fine. I won't ask again until the kid is hanging out of you."

"Nice outfit," Nelly says from his easy chair. "What'd you bring to eat?"

"I have no idea," I say. "Peter made it. But it smells good."

"You're lucky. Adam and I go to the brewery. Hey, Adam, why don't you cook for me?"

Adam turns from stacking plates. "Because you wouldn't appreciate it. You'd shovel it down and forget it took hours to cook on the woodstove."

It does take hours to cook. Sometimes Peter starts it on a kitchen shift and brings it home. I do the same when he's on guard, or I just grab whatever's on offer. I'd rather paint than cook. Once I finished Holly's portrait, I was deluged with requests from others. They hand me their creased, worn photos and I do my best to recreate them. I wasn't a portrait painter before, but I like being the conduit between the old life and the new. I won't take anything for the paintings unless someone has more art supplies, which I always accept.

Nelly tells us that the wildlife is making its way back to the area. They've bagged moose, and between that and Terry flying a hunting crew to the caribou herds, we have a lot of meat hanging frozen in the storage area. That salmon will not have to pass my lips is the best news I've heard since the zombies froze.

Liz perches on the arm of Zeke's chair with a hand on his shoulder. She looks softer, more feminine somehow, until she pinches his ear at a comment I assume was teasing.

"What's with that?" I whisper to Penny.

"I have no idea. They look happy, though."

I wink at Liz, who blushes—there's a first time for everything—and get up to help Peter set out plates and utensils.

"Check those two out," I murmur.

"I saw that coming a mile away," he says. I put my hands on my hips and frown. "If I'd told you, you would've done something stupid like lock them in a closet."

"No, I wouldn't have!" I push him. He twirls me so my back is to his chest and Jamie and Kyle are in my line of sight.

"I wasn't born yesterday," he says into my ear. "But I will say that they've gotten close. I don't think they're always together because of Jasmine and Nicki."

"Ooh, really?"

He nudges me forward. "Go do your thing."

It doesn't surprise me that our people are pairing up, even with all the new faces in the mix. Our voyage here may have been on land, but it brought about a sea change, strengthening our bonds. I think for a minute and saunter over to Jamie. "I thought we could have Jasmine and Nicki one of these nights for a sleepover. We'll make popcorn and play games. You can get them in the morning."

"That sounds like fun, but they don't have to sleep there. It might be kind of cramped."

"We have a floor. You could have an uninterrupted night of sleep. A big bed all by your lonesome." I spread my arms and let out a big sigh. Peter shakes his head like I'm overdoing it. I shrug. "Well, you guys let me know. Bits and Hank would love it."

I'm four feet away when Kyle says, "How about Saturday?" He glances at Jamie, who nods and concentrates on smoothing down her unwrinkled shirt.

"Perfect."

Peter returns my surreptitious thumbs up. He's getting into the spirit of things. I fill my plate next to Zeke and try not to smile. "So...what's new, Zekey?"

"Just say it, sugar."

"You and Liz are getting it on."

His entire body shakes. "Cut right to the chase, don't be shy. She's a great lady."

"I know. I'm happy for you. And very jealous. I thought we'd be together one day."

"You'll always be my one and only Sugar."

I pretend to sniff. "You can call her Sugar, too. Although she might punch you if you do."

"You got that right."

"You look happy, Zekey. You deserve it. Maybe you'll take that trip one day after all."

"You never know," he says, eyes twinkling. "She can ride, that's for sure. You deserve to be happy, too."

"I am."

I kiss his cheek before I make way for the mob of hungry people. That feeling of joy hasn't left me yet. The people, the mountains, and the town's quirky little houses have become home more quickly than I thought possible. Even Patricia has warmed up, or at least she doesn't scowl when I call her Patty, which I do at every opportunity. I may complain that the weather is my worst nightmare come true, but I don't even mind that so much.

CHAPTER 61

Barnaby and Peter don't stir when I get out of bed in the middle of the night. The Leonid meteor shower should be starting around now. I want to make sure it's in full swing before I drag the kids out of bed, and I want one night to myself before that. After the kettle is on the stove, I walk into the dark. I don't need to go far; the porch steps are swept of the last snowfall and there's plenty of sky that can be viewed from the clearing in the center of the cabins.

I sit on the bottom step and lean back on the porch. We watch the stars as much as possible, although the weather makes it less enjoyable. The only drawback of Alaska is that the summer nights are light. I might not see all the summer stars again if I live here the rest of my life.

The first meteor shoots across one of Andromeda's chained arms. I imagine it cutting her loose, the cord snapping the way my bootlace did. Maybe I never would have fought back if it hadn't been for her story—for Dan—and I hope he knows how thankful I am that he was in my life.

A few more meteors zing past. I wished for so much on the way here, but now I can't think of a single wish except that I want things to stay the same. Maybe that's as good a wish as any.

The door opens, lantern light spilling onto the porch. "Everything okay?" Peter asks.

"Fine. It's the Leonid meteor shower, I think."

"Oh, okay. Don't freeze to death."

"Want to watch with me?"

"Sure. Let me get dressed." He comes out a few minutes later bearing mugs of tea. "I thought you could use it. I didn't think you'd be out here."

"Dan and I had a date to watch the Leonids. I wanted to keep it."

"I don't want to intrude."

He starts to rise, but I tug him down beside me. "No, stay. I thought I wanted to be alone, but I don't. I wanted to give him this night because I'm probably the only person left who thinks of him. There are so many people...he gets lost in the shuffle." I scoop snow off the ground and toss it into the dark. There are so many people who have no one to remember them. I don't want one of them to be Dan.

"I think of him. He didn't have to stay to help us, but he did. You and Hank might not be here if he hadn't. I think he really did love you."

I shrug. Not because it doesn't matter, but because there's nothing to do about it now. "You know what he once said? That maybe the world ended this way so that the people who belonged together would find each other."

"Was he talking about the two of you?"

"We were talking about Caleb and Liz at the time."

"That match was not made in Heaven," Peter says.

"It was most definitely not written in the stars," I say with a laugh. Zeke is much more Liz's speed than overeager, nineteen year-old Caleb. "I don't know that there is such a thing, but I'm still sitting here just in case Dan can see. I think we go on in one form or another. I hope so."

I know that if Adrian is watching, he'd understand why I want to remember Dan. Adrian wanted me to live, and Dan is one of the reasons I'm still alive.

"Reincarnation, maybe," Peter says, and sips his tea.

I groan. "Don't say that. I am not coming back to this wasteland."

"I would."

"Well, you're crazy," I say. "Why would you do this again?"

"I want more time. I'm not ready to give this up."

"I want more time with you guys. But when I'm done, I'm done. Imagine being born into this world? Imagine having a baby? Starting a family?"

Peter's quiet before he says, "It's a leap of faith."

"It's a trans-Atlantic flight of faith," I say, to which he laughs. We watch the stars in silence. "Want to know what you're looking at?"

I lay my head beside his and move my finger as I tell him the stories. He's gotten quite a few down by now. "You really do know them all," he says when we're finished.

"Not all, but I will one day."

Peter points to just above the trees. "Is that what I think it is?"

A faint green line has rippled into the dark. It's followed by a shimmering yellow cloud and then another. A reddish cast slowly appears and unfurls like a ribbon. They pulse and shift and light up the sky. I could almost believe they're made of fairy dust.

"We should wake the kids," I say.

"I'll get them."

Peter brings them out a few minutes later, and they watch the Northern Lights in awe before Bits whispers, "I'm going to make my wish. Are you?"

"Sure," I say.

"It has to be good. You only ever get one."

"I'll think about it." The red turns to fuchsia as I try to think of a big wish, but it's the same as earlier. I make it anyway—it's the only thing I want. I pull Hank close to me on the steps and ask, "Did you make your wish?"

"Yes. I wished for X-Men comics."

"Hank!" Bits gasps. "That was such a waste!"

"It doesn't work, anyway. But I really do want them."

Bits sighs. "Did you make yours, Cassie?"

"I did. And Hank can wish for whatever he wants. It's his wish." And now I have to find X-Men comics if it kills me.

"I wished for Superman comics," Peter says.

Bits laughs at his joke. "That's the best you could think of, Hank? How about graphic novels, at least?"

That whole portion of sky is alight. I want to wake up everyone so they can see, but I don't want the noise and commotion. There'll be other nights. Right now I'm happy to sit here with these three, even though two of them argue cheerfully about the best graphic novel choice for a wish this grand.

"Sorry we've crashed your party," Peter murmurs.

"This is much better," I say. "It's exactly what I would want to see if I were looking down from...wherever. You know we have to find him X-Men comics now, right?"

"Maybe in Anchorage."

They're making a trip south on snowmobiles, which means we can't bring much back, but the plan is to kill whatever's frozen in the infested places and then return with trucks in the spring. As First Guard, both Peter and I are invited.

"We're bound to find something good down there," I say.

"You're really coming? You know it's going to be cold, right?"

"How cold could it be? It's already like hell froze over."

CHAPTER 62

The answer to "How cold could it be?" is "Extremely fucking cold." I had a vision, admittedly a ridiculous vision, of reaching somewhere warm upon arrival at our destination. But it's dark stores and snow and frozen zombies all around when we reach the first shopping center. My first order of business is to make a trashcan fire and stand shivering over the flames until my hands work again.

It's peaceful, though, and the mountains outside of Anchorage are stunningly white. The only difference in temperature between indoors and out is the lack of snow, but I kind of enjoy walking around the empty stores. Every kid has dreamt of having an unbridled shopping spree, and each of us gets to fill our backpack with whatever we'd like as long as we can wear it back.

But first, we have to kill all the Lexers so we're not unpleasantly surprised come spring. Fred Meyer is empty of food but full of things that might come in handy, such as tools and garden supplies. We start at one end and sweep the store with our spikes until someone calls the all-clear, then it's on to the next store once we've locked up.

Peter and I head to a bookstore for comic books, where he laughs when I scare the crap out of myself twenty times. I know the Lexers are frozen, but that doesn't stop my natural instinct to jump when I see one unexpectedly. We stuff X-Men comics and graphic novels in our bags. Now, besides baby stuff, I only need an espresso maker for Peter.

We clear an outdoor store and a supermarket that has enough food to make killing a whole lot of zombies worth our time, but I'm no closer to finding what I need. I'm so cold that I've decided to give up and think of something else when I see a gourmet cooking store tucked into a high-end strip mall down the way. It's my last hope, and I make an excuse to plod through the snow with Nelly.

"What do you need over here, anyway?" he grumbles.

"It's for Peter. For Christmas."

"What about me?"

"Pepsi, remember?"

We break the glass door and peruse the rows of wire racks filled with fancy kitchen equipment. I wander around all the shiny steel and enameled pots until I find a small Italian stovetop espresso maker in the back. I shove it in my bag and pick up a Dutch oven that weighs a ton and cost over $300 once upon a time. It won't fit in my bag, but Nelly has room.

I put it in his arms and say, "Please?"

"No way. You know I have to wear this thing all the way back."

"Pretty please?" I clasp my hands together. "It's not for me. Peter used to have one the same color."

"Another thing for Peter? And all I get is Pepsi?"

"A lot of Pepsi, which is the best present ever and you know it. This is from the kids. Can you just do it already? He did save your life, you know."

Nelly drops his head back the way he does when he's going to give in. "Fine."

By the time we've gotten back, I'm frozen to the core. It was slower going with the full trailers, and my special fur boots and mittens and face mask did the job of keeping frostbite away, but that's about it. I stand in the cabin, too cold to undress or take off my backpack or do anything except want to die.

"What'd you get?" Bits asks.

"It's a secret," Peter says.

"What's wrong with Cassie?" Hank asks.

Peter knocks on my head. "She's frozen solid."

He helps to remove my backpack and coat, and then seats me by the fire while he wrestles with my boots. It takes him, along with Bits and Hank, a good five minutes to figure out my double knots. My mouth has lost the range of movement needed to form speech, and I watch them and quake until I've regained feeling in my face and limbs.

"I am never doing that again. Ever," I finally say. "Thank you. I would've stood there all night."

"For a minute there I thought you'd have to wear those boots all night," Peter says, and shakes out his fingers. "All right, time for bed, guys."

The kids go without a fuss because they know there's Christmas stuff in the bags. I head for bed and huddle under the down comforter, but the cubes of ice at the end of my legs, formerly known as feet, won't warm up. Peter brings in the lantern and gets on his side. I hear several pages of his book turn before he says, "What are you doing? Dancing?"

"I'm putting my feet on my calves to warm them, but I have to keep switching."

"Put them on me."

I was going to ask, but I didn't want it to be weird. Nelly has made me very conscious of what's over the line and what isn't. I'm not even sure what's over the line anymore. "Are you sure? They're really, really cold."

"Yeah, yeah, I know they're cold. I've felt them before."

"It's your funeral," I say, and press them to his side.

He jumps. "Holy shit!"

"I told you. It's a whole new level of cold." He clamps his elbow over them while I bury my head in my pillow to wait out the pins and needles. When feeling has returned, I pull them back. "Thanks. Where's Barnaby when you need him? It's a one dog night."

"He's still by the fire."

"So you filled the role of dog," I say, and reach to ruffle his hair. "Good boy."

He catches my wrist and holds it in the air, wearing his usual teasing half-smile with a slightly-cocked eyebrow, but my reaction is anything but usual. I notice the shape of his lips and the way his t-shirt is just fitted enough to hint at what I know is a lean and sculpted chest. I imagine him pinning my hand above my head, those lips and that body on mine, and remember the taste of his mouth with sudden clarity. A flush rises from my abdomen to my cheeks when I allow myself to wonder what being with this version of Peter would be like. There are so many reasons it would be a bad idea—Ana, our friendship, Bits. Once it was done we couldn't ever go back.

I realize I'm staring when he lowers my hand to the bed with a friendly pat, but not before I see something flicker in his eyes—surprise, uneasiness or maybe even the same desire. The air is charged like that day we first saw the Rockies. And it strikes me, like one of those bolts of lightning that flashed overhead, that Peter already has my heart, and I want to seal the deal with my body.

"Should I get the light?" he asks. The set of his features hasn't changed and whatever I thought I saw is gone. But when he averts his eyes and waits patiently in the few extra seconds it takes me to find my voice, I know I saw something.

"Sure," I whisper.

I lie in the dark, wondering if he felt what I did. I'm afraid he didn't and afraid he did at the same time. I've been convinced that I love Peter in a way that isn't romantic but not exactly the way I love Nelly. We have a connection that I attribute to Bits, but maybe it's been there since the night we met, when he gave me a glimpse of who he really was—who he is now. He would draw me in, but he also pushed me away so consistently that I'd finally decided he wasn't worth my time, energy and love. I was wrong.

I watch the sky through my window and wonder if this could have been written somewhere up there. If it's possible the stars have led me to a cabin in Alaska and a bed shared with my best friend. It doesn't lessen what I had with Adrian. Maybe love doesn't have to be quantified as more or less—it's just different than anything I've ever felt. This has grown out of heartbreak and friendship, out of forgiveness and being truthful about our real selves. I've been around for Peter's worst moments as well as his best. And I love everything about him. He's perfect for me.

CHAPTER 63

There's one good thing about living with the person you're secretly in love with, which is also the most torturous—they're always around. I can hide my feelings and act normal for the most part, but when I find myself swooning at the muscles in his forearm that still has a trace of summer tan, I tell myself to get a grip. I force myself not to daydream about what I want his rough, capable hands to do to me. And I know from past experience that they're extremely capable.

I would move to the couch rather than lie awake at night with every nerve ending tingling in anticipation, but I'll take a platonic bed-sharing arrangement over nothing. I'm thinking on this while I make the bed—or as close as I get to bed-making, which is to confirm the covers aren't in a ball—and freeze with my hand to my mouth. I've become Dan, waiting for someone who might never be ready to love me back. It's not the most uplifting of thoughts.

I have the day off and plan to paint while Hank and Bits are at school and Peter's on guard. The kids are already gone and Peter's lacing up his boots in the living room when Nelly, who sees the door as a formality with which he'd rather not be bothered, breezes in. "What are we doing on our day off?" he asks me.

"I'm painting," I say, and point to the corner window where I like to paint in what little light we get this time of year.

"Bor-ing. Let's do something fun."

"Does it involve going outside? Because I wasn't planning to do that until dinner time."

Nelly sinks to the dining table with his chin in his hand. "Stop being a hermit. C'mon. We'll bother Pen or something."

"Working," I say. "She's on lunch today."

"They're like slave drivers here. She's about to pop and they're making her work?"

"They are not, and she still has almost two weeks. Stop being so dramatic." I sit at the table and decide Nelly's right. "So what are we going to do?" He whoops in delight.

Peter dons his coat and covers his hair with an equally black hat. "All right, have fun whatever you do."

"Don't forget your water bottle," I say.

He touches my shoulder on his way past. "Thanks. We'll meet at dinner?"

"Yeah. I'll bring the kids."

"Okay. See you then." Sometimes, when he looks at me like this—dark eyes locked with mine—I think that maybe it's not just me. It's probably wishful thinking. And although Hank is probably right that wishes don't work, I could kick myself for wishing that things stay the same because I want things to be very different. I watch him leave, trying not to think about how his shoulders are solid under his coat and how his jeans sit low on his hips and slouch perfectly on his shitkicker boots. To think I once made fun of those jeans.

"—it warms the cockles of my heart," Nelly finishes.

I return to the conversation. "What does?"

"To see you guys playing house."

"We live in the same house. What are we supposed to do—ignore each other?" I stand and stack dishes next to the dry sink so I don't have to look at him. I know Nelly can read me like a book, but I wonder how obvious it is to the rest of the world.

"The lady doth protest too much," he says.

"Whatever, Shakespeare. Where are we going?"

"Let's stay here and chat." His boots hit the table and he leans back with his hands behind his head. "Sit down, darlin'."

"You're supposed to take your shoes off when you come in," I say, dodging his request. "I'm tired of washing the floor."

"You've never washed a floor in your life."

I ignore him and step into my boots. Nelly's like a bloodhound on a scent, but he bides his time and attacks when you least expect it. I'm going to have to be on my guard. He looks at me for a long moment before he strolls to the door. "Let's see who's at the clubhouse."

The clubhouse was once a restaurant and now where they feed the overflow of people at meals. At other times of the day, people hang out at the tables and couches. It's the social hub of Talkeetna, and while I like to visit, I'd rather spend my free time at home or with small groups of people. Sometimes I worry that I won't be able to hear something coming. It may not be a concern in the winter, but old habits die hard.

When we enter, we're deluged with offers to get in on a card or board game. Nelly leads me to a couch where I lose at poker with Tara and Philip before they leave for their street shoveling shift.

Patricia strides our way, turns a chair backward and pushes her hair off her face. "What's up?"

"Hey, Patty," Nelly says.

"Stop with the Patty already," she says.

"Terry calls you Patty," Nelly says. "You don't seem to mind."

She flashes a look that says to tread no further, which goes completely over his head.

"You know, maybe you two gals should think about dating," Nelly says to us. "You could have your pick of the litter. Like, for instance, Patty and Peter would look good together."

Here it is—the attack. I shrug and find it easy to be dismissive since I know she has no interest, but it still makes my stomach roil.

"No thanks," Patricia says.

"Or you and Terry," Nelly says to me. "You seem like his type. Should I see if he's interested?"

I elbow his side when Patricia looks like a kid whose birthday was canceled. "I have no interest in Terry. He has no interest in me. You know that."

Patricia bolts from her chair, mumbling something about guns, and I sincerely hope it wasn't something about coming after me with one later. I pull him up by his sleeve and push him into the snow-covered street. "You're an ass! She's so in love with Terry she can't see straight."

"Shit. I had no idea."

"You know, for someone so observant you can be completely clueless when you want to get your way." I sink against the side of the building, heart drumming and mouth dry. I don't want to say it aloud and make it real, but Nelly will never stop pestering me until I do. "So just do it. Say what you want to say. Ask whatever you want to ask."

Nelly rubs his cheeks and deliberates before his sky blue eyes meet mine. "No."

"No?"

He puts his hands in his pockets and shrugs. "You'll tell me when you want to."

I'd like to walk because I'm freezing, but I'm frozen in shock. He must have something up his sleeve. "Seriously?"

He takes my arm and wanders back toward the cabins. "Yup. So what shall we do next? The world, or a small fenced-off part of it, is our oyster. We have three hours until sundown at the ridiculously early time of 3:30."

"Let's go to the big cabin and see who's there."

"Your wish is my command." After a block, Nelly clears his throat. "So, anything you want to tell me?"

"Can't think of anything," I say.

He throws me into a snowdrift and laughs while I splutter obscenities. But, to his credit, he doesn't ask again.

CHAPTER 64

We have a Christmas tree. Really, it's the top of a fir tree that'll be kindling next year, but it's pretty with the decorations we made during art class at the school.

"Did we get Barn a present?" Bits asks. She lies on the floor next to the dog, fiddling with the earrings Penny and I put in on her birthday, and Peter followed with a French fry and vanilla milkshake party. Making ice cream is easy when your entire world is snow and ice.

"We'll give him a bone."

"How about Sparky?"

"Also a bone," I say.

"Did you get something for Peter?"

"A bone. Everyone gets bones this year."

She giggles. "He'll make soup with it. And then he can give us soup for Christmas."

"Perfect," I say.

Hank pokes his head out from the loft. "But did you get him something for real?"

"I have something from you guys. It's a pot. He really can make us soup."

Bits rolls on her back and looks at me upside down. "A pot? Why on Earth would you get him a *pot*?" I'd like to ask her where she got that tone, but it's like listening to a recording of me.

"It's a fancy pot, like hundreds of dollars fancy. It's turquoise."

She stands. "Can I see? Hank, come and look."

I take them into the bedroom and pull it out of the closet. They like it but look unimpressed. "You know how I love art supplies? Well, cooking's an art, too. The most famous chefs in the world used pots like these. People would travel all over just to try their food."

"Really?" Bits asks. "Maybe they'll come here one day just to try Peter's food. It's good enough to fight zombies for."

I kiss her cheek. "Tell him that, he'll love it."

It's true. The food here was decent but boring, especially made in large quantities, but now the restaurant is always full when people know he's on.

"So he'll really like this," Hank says.

"Thanks for getting it." Bits grins, eyes the same color as the Dutch oven. "Can we wrap it?"

The cabin door opens in the outer room. Bits places the pot on the closet floor and then yanks most of my clothes off the hangers to throw on top. Like I need any help being a slob.

"Hello?" Penny calls.

I follow Bits to the living room. She shows no interest in cleaning up the clothes even though it's not Peter. Another wonderful habit inspired by me.

"Hey, Mama," I say. "Anything?"

She sinks to the couch. It was her due date almost a week ago. "Nothing. Nada."

"It can only be a couple weeks at the most. Glory's never seen anyone go more than three weeks past."

Bits wanders back into my bedroom when Hank calls. "Hey, pick up those clothes," I yell after her. I'm met with a non-committal reply.

"Glory says to try sex," Penny says. "This is easier said than done, but I've told James he's on tonight. He looked a little frightened."

I snort and throw a log into the woodstove just as Nelly enters in his usual sweep of wind and snow. "Shoes!" I yell, and he stops to remove them before he launches himself onto the couch next to Penny.

"I bagged us a turkey for Christmas," Nelly says.

"What?" I ask. "I didn't think there were wild turkeys in Alaska."

"I didn't shoot it, I won it in poker. Peter's going to cook it in the kitchen the night before."

We're having Christmas dinner at the big cabin. Chuck and Rich are invited, along with a few others besides our group. It's such a large town that everyone couldn't eat dinner together anyway.

Adam walks in and removes his shoes, unlike his other half. "It's so warm in here."

I wedge another piece of wood into the stove. "But the bedroom is still cold, even if it's ninety degrees out here."

"Why don't you snuggle with Peter?" Nelly asks. "That'll warm you."

"Would you stop?" I ask, and head for the kitchen without looking up because I know they're all staring and my face is a dead giveaway. I'm most afraid of Penny thinking I'm usurping Ana, or that I don't miss her.

Adam sighs. "Nel, shut—" He breaks off when Peter walks in.

"Hey, are we having a party?" Peter asks.

Adam stands and drags Nelly to the door. "We were just leaving."

They say their goodbyes, and Peter moves to where I'm wrapping up what's left of dinner, my cheeks finally cool. "Dinner was yummy, thanks," I say.

"I knew you wouldn't leave the house in this, and then you'd eat something crappy."

A layer of ice swooped in this morning, and with my walking skills being what they are at times, I came home after breakfast shift and art class. "It's a good thing. We were going to eat your cookies."

His mouth drops. "You wouldn't."

Peter may love Bits more than life itself, but he doesn't share his Oreos. I refused when he offered me some because I never would've enjoyed the corn syrup as much as he does. I like to tease him, though. As long as I keep things silly, I don't worry that he'll see how I feel. I stand on my tiptoes and pretend to reach for their hiding place in an upper cabinet.

"You wouldn't dare," he says, and spins me around by my belt.

I lean against the counter and smile up at him. "You don't know what I'm capable of."

It comes out low and flirty instead of silly, and his eyes darken in response. His hand is still on my waist, its warmth radiating through my shirt to my skin. I think he wants to kiss me, and I'm pretty sure I'm failing at hiding how much I want him to. His gaze lowers when I moisten my lips, his fingers digging into my waist.

"Well, I've got a date," Penny says.

We jump and turn to find Penny standing, fingers on her glasses. I'd forgotten she was here, and so must have Peter, because his hand drops like a stone and he takes a step back. My throat tightens when I think about how it must look that I sleep in the same bed and spend most of my time with her dead sister's boyfriend. How obvious my desire must have been to the both of them just now. It doesn't matter that I haven't done anything to feel guilty about; wanting it makes me guilty enough. Even if Ana did say she'd want Peter to move on, even if I truly think she'd be glad.

Penny eases her feet into her soft boots and heads to the door. Just before leaving, she smiles our way, although it's tinged with sorrow. It doesn't exactly give me the go-ahead, but maybe it says she wouldn't hate me forever. I can't tell if Peter's noticed since he looks everywhere but at me.

The kids come from the bedroom. Bits's eyes widen when she sees Peter, and she holds her arms straight by her sides. Peter clears his throat. "Everything all right, baby girl?"

"Yes," she says. "We were in your room for a reason."

"Okay. Do you want to tell me the reason?"

Hank shakes his head at Bits, who will blurt out everything as if under torture with almost no prodding. "No. It's a pot for you," she says, and slaps her hand to her mouth.

"You're the *worst*," Hank says with a groan. "I should've wished for you to be able to keep secrets."

I burst into laughter while Peter bites back a smile. He meets my eyes and the awkward moment passes. Peter's still my best friend, and I don't want to lose that. If he doesn't feel the same, I'll have to find a way to let this go.

I lose at Monopoly for the thousandth time, even using Hank's secret system, after which we head to bed. I'm almost asleep when Peter's hand brushes my hair. I don't know if it means we're back to normal or if we're heading somewhere new, but either way, he's with me.

CHAPTER 65

Barn and Sparky devour their bones while Bits and Hank tear through their presents. Hank holds up the X-Men comics and raises his eyebrows at Bits. When he gets to his stocking, he sits quietly with the small portrait I made of his family in his lap. I'm never sure if it's a good idea to make a portrait for someone who hasn't asked, but so far it's always been appreciated.

I sit on the floor behind him. "I thought you might want them here today. I was going to wait, but…"

Hank nods and moves into my lap. It won't fit in a pocket like Bits's locket, but it's small enough to tuck in a bag if we have to leave.

"Sometimes Christmas can be hard," I say. "It's when we miss people the most."

"I'm excited it's Christmas, though." His voice cracks. It's been doing that occasionally, but this isn't puberty.

I twist one of his dreads. "It's normal to be a whole lot sad and be happy at the same time. And it's normal to feel guilty about being happy."

"It is?"

"Absolutely. But your dad would want you to be happy. It wouldn't hurt his feelings. I know that for a fact."

"Okay." He traces Henry's and Dottie's faces with his finger and stops on Corrine's purple shirt. "How did you know Corrie liked purple?"

"She kept wishing she'd brought her favorite purple shirt to the campground," I say. "She told me all about it, so I made it up from her description."

"It looked just like this. She wouldn't shut up about it. I forgot about that."

He rests his head on my collarbone and doesn't move for a long while. Finally, he goes up to the loft and comes down empty-handed. "I put it by my bed. It's near my bag in case we have to go."

"Good idea," I say. "But I don't think we'll have to go anytime soon, and I can always make another." He's slow to smile, but when he does like he is now, it lights up his face.

"Open yours, Peter!" Bits says. Peter winces when she drops the heavy pot in his lap.

"Whatever could this be?" He unwraps the fabric we've wrapped it in and looks my way. "You remembered the color. I love it, thank you." He hugs the kids and admires his pot some more, then passes me a package. "Here."

It's a large canning jar full of something thick and brown. "What is it?"

"Poop. We made you a jar of poop," Peter says, which sends the kids into hysterics.

I dip in a finger and groan in pleasure at the buttery caramel but screw the cap closed before I eat it all. "That's good poop. Thank you."

"I told you I'd make you caramel sauce one day."

And I told you I'd love you forever if you did, I don't say back. I'm sure he doesn't remember. "Wait!" I say as he hands me a jewelry box. "You have to open your other two."

He unwraps the espresso maker and then the box with the espresso beans I hoarded, of which there are more at Nelly's. I hold up the caramel sauce and bounce. "I see a caramel macchiato in my future!"

"Hey, is this present for me or for you?" Peter turns the espresso machine over in his hands and smiles. "You were right when you said to keep it. Thank you." I'd hoped he would remember our conversation in the RV. He points to the box in my hand. "It's just a silly present. I found it in Anchorage."

Under the lid is a silver half of a heart on a bed of cotton. It says *Best* and has a few tiny cut-out stars. The edge where the other half of the heart would be is curved, waiting for its mate.

"It has stars, so I couldn't resist." Peter digs in his jeans and pulls out the half that says *Friends*. "I keep it in my pocket."

I smile in thanks, but my throat closes so that I can't say a word.

"I want one for me and Hank," Bits says.

"Only if I can keep it in my pocket," Hank says. "You must be crazy if you think I'm wearing a heart necklace."

Peter laughs at the exchange. I head to the bedroom before anyone sees my tears, but Peter is there a minute later. "Shit, I'm sorry. I thought it would be funny."

"It's not funny." I touch his arm when his face tightens. "It means more than you know."

It's as much as I can say without treading into dangerous waters. My heart is full. It's grown back like that lizard's tail, but it's not a shoddy facsimile. It's different for sure, but it's better.

"I heard what you said to Hank. I know you're right, but it's hard to do." He looks as if he wants to say more, but he doesn't.

"It is," I whisper. It's a mixture of betrayal of the person who's gone and the fear that you'll lose the next person, too. I know it well—I still have the fear, if not the betrayal. "Thank you. Really. Thank you. Sorry I'm such a nincompoop."

"You're not a nincompoop." He takes my chin and looks into my eyes. "You're a weirdo."

I'm so surprised that I laugh. I'm even more surprised when he kisses me softly on the lips, then smiles and walks out.

***

We're all full to bursting. The turkey has been reduced to bones and all the dishes people brought to Christmas dinner have been demolished.

Penny slouches in a chair, looking as if she might burst for real. I sit at her feet and rub her knee. "So, maybe no Christmas baby, huh?"

"I'm going to be pregnant forever. She'll grow up and go to college without ever being born."

"I'm calling New Year's," James says.

Penny's eyes well up. "Don't say that. We'll miss the party."

We've heard all about the New Year's party of last year, with its alcohol, music and bonfires. The entire world is frozen and there's no need for quiet. Apparently, it's a bit like an office Christmas party, and the kids sleep in the upstairs of the brewery while it rages all night long.

"There'll be other parties," I say. "At least you won't have to go to college with her if she comes out."

"Her wedding night would be super awkward," James says.

Penny laughs and turns to me. "It would ruin your New Year's, too."

"It's just another night. We'll have our own party later."

"Well, just so you know, I'm not making out with you at midnight," Penny says.

"There goes my New Year's wish."

Penny's eyebrow arches. "Maybe you can think of someone else you'd like to kiss. There must be someone around here somewhere."

Her smile says she's enjoying getting me back for the years I've spent torturing her about bases and the like. The conversation moves to another topic, but I don't hear a word. As much as I want to find a rock to crawl under, I feel as if another rock has been lifted from my shoulders. I think I might have just gotten Penny's blessing.

After I've made the rounds, I stand by the window and drink the one beer we were each allotted. Usually we don't light many lamps, but tonight the entire cabin is aglow like the old days. I pull out my phone and snap pictures of Ash and Nat giggling in a corner. Jasmine and Nicki show off their presents while Jamie and Kyle look on. They haven't jumped into anything, but he smiles a lot more these days, especially at her.

Margaret sits on a couch, new hairdo framing her face. She's being her usual quiet self, although she's quiet in a way that says she's drinking in the festivities rather than holding herself apart from them. I walk to where Rich leans on a wall, also peacefully watching the fun. "Have you met Margaret?" I ask him.

"Sure."

"Have you *spoken* to Margaret?" Rich shakes his head, lips twitching. "Well, come meet her again."

I pull him across the room and plant him on the arm of the couch. "Margaret, you know Rich, right?" She nods. "Well, you guys grew up near each other. I bet you know some of the same people. Rich, didn't you once say you liked classical music?"

"Yup."

"Margaret used to play violin."

He raises an interested eyebrow, but neither of them speaks. This might be more work than I bargained for. "I'm sure there are tons of things to discuss in the world of classical music," I say, out of my depth now. "You know, like composers and symphonies and stuff."

"The first time I met Rich he was blasting Verdi's Requiem to lead away a pod," Peter says from behind me. I turn with a grateful smile.

"That's quite a piece," Margaret says. "What orchestra?"

Rich mumbles something I can't hear, but Margaret must have because she answers. I slip back to the window. Peter comes with me, and I nudge him when Rich moves to my empty spot. Rich's mouth opens and closes, as does Margaret's, so I can only assume they're having a full-fledged conversation. A very slow-paced conversation, but a conversation nonetheless.

"You think?" Peter asks, eyes on the pair.

"It's worth a shot. They can be quiet together."

He finishes his beer and wipes his mouth. "Good point. Is there anyone here you haven't tried to pair off?"

I take in the room, ignoring the glaringly obvious answer that stands next to me. "Mark. I haven't found the right lady yet. Zeke and Liz did it on their own. I'm still working on Patricia and Terry. Chuck."

"Work on Chuck. He deserves someone."

"I have a few candidates in mind."

"Of course you do."

I'd thought it might be sad tonight with all the empty spaces where people should be. But what I said to Hank was true: I know that if they're somewhere, they're nothing but pleased. Ana's probably screaming at me to stop being such a wuss. I toast the air and drink down the dregs of my beer.

"Tired?" Peter asks.

"Nope."

"Good. You still have another present coming."

"I do?" I ask.

"Yup. It's a long one."

"How can a present be long? Is it a measuring tape?"

"Great, now you've ruined the surprise," Peter says. "I know how much you love measuring things." I push him with my shoulder. He gets me back and says, "Let's go home and find out."

Bits and Hank go willingly, worn out by excitement and turkey. Once they're in bed, Peter says, "We'll have to do it in the bedroom so we don't wake them."

I stare at Peter until he's pinkish and walk to the bedroom, where he arranges pillows at the head of the bed. He tells me to put on my pajama pants and read while I wait. "This is getting weird," I say, and he leaves with an enigmatic smile.

I pull up the blankets and stare into space. Obviously, this is not some sort of seduction present, unless Peter is suddenly turned on by ugly pajamas. My lips still tingle from his kiss this morning. It could hardly have been more chaste, but I think it held a promise—a promise I want him to keep.

The aroma of popcorn seeps into the room. Finally, he opens the door a crack. "Close your eyes."

He sets something in my lap and I hear a soft electronic beep after he settles himself beside me. "Comfortable?" he asks. I nod. "Okay, open them."

The first thing I see is the bowl of popcorn in my lap. The second is the tablet that Peter holds, *The Big Lebowski* beginning to play on its screen.

"You didn't!" I screech and cover my mouth. The last thing I need right now is two woken-up kids.

"I did. And there are two more movies besides this one."

He shushes me when I try to thank him. I watch the first five minutes in silence, wondering how he managed this, how he remembered it at all and how I deserve someone so incredible, even as a friend. He props the tablet on his knees and puts an arm around my shoulders the way he used to, when he'd say I fit right under his chin. I can remember all the good things about Peter these days.

"Thank you so—" I begin.

"Shhh. Don't talk during the movie." I try to speak again, but he covers my mouth. "Movie."

I pull his hand away. "I can practically recite this movie. Would you let me say thank you?"

"Okay." He waits a beat and asks, "Well? I'm waiting."

I laugh. "Thank you. Very, very much. This is the—"

"You're welcome. Now watch." He shoves a handful of popcorn in my open mouth. And Heaven help me, I think I've just fallen in love a tiny bit more.

CHAPTER 66

I'm enjoying a New Year's Eve bath when Bits flies into the steamy room. "Penny's having the baby!"

"What?" I ask. "Now?"

Bits spins around. "Yes! Come on!"

I arrive at Penny's cabin with my hair frozen solid and burst in the door to find her on the couch reading a book. "What's the matter?" she asks. Her eyes widen. "Oh God, I shouldn't have sent Bits. It's going to be hours and hours. What did she say?"

I plop down next to her and try to regain my breath. "Basically that a baby was hanging out of you. But it's happening?"

"The contractions are five minutes apart. But they aren't bad—I just have to breathe through them. There's one now." She puts down her book and inhales through her nose.

I wait for it to end and ask, "Is Glory coming?"

"She was already here," Penny says with a shrug. "Said to get her when they were three minutes apart and lasting a minute. Sooner if I wanted her here." Penny's been stressing about this day for months and now we might as well be discussing what to have for lunch.

"Do you have a watch?"

She looks around in a half-assed manner and shrugs again. "I don't know where it is. I figured we'd count. I forgot to ask Glory for hers."

"Where's James?"

"I made him go get me food. He was hovering."

"Are you okay to be alone? I'll go get Peter's watch or my phone."

She puts a hand on my leg. "I'm fine, Cass. Take your time. Sorry that it's starting now. You can go to the party if you want."

"Are you crazy? I wouldn't miss this for anything. Are you sure Glory didn't give you drugs? How are you so calm? It's scaring me."

"I've been waiting so long that I'm not worried anymore. I just want it to happen." She goes back to her book and barely takes notice when I leave.

I find Peter at the brewery helping set up for tonight. "Hey, Penny's in labor and we need your watch."

He sets down a chair and hands it to me. "I know. I just saw James. He's freaking out. How's Penny?"

"Eerily calm." The lights of the restaurant flicker on and classic rock blares from the overhead speakers. Cheers from the workers drown out Peter's next words. "What?"

He pulls me into the kitchen. "So you might not be here tonight."

My weeklong daydream of a New Year's kiss is going to remain just that, but I'm too excited to be disappointed about missing something that might not happen. Between night shifts on guard and the kids watching *Groundhog Day* with us, it's been friendly and cozy but nothing more. I'm trying very hard to remember patience is a virtue.

"Probably not," I say. "Have fifteen beers for me."

"Fifteen? You're a lightweight. That'd kill you."

"All right, four."

"You never know, maybe you'll get here late. I'll save you your four beers."

"Better make it five," I say. He laughs, but he looks disappointed. It pleases me more than it should. "Okay, I should get back."

"You'll let us know when the baby's born?"

"Of course." I give a little wave and spin right into Terry, who drops the boxes he was carrying.

"Sorry!" I help pick them up and restack them in his arms.

"It's all right. I heard about Penny. Tell her good luck from me."

"I will. I'm on my way back over there now." I pull his sleeve carefully so I don't send his load down again. "So, who are you kissing at midnight?"

"Why?" Terry asks with a wink. "Are you looking for a kiss?"

"It's tempting, but I value my life far too much," I say. He looks mystified. "Patty would kill me."

Terry makes a *pshaw* noise. "She doesn't date. She told me that once."

"I think she might have meant she doesn't date anyone but you. Trust me. Right, Petey?"

"You're missing out, man," Peter agrees.

I do an excited dance when Terry walks away with a spring in his step. I think Patty's going to be surprised come midnight. "Okay, now I'm really leaving. My work here is done."

"What work?" Peter asks.

"I've got people to hook up, babies to deliver—"

"Boxes to knock over."

"Ha. I'll see you later."

"I hope so."

I look into those dark eyes. He knows how I feel, and I don't try to hide it. I'd swear he feels the same. "Me, too."

CHAPTER 67

By nine o'clock, Penny is not as serene as she was, but she's calmer than James at the contractions that have grown increasingly powerful. She plows through each one the way she did in school—focused and with determination to get an A. It's quieter and less messy than I thought it would be until the very end, when Penny gives a final yell and a push that results in all sorts of gunk along with a tiny, slimy baby.

Glory sets it on Penny's chest and rubs it with a soft towel. "Beautiful," Glory says. "A beautiful little girl."

Penny rubs a finger along the baby's tiny cheek, looking exhausted and overwhelmed and completely enamored of the person we've been waiting to meet. I wipe my eyes, but not because I don't want to cry; these are exactly the kinds of things I want to cry about. I kiss the happy parents' cheeks and clean up while Glory deals with the afterbirth, which I've decided I don't need to see in detail.

"I'm going to leave you guys alone," I say when everything's been put to rights. James and Penny are tucked into bed, gazes riveted on the tiny bundle in her arms. "I'll be back tomorrow to annoy you."

"Do you want to hold her?" Penny asks.

"You know I do." I snuggle the baby to my chest and admire the face that's squashed the way all newborn faces are. I can tell she's going to be pretty, though. She has the Diaz features—small nose and not-too-full lips—and two tiny licks of hair that look to be closer to Ana and James's lighter brown. I wish Maureen were here to see this, but I find solace in the thought that she may be holding her own granddaughter right now.

"She's so—" I begin.

"Purple," Penny says at the same time as James says, "Frog-like."

"I was going to say gorgeous." I shake my head. "Maria, do you hear what they're saying about you? Your auntie will always think you're gorgeous, even when you look like a purple frog." She mewls and opens her tiny mouth, eyes scrunched, so I hand her back to Penny to nurse.

"Anamaria," Penny says. "We decided to name her Anamaria."

"I love it. I really do."

Penny and I smile through our tears. There are times in life when things seem to come full circle. It doesn't all suddenly make sense—how could it?—but it feels as if there might be something or someone out there that provides us with just enough good to endure the bad.

James hands me Peter's watch. "You can probably make it for midnight."

"I have to change first, but I can if I hurry. I'll see you tomorrow, Anamaria." It rolls off my tongue easily, not getting tangled up in the names of two people I loved who are gone. I kiss her soft head and get ready to leave.

"Cass," Penny says. She holds the baby to her breast in the golden light, a Renaissance painting of Madonna and child. "Go get your kiss."

I freeze with my zipper midway. "What?"

"Go get your New Year's kiss from Peter," she says with a beatific smile.

"I'm not...really sure—"

"I have never seen anyone want to kiss someone more than that man wants to kiss you." It's a good thing she's cut me off—I might've stood here stammering until midnight. I prickle with happiness that she's given me her blessing and that she sees it, too. And then Penny leers in a way the Blessed Virgin never would. "Who knows, maybe you'll hit a home run."

James laughs his ass off while Penny giggles. And although she's torturing me, I blow her a kiss before I leave. I want them to always be this way—a family full of joy and promise, unafraid of the future. I trudge through the snow past the noise of the party and wonder what this world will be like when Anamaria's grown. I believe we can give her a future that's more than just survival, if we have the courage to keep fighting. Maybe it's an act of courage in itself to believe there can be a future, to accept the challenge of protecting something so small and helpless. Maybe it's an act of courage to love again and again, no matter how many times your heart has been shattered.

CHAPTER 68

I expect to find the cabin empty, but Peter kneels at the woodstove feeding logs into the fire. He spins and looks at me expectantly.

"It's a girl," I say. "Everybody's fine."

"Wow. That was fast, no?"

"Believe me, Penny isn't complaining. Why are you here?"

He tosses another log in. "I didn't know when you'd be back. I thought you'd be cold."

"Where'd you get a crazy idea like that?" I ask. "Thanks. But it's almost midnight. You might've missed it."

"I was just about to head back. Do you want to go now?"

"I have to change first. I can meet you there." I want to tell him how beautiful it was to see something come to life that wasn't dead. Instead I blurt out, "They named her Anamaria."

I expect to see grief settle on his features, but he stands and brushes his hands on his jeans with a soft smile. "That's...perfect. I always thought I'd name a daughter Jane."

"Eric," I say. "A son, I mean."

He laughs. "I figured. Go change, I'll wait."

I throw on the shirt Patricia loaned me and abandon my original plan to apply makeup. One glance in the dresser mirror makes it clear that saving my frozen and thawed hair is hopeless if I want to make it there for midnight. And I do—I'm going get my New Year's kiss.

"You look nice," Peter says when I've entered the living room.

"This is as good as it's getting." I wipe my now sweaty palms on my jeans and make a joke so he can't tell how nervous I am. "Wait, was that the automatic you-look-nice reflex?"

"Yes." He moves closer and brushes my hair behind my ear with feathery fingertips. "It's always automatic. Because you're always beautiful."

I would deflect the compliment if I weren't breathless from his words and his touch and the desire on his face. The distant blare of music stops abruptly and a multitude of voices begin to count down from ten.

"We'll never make it," he says. I shake my head in agreement because I can't say a word.

I count along silently, keeping my eyes on his. I know by now that life is messy, filled with doubts and guilt and conflicting emotions, but I have no doubt he's going to kiss me. No doubt that he's ready. My stomach churns out warmth that travels to the tips of my fingers.

"Four," I whisper. "Thre—"

Peter brings his mouth to mine, pulling me close with a hand wound in my hair. Nothing about his lips and tongue is tentative, and there's nothing tentative in the way I respond. I'm done with saving things for later.

His hands are as capable as ever. Somewhere along the line both our shirts disappear, and I moan when he runs his mouth along the swell of my breasts. He must take it as a sign of protest because he asks, "Is this okay?"

"Are you kidding?"

Peter's breathy chuckle on my neck sends a shiver to my toes, and I start to work on his jeans in case my answer wasn't clear enough. A low groan rises in his throat, and when he breaks our kiss to grab the lantern, my moan *is* one of protest. I yank him to me, fitting his hips to mine, his lips to mine, his free hand to anywhere it wants.

"Bed," Peter growls into my mouth. I allow him to seat me on the edge, where he kneels to remove my boots. After a minute of struggle he looks up, breathing hard. "For someone who can't tie shoes, you can knot them just fine."

I fall back on my elbows and crack up at the half-amused, half-exasperated expression that's become so familiar. It doesn't ruin the moment. If anything, it tells me that Peter's along for the ride to wherever we're heading. He smiles the way he used to—soft but cautious, like I had the answer to a question he was scared to ask. Maybe he wanted to know if I could love him, if he was visible.

He was always visible. And maybe I could have loved him then, or maybe it took the end of the world to make this possible. The words stay on the tip of my tongue—I'm fearful to be the first to speak them. I kick off my boots and pull him to me, hoping he can feel what I don't say. The old chemistry is there, although those times when I'd thought we'd connected were nothing compared to this. There's no going back, but I don't ever want to.

✶✶✶

Afterward, the fear creeps in and whispers that I'll most likely lose him. My heart could be re-broken and never grow back—I'm not sure how many times the tail can regenerate before the lizard allows the missing piece to become a memory. I chase the thought away; I have faith it'll be all right. Peter didn't promise nothing bad would ever happen, but he's shown me how to make the best of it.

"I love you," I say, and fight the urge to protect my heart by looking away. I'm rewarded with a smile I've never seen—it could be I've answered his question.

"I love you," he says, face so tender that my chest flutters.

I can see it in the liquid depths of his eyes and in the gentle curve of his lips, can feel it in the way he touches me, but I still ask, "Really?"

"Really," Peter says softly. "I love the way you talk to inanimate objects. I love the way you tie your shoes like you're five. I love the way you joke about anything and everything, even if it does drive me out of my mind."

He traces my lips when I laugh, and then he says, "Promise."

The flutter in my chest becomes a loud thrum. "You promise all kinds of things."

"Maybe," he says. "But I always keep them."

He does—every single one.

EPILOGUE

I grab the toddler just before she hits the puddle on Main Street with both feet. "Caught you, you little stinker!"

Anamaria shows me her twelve teeth and bats the lashes that frame her big, brown eyes. She has Ana's ability to flirt her way out of any situation and a bit of a wild streak, but she's as sweet as Penny—when Penny's not pregnant.

"That doesn't work on me." I plant a kiss on her nose and take a hit of her toddler scent before handing her to Nelly. "Here, go see your uncle."

"Uncoo Newwy," she says, and pats his cheek with her chubby hand.

Nelly sighs at me over her head. "Did you really have to teach her that?"

"That's your name, don't wear it out."

"A whole generation of children will be calling me Uncle Nelly."

"You're the one who said you wanted to be the gay uncle." He grumbles at me, but he secretly loves it.

"Hey, *Nelly*," Adam says. "They want you inside."

Nelly places Anamaria on the frozen ground and lifts her chin with his finger. "Stay right here, okay?"

She nods like an angel but takes off the second his back is turned, only to stop and watch Bits and Jasmine raise their faces to the sky and stick out their tongues for a snowflake. There've been flurries all week, but it hasn't stuck. Anamaria opens her mouth and leans so far back she lands on her diaper. Bits picks her up with a laugh and shows her how it's done.

Bits is still small at almost eleven, but she already has a gangly teen look about her. She reminds me of a newborn colt trying to find its legs, especially with the long, shiny mane of brown hair she always wears loose. She's kind and smart and beautiful. Hardly anything scares her now.

Hank stands behind them, hands in pockets, and glances around before he sticks out his tongue. He's growing into his dreadlocks and glasses. We've managed to inject a little silliness into him, or at least a willingness to catch snowflakes and make the occasional wish.

Bits leads Anamaria my way. "Cassie, we're going to the library to work on our comic during the meeting."

"We have a deadline to meet," Hank says. His twelve year-old voice is deepening and sounds a lot like Henry's, but he'll be taller than his dad for sure.

"Home for dinner, though. Jasmine, I know Jamie and Kyle want you home, too." I wave a hand. "Go forth, my children."

They allow me to kiss their cheeks after they ensure the coast is clear of anyone their age or, God forbid, older. They still have a business selling their comics to the other kids. Commerce around here generally involves homemade goodies, books and favors, although Peter was thrown for a loop when Bits traded for some old makeup last week. He doesn't want her to grow up, but I love every stage, even this awkward one. Every year that passes is another year we're alive. I can't help but be thankful for that.

"Now, where's your mama?" I ask Anamaria.

She points to where Penny and James stand by the entrance to the brewery. James motions at the train tracks while Bernie and Terry nod. Part of today's annual fall meeting is about James's grand plans for rail travel, and I have no doubt he'll get whatever scheme he's cooked up to become a reality. The other part concerns our food stores, which are going strong, and the latest news from survivors outside Alaska. I was on the radio earlier, when we received one of our rare calls instead of the usual static. Sometimes it's bad news or someone looking for help we can't give from afar, but today it was news I'm delighted to share.

I make sure Penny has Anamaria in hand before I let go. The kid is fast, like her namesake. "Thanks for babysitting," Penny says. She's pregnant again and feels no better than the first time.

"Anytime. She had a great time with the old radios. Did you get any rest?"

She nods, but she looks like she could use a month of sleep. "I can't believe I did this to myself again."

"Hey, you did it on purpose this time."

She gazes down at Anamaria. "I know, right? How stupid am I?"

"Pretty stupid." She kicks my shin, and I level a finger at her. "Why do you kick me when you're pregnant? You'd better look out in seven months."

The wind gusts and with it comes a swirl of white flakes. It's time to whip out the puffy parka. I'd been putting it off, not wanting to concede to winter, but winter's going to win this one. I lean into Peter's warmth when he comes up behind me.

"Cold?" he asks.

"Just chilly." My blood has thickened a little over the past two years. Not a ton, but enough that I don't complain constantly, much to everyone's delight.

"How's my girl?" he asks Anamaria. She looks up from digging in the dirt with a stick and blows him a kiss. He catches it and makes *nom nom* noises. "How's Mama?"

"Don't ask," Penny says.

"Oh, I almost forgot." I hand her a bottle of ginger lemonade from my bag. She sighs in thanks. "The ginger went crazy this year and the lemons in the greenhouse are dehydrated, so you can have as much as you want."

I think Dan would be pleased to know his concoction has helped several pregnant ladies. Except for Jamie, who's in her fifth month with not a bit of sickness. He'd be even more pleased to know that I teach the kids astronomy as well as art. It's always been useful knowledge, but it's more important than ever now that they're what are left to guide us.

Peter snuffles on my neck until I turn for a proper kiss and tuck my icy hand in his shirt. He doesn't mind as long as I let him do the same with his warm one, which is never a bother.

"Get a room," Penny mutters.

I laugh. "Pregnant Penny's back. You really want to see me like that, Petey?"

"Nope," he says, and grins at Penny's scowl.

He'd like kids—a little Jane or Eric. I would, too, but I can't bring myself to intentionally add another person I love to this world—one more person who could be ripped away so easily. Peter tells me it was always that way and that if anyone knows it the two of us do, but I'm holding out.

Nelly opens the brewery's door. "You guys coming in or what? The rumors are flying fast and furious in here."

James throws Anamaria over his shoulder and leads Penny inside. I turn to look at the streets that make up this tiny village I love. And although I'll always miss Adrian and Ana—and all the others I loved who didn't make it here—I'm exactly where I want to be.

"Everything okay?" Peter asks.

I touch his cheek. "Everything's great. And I love you."

"I love you," he says. "Promise."

He always says that, and he hasn't broken a promise yet. I'm certain he never will.

"I love you more."

He leans on the doorjamb, eyebrow lifted. "More than all the stars in the sky?"

"Well..." I twist my mouth and pretend to think. "I definitely love you more than salmon."

"Thanks a lot, weirdo," he says, and pulls me inside.

The building is full, kids playing quietly in the back. They've spent so much of their lives being quiet. I'm waiting for the day they can be as loud as they want without fear. And from what I just heard on the radio, that day might come soon. The survivors south of us, those who have eked out an existence on the peaks of mountains and other inhospitable places, say that the mold is winning. We've seen it, too, on the few who make it to our fences before the cold comes again. The survivors told me of millions of bodies that have collapsed into black dust and bones under the summer skies, and that the remaining Lexers aren't far behind. They believe this will end next year or the one after that. It'll be all right.

Maybe we'll leave here one day. Head back east to more fertile soil and warm summer nights where the stars are visible. But, honestly, I don't care if I never see the summer stars again. Not if I have the people I love more than anything—more than all the stars in the sky.

ABOUT THE AUTHOR

Sarah Lyons Fleming is a wannabe prepper and a lover of anything pre-apocalyptic, apocalyptic, and post-apocalyptic. Add in some romance and humor, and she's in heaven.

Besides an unhealthy obsession with home-canned food and Bug Out Bag equipment, she loves books, making artsy stuff and laughing her arse off. Born and raised in Brooklyn, NY, she now lives in Oregon with her family and, in her opinion, not nearly enough supplies for the zombie apocalypse. But she's working on it.

Visit the author at www.SarahLyonsFleming.com

Other books by Sarah Lyons Fleming:

The *Until the End of the World* series
Until the End of the World (Book one)
So Long, Lollipops (Peter's Novella, Book 1.5)
And After (Book two)
All the Stars in the Sky (Book three)

The City Series
Mordacious (Book one)
Peripeteia (Book two)
Instauration (Book three)

The Cascadia Series
World Departed (Book one)
World Between (Book two)
World Undone (Book three, coming in 2022)
World Anew (Book four, coming in 2023)

ACKNOWLEDGEMENTS

Once again, I have folks to thank for reading and editing and helping me get this book done.

As always, my parents, both in-law and not, who read and comment and find those pesky typos.

Jamie A. Mcreynolds, who always reads and annoys the crap out of me until I give her a finished product—which is great. Tracy Nielsen, who gives me a lovely boost.

Danielle Gustafson, who sits to type my out typos and her notes. With four kids. FOUR.

Jessica Gudmundson, who, in giving me some Canadian expertise, became my lovely, funny internet friend. And, being Canadian, she's super nice (of course!).

Lindsey Fairleigh, a talented author and all-around wonderful gal, who gave me some advice and pointed out an inconsistency or ten (Read her books!).

Melissa Jane Keaton, who gave me some dental advice when I was unsure about just how much dentists know.

Charlene Divino-Williams, who offered to proofread and edit and gave me thoughtful, insightful comments.

John Evanston at Bi-Mart, for letting me wander around his distribution center and imagine standing just out of reach of hundreds of zombies. I know where I'm heading in the zompoc—wait, maybe I shouldn't have told you that.

Lindsay Galloway, who gave me some good Winnipeg-area advice for no reason other than being helpful.

Google Maps, without whom I would have had no idea about Canadian geography. We've become very close.

My husband, Will, who amazes me every time with his knowledge of grammar and his ability to see things others have missed, whether they be good or bad. A book isn't finished until he's worked his magic. I'm a very lucky lady.

Printed in France by Amazon
Brétigny-sur-Orge, FR

20010697R10198